Hex stared at the de[...]
which the eyes and [...]
listened to the demo[...]
into a dungeon place. [...]
on the ageless prison s[...]
of a multitude a-wan[...]
charnel odour seemed to saturate his very skin.

'What are you doing to me? I protest! I won't do business under this kind of coercion!' Hex yelled.

'You misunderstand, human, I have not finished setting forth my offer. I would give you the means of eternal life. I would tell you how to find Yana.'

'And in Yana?' Bramt asked.

'In Yana, the touch of undying is given to all who seek it . . .'

By the same author

Nifft the Lean
A Quest for Simbilis
The Colour Out of Time

MICHEAL SHEA

In Yana, The Touch of Undying

GRAFTON BOOKS
A Division of the Collins Publishing Group

LONDON GLASGOW
TORONTO SYDNEY AUCKLAND

Grafton Books
A Division of the Collins Publishing Group
8 Grafton Street, London W1X 3LA

A Grafton UK Paperback Original 1987

Copyright © Michael Shea 1985

ISBN 0-586-07145-8

Printed and bound in Great Britain by
Collins, Glasgow

Set in Times

All rights reserved. No part of this publication may
be reproduced, stored in a retrieval system, or
transmitted, in any form, or by any means, electronic,
mechanical, photocopying, recording or otherwise,
without the prior permission of the publishers.

This book is sold subject to the condition that it
shall not, by way of trade or otherwise, be lent,
re-sold, hired out or otherwise circulated
without the publisher's prior consent in any
form of binding or cover other than that in
which it is published and without a similar
condition including this condition being imposed
on the subsequent purchaser.

1
Bramt Hex Leaps to a New Life

'Will you take something with your wine?' the innkeeper asked with feigned offhandedness. Bramt Hex had been frequenting the inn for some weeks. He was always resolved to order wine alone, but the keep knew he could, with the slightest nudge, be stimulated to order a large meal as well.

'Yes, in fact,' Bramt Hex replied promptly, 'since you suggest it. A salad of spindlewort. The broasted homunculus as well, followed immediately by a chilled crab tart.'

'The domestic or the wild homunculus?'

'The wild, of course.'

'We cannot give it to you, sir. The trappers bring none in. The vampires have lately increased in the hills.'

'Do they feed on homunculi?' Hex asked with surprise.

The innkeeper shook his head: 'Trappers.'

'Of course. Well, I'll take the sausage then instead of 'munk.'

'Thank you, sir.'

Settling back, Hex looked out the window at his side. He watched the traffic the more closely because he did not wish to think about his studies. The meal he had ordered was costly both in coin and time. He concentrated but poorly with a full stomach, and wouldn't be able to return to his books for two hours after such a feast as he had just bespoken. And this inn was not his only new-formed habit, now that his Ultimary Examinations drew near. The harbour side in particular abounded with dissolutions he had lately come to relish, and he foresaw this evening's waste following this afternoon's. More unread pages to be added to the stack already two months deep.

Out in the street, three old breadwomen trudged against the onshore wind of Glorak Harbour's late afternoon. Hex felt a pang of envy, seeing the crones' stubborn fight against the backdrag of their black mantles, each hugging her deep basket of loaves. They were free, absorbed in their lives, thinking only of whichever of the dusk bazaars was their destination.

A wagon of jars, driven at reckless speed, careered round the corner. As it made the turn, a gust caused it to yaw from its course. It skated sideways and almost hit the breadwomen, who fled to the wall before it. The driver reined hard, straightened, flogged his plod anew and sped down the street, his jars bobbling in the cartbed, and his wheels barely skimming the noon-gilt cobbles.

One of the breadwomen, having spilled three loaves in her flight, gathered up two of them, but Hex could read her soundless curse as she found the third too dirty for salvage. She kicked it away with feeble anger, and turned to follow her companions down the hill. The spurned loaf rolled to the feet of a chained troupe of felons being led past by two Karbies, the giant escorts who took men to the skinfarms. One of the prisoners grabbed up the loaf, while the man behind him jostled his elbow coaxingly. The loaf's owner hugged the bread with greedy denial, bolting hunks of it as the Karbies led their party down the hill in the direction the breadwomen had taken – doubtless to the Inlet to take ship to the farms. There was a cluster of them just downcoast of Glorak.

There were some less free than himself, Bramt Hex considered. The breadwomen too, after all, were as much prisoners of their poverty as those men in chains were of the Karbies. Only the rich were free.

Meanwhile he at twenty-eight lived in the quasi-freedom of the student. He had held the scholar's midway position all his life: dwelling among the poor, while learning the arts and mysteries enjoyed by the wealthy; receiving simultaneously the proletarian's ardour and harsh humour, and the magnate's overview, wealth's fund of information. He was a man who could sit at ease in an expensive inn like this, and look with understanding on those in the street. The thought was bleached of pleasure. He could not congratulate himself on a role he was growing too paralysed to play. His spindlewort arrived, and he fell to it greedily.

Bramt Hex assumed that he looked as at home as he felt in both social strata. In fact, he seemed slightly out of place wherever he was. He was a tall, plump man, whose reddish beard and blond moustache contrasted subtly with his brown hair. His tunic and cape of black velour, which he believed to appear as costly as they had once been, looked both quaint and well-worn. He considered himself skilful in dealing with people; the truth was he had the quirkish manner of a solitary. He was both withdrawn and obtrusive, an oblivious and conspicuous man.

He did not know he was fat. He sometimes glimpsed the fact – when he leaned over the Academy fountain to feed the waterbrats, or when he walked, conversing with Lamkin Bont in the morning on the Academy quay, and saw his thick shadow beside his friend's narrow one. Large and sturdy of frame, Hex was actually an ace short of full obesity, but even his heaviness, though glanced at, never entered his idea of himself.

He found scant forgetfulness in his food. The knowledge that he must change his life nagged him. The Ultimaries came in three weeks. It was still just possible to cover two months' material sufficiently to pass, but it was all too likely he would not summon the will to do so.

Never in his life had Bramt Hex read so widely as now, when everything depended on his reading narrowly. He found himself fascinated by *any* topic, so long as it was unrelated to his studies.

His course as a scholar had never been smooth. It had taken him three years longer than the usual period to earn his First Seal. Only his high achievement had redeemed his slow pace. Now, in the morass of infra-magus scholarship, the pace had become more demanding even as his devotion to his studies had begun to disintegrate.

He gobbled with diminishing pleasure, and found the sausage fatty. He ordered a double bitters for desert, and stared gloomily out the window. Out in the waning light of the street an elegant coach, bearing a coat of arms on the door, skidded around the corner, caught by a gust as the jar-cart had been. It was fortunate that the street was empty just now, for this high-wheeled vehicle was blown so completely out of control that it slammed sideways to a stop against the opposite wall. The coachman, a small, lithe man, jumped from the box, cringed up to the window of the coach, and spoke to someone within. Bramt Hex sighed.

Wealth! How utterly it would erase his woes! He had a small stipend, won by his early brilliance. If by a miracle he passed the Ultimaries, his wage as an infra-magus would be perhaps three times as much – still a pittance. For this he was supposed to shackle his mind to some narrow speciality. He loved Lore and Letters. It was the act of specializing in itself he recoiled from – to slink through the wide world down one twisted little path, sneak through one's life, one's sole and unrecoverable life, as if it were a shop-boy's errand, strictly routed to a simple end! Meanwhile mere wealth – brute, meaningless funds – endowed a man with a free sky and all the fair earth's range of choices.

Outside the coachman, having remounted and gee'd up the matching pair of Slenders that drew the vehicle, had discovered that it moved with a severe wobble. He leapt down, found the left wheel badly bent, and cringed anew to the coach's window. He gestured at the inn Hex sat in, bowed at some reply he received, and opened the coach door, releasing a small set of steps hinged to its sill. A lady in a regal gown emerged. Easing a silver prow of multiple petticoats into the gale, she stepped down with a steady foot despite the wind's tug. Though her coif was also elaborate, she moved through the rushing air with a firm control that seemed to hold the elements of her attire together by a direct exercise of the will. She advanced unruffled while the wind rummaged at her clothes. Her hair was frosted and beaded with pearls, a style typical of the elderly rich, as was the deep black of her quilted sleeves – yet she moved with a vigour that seemed younger than her accoutrements, and the coachman had to spring nimbly to precede her.

The inn door banged open. The coachman strode into the public room and cried with a scowl: 'Keep! Hither!'

Out of the wind which had made his loose and somewhat foppish livery billow and banner, the coachman was rather remarkable. His small frame vibrated with tigerish power; his black eyes, under plucked, arched brows, had a gimlet stare, murderously fixed. He snatched up a chair, set it near the room's centre and, in the same motion, whirled to bow the entering lady towards this presiding throne he had arranged for her.

She glided in on a breath of wind. Her face was autumnal, but firm and handsome. She swept the room, politely acknowledging its other occupants, and Hex thrilled at the brief engagement of her eyes with his. The way she sat down made the chair seem a throne. The innkeep hurried to her side and executed a profound and vigorous bow. She murmured, gracious but brief. The innkeep bowed vigorously again, beckoned to the coachman and led him out the side door that opened on the stable-yard. The lady, whose aquiline profile Hex had been admiring, turned and settled her cool gaze in his direction.

Her gaze was clearly devoted to the window he sat by, yet he felt a second thrill. He asked himself why he should be so impressed with this woman. Though maturity had never been a bar to his lust, he preferred women of his own age. As for her wealth and station, he had always mocked fatuous reverence for the 'great'.

What affected him so strongly, he realized, was a sense of portent. A moment before he had wondered how he might change his life. Now this Embodiment, this mute sphinx of Wealth and Power, sat not five strides distant and practically solicited his eye!

With the suspended feeling of a man who makes a great first step, Hex rose in his place and made the lady a courtly gesture welcoming her to the view out the window. Almost imperceptibly she acknowledged him. Hex resumed his seat with a pounding heart. He noticed that the crest on the coach door outside had a black quarter-bar, denoting recent widowhood. Unmistakably, he was beckoned!

He must do something, make some further communication with this august Visitant – Hex felt this, yet dared not seem to solicit the lady's attention like a scheming commoner. He turned, and saw that the lady had already risen.

The coachman opened the inn's door and stood flanking it. His pose combined with the woman's strong presence to transform the public room into a rapt court viewing its sovereign's departure. Bramt Hex stood up and cried with feeling: 'Farewell rare lady! Your presence honoured us too briefly.'

The dowager paused as she stepped over the threshold. She looked at Hex an instant, then nodded graciously. In an instant she was gone.

So much from so little! The thought reverberated in him as he stared again at the street's traffic. The smile and nod were mere nothings. But seen another way, he had seen an omen, greeted it, and it had smiled back at him. His fate had invited him. Filled with this sudden, sensual tonic, he realized just how large a plan had been born within him in these last moments: to woo this dowager – win her and possess her, body and fortune. So much from so little!

He recognized his confusion of greed with desire, yet it thrilled him no less. Was she not a woman – strong-natured and probably fully awakened by marriage to sexual ardour? Was he himself not a handsome and cultured man? The annals of love had a thousand chapters about passions born from one glance, while convention permitted a poor scholar's acceptance as a suitor to one of the great, where it would forbid a man who was merely poor.

Luck was precisely in such moments of inspiration made real by daring. If – right now, tonight – he converted all his texts to cash, bought fine clothes and assailed the dowager with hot avowals – if he threw all his poetry and persuasion at her, he could quite possibly, by force and charm, fan the lady's benign, brief attention into a fire.

Of course he had long deplored the evils of wealth. It would be more consistent of him to hatch plans to sabotage the skinfarms, and free such men as he had seen pass in chains, than to chase after the titled oppressors.

But wasn't he debating a total change of his life? Let his leap be a great one, then! Let him try on a new way of thinking. To hell with altruism – it had been a mere habit, more talk than action. Let him now take up an unsentimental realism. He would go forth, keep his own counsel, devise his own stratagems, and win what could be won of the world. This had been the way of many great men.

'Innkeep!' The keep appeared at Hex's table, and delivered the less athletic bow he reserved for customers who were not dowagers.

'That lady, innkeep. I had the impression you knew her, knew of her, I mean.'

'That is correct, sire.'

'Well then. You see, I am curious to know her name, her residence.'

'Indeed? I see, sire.'

'You say you see, and you tell me nothing.'

'Perhaps there is a reason for that, sire.'

Sourly, Hex counted one and a half times the meal's cost on to the table. The keep bowed with more energy. 'She is the dowager Poon, widow of Orgle Poon, the homunculus magnate. Her house is a prominent one in the Scarp Heights quarter.'

When Hex subsequently stepped out under the first stars, he could see Scarp Heights from where he stood. It was in the arc of hills that protected the half-basin of Glorak Harbour from the open sea. The inn stood in the well-to-do footslopes of this range; Scarp Heights lay among its exclusive crests. A fang of rock, the Scarp, protruding from a line of more rounded summits, marked its centre among the sparse window lights of wealth's well-spaced properties.

Below on the shoreside flatlands where he must now go – the bottom of Glorak's broken bowl – the lights lay thicker. Torch yellows and the red of braziers freckled the square zones that Hex knew were the dusk bazaars; the taverns had their oil-lamp clusters of whiter light, and also white were the quayside lamps that fringed the Inlet, a black swordblade of sea thrust deep into the city's flank. The Academy's Great Mamble Beacon burned orange at the inlet's mouth.

He had always loved the Academy's position on its corner of land, with the sea to one side and on the other, the inlet, down whose corridor incessant ships took the somnolent last steps of voyages from worlds that were bare names to him. He realized as he stood staring that he was summing up, taking a kind of leave of the years he had lived there.

Did he expect so much to flow from this slight thing? A pang of fear told him that he did. This, if he made it so, was a real turning, a real end of a life, whatever might happen with the dowager. If he went down there now to his quarters, and sold his books and his chamber-right, he would be shutting himself out of his present existence as effectively as if he had had himself transported by a wizard to another land.

However it was precisely in the completeness of the risk that his luck lay – he felt sure of it. The alchemy of daring could convert this fantasy to glittering fortune. Failure would merely be a harsher brand of success, leaving him to find *some* new life, will he, nill he.

For that was where salvation lay – in the leap more than the landing! He shivered to see this so clearly now. Like a sleepwalker waked at a chasm's edge, he looked down upon his twenty-eight years of habit and routine. If he turned twenty-nine in that gulf of lassitude, his soul would surely die.

He felt welling in him precisely the recklessness and humour with which his court must be paid to the dowager. That he laid his life at her feet would be the simple truth, and he knew exactly how he would say it. He moved forward, and the wind's rush felt like the sky's assistance to his steps. 'But such a scheme!' he muttered, grinning. His heart stretched in him like young wings flexing away sleep. 'Madness!' He began to stride.

2
A Misadventure with a Melancholy Melodeon

Lamkin Bont sat hunched on his pallet, the scroll he had been reading laid by on the blanket. 'It does not sound very passionate, Bramt Hex. I mean, you all but *decided* to desire her . . .' He raised his faint eyebrows only slightly enlarging his habitually squinted eyes. The rest of his narrow, lantern-jawed face was inert – as usual. Hex laughed, more at the thought of Lamkin, at his stolid sunniness through all the years they had been friends, than at the accusation.

'It's true, I did decide, in a way. It's such a mix of lust and greed and ambition. Shameless! But I've got to get out of this narrow little life. My soul depends on it.'

Lamkin looked at his nails, an expressive trait; Hex saw he had been offended. He added, 'Narrow for me I mean, naturally. I'm just hiding out here. I don't want to work on pandects or master text analysis! I love my books, but I could read them anywhere! I'm playing it safe here and I've got to stop.'

'It's only a narrow little life to those who let it become so,' the myopic scholar said, only now looking at Hex again with relenting humour. 'Well then. Bramt Hex is now at large in the world. That honest, tumultuous man! If the near-sighted Lamkin Bont could do it, he would willingly shower good luck on the head of Bramt Hex, with both hands.' Bont squinted at Hex and wagged his head slightly, solemnly. 'Blessings will have to do. Who knows what things Bramt Hex, that large-witted, touchy, stubborn man, is going to see in his new life?'

'Maybe one of them,' Hex replied, 'will be Lamkin

Bont, that redoubtable scholar. After all, maybe I'll succeed, and live in Scarp Heights.'

'And maybe you'll end up with nothing but a suit of expensive clothes.'

'Then I'll sell them for a staff, sword, boots and steerage to the farthest large city I can afford to get to. It's got to be all-or-naught. But if you could only feel my sense of luck, Lamkin! I hardly feel like I'm taking leave of you at all.'

'Still, *different lives, different paths*, as Nab the Trickster says. Shall I sell your chamber-right for you, and give you the money for it myself?'

'Bless you. Here's my token. Now I'm taking these' – he pointed to the bundle of his texts – 'to Rouchernod's. Thanks.' Hex pocketed the fifty lictors Lamkin gave him. They shook hands. Hex felt sadness as he flipped up with his toe the trap in the floor. Voices, and the clatter of rune-bones on playing boards rose into the room from the scholars' refectory downstairs. Hex paused before walking straight out of Lamkin's life but, dreading to show his doubt, he climbed hastily down the ladder.

His happiness returned with the wind outside. He decided to stroll down the Academy Quay as a ritual of farewell. On the way there, he made humorous partings with various acquaintances he met on the streets of the quarter. He reached the waterside in time to see a ship gliding berth-ward, her lanterned masts on a level with the quayside lamps. Another omen? Yes – he must include a scale doublet in his wooing-outfit! At this moment the moon – just off the full – began its rise from the sea's edge – propitious.

The parchment broker converted Bramt Hex's library into a hundred and fifty lictors. At the haberdasher's, Hex converted sixty of these into a wardrobe that scorned any appearance of self-effacement – for had he not chosen a bold role? He emerged from the shop in boot-length moccasins, pleated hose, and a hooded cape of lavender velour. A collier-scale doublet was the jewel of his attire. Its flexible, rainbow-coruscating scales, each as big as his palm, were woven to overlap, like those of a fish. On Hex's bulky frame, it looked like a glittering barrel. Still, with his cape closed against the wind, he looked heroic enough.

A melodeon was next to be found. Among the student population, this custom had long been thought comic and passé. Hex, however, felt sure that the practice was still much used among the affluent, whose mores undoubtedly changed much more slowly than those of poorer, more experimental folk. He began his search in a district that abounded in taverns, for the keepers of melodeons were notorious drinkers – a habit due, some said, to their emotionalism, which gave them the empathy necessary for a rapport with the tender-voiced, quasi-verbal breed they handled. Indeed, Hex found a melodeon-keeper with his beast at the fourth tavern he tried, sitting on a bench in the stable-yard.

He had not looked in the yards of the previous inns because no keeper would have thought of tethering his beast – they formed a proverbially inseparable pair. But, as he crossed this yard, he heard a soft, gulping yodel from one corner, and saw there a melodeon and keeper sitting side-by-side in the shadow, backs against the wall. It seemed that the keeper comforted the creature.

'. . . water under the bridge,' Hex thought he heard him say, as he approached. The keeper looked up.

'Good evening,' said Hex. 'What's your fee for an evening of melody?' Hex thought the man shot his beast a dubious look before answering.

'Seven lictors, sir.'

'And what is the price for a shorter bout – three hours say?'

'Five lictors.'

'Consider yourself engaged, friend keeper.'

The keeper nodded, and turned to whisper to the melodeon, which sobbed faintly as it listened. Then, gently, the keeper hoisted the melodeon into the leathern papoose-frame which keepers wore always on their backs.

If the melodeon's trunk, legs and loins had matched the proportions of its huge, sleek-furred head, it would have been able to carry the keeper. But the beast's shrunken lower half – specially bred into the strain – rendered it a helpless infant, utterly dependent on its human partner. Its sad monkeyish face looked infantile.

The keeper trudged behind the scholar up the windy streets. Because of the beast's intermittent sobs, Hex was moved to ask: 'Is your melodeon in spirit tonight? I want to impress someone whose taste is as exquisite as her rank is high.'

'My colleague is perfectly well, sire.'

Hex thought the man sounded hurt.

'Excuse a distracted suitor,' he said. 'I certainly don't mean to slight your companion. He is a handsome creature, I notice.'

'Indeed he is,' said the keeper with relenting warmth. 'You see, their nature is finely tuned. You ask if my Molinor is in spirit because you have heard his sounds of grief. Molinor will rise above this sadness, because Molinor is a true performing artist.'

Hex could detect that the keeper's words were aimed as much at the melodeon as at Hex himself. It worried him that the man was still trying to enspirit the beast.

'And what was it that caused Molinor's sadness?'

'My own negligence!' cried the keeper with anguish. 'I left him in my seat at the tavern a week ago – briefly, to relieve myself. But there was another melodeon, a female, on the premises, and by the time I returned, the two of them had consummated their instantaneous love under the table. The other's keeper, you see, was in a stuporous state. Of course Molinor still pines, for his breed is an ardent one, but he is a noble creature, and will answer the call of his Art, leaving his pain aside for the sake of song.'

Again the melodeon was the intended audience of these inspirational words, and Hex felt renewed misgivings. The melodeon's song was directly connected with its passions. Indeed, its music was no more than its richly varied courting cries, slightly improved by training. They came in view of the escarpment that gave the Scarp Heights district its name.

The street, flanked by the spear-tipped palings of broad, landscaped grounds, rose steeply to the foot of the starlit crag. Hex had often enjoyed wine and daydreams sprawled on its crest, with Glorak's great half-circle at his feet, and the Glides coasting past at eye-level, riding the updraughts from the hills. Now, it looked grim – the sentinel of the great properties surrounding it. The wind at Hex's back almost cancelled the effort of climbing the slope; he felt he was being borne up towards the Scarp's black, fang-like form.

A man in a cowled cape emerged from a side street and proceeded downhill towards them. He crossed the street to meet them. When he was near, Hex saluted him.

'Good evening, sir! May I detain you in such impossible weather? I am looking for the house of the Dowager Poon.'

The man halted before them and bowed decisively, as if it had been his own purpose to stop and talk with Hex. 'I am delighted to be able to help,' he said. He simpered as if swallowing a giggle. 'The esteemed widow, sir, of the late Orgle Poon still lives in the mansion he built for them. I knew him well, sir! Ah, Poon, Poon! You preposterous bag of slag! Whither blown, foul-wind? For his breath, sir, earned him the fame of having a bunghole at both ends, while his body reeked with ancient greedy sweat, more offensive than any other kind. His strong-stomached lady survives him and still lives, as I say, in his house. Are you a man of business, sir?'

Hex answered simply: 'No. I am, and have long been, a scholar.'

'You are not a man of business. I see, I see. You're one of the parasites then, you say? Sucking life out of the blood of the men of business, drinking their sweat and cursing them as you feed? Well, well, I am intensely delighted to meet you sir, intensely.' He spoke with unmistakable warmth, seized Hex's hand and pumped it cordially.

Uncertain whether the man was mad or jesting, Hex pulled his hand away.

'Listen sir,' Hex said, 'I am no parasite. If anything it is the men of business themselves – I take it you are one? It is just such men as yourself who are parasites upon *my* kind. For my kind live on scant scrapings and till the fields of speculation which bear the fruits of culture and insight which you, greedy privateers, buy up for a song with your blood-stained millions.' Hex had argued this case before, but still he felt pleased with the fire of his delivery. The plump stranger, beaming, shook his head.

'No, no, no sir. It is we who wade in the muck of murderous realities, winning the fortunes that someone must win, while such scholarly scum as yourself, sweet sir, sit curled up with pipedreams and noble fantasies, which you sell to the brainless *wives* of the men of business, forcing us to tolerate you for the sake of peace at home!'

'Muck! What muck do you wade through?' Hex's temper was coming up. The melodeon behind him whimpered, and the keeper murmured to soothe it.

'What muck?' beamed the stranger. 'You ask what muck, and know of Orgle Poon? The illegal aphrodisiacs of his homunculus farms? The sick meat of over-breeding that swelled his productions? What of his rape-and-murderees? Supported in luxury to a contractual age, then his sole property, and object of his degenerate lusts? All, all truths of common knowledge and officially blinked at! If Poon had not stooped to these revolting practices, unthanked, day in and day out, getting that he might spend, then vast sums would be out of circulation, thousands would starve outright for lack of diseased meat to prolong their miseries! Such was Poon, self-crucified in a wallow of bestiality, solely that the vast idle, begging populace might not starve. He dredged the seas themselves for new infamies, and scoured the highest peaks! Ah, Poon, where now your waxy snout, and brow sweaty with recent gorging? Incorrigible cornholer! His grim-faced widow survives him, sir, and continues still in the house he built. Do you know who I am, sir?'

'No, I do not.'

'I am the greatest muckmaster of them all! A thousand times greater than the piddling Poon! I am Arple Snolp.'

'Gratified, I am sure. I am Bramt Hex.'

'You do not understand! I am *Arple Snolp*. I have bottled and sold the plague to destroyers of cities! I have sold to ravenous populaces tons of a confection whose main constituent was loon-excrement! I am king of the immensely lucrative lines of gladiators, torturing implements, and peel. Poor Poon! I hate to say it, for many's the time he buggered me, dear man, but he was a mere nothing compared to me. He merely rubbed his jowls against dung I've wallowed in! But please! Merely ask the Dowager Poon when you see her if I have not spoken the plain truth in all respects. You will find her, as I have said, still living in the hall Poon built for them. And so, good night sir!'

'But where *is* Poon's house?'

'The first to the left of where this street ends at the crag,' Snolp called as he marched on down the walkway.

'Madness!' growled Hex to the keeper, who shrugged and continued speaking to his beast in whispered exhortation. Hex strode on; despite the ugly outpourings with which he had just been regaled, he must sustain at all costs his precarious momentum, his fragile romantic feeling, or the unlikelihood of the whole project would overwhelm him.

The iron palings which surrounded the property contained a dark zone of lush shrubbery from the centre of which the mansion rose, a four-tiered pyramid. The terraces of its two upper tiers bristled with yet more plantings. The house was huge, its monolithic impact modified only by the immense presence of the Scarp, its backdrop. From the gate Hex could see – at the end of a frond-bordered lane – the main door, a high, two-valved portal flanked by torches and bearing the Poon crest. Hex turned to the keeper.

'That is what we, my friend, by the sweetness of your melodeon's song, must open. Music's a potent key, but then, that's a heavy door. Can we do it? I think so, by all the powers! Let's begin!'

The man unfolded his little portable stool, sat down, unslung the melodeon and settled the creature in his lap. He stroked the beast's sleek-furred throat – which still rippled with suppressed sobs – to prime it, and then nodded his readiness to Hex. Hex advanced to the gate and cried out – fervently, he hoped –

'Incomparable Madam Poon! Poor Bramt Hex, a scholar of renown, is heartstruck! He has abandoned his books, put by his pandects and his scrolls! He has set his life aside, and come to sue for your love. Hear his song, oh adored and lofty Lady!'

The melodeon lifted its song, and Hex's heart sank. Plainly, the animal was near emotional collapse. It opened with the traditional boom warble. But its boom, instead of the plangent and cavernous hum so justly esteemed by connoisseurs of sound, was a broken, rheumy groan, a dank, rocky noise as deep as a tomb; while its warble – no soaring, sweet falsetto – was a shrill and gassy squeal, the searing soprano of a thing in torment. Moreover, seeming to have forgotten the development of this passage, the melodeon repeated it, starting anew each time it faltered.

'Enough!' Hex rasped. 'It's dismal, a mockery! Silence it!'

The keeper hissed reproachfully, but the animal had heard the slur, which snapped the last frail threads of its self-control. It abandoned the pretence of song, and gave way to its grief. Escaping the keeper, it scuttled to the gate, whose bars it clasped with all four of its spindly limbs. Hex was awed by what now rose from its throat, an oratorio of mind-stunning volume and repetitiveness. This consisted of an acidulous wail which collapsed, in its latter half, into a gargling, flatulent racket that sounded like a bull bladderfish caught on a reef.

Almost immediately a small lozenge of light appeared in the left valve of the great portal: a man-sized door opening in the larger. A stout female silhouette filled this.

'What are you doing? Take your murders elsewhere!' she bellowed.

'You misunderstand!' Hex shouted.

'What do you say?'

'Damn you, silence it!'

'How dare you, you saucy scum!'

'No, madam, please – I am a suitor!'

'A what?'

'A suitor!'

'I am married! Cease that din!'

'I want to see your mistress!'

'I want no mistress either!'

'SEE your mistress. Roast you! Begone, begone! I dismiss you!' Wildly Hex flung down five lictors. The keeper took this with a scowl, but he seemed unable to pry the melodeon off the gate – or unwilling to apply the necessary degree of force to his associate's frail body. Sunk in despair, Hex watched his all-too-gentle struggles with the thunder-throated jot of fur and flesh. With frantic invention, Hex howled to the figure in the doorway:

'Life and Death Message for Dowager Poon! Life and death! Admit me!'

The silhouette did not move for a minute. Then she marched forward, her swinging skirts leaving the fronds nodding in her wake. She was a squat, solid woman. She came up to the bars and thrust a ferret-eyed, knob-cheeked face up at Hex, who stood gripping a bar in either hand, like a prisoner waiting release.

'Silence that animal,' she said.

'It is not mine, I cannot. The pair followed me, Madam – they have followed me for some time. They plague and spy on me. They wish to prevent me from seeing the dowager.'

Hex felt each sentence he uttered locking him more and more irrevocably out of the dowager's mansion. He looked desperately for something tangible, a hard fact to convert his appearance of lunacy into one of persecution. 'Arple Snolp!' Hex cried. 'Arple Snolp, or so he called himself, set them upon me when I asked my way here.'

The stout woman cocked her head at this, a gesture both amused and canny. She hesitated, then unlocked the gate.

'Enter, messenger.'

And in moments, with an amazement his confusion could not wholly obscure, Hex found himself in the antechamber of the mansion, with a heavy door interposed between himself and the din outside. The room was barrel-vaulted, flagged with tiles stamped with the Poon Crest, and furnished round three of its walls with fur-upholstered benches. A door was centred in each of these walls.

The woman bowed Hex to a seat on a bench, then folded her arms and cocked her head at him when he was seated. She smiled broadly, revealing strong and evenly gapped teeth. Hex did not care for the rodentlike intensity of her black eyes.

'I am Korl, my lady's housekeeper sir. So. You have come with a message, of life-and-death weight, and with a malign melodeon pursuing you, trying to thwart your mission?'

'Unaccountable as it may seem,' Hex answered with a show of affront. He had just felt the stir of a suggestion, a plausible rearrangement of his wild statements. 'You're implying that my explanation is unlikely. I can't help the appearances. Here are the facts. On my way here with my urgent message, I asked the way of a passerby. This man launched an astonishing series of obscenities and slanders regarding the late Orgle Poon, and of himself to boot! He called himself Arple Snolp and boasted of great notoriety, though I had not heard of him.

'It was but a few moments after I disengaged myself from his fulsome particularizings that I found this keeper with his beast pursuing me. The man insisted on believing – pretending to believe – that I came as a suitor to the dowager. He ignored my rebuffs and clung to my heels with his offer of service. I feel certain this Snolp desires the failure of my message to your lady. Wouldn't you infer the same, given the circumstances?'

'Yes sir, from those circumstances.' The uproar, which the closing of the front door had lowered to bearability, suddenly receded, and then all but vanished, from which Hex guessed that the melodeon had been carried round the corner and down the hill by its keeper.

'They have given up,' said Korl with an ambiguous smile. 'Now what is your message, sir?'

'It is deliverable solely to your mistress. You may tell her it comes from Bramt Hex, and that I am an inframagus of the Academy.'

Korl nodded, smiling, but did not move to leave. 'Your hose are most imposing,' she said. 'Are they new?'

'Comparatively,' said Hex stiffly.

'And your doublet! It is a most admirable doublet. Nay, I will go further – it is a prodigious doublet. Surely *it* is new?' She asked this ingenuously.

'No – it is old actually. Will you take my message to the dowager?' Korl shrugged at this, stood smiling a moment more, and went out of the chamber by the door to the right of the entrance.

Hex sat, imagining the hugeness of this ziggurat he had entered. The thought of its sheer bulk pressed upon him. The dowager owned this outright, and vast holdings besides. She was a woman of great power, pure and simple. How callow to think her susceptible to poetic wildness!

The door opened and the dowager entered. Hex rose, looking desperately into her eyes, even as he bowed. The name of Arple Snolp had got him past her door. With it then perhaps he could jar that autumnal face's remoteness.

'Madam Poon, I lied to your servant. I didn't come as a messenger. But an ugly accident has made me one! You are in danger from a slandering madman. He called himself Arple Snolp. I'm stunned. The foulness of the man! And the incredible luck of my meeting him, so I could warn you! You see, I came as your suitor!'

He stared open-mouthed in her eyes, letting his preposterous declaration hang in the air, finding an unexpected rush of confidence and humour in the fact that it was now the dowager's task to meet his odd apparition with poise. He had seen Snolp's name find a nerve in her.

While she stayed mute he rushed on easily, knowing that each awkwardness or hesitation would fit his part: 'It is madness I know, marvellous lady. I've stood in amazement at myself since I saw you in the inn this evening! But all that concerns only me – I must put it aside. This lunatic Snolp walks at large. He slanders your husband to strangers on the street. I was so astonished by him, his prattling bland way was so hypnotic, I actually let him walk off without strangling him for your sake – that's the most surprising thing of all!'

The muscularity of the woman's jaw had become subtly more pronounced. Hex knew he had sketched a portrait she recognized.

'Do you tell me you come as a suitor, sir?' The cold, measured question was the first he had heard of her voice. It was an alto woodwind voice, its low clarity had a sensual graininess – an unexpected pleasure of a voice.

Hex's organ of mendacity moved smoothly in him now. If she threw him out, so be it. He urged his part, delighted at his own ease:

'Oh please, I see the insanity of it even more than you. My orderly life, thrown over! I was an infra-magus of no small standing – and now I am nothing. Forgive my crassness, but when I saw you, a craving filled me, and now I am not happy with my life. I had to tell you this, not hoping for anything at all – how could I – but merely because a man must declare such a thing, must attempt to have his happiness, or think himself a coward. I'm a bookish man, tactless and direct in the world at large. And so here I am, Madam Poon – Bramt Hex, utterly at your service, making his crazed avowal. I am luckless, as in the melodeon I chose to please you with – but in my own world I'm widely known for my work in lore and letters, it's only justice to myself to say so. And thus my short story's told, esteemed madam. I stand before you desiring the impossible, not hoping for it.'

With an effort, Hex stilled his tongue. It was harder to look in her eyes when he was not rapt in his performance. She advanced two steps. The neutrality of her stare was, he realized, a concession – anything but a curt dismissal at this point was.

'What did Arple Snolp say of me?' she asked evenly.

'Of course, that's the vital matter! Nothing at all of you personally, madam. That would have wakened me to outrage. But of your late husband! He spoke filth as I could never repeat to you. Strangely, he spoke of himself in the same terms – that was largely what baffled my anger.' Hex saw he had added another detail that she knew. She looked at him in silence, absently crossing her forearms below her bosom. Her black eyes canvassed him with candid freedom; they were eyes which from birth had enjoyed the right of assessing others to their faces. At length she smiled faintly.

'I thank your concern, Master Hex. As it happens I'm aware of Snolp's calumnies. I'm glad however to be warned of his promiscuous forwardness in urging them. As to your suit. I must ask – is this possible? I recall you from the inn, of course. Could such a project arise from so brief an exposure?'

'Ah! I marvel too! Perhaps it is my aesthete's life, my long training to exalt the spirit's highest feelings. Only a moment's exposure was needed, for a soul taught to seize life's greatest treasures quickly – I mean, of course madam, your person.'

'I hope you have no thought of seizing my person, sir,' she said coolly. 'The attempt would cost you your life. I am forced to say that you are overbold and naïve, Master Hex. I forbear to have you ejected only because you are obviously sincere and seem, outside your folly, to be a man of polish and culture. You put me in a unique position. Your chance service to me, along with certain of your qualities, demand my grateful acknowledgement. Your madcap proposal excites only my amazement.'

Hex sighed, sharing her amazement: 'It calls to mind those lines in the *Epic of Urkh* – you know them, I'm sure: ". . . the winds of passion pluck our souls – mere leaves, mere scraps of longing – on . . ."' He paused and looked at her intensely.

She stared back, scowling slightly. As if against a sudden draught, she hugged herself a trifle closer and spoke.

'Master Hex, I have decided to take a risk, and be the equal of what seems to be my good fortune. You may be a man who can perform for me a vital service. If so, if your character is such as I feel it, instinctively, to be, then a certain form of union is actually possible between us – all this provided that I act as abruptly as this opportunity has arisen, and take you on slight acquaintance into my confidence. I am resolved to do this.

'But first, to mince no words: I am cold-natured and without passion. Quell all loverly imaginings, sir. Still, as chance has contrived, a friendship close and enduring can be established between us.'

'Any nearness to you, madam, would be better to me than utter separateness!'

'Then, good Infra-magus, kindly return here tomorrow forenoon. In the meantime I may rely on your discretion?'

'Absolutely. I am a man practically alone in this city, but if I had a thousand friends, they would not hear of it!'

'I rejoice. I would dread undue publicity. Korl!'

The door opened behind the dowager. 'See Master Hex to the gate,' she said, and with a smiling nod, returned through the door the housekeeper had emerged from. The stout, ferret-eyed woman led him outside, and along the walk.

'Well hasn't it been a night?' she said over her shoulder. 'Imagine – a melodeon! I did not think the custom survived!' She opened the gate and stood aside. 'Good night, sir. Your doublet is quite splendid, I assure you!'

Bramt Hex set off into the night with a fierce stride. The wind framed his exultation. His fortune dawned more largely upon him the longer he thought of it. Spreading his arms he shouted at the wind-whipped stars: 'So much! And from so little!'

3
The Dowager's Whorehouse

Hex passed the night on the roof of an abandoned house. It was in a north sector neighbourhood of the Glorak Hills, where fishing tycoons had built with grand arrogance in the days before homunculi and the skinfarms. Near-standing trees gave him a couch of dead leaves from which, looking past the dark roofs of other derelict mansions, he viewed three adjoining immensities: the stars, the city, and the sea.

He navigated among them till the sunrise, steering smoothly from aerial voyages with hired wizards, down to cross-ocean treks in purchased exploring fleets, and thence to the secret chambers of power where the application of a pen-stroke or a flame to a parchment made or unmade hosts of lives.

He had walked this city end to end, dawn noon and night, and had thought he knew it, but he smiled at the thought now. To a man of fortune it would be new terrain, threaded by different paths. And the world at large, so fragmentarily known to even the greatest cartographers – what great new map might not be drawn of this, by a determined man with wealth behind him? The first torch of sunlight, kindling on the sea's rim, took him by surprise, though he had been staring for half an hour at the dawn's deepening saffron.

At an inn not far from the Academy quarter, Hex took an heroic breakfast, and bathed in a rented stall. For digestive reasons he walked to the dowager's mansion, whither he had planned to take a cab. The day was overcast, and all the streets were reamed clean and dry by strong winds – wet-smelling wind promising rain. Each prosaic step by which he moved towards unguessable rewards summed up the miracle of his leap to new life: simple, direct, complete.

At the mansion's gate he had reached for, but not touched, the bellpull, when Korl stepped out of the front door and swept forward. The fronds were still bowing crazily with her haste, a leafy accolade, as she ushered Hex back up the walk.

'You are resplendent sir – No! Effulgent. How your doublet takes the sun! My mistress will be dazzled! I'm sure you have breakfasted, but if you'd like to do so again, I'm instructed to offer you whatever you wish.'

'Why are you so sure I have breakfasted? I haven't, in fact, and I won't. There are certain feelings, you see, good dame, that have a way of killing hunger.'

'Oh. You haven't been dyspeptic, I hope?' She brought him across the antechamber to the door opposite the house's entrance. Opening this, she stood aside, and Hex passed through.

He entered a high-ceilinged room, triangular in plan. Its apex, where the dowager sat by a lively fire, lay towards the centre of the house. Three other such rooms completed the square of the pyramid's base, Hex guessed. The air was cool, but the chamber's field of colours was hot; it was carpeted in amberfur and the fat, abundant furniture was upholstered with off-shades of the same, or with the cornelian pelts of the rare fjord-otter.

The dowager's gown was silver, coolness amid heat, reflecting the wavering of the yellow flames stretching up beside her. Her smile and nod were effortlessly articulate, welcoming him, conditionally. Hex answered with a bow and advanced.

As he took the seat she indicated, he guessed she meant to speak first. A freshness surrounded her – the morning was clearly her season.

'Infra-magus Hex.' Her voice weighed the epithet

gently. 'I know enough to be flattered by the praise of discriminating men. Such I knew you to be. I have inquired. While you are not, in point of official detail, an infra-magus, you are unanimously reported to be a brilliant scholar, whose examinations are impending, and who is expected to pass with dazzling ease. The *Urkh* teaches us how to esteem learning:

". . . give me the man whose mind is tuned and true, whose gaze is turned
To the lore and lays and laws of humankind . . ."

Aren't those the lines?'

'Wamph's oration, letter-perfect madam.' His heart pounded with expectation. His one sally had set his luck in motion, and this woman's cool control, her studied preamble, told him that an offer was prepared for him. He added with an unfeigned fervour:

'Your openness puts me to shame. I confess the paltry lie – perhaps forgivable – that my knowledge of my own brilliance persuaded me to tell. But now I wish to emulate your honesty. Please go on.'

'I will speak quite candidly then sir, for I think much might come of a complete understanding between us. I have told you I am cold-natured and disinclined to passion. This was a polite understatement. The bare notion of copulation between two persons has always struck me as ludicrous. It is an activity whose grotesqueness has always, for me, been accentuated by the vigour with which it is customarily performed – to such a point that it moves me to nearly uncontrollable laughter.

'Banish forever all notions of physical union, then. This is an essential point. At the outset you must make clear you can accept this.'

Hex blessed her directness. He felt glib and sure now. They were moving towards some colder, more occult bargain than sex – one perhaps even deeper in the mysteries of wealth than he had imagined. 'It's as I've told you, dear madam. I've been for years a bookish acolyte. Restrained passions are sometimes more gratifying to me than fulfilled ones. I don't deny certain drives, but I've never needed crass possession to enjoy a cherished object.'

'Splendid, Master Hex. Let me then sketch my position. My current social objective requires that I have a husband. If you could know, sir, the joy with which I greeted my abominable husband's death, you would appreciate the strength of my desire for this objective, that it could move me to re-enter matrimony. I only do so resolved on certain conditions, and these are what make a close and fruitful bond possible between us.

'Moving through my own stratum I might find a match of suitable culture and polish – for this is one of my conditions. I might also find one who would grant me, in the union, the physical freedom which is my second condition. But I would be very unlikely to find one who would waive legal prerogative, and leave the bulk of my holdings in my sole ownership, my third condition.

'You, if I may remain candid, possess the mental refinements essential to my tastes, and at the same time have much more to gain from even a restricted union than would one of my peers. You would have neither power over me nor title to my properties. But you would enjoy an annuity of five million lictors, from which you could quickly build your own body of holdings. You would always be treated by me with unfailing courtesy and respect, but you would be in essence my hired companion. If you can accept this completely genial, but limited, post, Master Hex, then I have every hope of our speedy marriage.'

'Madam, I am stunned.' It was the truest thing Hex had said thus far. 'The proposal does me tremendous honour – '

'Not at all, sir. Connection with a man of learning

has long been regarded as acceptable, regardless of the savant's material status – especially once a publication or two have been financed, and his attainments given the airing they deserve.'

'Madam! You load an honest man with unmerited bounties!' He understood now that their exchange of words was mere trimming – the exchange of services was everything. He waited rapt, sensing that he must perform something more than she had named, feeling certain he would be able to. She paused courteously over his ejaculation, and then went on.

'Our way is clear then. One difficulty only remains, a troublesome inequity.'

'My own unworthiness of course, Madam Poon!'

Her headshake dismissed this notion; a gesture of her hand acknowledged it. 'In all that matters, Bramt Hex, we are peers. Nonetheless, this remains a situation in which you, at the mere asking, are to be blessed with the highest advantages and, more importantly, with intimate knowledge of my affairs. To put it rather brutally, what pledge have I of your loyalty in return?'

'I am ashamed that it was not I who spoke first, madam! How may I serve you?'

'Your warmth and tact amply reward my trust. And I confess I would never have called you to this interview at all, if I had not felt an instinctive reliance on your character. May I suggest a beverage?'

The dowager summoned Korl and bespoke hot morning wine. She and Hex discussed the *Epic of Urkh* a while. When Hex rose to feed the fire, she returned to the topic at hand.

'My late husband was a swinish man, Bramt Hex – no, a mannish swine. He was a bundle of ungovernable, degenerate lusts whose envelope alone was manlike. I brought our union a considerable dowry, and in Orgle

Poon's lifetime he involved many of these funds in disgusting properties.'

Hex took his seat again and nodded attentively. 'Yes – as I mentioned, this lunatic, this – ' He stopped, seeing her upraised palm and closed eyes signalling to prevent the utterance of a coarse word. After a moment she spoke it herself in a low voice. 'Arple Snolp. Please don't use his name, Master Hex. He is the major and foullest part of my present dilemma. You see, he heads a group of decadent wits among the elite who vaunt their own evils. They are fork-tongued persons with the hearts of lizards. They believe their own ill-won fortunes render them immune to justice, and they utter all the slanders they can against other fortunes which, being honestly amassed, these toads can't bear to see unmaligned.

'My husband, however, while he did not go so far as to boast of it, was as foul as Arple Snolp himself, and anything the loathsome man told you regarding him was probably the truth. It was my ill luck to be a woman in the eyes of the law, and, as I have said, my properties became enmeshed with his.

'And now the grand object that I spoke of, Master Hex. I have just advanced my candidacy for the Thetataliad. Not merely for the Thetataliad, but for the seat of Archia Thetatalia, whose vacancy Lissaba Marm's present illness promises. I am likeliest candidate – my line has held at least one priestesshood at all times for seven generations. The seat of the Archia is undisputedly my right by every consideration.' An intensity had entered her speech. She paused, and when she was calm again, resumed. 'I entered my candidacy the instant I learned of Lissaba's failing health. I alleged a private betrothal and imminent marriage, and the Thetataliad took me at my word, setting me down as remarried and thereby eligible. I had in fact no suitable husband in view. That problem, however, quickly gave way to worse.

'Just after advancing my candidacy, I made a devastating discovery. Over a hundred million lictors of my uncle's holdings outside Ungullion have been, these thirty years past, invested in the largest and most egregious brothel in all of Glorak Harbour. The moment Snolp's carrion birds get hold of this fact, the foul breath of their rumours will blow away my chances of the Chair in a single day.

'This then is the service – call it the pledge – you must perform. You must sign an antedated deed of title to this infamous property. The document would designate you the sole owner of it as of thirty years ago – I believe you are twenty-eight years of age?'

'Yes.'

'Your age will not come in question. I don't deny a remote element of risk. You will be committing a crime for my sake and in the unlikely event of discovery, would stand liable before the law, though of course you would enjoy the discreet defence of my fortune. But honesty has already made me exaggerate the risk. The overwhelming probability is that you will never be called on to answer any questions. You'll be selling the property on the same day you sign the deed, and that is today, if you are willing. The buyer you will probably sell it to is a denizen of one of the subworlds, whither the house will be transported this same day, if all goes as foreseen. I and my agents are certain that secrecy is thus far intact. Even if we assume the worst, that Snolp or his ilk have lately broached the matter, the empowering of bailiffs and drawing of charges takes time, and both property and deed would be days in hell before any doors were knocked on.

'I know you can appreciate the extent to which I have already revealed myself to you. I do so in certainty of your discretion, whatever your decision.'

'Can you doubt what that is? Let pen and ink be brought, and this danger to you speedily removed!'

'I was lucky in you, sir. I am a meditative person who keeps her dealings to herself. I rejoice that in this departure from my custom I didn't err, but found a true ally. We'll have the deed brought, and I'll explain how to proceed with the sale.'

Hex emerged from the mansion around noon. To the driver of the first cab he was able to find – some blocks out of the exclusively residential Heights – he needed say no more than 'the Marketditch Brothel' to be whirled on his way towards that establishment. He himself had known the place before the dowager named it, merely from the epithet 'the most egregious brothel in Glorak Harbour' – known it, indeed, inside and out, though he was no 'chipster' in the student parlance, having been there only a few score times during his Academy career.

It stood in a waterfront neighbourhood, a five-storey stone box. Small windows, tightly shuttered, were countersunk in its bare façade, and their great number per floor made it look hivelike. This character, accentuated by its swarming activity at night, was part of what made his visit of almost a year ago his last one to date. The girl had been fey and fat-breasted, and Hex had been just on the point of getting his money's worth. Abruptly he remembered his larger position. All around him, for two storeys above and below, in dozens of identical cells, others copulated. He was surrounded by a host of coupling strangers, each pair of them adding infinitesimally to a faint rocking of the entire building which he fancied he detected even then. A kind of earthquake-panic soured his pleasure.

He entered and found the mute desertion of noon – whores' night – but otherwise the place was just as it had been. Hex remembered leaning tipsily at the balustrades, peering down on this lobby with its pimp-counters abustle and its fat furniture filled, some of it by clients of a public taste who were actually enjoying their assignees: a vision of vague shapes in turmoil, senseless as the patterns in sea-foam.

The place was not wholly empty now, he found. At one of the bars sat a lean, hairless man, his skullish face intent on some work in his lap. Hex approached and saw that he was polishing the numbered plaques – chips – which the pimps hung under the numerous women's names on the wall above the bar, to reserve them to waiting clients.

'I don't come as a client today my friend,' Hex said heartily, 'though I won't deny I've done so in the past, on a whim.'

The man, whom Hex had now identified with certainty as the head pimp, tossed his chip into one bin and took up another from a second. 'I see sir,' he murmured to his polishing hands politely, not lifting his head.

Hex noticed another presence he had missed – a lone whore, bored, leaning at the third-floor railing, looking down at them.

'No, I come wearing a different cap today,' Hex said. He drew the deed of title from his doublet and stroked it slowly, consideringly across his left palm, as one who whets a blade. To his irritation, the pimp did not even glance at the document, but took up yet another chip.

'I've come to tell you that you must prepare for this house's transportation, this same afternoon. I've sold it to an Ungullion man. You see I am its owner. Slamp, the skinbroker with whom you have dealt with these past years, is my agent.' Hex thought his declaration echoed menacingly in the stillness and dark-curtained spaces of the brothel. He smiled, trying to radiate the bland, unfearful nature of the whole affair. The pimp, still polishing, did not look up.

'I see, sir. Plods or wizardry sir? Must we batten down?'

'Plods. The buyer's no spendthrift. Do batten down. They'll be here in two hours or somewhat less.' Hex repocketed the deed as he spoke, deeply dissatisfied. Such smooth concession did not speak well for the whores' compliance with the move. Pimps and whores alike were life-bound to the house, for all had submitted to a soul-shackling, and were incapable of stepping outside it. With it they had a free hand, and since the demon buyer, in his concern for discretion, insisted on the conventional mode of transport, they would have considerable latitude for resistance.

Unwillingly, he turned away, while the whore who had been watching from above came down one of the two staircases that flanked the entryway.

She was nude, saving a belt with a tiny curtain of crotch-bangles. She was Loopish, with the jutting jaw of that race. Her long thighs, the aureoles of fine, white fur round her nipples, and her restless, shifting stance were all equally characteristic.

'Who's our new owner, your eminence?' Her voice was throaty and strong.

'He's a downcoaster, Madam. A man from Ungullion.'

'Ah! Ah ha! Would you believe it? Someone whispered to me that he was a demon! What's the name of this Ungullion man, sir?' She came closer with the question, grinning up into his face. Hex smelled her musk, and felt the taunt.

'I'm not free to say, Madam,' he said stiffly.

'Few are free to do anything, precious few. Except for the rich. I'm Zelt. I'm a whore, not a madam, so call me 'whore', Your Highness.'

Hex stepped around her. She sprang ahead of him, cupping her breasts in her hands to run. She turned in front of the curtain, blocking his exit.

'Good whore, I must pass.'

'Good owner, all things must pass. You're selling us to

a demon. I've heard rumours. One gathers many things, lying on one's back. Demons have been in town, looking up skinbrokers.'

'Don't call me a liar, whore.'

'Demons, Ineffable One. Names. Dreadful, hair-raising names have been whispered. Names that could buy a city of whorehouses at a nod. How will it be with us tonight, after the sale? What'll be hugging us close, and where?'

'Get out of the way!' Hex raged, her ugly accuracy angering him to the needed force. She shrugged – a breast-bobbling operation – and stepped aside.

'Owner, my arse!' she called to his back. 'Poon's puppet!' Hex threw the door shut on the words, which struck him like a snakebite. Fears poisoned his cab ride back to the foothills, to Slamp's brokerage.

This was a two-storey house of weathered timbers. The man who opened the door was short. He wore a fur-trimmed robe. His moustaches were waxed, and his long hair was interrupted on the crown by a bald spot. His bow, courtly in intention, was evidently abbreviated by a stoutness which his robe concealed.

'Good day, I am Slamp. Whom do I serve?'

'My name is Bramt Hex. I own the Marketditch Brothel.'

'The Marketditch Brothel! I am honoured to meet you for the first time, after so many years of satisfying association! By the powers! Your brothel is just what absorbs me at present. I feel a great stroke of luck is about to fall on us both, Master Hex. Tell me quickly: do you wish to sell this property?'

'Why, yes! Yes, I do!'

'Now this is a rare crossing of paths, Master Hex! Would you believe it? A buyer desiring this very property of yours sits even now above, in my office. Will you join us?'

4
A Hard Bargain

Hex was not at ease as he climbed the stairs behind the broker. The dowager had told him to hold out for a hundred million, and to combine firmness and tact equally, which indicated that the transaction, though prearranged, was to some degree genuinely at hazard. Meanwhile Slamp's jovial pretence betrayed underlying fear. The man's voice was not quite steady. Moreover, there was a smell, an acrid, faecal stink, that teased their nostrils as they climbed the dim stairwell. It seemed to Hex a kind of sensory echo of the fear he felt infecting his host, and it grew stronger as they topped the stairs. He decided it was coming from a door Slamp now led him to.

The broker paused before this door, his hand above its latch, and Hex started. It was an ordinary wooden door they had approached, but what they stood before was massive, rusty iron, all rivet-studded and dank. That light, insistent stench that leaked from this phantasmal door seemed to be the source of the hallucination. Hex shook his head, and saw again the same wood panelling, as Slamp pushed it open and led him into malodorous gloom.

The room was an office, its windows heavily draped. There were a table heaped with scrolls and ledgers and several chairs, in one of which the demon sat. But it was also – fleetingly, in unpredictable pulses – a different room, a room whose walls were of oozing, earth-sunk stone and gapped with the mossy doorframes of long corridors that echoed, just audibly, with restless, shackled multitudes. Hex understood the demon was the font of this phantasmagoric trance, and it helped him keep a semblance of poise. He sat in a chair of padded leather (intermittently, a rusty iron stool) that faced the entity.

The demon wore – *was*, in a way – a black cape and a wide-brimmed black hat. White smoke swelled and tenanted these garments. The restless, ragged hands were smoke – fuming out of shape, reformed each instant. The face was smoke, in which the eyes and mouth were jagged gaps. The demon's upward-welling substance did not diffuse through the room, but gathered in a column over him and vanished neatly through a slit in the air. Slamp was saying something about wind, and, gladly, Bramt Hex turned his eyes to the broker.

'What wind, did you say?'

'A lucky wind, I say. That's blown you here. Master Hex, you see,' he told the demon, 'is the owner of the Marketditch Brothel. He has just come to me seeking a buyer for it!'

The smoke-buoyed hat nodded. A whispered voice replied: 'Splendid. A splendid stroke of luck.' The mouth squirted wisps and fumes with each sibilant and plosive. 'Assuming, of course, you ask a sensible sum, not exceeding seventy million lictors.'

Hex spread his hands helplessly. 'Alas. Our smooth-sailing luck seems to have struck a reef. You see, I have come here with an unnegotiable figure – one hundred and ten million lictors. Debate would be a waste of . . . breath.'

With horror Hex found himself sunk, deeply and prolongedly in the dungeon place, and found its features more starkly vivid than before. He could see white veins of nitrous encrustation splayed across the ageless prison stones, could hear distinctly the lamentations of a multitude a-wander in darkness without limit. The charnel odour seemed to saturate his very skin, and he could see down some of the corridors now, see torchlight puddled on the flagstones, and figures creeping through those little oases of light. He jumped from his seat, strode to the door, and pressed his back against it, feeling the delusion loosen and fall from him, as if it had been some physical envelope. 'What are you doing to me? I protest! I won't do business under this kind of coercion!'

Slamp had risen to exhort them, but the demon stilled him, raising a tenuous hand which tattered into fragments with its languid, beckoning wave. 'Sit, human. You have misunderstood me. I did not finish setting forth my offer.'

Hex returned to his seat, full of relief and self-congratulation. He would get Lady Poon's price. No! He would get more! He would bring her not only the ninety million (after commission) she expected, but a princely gift besides, fruit of his initiative. Bramt Hex, the cat's-paw? The Dowager's lap-dog? Not entirely, it seemed.

'I beg your pardon for my haste. What was the rest of the offer?'

'Why, not much. A slight thing. Simply, eternal life. To live forever. Never to die.'

After a pause, Hex found a crack in his voice when he used it. 'You would give me this?'

'I would give you the means to achieve it. I would tell you how to find Yana.'

'And in Yana . . . ?'

'In Yana, the touch of undying is given to all who come seeking it.'

'Is it far?'

'Very far.'

For just a moment, his mind hung amazed. Even as the door to wealth was opening before him, to have the door thrown open on a second and greater wonder! Where might the bold spirit not soar? But then the free flight of ambition became a dread that he should fall. The revelations of demons were murky, doubtful things – fool's bait. The enterprise in hand was real, and great enough.

Not to be jeopardized for the sake of a treacherous rumour, no. It was time to state the price he really aimed at and wrap things up before his adversary worked further mischief on his imagination. He nerved himself to be firm and brusque:

'I am sorry, sir. I feel that you simply refuse to understand me. I will, in the spirit of compromise and goodwill, go down to a hundred and one million lictors, but not a lictor less will I accept. Please do not try me further.'

In the cold, stinking silence that followed, the demon's cape shuddered and boiled; his smoke raced more thickly up to the air's seam like a mute, reversed waterfall.

Then he replied. And throughout his answer Bramt Hex – for as long as that unhuman gasping filled his ears – was again in the demon's vault. He could see it yet more clearly than before. He had time, while he listened, to determine that the movement in the torchlit corridors was that of huge, multibrachiate shapes, all crawling now towards the chamber he sat in.

'I accept the offer, human. You put your terms insultingly. Hear mine. The house must submit to sale. There must be no displays. Neither alarm nor rumours must be raised. This is your responsibility. You will see it met, or suffer indescribably.'

The portals of the demon's clothes erupted gouts of smoke. The cape collapsed, the hat fell to the floor, and a last thick cloud vanished through its eerie vent. Gasping relief, Slamp rose and tore aside the drapes, thrust up the windows. The breeze rushed in, along with the sweet, wholesome sunlight of the upper world.

Slamp was subdued as he gave Hex the instruments of exchange to sign. When he drew up the bill-of-draft for the payment, Hex asked that he draw it for ninety million, and that the 'slight remainder' be given him in specie.

'I plan to purchase a surprise for a certain noble lady

who stands high in my esteem,' he explained with shaky gaiety. Slamp glanced at him, plainly aware of an irregularity, but just as plainly deciding it was only the dowager's business. It was clear that his responsibility to the other principal of this transaction was what engrossed him. He provided Hex with a stout satchel for his draft and his coin, then led the way down to a stabler who kept a coach and driver for him. As they rode together to the brothel Hex, made uneasy by the broker's gloomy silence, tapped him on the knee.

'Listen, good Slamp. This is foolishness, this idea that using a wizard would be talkmaking or flamboyant. It's quite common nowadays! Why invite trouble with a protracted plod-move? I'll gladly share the cost of a wizard.'

'I'm sorry. The buyer was too particular about this. Too many tongues are wagging lately of subworld encroachments. For my own part, I think you are perfectly right. But I stand even more liable to him than you do, my friend. I dare not violate his instructions.'

The first teams of movers were already on hand, stringing traffic barriers at both ends of the lane in front of the brothel, and they told the broker that the plods and earth-saw were on the way. This transportation-readiness plainly betrayed the prearrangement of Hex's and Slamp's 'lucky' encounter, but the broker was oblivious to the scholar's grins. He led them to the brothel's door, and through it. Pushing past the curtain and crossing the antechamber, they found they had the rapt attention of three hundred souls.

The house's denizens were draped all over the lobby furniture, sat hugging their knees atop both bars, leaned at every railing around the shadowy well of the central shaft. The focus of this conclave was obvious: Zelt, standing in a half-crouch, atop a chairback in the lobby's centre. She had turned her raging, gibbous eyes on the pair and now she shouted, pointing:

'Ask them! There they stand. Our fat Highness and Slamp, his sawed-off catamite! Isn't it true, Immensities? That we're being transported to the subworlds?'

'Madness!' Hex cried. 'What did I come here earlier, expressly to tell you? You're being moved to Ungullion. Why, it's even pleasanter than Glorak, a greener city by far!'

'Greener!' Zelt shrilled gleefully up at the shrouded skylight. 'Plod-flop is green, Your Maggotcy, and you're a liar! A demon has bought us – isn't that so?'

'You brainless slut!' As he shouted this, Hex envisioned with fearful clarity each foot of distance separating him from the door behind them. Within these walls, they could be torn to pieces. 'Consider what you say, fool,' he went on. 'Do demons use plods and earthsaws to move property?'

'Yes! Yes!' The Loop fairly danced on the chairback. 'They do if they want to avoid a stir, and squelch rumours! And isn't it also true, what they say about demons? That they fasten in swarms of lice and couple by feeding? That they cling to a body as fiery scabs, as gangrenations of the flesh? And isn't it true that it's demons who bought us?'

'Rubbish! You will obey!' It was Slamp who exploded with this, causing Hex, but no one else, to jump with startlement. The shrillness of the man's voice aroused laughter, which brought his wrath to a peak. He tried to shout, but was speechless, and turned on his heel for the door. Hex, not expecting to retire so abruptly, stumbled in his haste to follow. They dived through the chattering curtain with universal jeering at their backs. 'Oh sir!' cried a voice. 'Your doublet quite kills me, I'm weak at the knees!'

Outside, they congratulated each other on their

firmness, cursed the whores, and rushed to meet the movers' engineer, who had just arrived with the titanoplods. The shovel-jawed quadrupeds, one behind the other, trundled the earth-saw's forty-foot, circular blade between them. They could not have moved abreast, for either of them alone nearly filled the street widthwise. Their top-set eyes had a mournfully pious look, and their movement had a creaking pomp, an air of clumsy consideration. First they would operate the saw with their armlike forelegs, cutting free the block of pavement and earth the brothel was rooted in. Then they would work the windlass of the great boom whose top, slowly swaying, was even now visible above the rooftops some blocks away. The infamous structure would then be hoisted on to the wheeled platform that was the crane's foundation, and borne down to a barge already moored in the inlet.

'Set them to it at once,' Slamp told the engineer. 'We want to catch the early tide, and still might!'

The flagmen and goaders, directing the beasts by signals, specially inflected cries, and prods, faced them off on either side of the saw, and guided their positioning of it before the brothel. The giants lifted their forepaws to the two-handled crank. There was a sharp clapping sound as all the shutters of the top three storeys of the brothel were flung open.

Perfume jars, bottles, cosmetic boxes, phials, and jets of foul-coloured fluids smacked and spattered down – not against the plods, but aimed with fair accuracy at the flagmen and goaders. Several of the latter cried out; a flagman fell stunned, and was dragged to safety by two others. Both teams of workmen retreated, leaving the behemoths, blinking and immobile, under the windows. Zelt's head thrust out from one of these.

'Bedpans and bottles,' she cried down. 'Trash on your heads, fatcats! We won't be sold away to hell!' She pulled her head in. A flaming mattress was thrust out.

Unfolding in the air, the smouldering pallet flopped squarely on the upstaring eyes of one of the plods. The mountainous animal reared up screaming, flinging the mattress off its face. This movement knocked over the earthsaw which, falling, scored the flank of the second beast. This latter, mad with pain, leapt to one side and collided with a garden wall across the street, leaving a huge crack in it. The engineer sent flagmen and goaders to the beasts, who stood waggling their ears with amazement, and had them brought back from the house. Then he descended angrily on Hex and Slamp:

'Gentlemen! No mention was made of danger to my beasts and men! These people must be brought in hand, or we work no further!'

The labourers, recognizing that a pause had been reached, already stood around in relaxed groups, gossiping, breaking out loaves and cheeses. At various windows whores leaned out to shout jeers and insults. The workmen, munching, shouted cheerfully back. A carnival atmosphere was spreading, a maddening air of ease and jocularity. Hex – glum, void of ideas – watched his swift-moving good fortune grind to a halt before his eyes.

'Slamp,' he said. 'Wait here with the crew. A plan has been prepared for this contingency, and I must go to set it in motion. I'll be back within the hour.'

The engineer's protest at the length of the delay was silenced by the broker. 'I know whom you go to see,' he told Hex, a light in his desperate eyes. 'Take my coach. Explain the need of . . . emergency disciplinary measures. We will wait.'

At the Epicure Inn the dowager awaited Hex's completion of the sale. The place enjoyed one of Glorak Harbour's most breathtaking views, but as he was whirled up the ever-steeper streets, he hardly saw the brilliant sprawl of sea and city that spread below him. The dowager, a veteran in the ways of wealth and power, could surely untie this little knot in their proceedings, but at the same time, it shamed Hex to be running back to her like this. To play such a craven role, the Novice, returning for new orders!

She was in one of the inn's reserved rooms, her coachman standing at the ready by her table. Hex bowed.

'My lady, I bring good news mixed with slight difficulties. First, the sale is made.' He produced the bill-of-draft from his satchel. The dowager did not move – the coachman plucked it from his fingers. Seeing her cold, level stare, Hex cleared his throat and went on:

'The inhabitants of the property – they have resisted their transportation, Madam Poon. Their missiles have forced the plods to be withdrawn from the work. I have, discreetly of course, sought your advice. None knows where I am.'

'They resist, you say?' the dowager asked.

'Yes, Madam. Under the instigation – '

'The whores and pimps, you say? They resist their sale?'

'Yes, Madam. The whores and pimps.'

The dowager's eyes registered only well-bred disgust and irony. But Hex could discern a simple, unrefined rage. Startled, he asked:

'May I speak a thought of mine?' – and rushed on to do so. 'The buyer, as you . . . predicted, dislikes flamboyant means, fears publicity. But his fears distort his judgement. Many respectable brokers use sorcery in transport, that's well-known even to men untrained in finance, like myself. It merely means the buyer and seller are in haste, and is not interpreted as masking black purposes. To insist on plod transport means a prolonged confrontation, ensuring a notoriety which the use of wizardry would never stimulate. Why, as for the added cost, I think you may be pleased to – ' the happy memory of the excess lictors had struck him, but the dowager cut in:

'Master Hex. I thank you for your services. You can do no more in this matter. I will go to an agent of mine who has greater experience of these accidents. Trouble with it no further. Take any refreshment here you desire and charge it to my account. Then take a coach to my house and await me there.'

She had risen as she spoke, and her coachman was already officiously preceding her to the door. Hex could only rise and return her salute with a bow.

5
Transportations – Foreseen, and Otherwise

The dowager, as she sat in her coach, held a lace handkerchief between her hands. In the course of her ride, she tore this meditatively into seven almost perfectly equal strips, each of which she let fall to the floor. Her hands were patient in the task; her fingertips, white-and-red with strain, worked through the lace's unequal toughness in a line almost scissors-straight.

When they arrived, the coachman had scarcely dropped the steps and touched the handle of her door when she flung it open and stepped out, ignoring his proffered arm. Slamp was already hurrying to her.

'Madam?'

'There is rebellion here, Master Slamp?'

'Yes, Madam! Murderous insurrection! Foul revolt! Hear me, for my life, something must be done! You know the buyer I stand before – '

'Don't dictate to me, greedy maggot.' She spoke softly. The coachman leapt in front of her. He dropped to a light crouch, and from that stance fired two near-invisible blows up into the face of the skinbroker. Slamp was lifted from his feet by the first and jerked sideways in the air by the second. He crashed on to the street, a pile of unknit limbs. He lay shaking his head until the glaze left his eyes, and then got humbly to his feet. Both his cheeks, where large gouts of skin were missing, bled.

'I meant no . . . Excuse . . . Only that . . .'

'Attend me,' said the dowager to the coachman, and swept towards the brothel's door. Though a black drape covered the coach's coat of arms, its advent had already been recognized as an event. The work crews, gathered round the legs of the withdrawn plods, gossiped busily; the whores had vanished from the windows to report within. The coachman, menacingly, took up his lady's vanguard, pushed open the door, and held aside for her the scale curtain. His posture was a footman's who announces an entering notable.

The house was even more awake than Hex and Slamp had found it. Shrill railleries were traded across the shaft by the whores leaning at the railings; cheesepots, loaves, and winejacks now had space on the bars along with the hairnetted pimps; the furry arms of chairs and couches were decorated with crumbs, butter knives, and greasy plates, and the dozens of whores who sprawled there munching – some in their skin-smoothing masks, others trailing blankets shawlwise – displayed a holiday mood. Crusts, cheeses and bottles were passed from diner to diner aerially, and went arcing unpredictably through the glee-loud gloom. The dowager steered her hooped prow through the anteroom, and stopped at the lobby's edge, with a motion as if holding her skirts back from the brink of a foul pool. The coachman stood beside her.

Their presence spread a silence through the house. Here and there the whores' noise flared up in exclamations, bursts of uncertain mockery. But in a few moments all had become the dowager's audience, submerged in the expectation with which her mute, arrogant stasis effortlessly filled the huge interior. She needed – and used – scarcely more than a speaking voice to reach every ear.

'By your own hands, and your own wills, you bound yourselves to this house. You scum. You thankless filth. For years you've had bed, board, and raiment here. For years, in payment of easy, honest work, you've had every benefit. You've had your bread, and hours of ease. You've – '

'Benefits! Did you say benefits? Or Pain and Fits?

Bread and Ease? Or Dread and Disease? For such have been your bounty, oh Enormity. Pain and Fits! Dread and Disease!'

These words were flung from the third-floor railing, and raised applause from the lobby. Zelt leaned from the balustrade, grinning down. Her breasts hung over wagging sarcastically with her vehemence. The dowager locked eyes with her. There was a pause, in which the assembly's noise fell to a murmur.

'Foul slut. Come down here to me.' Her voice was a velvety growl. It might have deepened the general silence, but for the quickness of Zelt's reply:

'Oh, readily, Lady Petticoats! Faster than you'll wish I had when I get in pissing range. Yes yes! Coming!'

The whore plunged into the crowd behind her. Her passage was marked by a stir and a tittering along the third and second balconies, while a merry babbling rekindled throughout the lobby. Zelt reappeared at the first-floor railing opposite the entryway. Positioned like a general in the midst of his force, the shaft's width from and a storey's height above her antagonist, she cried with expansively outflung arms:

'Come forward! Come and receive the golden rain! By the Powers, I'll water you till your hair shoots out and grows to your ankles!'

This raised an outright cheer, and the crowd's first direct taunts.

'Make way for the pious Poon who owns us!' shrilled a whore.

'This way, you elegant old gash!' cried a pimp, approaching within a few yards and delivering a welcoming bow. He never straightened from the gesture. The coachman sprang forward with all the suddenness and thrust of a leaping feline, bringing his feet forward in mid-air and tightening his body. His right heel loudly snapped the pimp's bowed neck. Before the corpse had settled to the carpet he leapt again – on to the back of a second pimp who had turned to flee. The coachman locked his knees against the man's lumbar vertebrae, hooked an arm round underneath his chin, and hauled back. The pimp's heels snagged in the carpet, his body arched forward, his spine snapped. The coachman rode him to the floor and somersaulted off.

He landed on the balls of his feet and, with a seemingly random fluidity, dodged a heavy perfume jar thrown from above. A whore was just struggling out of an armchair to his right, and he killed her with a blow to the diaphragm. With a side-skip and a kick of his left foot, he crumpled the rib cage of a tall, small-breasted redhead who had just lofted a wine bottle to throw at him.

All in the lobby scrambled to flee, but the abundant, bulky furniture baffled their panicked – and, in many cases, tipsy – efforts. As the dowager stared on, not moving, the coachman now vaulted atop the furry maze of couches and chairs. Nimbling across their backs and arms he did his jerky dance of death, striking his victims' vainly shielded heads and throats, dodging a rain of missiles from the shaft as liquidly and unpredictably as he moved from prey to prey. Then, as he bounded off a couch-cushion, his feet were snagged in a shawl left sprawled across it. His takeoff was marred and he fell short of the armchair he aimed at, just managing to hook an arm across its back as he went down. In that instant a heavy coffer struck his shoulder with a meaty crunch. The coachman dropped to the floor behind the chair.

'Ha! Got you square and hurt you bad, you nasty little ghoul!' Zelt shrieked down, hopping with excitement as, enspirited, those who had fled the coachman now turned and reconverged on him. He regained his feet. He was groggier now – one arm dangling, his face sweat-bright – but still lethally poised. He flourished his good arm and spread his fingers. From their tips sprang six-inch razors, hooked like claws. Like a man fighting off a cloud of hungry blood-flies, he began to rake the air in all directions. Men and women fell clutching at their whistling, spurting throats, collapsed on legs that folded like scythed stems. Still lithe – though less quick – the coachman moved back across the lobby. Leaving a redder wake than he had made going out, he returned to the dowager, and resumed his station at her side.

The dowager languidly raised her hand towards the dead in the lobby – a gesture of presentation. She scanned the faces of shadow-etched alarm that crowded above the railings, and met Zelt's eyes. Under the lamplit gloom of the great, shrouded skylight, the fallen – there were more than a score of them – had an orgiastic air. The self-abandonment of death's postures, the outflung limbs and impossibly back-bent heads, suggested revelry. Some still feebly moved.

'Can't you see, you degenerate fools?' Lady Poon's voice was grave but mellow, almost lilting. 'No waste sickens me more than the waste of lives. This is your achievement! It's the image of your madness!'

'Then let there be no waste! Yes! Let there be none for you or us, Majesty!' Zelt leaned from the balcony with perilous eagerness, crying this. 'Sell us to ourselves! We'll pay the same this demon gives! What is it – ninety, a hundred million? At double shift and quarter ration, we'll bring you that much in one year – that much above and beyond the normal gate!'

The dowager stared up into Zelt's face so long a murmuring grew along the railings. There was movement in the crowd filling the corridor behind the Loop, as well as a cautious advance of onlookers down the two staircases flanking the antechamber. To this latter movement the coachman attended calmly, not moving from the dowager's side, though through the antechamber lay their sole retreat.

'Sell you to yourselves. Double shift and quarter ration.' The dowager still stared at Zelt as, with a low tremor, she returned her words. 'Do I actually stand here to hear terms bandied by a slut I own – skin and soul, living or dead? Hear me all. Thus it stands with no more said: you yield, all of you, now, or you will be burnt to ash.' She turned, and the coachman with her, ignoring the Loop's shrill answer:

'Own us? How do you own us – did you swallow us down? Oh, you could never swallow the things *I* have, your majesty.' Even as she shouted, Zelt jumped to one side, and her place at the railing was filled by a tall zanobian female with a crossbow.

Though the exchange was nearly soundless, something alerted the coachman, who whirled as the bowstring hummed. He completed his turn in time to fold himself neatly round the shaft that sprouted from his diaphragm, and fall. He folded and unfolded several times more on the floor, and was still, while pimps and whores rushed down both flights of stairs and filled the antechamber, blocking the door, whose bar was heard to crash into place.

Lady Poon watched these manoeuvres coldly, as though none of them personally concerned her. Looking back at Zelt she began a stately, deliberate progress towards the centre of the lobby.

'So. Not only do you keep weapons here, but you actually seek to detain me. You debauched, lunatic bitch. It seems that violations of contract mean nothing to you – violations of your solemn oaths of indenture.' She seated herself calmly on a couch where all rebellious eyes might fix directly on her. She turned her own eyes, remote and scornful, on the activity around her, seeming a playgoer who reviews a distasteful presentation. The dead were being carried off, and the lobby reoccupied. But those who returned – for all their more truculent looks, and harsher taunts – still left an empty zone immediately around her. Even a weeping whore, who cursed and kicked the coachman's corpse, flinched from the Lady's eye, and said nothing as she dragged a dead friend past her.

'*Contract*, you say,' Zelt howled. The Dowager's calm unassailability threatened to deprive the revolt of its centre. The more everyone sidestepped her, the less was their many-voiced anger able to focus; it stayed at the level of a mutinous but impotent hubbub. As the Loop continued, her voice grew shrill, and almost frightened: 'What of *your* side of the bargain? Assumed, if never specified? That we would mate with humankind? Where you're sending us, we'd suffer daily murder! Demons rarely copulate as flesh, and when they do, it's flesh you'd shake to look on! More often, they enter your blood as ague, or burrow into the soles of your feet as worms, or eat, digest, and vomit you whole again! And worse than all of these, of course, are the ones that enter you as dreams.'

'Your life, whore,' said the dowager, 'is forfeit. You will die. I don't know why you have concocted this lie of demons, but you have already cost a score of your friends their lives and you will pay for this. The rest of you, all the rest of you, I will excuse with a hundred lashes and half rations for one year. Your fears, played upon by this lunatic, urge me to this mercy. Strict justice demands your lives with hers. There is not one among you who did not bind herself, out of her own free choice and will, to my indenture.'

The hum of reaction to this was fierce, laced as much with laughter as with doubt, but no voice was raised directly against the speaker. Zelt's answer came raw and angry, an underdog's blows, slightly wild and wide.

'Our own free choice, rot you? Did you ever crouch

for your life on a blind, fat, foggy street? Where I come from, they laugh at the term "hill vampire" – there, the Sucks walk right up and try your windows and doors, and you'd better *have* windows and doors! There were norns galore, and ghouls, ten times nastier than yours, oh eminent bitch! And you sold your skin quick there just for the sake of a room at night, sold it to whoever was buying!'

'My answer is a simple matter.' The dowager looked coolly to the house at large as she spoke. 'Accede to your sale, vote now to cooperate in your transportation to Ungullion, and surrender this villainness to me. Your punishment will be no more than I have said, though I'll see to it that the new owner inflicts it: I'll make its enforcement one of the conditions of sale. Your alternative is to be burned alive. Yes! For I have been, all along, in mental contact with my wizard. I have endured what I have only to gauge the extent of your madness, and as I find this Loopish slut to be its real instigator, I remain willing to excuse the rest of you. But defy me further, and I will annihilate the lot of you. Depend on it! I have too many holdings to allow the deadly precedent of such insurrection.'

'*Annihilate?* Idle threats! Bluff and bluster!' There was a note of resurgent glee and confidence in Zelt's voice. 'She came in anger, friends, unprepared – thinking to face us down by her mere presence. She's trapped now, and burns with rage, but dares not show her hand. Believe me, for I know her! I have known her *intimately*. She's the Veiled Lady, my friends! The Veiled Lady!'

At last Zelt had kindled a real outcry. Here and there came joyful hoots of recognition, and explanations were passed round with an excited warmth. The dowager did not move, but her careful immobility was a kind of betrayal. She glared up at the whore, who was gleeful again, and recovering her oratorical rhythm:

'What? Do some of you not know of the Veiled Lady? My most mysterious Regular? My most dread, exalted Regular?' Shouts begged the details, other voices crowed corroborations. A mimic wail topped all other noise, issuing from some upper balcony:

'Pleeeeeeeese. Oh! Don't annnn-nyyyyyyye-ulate me! Pleeeeese!'

'Just so! Just so,' howled Zelt above the laughter. 'One of your squirmers and pleaders she is, this Veiled Lady I'm talking about. One of your wiggly writhers who pays to beg mercy and be denied! No chipster, mind you – she has me on bimonthly exclusive! Oh, she's top rank, all right, and the rankest kind of bellycrawler! A tall, firm party – I can tell she's grey-haired through the veil. An escort always brings her and waits outside. By his tread, though I never see him, I judge him to be a small and agile body. I mean, judge him to *have been* such! Oh, how could I not have recognized your voice till just this moment??!'

The dowager's surrounding zone of awe was gone. A whore vaulted on to the back of a chair quite near her, struck an imperious stance, and flourished the blanket she carried like a whip above her head. A second and then a third whore imitated the first, and a hairnetted pimp thrust his face into the dowager's and shrieked conspiratorially:

'Oh! Isn't it *delicious*??'

The dowager apportioned each tormentor one close, cold look, and returned her eyes to Zelt. The Loop seemed irked at the dowager's silence. Lacking the counterpoint of denial, she lashed down her strokes more fiercely:

'Oh, how you've wagged that bottom up at me in supplication! Oh, with what sincerity I've scourged it! "Oh, oh, oh," you've quavered, "Oh brutal, beautiful, merciless bitch, don't crush my body utterly, don't grind me out of existence!" Wag your royal rump for us now – yes, wave it, do! That fat flag of surrender that beseeches more blows!'

Whores up in the shaft now postured, hanging from their railings with one arm akimbo and scowling erotically. The pantomimers perched on furniture near the dowager had doubled.

Madam Poon's hand rested on her bodice now, as she stared a moment more up at Zelt. Then her hand came away from her bosom and she smoothly, unhurriedly, stepped sideways, and swung at the legs of a taunting whore. Though the blow seemed to miss, the girl's left leg collapsed and she pitched to the carpet. With a curtsy-like sweep of her skirts Lady Poon stepped back to let her fall, swept in again to straddle where she sprawled, and gracefully stooped over her. There was a punctured scream. The dowager rose and wiped her stiletto blade on the back of a chair, looking coolly up at the Zanobian who aimed the crossbow down at her from Zelt's side.

'I am leaving now. If my departure, and the movers' work, go unopposed, and if you, Loopish filth, are surrendered, bound, to my agent within the next half hour, then all the rest of you will live.' Lady Poon turned and moved grandly towards the antechamber. The first whores she met gave way, staring.

'Lies!' Zelt screamed. 'Do you think she'll let any of us live now that we've unveiled and mocked her? If she passes that door, we're all fried, my friends – every last one of us. Our only hope is to hold her and compel her to a contract freeing us, and guaranteed by sorcery!'

Several of those blocking the antechamber hefted stools as shields against the Lady's knife, and nervously stood their ground. A general stir, raised by Zelt's rallying cry, was not precisely caused by her words themselves, but by her voice, for this had echoed very strangely in the lamp-lit gloom. Indeed, the crowd's own murmurs had the same uncanny resonance to them, a circumstance that increased their volume and perplexity. The Loop did not yet notice these echoes, nor did the Lady, who whirled back to face Zelt wearing – for the first time – a smile.

'What? Can you think I care what any of you knows of me? You? Who are all the merest scum and insignificance? It is only from such as you that perfect humiliation can come, and that is why I bring those odd cravings of mine to you and none other! Mock me, you say? Who cares what noise the muck makes when it bubbles? Ah, the consequence you give yourselves! It's almost charming.'

Still smiling with what seemed genuine, mad mirth, Lady Poon returned a few steps more across the lobby towards Zelt, whom exclusively she addressed. The Loop returned her stare, but sweat shone on her face. She too now had caught the eerie reverberation of the Dowager's words, which went twisting up through the shaft in cracked and shimmying fragments of sound. The whole house buzzed with the queasy strangeness of the air and Zelt gripped the rail to concentrate on her antagonist who alone, rapt in the passion of her diatribe, still failed to notice.

'You talk to me of miseries?' she continued, crowing. 'Imbecile! No one has everything, and therefore all lives are miserable. Self-pitying swine! You've sheltered here! You've guzzled and coupled and slept here, dry when it rained and warm when the wind blew! What more do you think one gets? Worms in the feet, you say? Bad dreams . . . ?'

But now she too had heard. She stood amazed, jaw hanging, listening to her own last words – wrenched into a ghastly, senseless ululation that went twisting up into the shaft. Then the galleried faces above her screamed as the dowager, and the furniture around her, were drenched with a splash of crimson light. The skylight's black shroud was on fire with strange, smokeless flames of the deepest blood-red. A holocaust of sound – a vast droning like the after-hum of an immense bell – engulfed the house.

The building's walls, suddenly frail-seeming, pulsed like living membrane within that hell of noise. Whores, pimps, the dowager – all writhed, clasping their ears and making bent mouths of panic in the undulous red light now flooding the shaft – for the shroud was already consumed, and the unearthly flames still raged fuelless from the glass of the skylight itself.

Then, abruptly, the skull-numbing din sank in volume till the whores could hear each other's screams and – more – could hear outside the house the sound of an endless conflagration – the hiss and flap and crack of a thousand-league waste of flames.

There was a groan of ruptured steel. The people massed in the antechamber were exploded shrieking into the lobby as the front door was burst inward and three flaming tentacles, each thicker than a man, poured coiling into the antechamber – swaying, probing, seeking.

At her railing Zelt danced with terror and glee.

'We're there already! We've arrived! Hail to our new lords! This way, masters, this way!' She pointed down to where the dowager stood gaping. 'That one is fresh!' Zelt screamed. 'Feast on her first, my lords! Feast on her first!'

The address of Antil the Elliptical – which, along with his name, had cost Hex ten lictors – was near the inlet's western end. The still legible 'Goodsharbour' painted across the whole width of the building's second storey attested to its having been a warehouse. There was a bank of windows along its third and top floor, and a man darted across one of these, and disappeared, as Hex approached the front door. This latter he found open, surmounted by an 'Enter' sign.

The ground floor, vast and unpartitioned, was a forest of rampways, chutes, and slides. From the ceiling they dropped down to and often through the floor. They were arced, parabolic, straight, helical; they stood so thickly on all sides that Hex could see almost nothing of the room's farther walls. As he stepped hesitantly inside, a man dropped out of the ceiling and sped down a spiral chute. Hex gathered as he came through the first curve that the man was dancing madly atop a spinning red sphere the size of a melon.

The man in his turn saw Hex, and addressed him as his last three swift orbits permitted:

'Greetings! . . . Join you . . . Upstairs' and just before he sank through the floor, he pointed to the room's centre, where Hex noted a staircase, the sole sanely pedestrian accommodation in the place.

The second storey was like the first; the third presented Hex, at the landing, with three doors, only one of which was open. Within this was a large, nearly empty room. In one of its walls was the bank of windows he had seen. In a far corner were a pair of settles and an armchair. The vacant floor featured some two dozen trapdoors without latches, which Hex carefully avoided as he approached the windows.

Past some intervening rooftops he could see the inlet, looking down the long axis of that marine corridor. In the vigorous late sun, churned by the post-pluvial wind, the sea was a foam-marbled jade. He felt suspended over a host of possibilities, a multitude of epic acts now accessible, numerous as the waves of the open ocean. The nine-hundred and ninety thousand lictors in his pouch burned against him, a lump of sheer thaumaturgical energy. The dowager's far vaster sum had ridden there and he had felt it far less vividly. These fewer lictors were his own, the fruit of his initiative, and they, properly used, were going to command that arrogant woman's respect and erase from her lips forever all such cool dismissals as, 'you can do no more in this matter!' Decisive action had borne him this far, and now it would secure to him forever his lieutenancy on the winged vessel of Fortune.

One of the traps in the floor snapped up and the lean, bearded dancer hotfooted out of it. Hyper-nimbly he rode his spin-blurred sphere around the floor, dodging trapdoors with every swivel.

'Antil the Elliptical?' Hex asked with a bow.

'The same! A moment please,' cried Antil, still attending to his ride. He dropped through a trap. Some fifteen seconds later he popped out of another one, jumped off the sphere and kicked it smartly. It sped to a far corner, where it hung, still spinning. Cordially Antil indicated the furniture in a different corner.

'The flesh must be kept fit, you see!' he said cheerfully as they seated themselves. He had an anaemic look; his beard was scraggly and his thin, pronounced nose had a rubbed redness about the septum and nostril. His eyes were liquid, suggesting, alternately, sanguine emotion, or an imminent sneeze. 'Decay must be fought with exercise, oh, yes yes – ' he continued, with genial disclaimer of an objection Hex had not raised. 'Even a wizard's flesh dies, my friend, though somewhat more slowly than other men's. All flesh dies. Unless of course it has had the touch of undying.'

'I can see that you are remarkably fit, honoured Antil. Such exercise as I saw you doing is certainly terribly demanding. What do you mean by the touch of undying?'

'It certainly is demanding! And even so, it is much below what I could do as a youth. As a young man, I exercised on a sphere no larger than a kickle-nut. Age has forced me to this gross globe you see.'

Hex nodded with interest. 'Still, I see you scarcely

sweat – surely you're quite hale. You know, I just this morning heard mention of a touch of undying.'

'Yes.' Antil nodded energetically. 'In fact it would take me a whole morning's dancing to work up a sweat. You know, if you'll pardon my saying so, you are yourself carrying quite a load of flesh you'd be better off without! You're sturdily made, shake a leg, sir! I'm convinced you'd shape out just wonderfully with a little discipline!'

'Ah yes!' Hex assented with tepid joviality. 'There's more of me than ought to be, sad truth. You did say something of a touch of undying, didn't you? Is this perhaps connected with a place called Yana?'

The wizard stared back at Hex. All conviviality had left him.

'Is this the service that you seek of me – knowledge of Yana?'

'In fact no, there is another matter . . .'

'You must pay for each service I render.'

'Well of course; there's really no need to – '

'My fee is nine-hundred ninety thousand lictors per service.'

'That is the precise amount I bear,' Hex said quietly, after a pause. Antil nodded.

'Had you more, the price would have been that much higher. Which is your desire then – settlement of the brothel's difficulty, or answers to your questions about Yana?'

He resented the wizard's prying insights, and his cavalier use of them, but apprehension as to how much liberty one might take with a wizard kept his voice mild in reply.

'Naturally, I can't seriously consider abandoning business at hand for the sake of specious rumours. Kindly transport the brothel – doubtless you already know the details?'

'Perfectly, and I accept the commission. Ah, you've chosen oddly friend, though I must say most men in your place do the same!' The man's warmth had returned. 'Well! Do you care to pay me now, Bramt Hex?'

'Ah, payment in advance? Very well.' He spoke stiffly, irritation testing his control. Antil shook his head.

'On the contrary. I perform all commissions co-instantly with the acceptance of them. Pay me. I will show you.'

Paid, Antil flourished his right hand at Hex. A dense scribble of purple lines leapt forth and enmeshed the startled scholar.

Hex's sense of body vanished. He was eyes and ears only, mute, a weightless awareness towed like a balloon behind Antil, who strode to one of his windows, opened it, and leapt out.

Hex was plucked through the air. He could read the wind in the inlet's churning, but felt nothing of it. They crossed tracts of waterfront rooftops, lead-shingle dells, and thickets of stubby chimneypots. Then they paused in air, and plummeted. Pavements next to a gaping hole grew huge beneath Hex's sight. Then he stood, flesh again, on Marketditch Street.

A titanoplod's hindquarters were just vanishing around a corner. Farther off, the slowly receding boom rocked above the grey wharfside skyline. Antil was nowhere.

Hex returned to the dowager's mansion on foot, the better to digest his excitement. There would probably be some difficulties with the buyer, but these would yield before a description of the whores' rebellion and the dangerous publicity it promised. The consensus would surely be that he had risen to the occasion.

The sun was westering when he reached the palings of the Poon house. On an impulse he tested the gate, and found that it opened compliantly. He strode between the gilt, wind-stirred fronds. The mansion's portal opened before him, and Korl beamed and bowed him into the antechamber. 'Eager welcome, sire Hex. You're later than expected. The lady's not back yet. Will you dine, sir?'

'Good evening, Korl!' Hex felt expansive. 'Tell me, Korl, don't you find my doublet prodigious?' The raisin-eyed woman nodded with bright vigour.

'Indeed, yes sir!' she cried, bowing him ahead through the central of the inner doors. Hex stepped, chuckling, into the room. An earthquake of white pain wrenched his neck. As he plunged, lax, into the arms of gravity, the busy, humorous hum of his fantasies became a long, white numbness.

6
A Wizard Saves a Life, And Vampires End Two

Deep in a great swamp, freezing cold and utterly black, a solitary fire burned. Coiling snakes of greasy smoke it sent into the featureless dark.

Bramt Hex grew a little more conscious – enough to recognize this landscape as his own body: a hot, smutty focus of nausea, which coiled up through a still-boundless swamp of awakening nerves. He could not yet find the delicate filaments of control that would open his eyes, but he did discover the indistinct, outlying masses of his limbs. He stirred them. His body – a strengthless sac – rolled until it came up against iron bars. Between these, he vomited.

These bars would be the palings outside the dowager's mansion. The thought was the one particle of clarity in him as he shuddered and heaved the cold swampwaters out, but even before his convulsions had ended, he realized the unlikeliness of this.

He opened his eyes. He was in a cage. It looked just high enough to sit upright in, and somewhat less than his body's length on either side. This cage stood on the side of a hill, and under a star-cobbled sky. The breeze, which he felt keenly through his scale doublet, smelled of lush grass and – more elusively – of the sea.

He heard the mutter of burning wood, and then saw two silhouettes just downslope. They sat with their backs to him, screening a fire so small its red glow barely limned their hairy outlines – their batwing ears, their manes that merged with the thick tresses of their shoulders and backs, their barrel-chests thick-staved with prominent ribs.

A new tide swept through Hex, one of horror and misery that could not be vomited out. He had been sold to the skinfarms.

'Help!' he croaked. 'Water! Please! Where am I?'

One of the silhouettes towered upright against the fire's faint backlighting, and strode upslope. The giant had to squat low to present his shadow-face at the bars near the top of Hex's cage.

'Listen closely, my friend.' The voice was gravelly, the words freighted with warm gusts of wine as they fell down on Hex. 'You cried out. This you must not do. Never. Your next loud sound we will punish by crushing your feet, gagging you to mute your moans. Terribly painful, but we'll have no choice, and your feet needn't be intact for our purposes.'

'You are selling me to the skinfarms then?'

'Yes. My condolences. Don't be downcast. At least it's a secure living. But keep firmly in mind this matter of noise. The night is alive for leagues around. If you could hear as we, and follow the stirrings which we've been listening to, you'd want no threats to keep you still. We're not of a timid species, but things are abroad tonight that we don't want to invite here. Do you understand?'

'Yes.'

'Here. This is your ration for the next day. Be sparing.' The Karbie thrust a wineskin between the bars, and returned to the little fire.

Hex used his entire ration that night. A little he splashed on the bars where he had puked. The rest he drank, numbing his thoughts, which kept bobbing horribly to the surface, till at last he passed out, hugging the deflated skin.

Morning brought an agony freshened and sharpened by sleep. In the freezing dawn he urinated from between the iron bars on to the dew-charged grass, then crouched in the middle of his cage, his throat a knot of thirst and his skin cringing from contact with the surrounding metal. Awareness of the misery of cold was intermittent, however, and came as a respite from his thoughts, which crystallized out of a welter of pain, and dissolved back into it, incessantly.

His rage at the dowager racked him. He imagined revenges, ladled upon her pinioned nakedness the orifice-seeking ants of Rasch, even as Smapp does to Grudjin in the *Epic of Urkh*, or infected her and watched her swell with the scabrous influx, at her every pore, of the Dismal Reverse Sweats. But the impotence of such revenge was in its turn as excruciating as his rage. Shame choked him, and led to the tortures of contemplating his astonishing gullibility and perfect pliancy as a tool in the she-monster's crime-stained hand. His own guilty role in the dooming of the whores was but a thought away, and he considered that for a while. Thereafter he had his now-imminent fate, its horror and revulsion, to study, until his wrath at the dowager rekindled, and he fell to reviewing such subworld sexual monstrosities as the whore Zelt had put him in mind of the day before, searching for an appropriate punishment for the treacherous, withered ghoul.

He bestirred his soul to escape this treadmill of despair, charged himself to see the symmetry of justice in his situation. With a flourish he had sold three hundred people into hell; with a swagger he had personally arranged their transportation thither. He had used them as chattels. Now he was the same, boxed, as good as limbless already.

In the skinfarms he would have no movement, but there would be thoughts, memories, dreams, fantasies. A minimal life, but guaranteed at least against the horrors of an uncertain world. Hex tried to look on his future with acceptance.

But when the sun rose, and washed gold across the crests of the hills, he felt something like death, seeing the life ahead of him all too clearly: the incessant amputations, the stink of anaesthetic, the eventless decades amid the fetor of a thousand rooted neighbours, all too slack-jawed with skin-loss and ennui even to converse.

'What? Have you finished it?' The Karbie's grainy voice brought Hex's eyes up to where the giant face loomed at his cage bars. Save that his beard covered his cheekbones and rounded his orbits to join the brows, the Karbie's features were manlike, with a fat, bibulous nose and a sarcastic mouth of bawdy flexibility. 'You'll get no more, my friend. That little lard-pot of Lady Poon's drove us a stingy bargain. We can't be stuffing you.'

'What'll he care about eating?' the second Karbie down by the fire said. 'In a few days his stomach'll be re-routed. Listen, human, practise feeding like a flower – on sun and dew! You'll have roots yourself by week's end.' Both giants laughed.

'Honourable Karbie, listen to me,' Hex blurted to the one at the bars. 'You're throwing away money by selling me to the skinfarms. I'm an infra-magus, I hold seals in lore, cartography, and incantation. Think of what I'd bring as a slave-tutor on some rich estate – say in Ungullion!'

'Think, you say?' smiled the giant. 'We have, be sure of it, thought more about the body-market than you've ever done. Alas, if the world were air, my friend . . . ! But the fact is that a man with five seals, not just three, fetches twice as much on the meat market as he does on the slave! Melancholy, by the dark ones! But you're bound for the farms.'

'Klar!' said the Karbie downslope. 'What's that?' He pointed across the hillsides to where – bright and distinct in the early sunlight – two bodies sped towards them across the grass. In its pearly wetness they left behind them two tracks of darker, trampled green. They must have been half a mile distant when Hex first focused on them, but such was their speed that within a scant two seconds of this, they had crossed an entire hillside and vanished within a nearer cleft.

When they reappeared, much closer, they were identifiable. They were a man running alongside a dust-devil – a miniature cyclone that raced across the slope despite the absence of either the wind or the dust to warrant such a phenomenon. Again they plunged out of view, and re-emerged yet nearer.

The man was not running, Hex realized. With madly pumping legs he was keeping a small, red object under his feet and this, in some impossible way, was his vehicle. As for the foggy spiral of wind that kept pace with him, it was not merely air and smoke, for some large form was suspended within its swirling mass. The speeding pair plunged into the last hollow between them and the watching trio. The Karbies had both drawn their huge broadswords, and Hex's interlocutor now rejoined his partner by the fire. The racing pair burst upon the far side of the slope. The dancing man was Antil the Elliptical, atop his exercise globe. As for the little maelstrom of wind, the shape suspended within it was clearly a man's.

'Look out! Stand aside!' shouted the wizard, waving an arm. 'You're blocking the goal!' Hex had freedom, in his bemusement, to think it odd that the Karbies stood aside at once. Both the wizard and the strangely purposive whirlwind leaned forward in their last uphill drive towards – it seemed unquestionable – Hex himself. As he watched, Hex noted dreamily behind them the faint, settling mist of the exploded dew. Antil, with a sudden rictus of triumph and exertion, leaned almost parallel to the ground as he and his competitor ploughed through the Karbies' fire, whose burst coals were still rising like comets when the wizard's hands struck the cage bars a fraction of a second before the freezing cyclonette hissed up and hung revolving with a frosty rush.

'I won! I won!' crowed Antil. The rheumy wizard was transported. He nimbled his sphere through a wide, careering joydance, circling the cage and the staring Karbies. Hex saw this only peripherally, because of the horror-trance the whirlwind held him in.

The man who hung inside its wheeling opacity was Slamp, the skinbroker, nude. Spread-eagled, upright, he had the pallor – the bloated, sodden fixity – of the long-drowned, but his eyes were open and his lips under the dandyish waxed moustache, moved in a mumble. Minute insectoid forms criss-crossed his body – they threaded his pulpy skin with their crowded paths, which latter connected every conceivable orifice – nostrils, ears, the undersides of his nails, the end of his sex – all were the trafficked tunnels of this swarm. Meanwhile, Hex perceived, this whirl of air was more than air. Its spumy substance displayed a jellylike, quasi-viscosity. Ropy features, roots or intestines, became apparent within it – all anchored in the broker's flesh. By its fetid stench – an acrid, faecal smell – Hex had understood its provenance from the first.

'Avaunt now, friend, no nearer!' Wheeling with lazy jocularity, Antil coasted back to the cage with this cautionary remark to the whirlwind. 'I won fair and square! Master Hex is mine now.' The wizard jumped off his ball and stood, arms akimbo, beaming at the ghastly turbulence.

There was a pause, during which Hex felt waves of icy, intense concentration wash over him, emanating from the poised vortex. In that moment Slamp's eyes found and focused on Hex. In dread, Hex saw the swollen lips move more urgently under the waxed moustache; faintly, the bleached, sausage-fingered hands moved, still blackly acrawl. A choking gust of hate concluded the vaporous entity's pause; it spun away, climbed the slope. Hex saw a last brilliant view of the spread-eagled, naked Slamp, and then the broker was snatched from sight below the hilltop. Hex heard a nearby concussion, winced and turned. One side of his cage had fallen away, and the wizard beckoned him forth.

He stood beside Antil, whose mild gaze was turned upon the Karbies. The giants remained downslope; their swords were drawn, but not held at ready. One of them now performed a stiff courtesy to Antil.

'Good morning, lord wizard. We hope you don't mean to take our cargo, sir – we've paid our whole capital for him, invested all we own.'

'You *hope*, sirrah?' The wizard spoke musingly, amazedly. 'You *hope*, you say, o gross, towering, perambulant scum? *Hope?*' He turned to share an incredulous smile with Hex, who returned a nervous version of same. Antil looked sharply back at the Karbies. 'You could do far better than to waste your hope on such futilities. Why not hope instead that you escape with your life from our visitor?' Antil pointed, and Hex and the Karbies alike jumped to see, not twelve feet up the slope, a lone vampire, who gave them an obsequious bow of greeting when he saw he had their attention.

Like most of his kind, he stood under five feet high, and wore ragged trousers of human skin which were supported by a single greasy shoulder strap that crossed his narrow, hairless chest diagonally. He had the typical, unimpressive face: a receding chin with an underslung, flabby-lipped mouth, a ratty snout of a nose and little dull eyes. His feet, bare, were deeply arched, with finger-long toes, and grasped the ground with handlike prehensility. 'Good morning, gentle giants,' he said in the species' snotty, wheedling voice. His bow had included Hex and the wizard, but his concern seemed solely with the Karbies. 'May I speak with you for a moment, sirs?' The vampire advanced humbly as he asked this. Both giants crouched sword-ready. Hex saw something rise from the grass behind them a moment before they became aware of it. It was a second vampire who with one hooked claw plucked through the leftmost giant's hamstring. Even as his stricken leg buckled, the hyper-alert titan, with a hop on his good leg, turned and brought his broadsword round with a booming whirr, sweeping low and halving the vampire at the rib cage with a meaty, split-melon noise of impact. Still hopping on one leg, he turned his back to his partner, and they divided the compass between them. Six more vampires had stood up from the lush grass, and were now circling the pair.

'By Nab!' exclaimed Antil to Hex. 'It must be said – there's strength in the old stumps yet!' He indicated his legs, with a headshake of admiration. 'The challenge of it was half my motive. Of course I had a thought to you too, good Hex. You may well do a rare thing, given the chance. I felt that from the first.'

There were too many vampires standing too near, for all that the giants seemed to absorb the bloodsuckers totally; Hex could not concentrate on what the magician said. They circled the Karbies, feinting, shuffling sideways, feinting again.

One of the giants leapt forward to break through their encirclement. It was a powerful spring, marred only by the fact that his feet refused to leave the ground. He stayed upright only by driving his swordpoint against the earth, and scarcely re-elevated the weapon in time to impale a vampire that had launched itself towards his throat. The other Karbie found his good foot similarly rooted, and only kept his balance by occasional – and clearly agonizing – use of his crippled leg. The ring of vampires tightened.

'I recommend Ungullion,' Antil went on, after watching the deathdance a moment with Hex. 'Get right out of the hills. Get down to the beach – it's scarcely a league from here – and follow it south. South to Ungullion, that's my advice.'

Two of the vampires feinted inward, then sideways, drawing the giants' swordstrokes. The wounded one had trouble recovering from his sweep.

'Come now, sirs!' cried the vampire who had been first to appear. 'You're hacking and slicing at us – it's brutal and cruel! We just want to get close and talk! You probably think we're vampires – everyone does. It's an accidental similarity in our appearances. We're harmless Eripmavs, in actuality!'

'To Ungullion?' Hex asked in belated response, tearing his eyes an instant from the scene. The wizard was looking at him with the beginnings of displeasure. 'Honoured Antil! You've saved my life, and I'll do what you say, but must I go to Ungullion? Can't I go back to Glorak Harbour?'

'Go *back*, you ask? Go back?!' The thin, raw nose grew subtly thinner – bladelike – with the wizard's disapproval.

'Great magician!' boomed one of the Karbies. 'We humbly beseech you to unroot our feet! A fighting chance is all we ask!'

Antil did not even turn his head. 'Go back to Glorak Harbour, is it? Don't you suppose that the Dowager Poon – assuming her not to have altered in some miraculous way since yesterday – would be a sufficiently dangerous enemy to share a city with? And don't you think that if she *were* your enemy there – ' and here Antil nodded towards the broken cage from which Hex had just stepped ' – that she could make even Glorak too small, too close for your comfort? Mind you, I *advise* nothing. I do not *tell* you what to do!' The wizard grew even more irritated as he uttered these two denials, and then broke off to follow the struggle anew.

A vampire had just dived suicidally close to the wounded giant who, with expert wrist-action, brought his blade inward and clipped off the vampire's forearm. The move was unfortunate. It unbalanced the Karbie, and brought him full-length to the ground. While he was struggling to his knees, a vampire charged his partner, then ducked the full swing of his warding blow. The blade came round and, just as the fallen giant was rising, his neck received it, and his head jumped from his shoulders. With a curse, the survivor began sweeping his sword as widely as he could, but immediately a vampire sprang on his unguardable back, reached round with one hooked claw, and plucked through his jugular. Unstrung, the Karbie knelt, and was overswarmed.

Antil had remounted his globe, and was performing lazy zigzags on it. Idly, as it seemed, he told Hex: 'No, I'm no meddler – certainly not. But I must say, speaking in a general way, that for you the bolder thing, the worthier thing, seems to be travel – to keep trying your fortune. In any case, whether you go north or south, if I were you I'd take the coast from here. These hills are nowhere to be walking.'

Hex looked at the supine giants who – one still feebly struggling – were now blanketed by the dozen smaller forms. All of these lay face-down, seeming to kiss various parts of their victims. Antil was already moving away across the slope.

'Antil!' cried Hex. The wizard, though he did not pause in his mincing footwork, looked inquiringly back as he danced away. 'Honoured Antil! What is this rare thing you say I might do?'

The wizard merely stared back a moment longer, then faced north and began to skim away in good earnest. Hex, with a last glance at his erstwhile captors, began to run downslope, eastward, towards the sea.

In his flight, in fear, Bramt Hex truly knew his heaviness, for he became a man of two parts. His fear was fleet. His fear was an athlete, swifter than a wolf. His flesh was something else again. His flesh jerked and wobbled, hung on his speedy fear like an anchor, a grotesque overcoat encumbering the wolf. Divided man, a quick will in a lagging frame, he fled. The dew-wet grass, like skinny, sweaty fingers, clutched at his heels as he bounded downslope.

But at length, surprisingly, his flight began to cure him of his fear. As he hove in sight of the blue horizon and then – crest after descending crest – brought the sand-dunes and the beach itself into view, he grew amazed, and then intoxicated, with his own endurance. Sweat oiled every inch of him and his shoulders ached, but his legs – long, city-rambling legs that they were – never faltered, and his lungs supplied him with a tough, untiring ease. His life had made him fleshy, but not weak. And his luck – surely it thrived with similar vitality! He was alive and bounding through sunlight. He was neither sprawled bloodless in the grass, nor rooted at the ankles in a plasm-bed. And so he charged towards the weed-tufted dunes, gulping down the sea's tang, and his surge through the undulant grass might have been that of a great, silver shimfin at play, bursting through the crests of waves.

On the beach he found a stout driftwood club, and strode south. Thus, simple was it to shrug off an old world and march towards a new. For could such intercession as Antil's be anything less than a destiny-signpost – one of those vital clues that the daring earn by an initial risking of the unknown? He was obligated to accept it promptly, gratefully. He blushed to have balked at the wizard's advice. He'd hardly even thanked Antil for saving him!

Throughout the morning, he walked, crossing cove after cove, rounding small headlands just as smoothly as he might follow some character from line to line through his exploits in an old saga. An offshore breeze woke. Out to sea, he admired the blown-back spume of the waves – like windbroken smoke from the torches of messengers who rushed in from mid-ocean, collapsing as they shouted their indecipherable tidings from the Deeps. Along the sand, silver traceries of Glowfish skeletons marked the last high tide. Banded Scoops crash-dived for fish just offshore while Glides, with their more scythelike wings, cut precision courses overhead, scanning the surf-line.

But midday, and weariness, brought new anxiety. The great emptiness of his future began to tell on him. Compared to the void he marched into, the city on which he had turned his back clamoured after him, full of known places of shelter, known lines of work where a man might in safe anonymity amass steerage, and make a delayed but much more secure departure southwards. Surely he would leave Glorak – the Academy was too dangerous to return to, even if he demeaned himself to crawl back after his bold renunciation. But how quickly could even the dowager discover him elsewhere in the city?

His more heroic alternative, meanwhile, looked gruelling. Klapp, a mid-sized fishing village, lay another day's walk south. There, his doublet could be converted to sufficient cash to buy a cloak, a sword, and a wallet of loaves and cheeses. But thereafter? Two days' walk to Wibbles Jut, and thence another *week* to Ungullion. Moreover, since he must expect to arrive there nearly destitute, he would have to lodge in the city's poorest quarter – in the Tree-slums.

The sun had started sinking to the hills, and the sea took on a ruddiness suggesting blood. Hex jumped at every unexpected slap of wave to rock. These beaches, he reminded himself, were fairly safe in this season, but stripe-gilled crushers with tongue-lengths exceeding eight feet *had* been sighted hereabouts. He began to look for a place to sleep.

Near dark, in a small cove, he found a little cave in the sand-bluff that walled it. Curling himself up on the cold sand of the cave floor, he felt like a pauper testing a cheap grave for tenancy. He clenched his teeth against a surge of hopelessness. Tomorrow, he would turn back. His stomach, given only springwater and scant watercress all day, gurgled. Would he even be able to sleep? A moment later, he was unconscious.

The steel-grey light of dawn pried his eyelids apart – unless it was the sand that had invaded them, and every other inch of his flesh besides. Or perhaps it was the noise of his teeth chattering that woke him, along with the growling – vigorous now – of his belly. He rose to a squat to reduce his body's contact with his burrow's frigid floor. Cautioning himself to collect his wits before leaving his covert, he crouched there, bleakly ticking off a mental list of his discomforts. He heard, from just outside, a minute tittering.

He listened, frozen, till the sound returned – minuscule but quite distinct. Inch by inch, he emerged – crept to a rock that half-concealed the cavemouth and peeped around it with excruciating care. He had company in the cove. A small, one-masted sloop lay beached not twelve strides off.

Its owner was not in view. Shadowy bales, a heap of rope, and some small casks lay by the craft on the livid sand. The tiny giggling came again, clearly from somewhere in this little pile of stowage. Some merry but negligible vermin, then. The boatmaster must have gone inland for a warmer, drier shelter than the foggy shore afforded – a decision Hex envied him, whoever he was. He stood up from behind the rock, and just then something small moved amid the baggage – detached itself and wobbled a short way out across the sand. It was a leathern pouch.

After a second's immobility, the poke's drawstring mouth opened, like an unfolding blossom. Hex would have judged the pouch just large enough to accommodate his hands, clasped together, up to the wrists. But now a man's foot and leg up to the knee thrust out of the sack's open mouth. Another foot and leg followed, then the hindquarters and torso of a man perhaps five feet tall backed out of the bag. The head and arms still remained inside, but did not make the pouch look fuller than a handful of walnuts might have made it; there was further tittering within the bag, and a sound of scuffling.

Then the man drew the rest of himself out. He was bald, with a wispy, pale beard. Chuckling fondly he drew the strings of the bag tight, and tied it to his belt. Then he set about stowing his goods, and in another moment, Hex could see, would be righting his sloop.

Hex had hidden himself again, but indecision racked him. The old man had some sort of wizard's power, and to expose oneself would be to stand the target of that power if malign. And yet his appearance was unthreatening, and Hex realized that he did not really fear him. Might this not be a further stroke of that remarkable luck that had so far cancelled his misfortunes even as they had arisen? In so small a boat the old man would be coasting, and thus bound north or south. Let Hex step forward, ask passage, and take the man's destination as his own – invite fate once more to solve his dilemma. He rose and came forward.

'Sir! Good morning. You must forgive my sandiness, but you see I – '

The little man whirled, his face not startled, but surprised. 'Forgive your sandiness?' he asked with amazement. 'Why, right heartily sir. You are forgiven. No, no! Don't brush it off – I insist! Haven't I told you I'm not offended? Please! It makes you look quite splendid, actually, like an enormous sugared loaf! May I offer you breakfast, since the topic arises? A great, stout man like yourself – even if you've already eaten, why, I'm sure you'd be glad to eat again!'

'You're very kind,' Hex said a trifle frigidly.'In fact, I've eaten nothing for some time.'

'Wonderful! Come along. Take that keg for a seat. I have some morning wine and crumble. No, no! Don't brush it off, I insist!'

After an initial, gluttonous silence, the old man introduced himself as Kabrow. Hex gulping, supplied his name and followed it, irresistibly, with 'infra-magus'. After some further wordless guzzling, Kabrow leaned forward with a confiding smile.

'Friend Hex, I take it that you do not reside on this beach. Would you be en route somewhere – specifically, to the south?'

'It's interesting that you ask, good Kabrow, for I was just debating between north and south. You are bound to the south?'

'To Ungullion,' Kabrow nodded. 'And I have a post to offer you if you should choose your destination in that direction.'

Hex's heart leapt. Gone were his fearful temporizings of last night. Filled with happy fear, but trying not to seem eager, he nodded.

'What would be the wage?'

'Seven lictors, for one long day of nearly nonexistent duties. You see, below Wibbles Jut the coast swings so sharply west that this westerly weather sweeps you right along almost parallel to the shore. I'll lash the tiller at a slight angle and we'll hold a southwesterly course with almost no steering involved. For that's what I'd have you do, you see – sit the tiller while I, ah, retired.'

'Kabrow, you have been generous to a stranger, and I accept your offer. For in fact, one place is as good as another to a footloose man like me – erstwhile scholar, present vagabond!'

'This is remarkable luck then,' beamed Kabrow. 'You

will not regret taking the post. I'll bring us to Wibbles Jut before retiring, and you'll be free to rest and sun yourself. Now. Let's stow these casks under that stern thwart there . . . No, no! Please! Don't brush it off!'

7
An Encounter Involving Harsh Language – Bramt Hex Enters The Tree-Slums of Ungullion

Kabrow brought the sloop past Wibbles Jut in the forenoon. The town seemed little more than a pale lichen patch on the headland's great knee of rock. Below that promontory the coast swept southwest in a vast arc. In the stiff westerly breeze, Hex could see that a slight southerly set of the rudder would carry them smoothly parallel to the shore.

'What with the wind, the helpful current,' Kabrow said, lashing the tiller, 'I've often risked . . . retiring even when I've had no one to watch the course. You'll have practically nothing to do. There's the food locker, there the wine. Just don't let us get too much less than a mile off the coast. Let me know, of course, if there are any, ah, little difficulties.'

The old man placed his pouch on a cushion beside him and opened its drawstrings. In the manner of a man pulling one stocking on to both feet, he thrust himself knee-deep into the poke. With a second pull he hitched it up to his armpits, while causing it to look no fuller than before. He stretched both arms over his head and wriggled the rest of the way in, hooking the drawstrings inside after him and pulling them tight. The poke lay lax and unswollen on the cushion. There came a series of minute exclamations, pitter-patterings of pursuit, and amorous scufflings.

Hex undressed, washed himself with scooped-up handfuls of seawater, and dressed again. With a pile of netting he made a couch amidships, from which he could view coast, sky, and sea in comfort.

The green brocade of forests, velvet of meadows on the coastal hills, stretched league on league, impossibly distinct in the wine-clear air. His freedom was the world itself, spread unknowably wide before his choosing. Now he thought of the skin-farms, to a degree of detail which his horrorstruck mind had not previously permitted itself to imagine. He saw the gathering-leeches hanging from his body, tatters of black flesh swelling, plucked, replaced; the sweating-torches and buckets of the monthly salt collection; the tears-and-saliva taps, with their dangling copper coils.

Then the thought of Zelt and her colleagues came to him, like a funeral barge pulling up alongside the sloop, laden with melancholy ghosts. A faecal stench, laced with the odours of sulphur and scorched meat, wormed its way to him through the wash of the brilliant air. They now lived agonies quite as soul-wrenching as those he had escaped; and he had known them! He had fired his very seed into how many of them?!

He felt a grief and guilt which might have overwhelmed him had he been sitting in a small room. Out here, gliding through the gigantic fact of his liberty, he shook them off fairly soon. He had been as much a fool as a criminal. They had been property, and would have been used as such with or without his intervention. Hex laid back his head and shut his eyes against the sun. After all, he mused, would Antil have intervened so strenuously on the behalf of a worthless man, assuming the wizard to be as benevolent as he seemed? The Marketditch whores, of course, might not have deemed him benevolent . . . but who was Hex to plumb the motives of wizards? *A rare thing*, Antil had forecast for him. What was rarer than immortality, which had not gone unmentioned by the magician? Hesitating between these imponderables, bathed by the sun, Hex let his thoughts disperse, and dozed.

He awoke near noon, thinking he had heard a splash. Looking anxiously to starboard, he found them on course, the shore a mile off. There was one major difference, though. The sea's blackish-green had lightened to turquoise and its swell, though still regular, was radically reduced. For they were now gliding over a vast, uniform shallows, a coral plateau submerged beneath scarcely two fathoms of limpid water. Looking to port, he could see, just fifty feet off, the dark line where this plateau ended and the depths resumed, a line which the sloop's course paralleled.

He noted something else as well. For there, bobbing in the deep water at the shallows' brink and peering towards him, was an enormous head.

This head was barnacle-crusted, roughly pyramidal, with a single, opalescent eye set near its apex, like a beacon. For a nose, it had two nostril slits that opened and closed like wet shutters. A weedy, limpet-scabbed pair of lips some ten feet wide spanned its base. The whole loomed half again as tall as the sloop was from waterline to mast-top. Its mouth peeled open, and emitted a voice like glaciers calving.

'You! Come here! Quick!'

Hex seized the poke. He meant to shake it in his panic, and wrenched his shoulder as he discovered it was too heavy to lift. His attempt brought Kabrow's dishevelled head from within. The old man's wispy hair had been tied in love-knots, and small flowers had been plaited into his goatish beard. Hex pointed to the giant off the port, just as its avalanche of a voice again rolled towards them:

'Come here! Right now! I kill you quick!'

As the sloop's pace hadn't slackened, and the giant was still with them, Hex realized the giant too had been moving along the edge of the shallows. It occurred to him the monster had to stay in deep water. He was turning for the tiller, to steer them farther into the shallows, when Kabrow wriggled out of the pouch and grabbed it himself.

'Sit there!' snapped the old man, unlashing the tiller and steering them – not from, but *to* the giant. Hex sat, horrified, and watched as Kabrow, bringing the craft some twenty feet nearer the monster, shook his fist at it and shrilled out:

'Heap of faeces! Your mother was a jakes! Your tongue is a turd! Are you one-eyed from squinting up bungholes?'

Hex's hair stood on his nape. They had again turned parallel to the deep water, but were now so close Hex could see small crabs scuttling from barnacle to barnacle on the monster's jowls as it worked its lips in rubbery, quaking rage, booming wordlessly in its sunken throat.

'Fiery hells!' Hex cried at Kabrow. 'Are you mad, old man? You enrage it!'

'Of course I do, fool! Aid me! Do likewise, or we're lost!' Again Kabrow turned to the giant. 'Mountain of scum! Monolith of living garbage! For a thousand lictors I will piss in your nose, but not for a lictor less!'

The giant twisted its hill of a head from side to side, groaning with inarticulate wrath. Feeling he dreamed, Hex raised his own faint voice:

'Fool! Rascal! May you get your just deserts!'

'No, no!' Kabrow hissed at him. 'Much stronger, thus: Bowel movement that moves! Putrid pile! You were got on the Goddess of Stench by the God of Decay!'

The head shook, its anger an earthquake, and then a second titanic head erupted dripping and bellowing beside it – its twin in every feature. Kabrow gave a little dance of eagerness.

'Help me with a will now, Hex – safety's in sight!' He shook both fists at the cyclopean pair and jumped up and down till their mast swung with his taunts like a wagging finger:

'Cloaca with eyes! Sewage that sees! You do not live, you but putresce!'

'Scoundrels!' Hex quavered in his turn. 'Cads! I have no respect for you!'

The giants still kept pace with them, leaving an ever more turgid wake along the shallows' brink with the shaking of their submerged shoulders.

'Immense twin haemorrhoids!' howled Kabrow. 'Sacks of slag!'

The giants uttered a simultaneous shriek. They sank – so sharply it seemed they had been pulled under. A milk-white turbulence developed in the water where they went down. This was stained a murkier colour as it dropped astern of the still gliding sloop. Kabrow uttered a huge sigh and sat down on the steersman's thwart. His garlanded and tufted hair made him seem, with the smile he now wore, some benign sprite, such as might preside at orgies and revelling.

'You see, Bramt Hex, you must never give a Megalops time to think. They are stupid and lazy and their first impulse is always to call their prey over to them. Give them time to think, and they'll realize that they can climb on to the shoals and wade after you. If they do that, my friend, your case is closed, and your goose is cooked.

'Never flee, then – no! Distract their thoughts by getting close, and work on getting them mad. When they get mad enough, they always pull both heads out of the water, and forget to look where they're going as they wade along the shelf. And then it's only a matter of time before they blunder into the jaws of an Oscule.'

'An Oscule?'

'Yes, a species exclusively indigenous to the steep flanks of these shoals. Fortunately, it is sessile. But now you must be at ease, my dear Hex. Such encounters are rare. The odds against two in one trip are overwhelming. Until this evening!' Having re-lashed the tiller as he spoke, Kabrow crawled back into the pouch. Under the noon's blue dome Hex quickly shook off his fear. And as the boat continued to glide across the coral shallows, he found himself enjoying a delightful illusion of flight. The sunken green plains sped under the keel, and their watery atmosphere's twists of pallid light suggested wisps of cloud. Schools of Quicksilvers and lone Rays flew with him over the seamed topography, where crabs among the hairy sponges and Lung-corals looked like Ogres crouched in hillside thickets.

And he was flying in fact, was he not? On his luck? His freedom? Suppose that his hopes exaggerated his destiny, that immortality was not his prophesied distinction? Wasn't the whole, wide, mapless world his in a briefer but still intoxicating fashion?

His, perhaps, to *map*?

The idea's rightness stunned him. Years of inadvertent preparation for such a work lay behind him, for along with legendaries and sagas, cartographers' folios had formed his staple reading. He knew as much about the Great West Shore where Glorak and Ungullion stood as the most learned of his fellow citizens did.

This was but little in itself, of course, but still, even the greatest centres of learning could offer no more than a skeletal picture of the West Shore. As to the East Shore – or, indeed, the territories more than three hundred leagues inland from the West – these vast tracts were a blank, fitfully limned by such *ignes fatui* as the uncollated, contradictory reports of traders, mercenaries and pilgrims offered to the scholar.

But a *mobile* scholar, diligently compiling all he saw and heard? And suppose that scholar's first goal did happen to be a place called Yana? He could amass as much new data travelling in that direction as any other, no doubt. And then, if he *reached* it, what territory *anywhere* would long remain unknown to a man with a world of time to find and study it? Think! A comprehensive portrait of the world, given freely *to* the world – forever ensuring the giver's world-wide renown.

When, at sunset, Kabrow hauled himself from the pouch, he found Hex in an exalted, mysterious mood – smiling crazily at the sea and sky, clapping him on the shoulder in a greeting of unaccountable ebullience. The old man took scant notice of this. He was hollow-eyed, his temples sweat-plastered. He re-tied the poke to his belt, dragged out the food-locker, and gorged himself for half an hour, his jaw working ferociously under the glazed fixity of his stare.

Replete, the old man sighed. He motioned Hex to his couch of netting, hooked one arm over the tiller, and fell instantly asleep. His portly passenger lay amidships, long unsleeping, murmuring and chuckling to himself, and staring tirelessly up at the stars.

Eventually, Bramt Hex dozed. At least, the busy hum of his new, ambitious fantasies seemed to sink only briefly under the thinnest blanket of oblivion. Nonetheless, when he reopened his eyes, the sun was three hours high, and they were gliding into the harbour of Ungullion.

Like Glorak Harbour, Ungillion rose from a level shoreside zone to inland hills, though here the range was not curved, but formed a straight crest. The offshore view presented three sharply colour-contrastive strata. The hills, lavishly studded with marble architecture, were white, thinly veined with the green of parks and alamedas. Below this, the flat shoreside was a solid green of massed treetops, and this in turn was fringed with the harbour's curve of pilings, wharves, and warehouses, all in the browns and mouse-greys of weathered wood. The harbour waters themselves, like a second, leafless forest, bristled with the masts of merchant vessels. The verdure of the dense forest-slum crowded right up to the verge of the wharfside zone.

'Don't they dare clear even the harbour's fringe?' Hex asked. Kabrow shook his head.

'The last bit of major axe-wielding they tried here woke the trees to a riot that killed eleven thousand souls. That was nearly a century ago. The slum-dwellers have long considered the trees' incidental outbursts to be quite a sufficient misery.' The old man steered the sloop towards a small-craft pier whereon stood a clearing depot.

'What a place to settle!' said Hex. 'I have heard that the city's founders were pushed here by western hordes. But why didn't they take to sea and find a safer piece of coast?'

'They were uprooted inlanders without maritime skills, and it was an even more dangerous sea then than now. Besides, after several battles with the trees, and heavy casualties, they realized that the trees' life-pulse was slow and that they were indifferent to unaggressive habitation by men. Only assault roused them. So the folk's nobility moved into the heights and its commonalty occupied – cautiously – the forest.'

'And outbursts of destruction on the part of the trees have remained endemic since that time?'

Kabrow chuckled softly. 'Perhaps you won't be surprised, good Hex, to learn that there are two theories here regarding the stability of the situation in the slums. The trees scarcely reproduce at all, and the forest here is essentially the original one. Therefore, say the first group of theorists, since the trees' reactions grow slower with age, they are less apt to riot with each passing year, and thus permit a steady increase in slum population without an attendant rise in violence. This view tends to prevail among the wealthy, all of whom live in the heights, well out of the forest. The slum-dwellers, on the other hand, are likely to tell you that the older any tree grows, the more irascible it gets, and that riots have grown more, not less frequent, with the passage of time, despite the population's increasing skill in adapting to this tricky environment.'

Hex helped Kabrow carry several bales into the clearing depot, where the clerk obviously knew the old man. Hex could catch no glimpse of the voucher of lading, which might have enlightened him as to Kabrow's business. A direct question produced only the curt response:

'I'm a vendor of exotica. Come along.'

The old man led him into the tree-slums. The trees' major branchings began at some twelve to twenty feet above the ground, leaving room for a veritable labyrinth of shacks, shanties, and plank fences to cluster round their trunks. Above this, the boughs supported ramshackle structures at every groin and angle – a tacky maze of airborne hovels that was crazily interwebbed with ramps, catwalks, cable bridges, laundry lines, and guy ropes. Children moved monkey-quick along this network, crowded on swings in the highest branches, or waged nutshell-and-pebble wars between neighbouring rooftops. The noise of their play mixed with the shrill chat of women moving methodically up rope ladders with baskets of washing, and with the rumbling blather and boasts of men loafing on wineshop platforms with leathern jacks in their hands. Meanwhile all these sounds merged with the vast, gentle susurration of foliage – in much the same way as the yellow-and-rust dapple of the dead leaves deeply drifted on every level surface merged with the mellow dapple of sunlight everywhere admitted by the forest canopy.

The main avenues here – on the ground level, at least – were cableways, narrow zones of unbuilt earth to either side of ropes strung waist-high between posts set at twenty-yard intervals. Threading his way behind Kabrow, Hex enjoyed sufficient perspective through the tangled scene to gain a clear impression of the vegetable giants that thronged it. They were squat in profile, their width only slightly exceeded by their height, which averaged some sixty feet. Their thick, horizontally thrust limbs diminished only slightly in bulk towards their crests, and had a flowing, twisted line that unpleasantly suggested muscularity – an impression which their smooth, fine-pored bark reinforced. Though they created an airier environment than Hex had imagined they would, a slightly dark coolness lingered under their leafy ceiling. Still the vitality of the scene was dominant, and the bosky gloom he had expected of the place remained only an undercurrent of its atmosphere.

Kabrow brought them to a wine-shed near a crossing of two cableways. For a short while they leaned in silence at the counter, sipping a tart, pale vintage and gazing at the shady, murmurous traffic around and above them. Hex was framing various ways of broaching the question of Yana. He decided directness was best, that Kabrow would either tell whatever he knew, or he wouldn't, but as he opened his mouth the old man pointed down the cableway.

'The Leafmould Inn,' he said. The building indicated – of tar-caulked wood – was low and shapeless, and so sprawling, that it incorporated the trunks of three different trees, which thrust up from its mulch-heaped roof like grass stalks from snowdrifts. 'It's two lictors a night, board included. There's another matter as well, my dear fellow. I would really advise you against those festive boots of yours, and that . . . striking doublet. They will only excite the, ah, cupidity of strangers. You ought to sell them and get some sensible, plain gear.'

'Yes, I was already going to – '

'There's a fat man named Grossp who runs a pretty decent jumble-shop here – the goods are sturdy and he can be bargained with. Ask anyone for directions. Now I want you to take this little bonus with your pay, and to wish you all possible good luck.'

Hex was startled by a sudden air of haste in the old man, who had laid two five-lictor pieces on the counter and was already hoisting and draining his glass. When he thumped it down and turned to thrust his hand in Hex's, the plump scholar anxiously detained it in his clasp.

'Spare me another moment, honoured Kabrow! May I be blunt? I have just – '

'You *will* be blunt, I suppose, with or without invitation.' A wryness now tempered the old man's good humour, but he grudgingly half-resumed his stool.

'I have recently learned,' Hex said in an apologetically lowered voice, 'of a place called Yana, where the touch of undying is to be had. Clearly you are a man of powers, Kabrow. Would you tell me something of the place?'

Kabrow no longer looked at all grave, and yet neither was the humour in his eyes of its usual sunny sort. The jollity seemed faintly cruel now. 'Endless life,' he mused. 'I wonder what you'd do with it.'

'I would map the world and give it its first comprehensive cartofolio,' Bramt Hex promptly answered. 'Failing that, for I don't rule out the Infinitists' view that the world is limitless, I would give the world its most *nearly* comprehensive cartofolio.' He hesitated, then added, 'Might I, without impertinence, ask you what you would do with it?'

'More to the point to ask me what I *do* with it. Of course, I would not answer you.' Kabrow paused, as had the scholar's heart. 'Look down here a moment,' the old man murmured, indicating his own feet. Under the counter he discreetly pinned his left boot with the toe of his right and withdrew from it – first, a thin and uncommonly hairy ankle, and then a large cloven hoof. No sooner had he shown it than he rebooted it.

'You would map the world,' he marvelled. 'By my wrinkly rod, Bramt Hex, you are no wisher-by-halves. You're a perfectly charming man, I swear it, and I'd love to tell you a dozen vital things. Unfortunately, a great gulf separates us. The information you want must be purchased with risks. Still, I have a parting bit of advice for you – that you go to a bathhouse. There is a particularly suitable one just down the way from Grossp's jumble-shop. Good-bye now, my friend. All the best to you.'

Hex found himself a bit dazed by this short series of bizarre disclosures, and Kabrow was out of view before he could bestir himself. He bespoke another wine to accompany his chewing-over of what he had been shown and told. The only part of it he could do anything about seemed the least relevant – the advice that he should seek a bathhouse. To Grossp's he must go in any case, for it was time to see to immediate needs, and defer the larger issues for a while. He got directions from the tapster.

Grossp was a man of nearly spherical obesity who never left – probably was unable to leave without help – a hammock slung behind a small counter in one corner of his mountainously cluttered shop. Each article Hex considered had to be brought into Grossp's heavy-lidded view to elicit its price. This the man voiced with a languor Hex found intensely irritating, as the price invariably seemed high.

He decided to assemble a full outfit. When he had found a heavy trail-cape of Hill-Plod wool, kneeboots of stout leather, and a thick doublet of peel – a dun-coloured, supple material resembling suede that he had seen to be much used hereabouts – he took them to the counter to haggle over them *en bloc*. The offer, though somewhat better this way, still struck him as unfair: for his own boots and doublet he would receive with the new gear only twelve lictors change.

'It's just plain unreasonable,' Hex expostulated. 'For

that rate you must throw in a sword, with belt and scabbard, as well.'

'If that will content you, so be it,' breathed Grossp with oleaginous affability. Hex strove to conceal his surprise. He found a twenty-inch shortsword of tough, supple steel, firmly hilted in bone with countersunk copper rivets. Even without its scabbard it would be worth nearly fifty lictors in Glorak, but Grossp nodded serenely at its inclusion. When his purchases were donned, and his money pocketed, Hex felt free to comment on the cheapness of the sword, and Grossp felt free to answer:

'Ah yes. Well swords, you see, sell poorly in the slums. Violence here? Brawls and blades? It would be madness, would it not?'

After a moment, Hex understood him. He shrugged in a debonair way. 'Ah well! As I shall soon be on the open road again, we can both count ourselves gainers in the bargain. I'm a cartographer, you see. Not your stay-at-home kind, but peripatetic. An investigator at large.'

It would have been hard for a man to look less enthusiastic about an itinerant existence than Grossp did. Snugging his rotundity more tightly – if that was possible – into the hammock's vast hemisphere, he bestirred one hand to a faint, dismissive gesture and said:

'Good luck then. Travel multiplies the need of it.'

Nonetheless, outside, Hex remained exhilarated by his own verbal portrait of himself. He stepped into an adjoining wine-shed, where he sat regarding his surroundings with the smiling, canny eye of a knowing vagabond, seasoned to exotic sights.

And the scene, in the gold-lit, late afternoon, was a lively one. Clearly, this was a social hour in the slums. Knots of labourers trudged up the cableway, their peel belts clanking with cargo-hooks or fish-cleaning tools. Most – including many women among them – were thick, big-shouldered people with a splayfoot, rolling gait smoothly adapted to the root-swollen ground. All the wineshops were full, as well as not a few barber stalls – for though the folk here went as long-haired and full-bearded as those of Glorak, combing and delousing seemed an important service in this damp, sylvan environment. Outside the stalls, children shrilled and skylarked, vying for adult notice, or from nearby rooftops flung twigs and nutshells at the barbers' basins, fleeing with shouts when they raised a splash. Their elders smiled, took squirts of wine from the leathern bottles that hung at their hips, and resumed the endless gossip that seemed more than half their purpose in frequenting the stalls. The breeze jumbled their myriad voices with the leafnoise, and broadcast too all the classic smells of poverty: sweat, soil, wine, urine, and cheap cooking, all tangled with the fresh, bitter scent of foliage.

Hex expanded with affection for these people. Weren't the poor everywhere the same? Sturdy workers, merry when they could be, straight-forward as safety allowed? Stratagems and cold-blooded killing were the special toys of the powerful. Here, toddlers scrabbled in the dirt, and lean old women, mummied in shawls, walked with careful economy of movement, eking out their last few yards of mortal progress across that same earth. Sweet, sad, universal sight! Hex ordered another wine. As he drank it, he fell to studying the bathhouse Kabrow had told him of.

Some hundred yards distant, at a turning in the cable-way, it stood amid particularly venerable trees over eighty feet tall. At three storeys it was itself an imposing structure as slum-buildings went. Each storey sat slightly askew on the lower, according to the thrust of the branches of the two flanking trees that supported it. Between these the mossy building seemed to slouch like a drunk held up by his friends, while the sun-dappled water tank surmounting it perched aslant, as a sot's cap would. Had the old man meant something by recommending it? There had been a pointedness in his suggestion . . . In any case, Hex's last sketchy ablutions had been made with seawater, and he felt distinctly itchy. He finished his wine and walked to the bathhouse.

A caged booth in the anteroom contained the bathwoman. Beyond her, past a doorless portal, stretched an oil-lit maze of wooden bathstalls. Hex marvelled at the probable capacity of the first floor alone, and yet the silence told him that its recesses were deserted.

'Tell me, Madam,' he cried – wine-gay – to the crone within the cage, 'do you think I will have much of a wait for a bath? Heh, heh!'

'Why, what a refreshing sense of humour!' crackled the old woman. Her edentulous grin was the emblem of sarcasm. Hex shrugged.

'My apologies. I'm sure you can't be expected to think it's funny. I'd like a stall, please.'

'And you shall have one!' cried the crone. Her manner was that of one who is fired with a sudden and profound purpose. 'You shall have the best, by all the powers! Seven dhroons, please.' She dragged his coins off the counter and into a chest that sounded surprisingly full of others. She emerged from a door in the side of her booth with two large drying-sponges under her arm. Beckoning Hex, she stumped ahead of him into the labyrinth.

Her hair hung in a sloppy white tail knotted with a dirty ribbon. Her stride was quite vigorous, but even their combined treads echoed little on the sodden floor. The partitions of the countless stalls – all vacant – were splotched and zebra-ed with moss. At a cubicle no different from a dozen they had passed she stopped and turned sharply. Thrusting her face – warped like a raisin – into his, she motioned Hex inside. She laid the sponges by the tub. She unlocked a spigot on the wall, ran the tub half-full, relocked the spigot, and left.

Hex hung his clothes on a wall-peg and wedged himself into the water, which was tepid from the sunlight he had seen falling on the water tank above. Gratefully, he laved his grittiness away, and scrubbed the salt from his hair. The stall door opened suddenly, and the crone stood beaming at him.

'Such pink health!' she cried with rapture. 'Shining wet like that, sir, you look like a Bulge that's stranded at low tide because he's just swallowed three fishermen and their skiff to boot! Bless your fat youth, you'll live long!'

'Witch! What are you doing here? And what do you mean? Heavy I may be – I'm not the gross heap you say.' It seemed too womanish to try to shoo her out – it seemed more dignified to return, teeth clenched, to washing himself. The old woman became quite nettled.

'Why do you dispute me?' she cried. 'I have lived a long time! You have scarcely lived at all. It's impertinent! Of course you're not *literally* as fat as a Bulge. But your soul's being so fat, matched with your body's fat – why, I was speaking figuratively! It's such a good match, soul and body!' She had, by her own reflections, restored her good humour.

'The impertinence is yours!' cried Hex. 'Kindly get out of my stall!'

'The building is mine and I go where I like in it! But come, you cannot anger me! Your plumpness quite disarms me! You are as round and resplendent as a slug on a daisy at noon! For one lictor, O Pinkness, I will sell you knowledge of the touch of undying. Think of it! A clue to the possession of immortal life, for only a lictor!'

Hex's skin crawled. The hair on his arms stood up. He peered into the crone's grin-slitted eyes and did not doubt that he was looking face-to-face at his fate itself.

'Yes. Yes, beldame. Forgive my anger.' Strangely

unselfconscious, he stood from the basin and dug a lictor from his doublet on the wall. He handed it to her and then, because she took it and stood silent, began to dry himself absently, waiting. At last he asked, 'Well?'

'It is to be had in Yana, which is to the north of here.'

'Yana. Yes, I knew that. To the north of here. Is that all?'

'It is much! It cuts your search in half! Mind you, I do not even say which shore it is on – only that it is north of here.'

'Forgive me if I sound greedy – I have just come from the north – from Glorak Harbor at least . . . can you say no more? I ask with all respect – I'll give you another lictor.'

The crone laughed – gleeful wheezes. 'Oh!' she cried, 'another lictor! By the powers, a sore temptation! Greedy, you say! Oh, greedy indeedy!' She turned, still wheezing, and left the stall.

By the time Hex had dressed and returned to the anteroom, the old woman was not to be found. He left without much hesitation, for the significance of what he had been given was growing on him. A bit at a time – clearly this was the tacit law of his luck so far. That word of Yana should keep coming to him, and from such diverse sources – this was more momentous than the actual extent of the information at this point. Clearly, he must keep an enterprising spirit, and move where opportunity prompted, and more would be given him. His step grew buoyant. Without conscious effort he threaded his way unerringly back to the Leafmould Inn. The place was rough, loud, and malodorous, staffed by black-tattooed Cannibal Islanders six-and-a-half feet tall and wearing flimsy-looking leather muzzles, but Hex's ebullience was unimpaired – at least they kept the clientele in line.

He found the supper coarse but tasty. Given his doorbolt he repaired to his room. With the door secured, he tried his bed. It was lumpy, and the blanket thin, but somehow he found it quite comfortable. The noise outside in the hall was incessant – stumblings, vinous shouts, eructations – but somehow unobjectionable, even entertaining. He fell asleep soon, and smiling.

8
An Altercation With a Sylvan Setting

The crash of his iron door bar to the flagstone floor woke Hex. Though his cell lacked a window, he knew it was sunrise – the hour when the bouncers went through the halls and – keying each doorjamb from without – released each room's purchased bolt. Its fall was the roomer's alarm, telling him his protected tenure was ended, and he'd better get up and look to his gear before one of his neighbours slipped in and stole it. Hex had slept dressed. He rose irritated at the harshness of this ouster. He turned in his bar at the clerks' cage at the end of the corridor and went in to breakfast.

In the common room the bouncers doubled as waiters, and they flung the breakfast vessels down before their tenants with a vigorous clangour and frequent spills. When they lounged by the walls during lulls they watched the guzzlings of their clientele with a peeved and brooding air, gnawing absently at their leathern muzzles. Their scrutiny tended to hasten the breakfasters through their work and hustle them outside about their business. Though the fare had been adequate in mass and savour Hex, once outside, made himself amends for the meal's hectic mood by stopping for a secondary breakfast – a mere culinary footnote to the first – in a wine-and-fry shop just down the cableway from the Leafmould Inn. When, greatly soothed, he sat back from his platter, he asked the tapster about an elusive, smoky scent that had teased him throughout his degustation of the braised Lumpet.

'It's the Throttlers' smudgepots,' the man told him.

'The morning wind's onshore in the autumn. It makes the wharfsiders half-daft all season.'

'Ah. The smoke that drugs the Slothers? Slows them down?'

'If anything really does that. Look here.' He hitched his peel jerkin's demi-sleeve off a knotty, scar-silvered triceps muscle. 'Their flap-tips hug you here while you're strangling them – outsides of the shoulders. Lots of little things like sawteeth they have, there on their flap-tips. I was a good Throttler, but unfortunately I was a bleeder.'

'My condolences. At least it certainly seems to have made you strong.'

'It does that. You should see some of the *ladies* of the guild. They make the best Throttlers, really. More limber.'

Hex, reminded of the well-known savouriness of Slother, had turned half an eye upon the board of fare nailed above the counter. And thus he discovered a man slouched against a post of the shed's awning, smiling a faint, acid smile at him. The man was slight and lean, a dun-coloured figure in breeches and jerkin of much-scuffed peel. His face, hawkeyed, was to Hex a sudden window on earlier years. The plunge of its long, narrow nose was brought up short by the solid horseshoe curve of a stubborn jaw brambled with coarse black beard.

'Sarf Immlé. Sit, and imbibe, old friend.'

Though Hex's pleasure was real, 'friend' was a bit of a falsehood, which he felt as he spoke it. They had enjoyed a cordial competition more than a friendship – arguers over midnight cups in the bistros of the Academy quarter. Both had had team-mates in these liquorish sessions of ideological arm-wrestling. The polarization of their affable, inebrious debating society was a fundamental one in the academic population as a whole. Hex was one of those who regarded that institution as an emporium of cultural models – a bazaar wherein actual, past, and putative forms of human experience were displayed for the promiscuous self-enrichment of anyone anywise interested. Sarf had always been one of those who saw the Academy as an arsenal of information by means of which to besiege the citadels of the Real World – the *current* one – with the goal of its reconstruction along more ideal lines.

Still, it was pleasant now for Hex to eat and order wine for this man who had once been fond of calling him a 'hedonistic book-guzzler'. He felt raffish, a veteran knight of the road, to be meeting so far afield a man who had thought him a schoolish stick-in-the-mud.

'I won't ask what *you're* doing here,' he told Sarf with a grin, 'because if you turn the question around on me I'll hardly know how to answer. As a matter of fact – '

'As a matter of fact, Bramt Hex, if you *asked* me what I'm doing here, I wouldn't be at liberty to answer. You're looking very healthy. You've gained some weight, haven't you?'

'I doubt it. I've lost some, if anything. I've had some fairly rough going lately, actually.'

'Mmmm. Is it two years since I saw you last? I'm glad to see you've finally got out of Glorak. A man should do *some* travelling before he snugs his behind into that nice, comfy magus' chair.'

'What makes you so sure I've *been* in Glorak all this time?' Hex's hostly warmth had fled him. He now recalled vividly that galling calm of Sarf's arrogance – that stolid absoluteness born of the man's serene conviction that most of the world misread the game of life. But Hex smothered an urge to lie, and shrugged. Present needs must be kept in mind. Sarf had always been something of a vagabond intermittently, was locally well travelled. He might have a place where Hex could sleep for free. 'I *have* been, granted. But I've been planning travel for some time now. I was just lately working on developing some, ah, new income to finance it. But, essentially, the enterprise misfired in a big way, and instead of properly shipping out of Glorak, I barely escaped it with my life. And since it comes up, have you got some place you could put me up for a few days? I just got here and I'm badly short of money.'

Now the barest ghost of mirth haunted Sarf's broad mouth and solid, scraggly jaw, but Hex grew glad again, knowing his man. With Sarf refusal would be dry and direct. His droll gravity portended – after some aggravating catechism – compliance.

'Your outfit looks new,' Sarf offered. 'Costly shortsword, good boots. Are you really destitute, or only relatively destitute?'

'All men are relatively destitute. I have, oh Inquisitor, not twenty lictors to my name.'

'Still, you could have bought cheaper gear and had more cash left over.'

'The gear has to wear. It's likely I'm going to have quite a way to travel to reach my destination. It's a rather unusual destination, I can tell you that.' He sensed that seeming eager to talk about his project would prod Sarf to revert to his own, the mystery of which he had been so quick to allude to. He was not wrong. Sarf's hand made a sweep of dismissal and he sat forward.

'It's odd that you ask me to put you up, Bramt Hex, because I find myself in a position to do just that, while at the same time, there is what you might see as a catch in the arrangement. Would you like to go for a walk and talk about it?'

Out along the cableway, they wove through the sun-speckled shoals of slumfolk. Everyone was out. The elderly were abroad with their grandchildren, for it was peak market hour. At the same time many of the workers on the littoral – Throttlers and Spongers – were filtering back to their neighbourhoods to quaff the cup and cut the loaf at leisure while a high tide drowned their harvest grounds. It seemed a carnival crowd, genially boisterous, wearing its universal motley of leafshadow. A pale flurry of nutshells abruptly decorated Sarf's hair and beard, and a second later a melon rind jounced off Hex's shoulder. From the foliage above the scholars' upflung curses and shaken fists there rained down a multi-voiced snickering, and one shrill declaration – made zestily in a childish treble – was heard: 'Boy, I really got the fat one good!'

The pair proceeded. Sarf, promising fuller discussion at a wineshop he had in mind, remained mysterious during their walk. He seemed mainly bent on getting Hex to notice how much of the Ungullionites' gear – boots, caps, tool-belts – was made of peel. Hex soon lost patience.

'Do you have to be so portentous? I'm wearing the stuff, it's obvious everyone uses it here. Proceed to the point.'

'That place,' said Sarf, his air of portent unruffled, 'has a quiet corner in its patio. There's a local red that's very tasty hot and sugared.'

Hex followed, resigning himself to Sarf's pace as long as Sarf was treating. The wineshop he indicated had beside it a low platform offering drinkers tables at a slight elevation above the cableway. Down-cable from it was a zone of particularly big trees, grandfathers standing somewhat wider-spaced than the norm, and permitting cave-ins of gold noon light that drenched the earth around them. Through a high lattice of gaps Hex glimpsed – at not too great a distance – a watertank dappled yellow and green.

'I know the neighbourhood,' he began as they took a table at the corner of the platform farthest from the cableway.

Sarf waved this preface off. 'Some of the oldest and most irascible trees are hereabouts. They call the area

Wrestlers Grove for all the riots that have started here. That's why it's such a quiet neighbourhood – did you notice?'

Traffic *was* light, and the pitch of voices low, even along the cableway. Hex nodded. 'Then, surely, there's more danger here of being overheard – I mean, about this momentous business of yours?' He felt himself leering a bit, but couldn't help it. But Sarf's composure was, he had to concede, impressive.

'I'll let you tell me if it's momentous or not, Bramt.'

He broke off to order, bespeaking a pair of sweet mulled reds. Just like the man! Those rare times you could badger him into buying a round, he always ordered for everyone what *he* decided they should drink, rousing numerous outcries and boisterous reorderings. Now Hex let it ride, rather liking sweet-mull. When the tapster – a man whose dewy baldness proclaimed a certain nervousness – had retired, Hex bowed:

'Speak. Detail your marvels, by all means.'

'Fine. I will ask you to note the steps involved in the production of peel. Also note, please, the absence of polemic from this description. Hear how this lucrative fabric is derived, and then tell me if any moral judgements are suggested to you by the hearing. Agreed? Good. Ah! Here . . .'

They took up their new-delivered mugs, and clinked them. The trite gesture caused Hex a surge of pleasant humour. Eversour but not unbrilliant Sarf Immlé! Suppose he *were* on to something momentous? The mull's heat and sweetness were good, but its aftertaste was resinous, and kept one sipping to wash it out.

'Peel is made in Slimshur, Bramt. That's a commercial confederacy of East Shore towns that share a unique, hundred-league stretch of coast. The land there is naked bedrock that slants into the sea at a very gentle angle. All Slimshur's bays are wide and shallow – a man could wade a half-mile offshore before reaching a fathom's depth, though of course no man would *want* to wade offshore. All the towns there stand at places where inlets deep enough for harbours adjoin smooth and level slopes of rock into the sea. So much for the scene of the peel-harvest. I hope I have not been too ploddingly circumstantial so far?'

'You are a master of narrative.'

'The scene of the harvest, as I say. Now to the Seeding of the Fields. By the Fields I mean the long, gradual slopes that are one of the prerequisites of a townsite. These are seeded with men. Convicts. For mark you: Just inland of Slimshur lie the vast satrapies of Pil the Unkillable. Juridical excesses are the peculiar characteristic of all this empire. Courts are innumerable and statutes draconian. The convicted and doomed have become one of the empire's major exports, since they are so numerous that the Pillians have long ago discovered the expediency of selling the guilty rather than suffering the expense of executing them themselves. Slimshur lay at hand to embrace the practice, having used cattle to seed their fields thitherto. What had been a rather anaemic and localized industry swelled – once stoked by human fodder – to vigorous, full-blooded health. At present a certain notorious West Shore entrepreneur is the factor of the Slimshurians' product. Those industrious shorefolk pay the Pillians with this man's gold, and march their purchased human fuel to the shore, to those towns couched in their little bays and coves where those hard-working folk flourish. And when they seed their slopes with these convicts, they do what they call a distasteful duty – they will not hear it called a crime.'

'I must interject here,' Hex put in. 'Your remarks have *not* been without covert polemical touches. Still your account is intriguing. Get to the crime, then! How are these convicts used?'

'It is generous of you to ask. If you weren't Bramt Hex I might suspect you of some glimmering of social concern! But hear. The slopes of Slimshur are seeded with men twice a moon – at half and full, the latter for some reason, bringing the higher yield. One to three score convicts are chained to the slope about a quarter mile inland from the sea.

'They are set out just at dawn. In the early light they soon become visible to certain creatures which inhabit the coastal waters, called Shlubupps. When the Shlubupps descry the convicts, their eyestalks extrude from the water. The townsfolk, witnessing the harvest from their various city-walls, raise at this point the cry *water broken*. At this cry an instrumental ensemble, also posted atop the walls, strikes up music whose effect is to encourage the long toil of the Shlubupps out of the surf, and up to the slope to feed upon the convicts.

'Each Shlubupp is over three rods long, and a dozen might emerge at a time, more if the offering is greater. The creatures' bulk, normally water-supported, can be moved upslope only with the greatest labour. And so the beasts, in their toil, lubricate their passage with great volumes of frothy digestive slime – more voluminously the more difficult their progress. The thick layer they produce in their climb is First-Pile peel. The lighter layer they exude on their descent – already smoothed by the First-Pile – is called Second-Pile. Once beaten and dried, the two-ply stuff is peeled from the rock with winches. It needs only shipment, curing in West-Shore warehouses, and separation to be cut and marketed. So. The exposition is done. Are you moved to make any remarks on the ethics and justice of the situation?'

'Tell me first, Sarf – What offences are capital in the Satrapies of Pil the Unkillable?'

'Well asked. They include, among what we would call the more serious crimes, such peccancies as Mocking a

Social Superior, Coughing During Tax-Collecting Ceremonies, Left-handed Nosewiping, and numberless others of equal whimsicality.'

Hex paused before answering, and in this blink of silence an eerie, muted roar drifted towards them from Wrestlers Grove. It was a human outcry, a brief, throbbing basso raised in rusty, resonant complaint. Hex blinked, but Sarf shrugged and bade him with an arched brow say on.

'All right, Sarf. If all you say is truth I freely grant all three are murderers of equal guilt – suppliers, processors and purchaser. Is this the judgement you – '

The Tapster, who had just approached with the carafe at Sarf's signal, spilled some wine on the table top, apparently startled by a second blurred shout from somewhere not too distant in the woods. 'Eh? What is it?' Hex prompted the man with some pique, withdrawing his sleeves from the spill's vicinity.

'Some neighbourhood quarrel,' the Tapster said, looking graver than his dismissive tone. 'Forgive me.' He plied his sponge and withdrew.

'So you grant it's murder,' Sarf solemnly prodded.

'I just said so. Advance your tale, please, that I may get some grasp of its fundamentals.' This last was an old joke from their impudent and disputatious Academy days, though in fact Hex was impressed by the story thus far. Sarf refused to smile.

'One of its fundamentals, Bramt, is that the killing of murderers is not itself murder. You grant that, of course, don't you?'

'Well, yes, by and large.'

'Good. Then I can tell you what I and my associates have afoot. You're bound to secrecy of course, whether or not you join us?'

'Yes. So be it. So, where in this murderous peel-cycle do you propose to strike? The entrepreneur perhaps?

Wealthy world-manipulators were always favourite targets of yours.'

A sour pleasure somewhat warmed Sarf's eyes. Fractionally, he smiled.

'The foreseeable guess, Bramt – only right in part, and far less bold than our actual plan. It's a whole Slimshur *town*, a village full of the monsters' caterers we're going to kill. Yes. Those pimps of human flesh to the lust of homicidal worms.' Though it grew, Sarf's jubilation remained soft-voiced, an effect Hex found disquieting, even as he felt Sarf's words rouse his own enthusiasm. 'Now as to the right part of your guess, the peel we'll make of *them* – yes! – will finance a further assault on the entrepreneur. For Arple Snolp has long been our foremost adversary. His power compels any effective attack on him to be well-funded.'

'Snolp? Arple Snolp? I know this man, Sarf. I've stood near to him as we now sit, and talked with him at length.'

Visibly, Sarf in his turn was impressed. 'When? Where?'

'In – '

There was a shout and a sharp, splintering noise of impact. Their vigour and shocking nearness brought every drinker's head up, and the tapster out to half-crouch – taut and pallid – in his shed's doorway. A scrambling noise behind a shack across the cableway focused all eyes above. On the roof of the shack – which was perched some twenty feet off the ground – a man swarmed into view. He was small and monkeyish; his clothes were torn. He scuttled across the roof, ploughing up clouds of dead leaves, and with no slightest quiver of a pause he dived straight off its nearer edge, hands stretched towards a laundry-rope a good twelve feet below.

The rope groaned, but did not give. With a half-swing the man flung himself – heels first – clear across the cableway. He struck and clung like a cat to the railing round the patio. The tapster bustled forth with curious shooing gestures. The ragged fugitive jumped into the patio, threw off the tapster with one squirrel-quick feint, and vanished through the door into the wine-shed. Everywhere the drinkers were carefully rising to their feet. The shack across the way began to rattle and quake furiously. A second figure mounted its roof.

This was a large woman with jaggedly cropped hair and huge shoulders. Her massy neck was oiled, as were her naked, sinewed arms.

'A Throttler,' Sarf murmured thoughtfully. He and Hex stood now too, sensing that those around them were acting from experience.

'Dog!' the woman bawled. She aped her quarry's heedless plunge. The clothes-rope snapped – whip-loud – beneath her. With a meaty, smashing noise she dropped from view behind a plank fence marking the back of someone's property. Crunchings and growled curses followed. Then a grunt, and the fence exploded into splinters. The Throttler marched to the cableway and bellowed up at the wine-shed.

'*Here!* Oh yes, you sodden weasel! You *would* flee here! You snivelling wine-sponge! I'm going to rip this place down around your arse, and then I'm going to *twist* your wretched frame till the grog squirts out of your ears!'

Hex and Sarf, imitating their fellow drinkers, were clambering over the nearest railing and vacating the patio, discreetly withdrawing from the intimate marital discussion that was obviously about to take place. The tapster began to bleat some feeble dissuasions, but when she vaulted on to the patio he followed his patrons. She marched up to one of the shed's walls, thrust spike-like fingers between two planks, and ripped a six-foot section of siding off the structure's frame. Through this, disdaining the natural door, she lunged, and from the door, in the same instant, the ragged man darted. From the railing he vaulted back across the cableway. The Throttler re-emerged, roaring, a two-hundredweight wine cask brandished overhead.

'Is it wine you want, Wimfort? Well by the black, greasy Death, it's wine you're going to get!'

Tucking the cask under one arm, she vaulted from the platform in pursuit. The forest swallowed both.

'What strength!' marvelled Hex to a fellow-drinker who had shared the shelter of the same tree with them. The man nodded tiredly.

'He drinks; she beats him,' he explained.

The patrons, for the most part, returned to their tables, and Hex and Sarf with them. The tapster stood with sagging shoulders, mutely looking at his shed. The wall's breach had somehow slipped the rafters, and the roof now gently canted. Hex called him gently:

'I say, could you pour us another pair of sweet-mulls?' The man turned him such melancholy eyes Hex added, 'Best look to your custom after all. That's going to be costly to fix.'

'My counter's smashed,' the tapster reported when he brought the pitcher. 'That raging sow has been warned. I'm closing early today and lodging a formal complaint down at the – '

From deep in the trees a wet concussion echoed. A perfect silence fell on the patio. Four heartbeats later, a man said in relieved tones: 'That came from near Old Mangler. We can thank our – '

A crackling, wrenching noise – dreadful in its duration and complexity – sounded from the site of the concussion. The sound suggested the crushing of an extensive structure. The wail of many voices rose in accompaniment.

'A strangling!' cried the tapster. 'So near! If a riot

starts, I'm ruined!' He and the other drinkers were over the railing and swarming towards the uproar before the two foreigners dazedly found their feet.

'Come on,' Sarf said. They followed towards a noise so eloquently terrible Hex couldn't repress a qualm that they were hastening in the wrong direction. They quickly lost sight of the citizens ahead, whose powerful limbs took them smoothly up ladders and across ropewalks. While Sarf moved nimbly enough, Hex scraped a shin on the first fence he climbed, and had to fight the wobbly ladders for his footing. The incessant snap of shattered wood was beginning to be drowned out by a human din of shouts and screams. As the pair followed a high catwalk, the strangling came in view. The two combatant trees, in intertangling their branches, had shrunk by half their leafy volume, and their struggle was bathed in new-admitted sunlight.

Each multiple gripped the other, their branches groping with jerky flexibility, like spastic snakes. The jerrybuilt hives that crammed the groins and elbows of their boughs were now a mass of buckled walls that rained down in pieces, some glinting wetly red.

One tree seemed somewhat smaller, and at the same time more densely inhabited. The bigger tree neighboured two massive stumps, and thus was two-thirds surrounded by comparatively clear ground. Spectators filled this with a turbulent periphery, or stood on adjacent rooftops of buildings based on the ground. Everyone visibly shunned arboreal perches. Hex and Sarf took the hint, and went down to join the crowd.

There was a kind of beauty in that slow, majestic vegetal hate, that stubborn, murderous torsion of boughs thicker than a man's body, that Antaean power and multibrachiate complexity. But viewed from below, this beauty was obscured by the human ruin and pain that rained down from the battle.

The crowd cheered as a man, having wormed himself free of his house, dropped from the straining limbs of the battlers and sprinted over the trash-littered ground to safety. He was embraced with a fervour that expressed the crowd's general sense of powerlessness to help. The furious and unpredictable movement of the lower boughs made it very dangerous to stand under them. Nevertheless there must have been a dozen people with long poles darting in and out of the fight, and reaching up what aid they could offer those trapped above. With a thrust one man broke open the jammed door of a torqued hovel. A woman's hasty arms thrust two small children out, who were caught and borne to safety. The woman herself, making her leap just before her house collapsed, was harder to catch and seemed to have broken her leg, but limped out smiling nonetheless. Another pole-man, spying an arm thrust from some wreckage and groping the air for purchase, supplied the hand his pole tip. Firm hold was taken, a second hand joined the first, a man's head and shoulders were hauled free – and then the tree shifted its grip and crushed the prisoner's chest. He jerked, and slumped, and three runlets of blood poured out his sleeves and mouth, like rain from gutterspouts.

'An ugly irony.' Hex and Sarf turned and found the man they'd shared the tree with at the wineshop. 'For stability we have to build right at the joints and crotches, and of course that's where all the crunch is in a strangling.'

'It's monstrous!' Hex shouted, realizing the shock he was in. More quietly he asked, 'Can't they be saved?'

'The axe-squad will be here any moment. They might kill the littler one in time to snuff out the trouble before it spreads. The big one is Old Mangler. See those stumps? The Mangler's work – a very crusty, touchy tree and generally agreed to be one of the strongest in the whole slum.'

This man was slight and shrivelled but hale. His seamed

face had a tart, lemony pucker, a touch of satire in it. 'In a way there's luck in this spot – see how clear most of the near ground is? If the little one dies fast enough, the thrashing might not start any of the others off.'

'They ought to kill Mangler – it seems the more aggressive.'

'It would take far too long to kill a brute that size. Time's of the essence. Look, here's the squad.'

Men in black shortcapes, led by a cape-less man with a tall white plume in his hat, flowed speedily along a high catwalk and jumped nimbly down to the clearing. The crowd, cheering, clove to make a runway which the plumed man, after quick survey, designated. Here he stood his men in single file. They tossed back their capes to reveal broad-bit axes with three-quarter hafts strapped across their shoulders.

The leader turned treeward, studied his course to the giants, and sprinted in. Crouching near the smaller tree, he plucked his plume from his hat and with it smote the trunk, leaving a white slash of chalk-dust on it. As he ran back the first man of the squad sprinted forward, axe at ready. With strength matched only by his speed he crouched and gave the trunk two strokes, knocking a fat chunk from the wrestler's side. Pain rolled through its embattled frame, and wrung new sharps and flats of agony from its strange fruit, those eerie sandwiches of planks and men jutting from the clutches of its reptilian arms. Detritus plopped more thickly on to the sticky litter-heaps below and – unmistakable here and there in the sunlight – fell fine, whispery drizzles of pure blood. As the axemen hit a rhythm, darting dodgily to and from their frenzied, two-stroke assaults, the seamed man shook his head unquietly.

'That little one's tough, too. It's going to be a near thing. It's been so sunny and breezy lately – prime riot conditions. That raging sow! If a bough hadn't half-brained her, she'd have climbed up after him and carried her assault right into Old Mangler's lap! They bound and dragged her off first thing, and I hope they give her the gibbet!'

'What do you mean? Is he – ?'

'Oh! You didn't notice Wimfort up there?'

The acrobatic little sot was halfway up Old Mangler. A snarl of laundry line and ropework had him – he hung head down from a shifty cat's-cradle crazily strung between two restless branches. He couldn't just wiggle loose and fall – the fifty-foot drop would kill him. However, were he unentangled, there was – two boughs away – a branch less mobile than the rest that he might shin down thirty feet to a jumpable height. His fierce but eerily patient efforts to untangle his legs were a spectacle of painful fascination. In tearing his eyes away Hex saw, in the crowd's front rank, the bathcrone of yesterday. Her walnut-in-white-wool head was tilted back – she was talking to someone trapped above, and . . . laughing? And what was this? Was that other, pilloried twelve feet overhead, also laughing?

'Back in a second,' he told Sarf. He moved towards the old women, for the crone's interlocutor was another crone, though her face was festively – even garishly – refeatured with cosmetics. A rampway of rope-strung slats, anchored at either end to flexible and active boughs, had flattened her shack against a straighter, less mobile limb that jutted between them. The woman had got her upper half out of a narrow gap in the pinch of her walls, but then Old Mangler's wakening rage had stopped her at the hips. Like a bright-painted puppet clutched in wooden fingers, she clapped her hands and sent down squawks of laughter to her friend at some joke the bathcrone had just told.

'Oh peace, peace! If you make me laugh any harder, you'll unmaiden me before this tree does!'

At this both shrieked anew – the bathcrone doubled at the hip with laughter, echoing how the trapped one too was rocking.

'What rogues and vixens we were!' the bathcrone fondly cried.

'Well, you at least still *are*, dearie,' the other mocked. 'The fruit being somewhat wrinkled, of course, you'll have fewer nibblers squeezing it.'

A groan, thousand-throated, caught their attention. A downward spasm of a lower branch had brained an axeman going in. Hex just saw the man's fall – his legs still staggering a moment after his skull flattened and his brain diffused through the circumjacent air. The smaller tree's pale wound was two feet deep already, and the pain-fluxes it sent skyward were, unavoidably, productive of greater torment for some of the victims. The pain-chorus there kept bansheeing into the upper registers. Ribbons and rivulets of dark blood now thickly zebra-ed its half-cloven trunk. A thicker rain of more grisly trash pattered around it.

'You know, dearie,' the merry, kohl-eyed hag called down in a more musing tone, 'I've often wondered why I never got back. Remember how we both swore that we would?'

'And *I*, at least, still might!' the bathcrone crowed, mocking her friend's previous words. Both laughed again, shaking their heads as at some enduring folly both shared knowledge of. Something in the easy intimacy between these two, a shared remoteness from the enveloping disaster, held Hex half-rapt, watching them as much as the cataclysm.

'It *is* strange, though, isn't it – how we never went back?' the victim prompted.

'It is that, dearie.' The bathcrone, grave now, nodded.

Something caught her eye. 'Oh my! Hang tight, dearie, I fear it may come soon now.'

'I hope it doesn't hurt too long,' the other said, and gripped her coffin's edge. Hex saw where a dozen bystanders had been knocked forward off their feet. The Throttler, trailing broken cords from her arms and wrists, surged roaring into the battle zone.

"Wimmy!' she thundered, looking up to her rope-webbed mate.

Wimfort had, in fact, just plucked his left foot free from his body's last entanglement. Clamping one writhing bough with both legs, he had reached both arms at a perilous stretch and half-hugged the next bough over, also writhing. He had just loosed his straining thighs to make the giddy transfer when his wife's thunder jolted him with a powerful reflex of recoil and escape. Both his arms' and legs' grips equally dislodged, he scrabbled one suspended instant to catch hold with either set of limbs, and then dropped. Skidding twice down the back of a pythonesque branch, he lodged in the crushing crotch of the giant and there, an instant later, was pinched in half.

The Throttler's anguish tore the sky far above the leafy turmoil.

'Wimmy! Oh my Wimmy! You! You wooden vermin!' She now addressed Old Mangler while, reaching down one hand, she took up the dropped axe of the brained squad-man. 'You cankered splinter! Log of Hell! Eat Steel!'

Lunging forth, brushing aside like chaff the axemen who rushed to intercept her, she, at full run, flung the axe two-handed at the tree. Its crescent bit slammed so deep into Old Mangler's trunk the head was wholly swallowed, and the haft left quivering like a down-grown branchlet of the giant. Geyserlike, a wave of pain billowed up the gargantuan vegetable's anfractuous skeleton, and made its leafy top snap like a whip. The bathcrone's friend got half a cheery chirp out, a truncated squawk of good-bye, and then the tree's surge hauled her up and inwards, breaking her against the bough that racked her, and she died very quickly indeed.

The bathcrone, with a grieving twist, turned her face aside and downward. Looking up, she stared unseeing in Hex's eyes a moment, till presently humour rekindled in her own.

'You'd best be away, dear Pinkness! This town can't serve your purpose now.' She pointed to Old Mangler, and turned away.

The giant had killed the Throttler with one downward spasm, the merest footnote to its rage, which was all now bent on its opponent. Before, its reptilian digits had bored and rooted and gouged for their purchase. Now the Mangler's smallest twiglets lashed and twisted and tore at the smaller tree. Now its vast, knot-muscled arms ripped, wrenched and ransacked the foe. In a moment, its convulsive wrath had torn a major bough from its weakened and half-felled adversary. A forty-foot length of living limb, weighing tons, was ripped free and flung triumphantly abroad by the frenzied titan. Like a sundered lizard's tail it galvanically thrashed in the air before striking two neighbour trees simultaneously. Its contortions, smashing ground-level shanties to bits, woke both trees to a furious, wrestling assault on anything they touched. Hex jumped to feel his arm clutched.

'Foreigners have no place here now,' Sarf told him. 'Soon there'll be all too little room for all too many workers. Give me an answer about joining us, and I'll take you to our movement's headquarters. It's waterside, and out of this.'

'What's this, extortion? Give me more details before asking me to decide.' He paused, struck by a thought. 'Mainly, I need to know more of the precise location of Slimshur.'

Sarf gave a laughing snort. 'Join or not, you should come waterside. Come on and I'll tell you more.'

Walking seaward was an upstream fight along the cableways, for civic attunement to conjoint action in these crises was intense. They were lithe, however, these half arboreal folk – fluid in the tightest bottlenecks, deft in making room for each other in even the closest defiles. Still, the pair made no better than a stroller's pace, and the splintery noise of riot could be heard behind them, broadening, probing outwards through the woods, its leaping, cancerous spread sounding even swifter than fire's.

Most of what would follow would be property damage, for the alarm had long been sounding overhead – a sweet, brisk trumpet melody, its tunefulness, Sarf explained, designed to carry without aggravating the trees. For these were known to share some tenuous, empathetic field, and grow generally more restive at any local flare-up. So the horns' incongruous sweetness soared overhead, and the slumfolk rivered riotward, as smooth and agile in their urgency as the sprightly brass that summoned them.

The pair made steady way, sometimes sheltering in side eddies.

'What makes them *live* here?' Hex asked, curiously vexed by the suffering that thrived around him. Sarf grimaced as if to greet a reiterated idiocy.

'Why do the poor live anywhere? Look you, friend scholar. Who consumes the most slother and marinated eel locally? Who owns the ships that carry excess slother and eel abroad? The rich upon yon heights. Where else is it *convenient* for these poor to live, save in these slums whence they can both farm the littoral and serve the ships as longshoremen?'

'Why not live inland of the heights – come shoreside just to throttle and sponge?'

'Inland of this range is Vampire Valley, where they ineradicably thrive. And nerve-grass grows so lush there you can't take a step without the thickest hip-boots.'

En route to the harbour Sarf added various details to his description of his movement's enterprise, but there was only one which really penetrated to Hex through the excitement of the wakened woods around him: Sarf was fairly sure that Slimshur, while it lay of course more than a thousand leagues east, also lay some few hundred leagues *north* of Ungullion's latitude.

'Then your enterprise fits mine as well as any,' Hex announced on hearing this. An ardour woke in him. 'It coalesces, Sarf! A certain clue I received yesterday, then this fortuitous . . . eviction from the city just as you come along with this intriguing northbound mission.'

'Only the most niggling cartographer would call it anything but an eastbound mission.'

'Better and better! Even your casual words ring like omens in my ear. Of that more later. Right now I can say, count me in! What have I to lose? I am rootless, a scholar at large in the world. Men of my kidney do not cringe from the cup of Chance, but boldly grasp the goblet and quaff the dram!'

'Fine. Come on then. When you meet the league and take the oath you should stress your enmity to Snolp and not your scholar-at-large character. I don't care about your motives. I just want you aware that it's a dead-serious allegiance you'll be swearing.'

9
An Early-Morning Incident

'They always wear such an astonished look,' Jazm said, smiling, of the harpooned slouch-calf they towed astern of their skiff. He stowed under a thwart the megaphone through which he had uttered the flatteries that had brought the creature – after the wont of its kind – within their range, bubbling shy disclaimers as it came. Its ears, which had stood erect to catch the fatal blandishments, now floated limp on the placid waters that muttered against the scattered crags through which they rowed. The man at the oars, Hossle, did not want to talk about their catch. He reverted to the talk their sighting of the calf had interrupted.

'Jazm, I'll speak straight to my meaning. I'm a blunt man and you'll just have to excuse it.'

He *was* a block-torsoed man, and his head of short grey hair was squarish. Blunt too were the fingers with which he counted off his points while the younger Jazm whose gold-clasped shoulder braid of black hair bespoke a certain sportive élan – wryly bowed acquiescence.

'Your friendship with Quad is solely due to his being quartermaster. Reason: quartermaster's recommendations nominate second mates. Further: this ambition for second mate is part of your larger ambition to captain the *Oriaph* outright.'

'Well, have I denied it?' Some weary pique was evident in Jazm's voice, though he strove for humour. 'Let's really be frank. Under these upbraidings, Hossle, lies the tacit reproach that *we* are friends only because I wanted your voice to get me my thirdship. Openly now – you think me a climber?'

Hossle snorted. His humour looked realer than Jazm's. 'Well of course you are, but who objects to that? You're a friendly fellow and like me well enough into the bargain. It's your goals I upbraid, not your drive.' Jazm laughed, not displeased by this candour, but Hossle pressed on, not to be interrupted. 'Consider. A *captaincy* of one of these peeling scows? Your status is bound to your boat. If peel should go out of fashion, what's your commission worth then? Young men never think of change. Suppose Snolp sniffs more gain in some competing fabric. Remember coiler scales? Everywhere you – was that a man on that rock?'

The question startled Jazm. The peaceful, rock-fanged shallows, gold and red in the new morning light, grew eerier with the thought of some fourth inhabitant besides themselves and their buoyant prey. Though in less than four fathoms of water they were two miles offshore. The *Oriaph* and her companions (the *Wollikan*, another peeler, and a nameless transport of snolpian mercenaries that no one knew the reason for) were anchored five miles south, awaiting the harvest to follow tonight's full moon. Jazm scanned, finding the half-gilt rocks around them vacant, and the wide whisper of waves unmarred by any sound.

Hossle shrugged, seeming embarrassed. 'I'm glare-blind, I guess. But let's not lose the thread – it was in your own time, while you were growing up – all the world was coiler scales, the ultimate gaudy gear, fops would never wear anything else again! So what of all those career coiler-captains? Look for them now – poor, grounded popinjays, shorn of every plume, guzzling cheap gut-stiffener in wharfside tumbledowns! But now, what of all the coiler *navigators*? Everywhere on any kind of ship, easily steering the tides of change. It's why I keep harping – the science before the ship itself. It's in honest counsel, and not pride of post, that I speak. If the *Oriaph*'s ever deassigned, I only – '

'Did you hear that, Hossle?' Jazm was hearkening towards the big crag – a fractional island, really – where Hossle had thought to see a man. Glides wheeled above it – rather thickly?

Yes.' Hossle was taut now, his whisper fierce. 'It's oars in locks – a lot of them.' Digging one of his own oars in he began to wheel them around with the other. 'Cut that bloody slouch loose.'

Before they had even half come about, a forty-oared two-master slid from one side of the crag, followed instantly by a second from the other side. The overlooming hulls converged to bracket the skiff. Their glinting oars chopped the water so near the skiff they smote and then imprisoned Hossle's oars.

Standing amidships, Hossle told Jazm in a mutter, 'Dig out our ensign, it's in the gear!' Crying upwards, his voice echoing between the two ships, he displayed the emptiness of his hands: 'Ahoy! We are Snolp's! We're with the peeling fleet nearby! We mean no harm!'

Through the strangers' oarports he could glimpse single eyes, fragments of bearded profiles. Jazm was just digging out their banner – a black A and S entwined on a blue ground – when from both unseen decks footfalls flurried. Along the gunwale of one ship a dozen archers appeared, nocking arrows to the strings of horn-tip bows, and to that of the other surged a score of men hoisting casks and bags of ballast overhead. Hossle stood paralysed with amazement.

'Wait!' shouted Jazm, jumping to his feet. Arrows snickered down and a fang of pain sank through the small of his back. A cask jounced off his shoulder, knocking him to his knees. He looked up as, just above him, a large, plump-faced man raised a box. Jazm's expression of astonishment precisely mirrored the plump man's as the latter's arms thrust a growing shadow down against Jazm's sight, and Jazm's thought was crushed.

The hammocks were slung amidships of the second deck, below the main deck and above the oars. Hex lay in his, musing.

It was scarcely noon. The rest of the crusaders were topside still gossiping in the bows about the kill, each still busy establishing his or her part of the exploit. Though Hex, in the weeks of crossing, had grown quite cronyish with some of them, he felt no stomach for this discussion, perhaps because he had had a more unmistakable hit than the rest of them.

The image of that impact was vividly recurrent to his mind's eye, and he had counselled himself to this retreat, to divert himself by going over his cartographic notes. These he kept in a peel pouch that belted flat to the small of his back, safe from theft and weather beneath his doublet. There was little to them at present, a slim packet of his jottings of any yarn or anecdote or datum he had come by with any bearing on places and their customs. He was not studying them in any case. He had his shortsword out of its sheath, and was perusing it. It seemed to him somehow heavier and sharper since this morning, oddly realer, as did the fact that he would have to use it – directly or as a prod – for a killing-tool tonight.

It still made him a little giddy, the oiled ease with which he had brained that man. He keenly felt the larger human machine he had been sucked into – which surrounded him and even plied his limbs to its ends. For the first time he appreciated the degree of surrender his enlistment had involved and, all too readily, some of his initial misgivings about the enterprise returned to him with great clarity.

The movement's headquarters had been in a defunct dockside eel-picklery. Overturned pickling vats had served for the tables at which various preparations committees had stationed themselves. The rank-and-file dossed down here and there throughout the big, lofted, unpartitioned interior – napped on sacking beds or lounged on crates in merry or disputatious gaggles.

Here had been a general ambience neither unknown nor unpleasent to Hex. That atmosphere of brash articulacy, that carnival variety of sartorial and tonsorial affectations – all smacked of the Academy so lately left. He even recognized a face or two from Glorak. If there was some fleeting pique at this familiarity where he had looked for unguessed challenges, there was comfort by the same token. It was when he and Sarf had to slog through a series of induction procedures that a lively disdain for some of these crusaders was wakened in him.

From table to table they inched to be dipped in vat after vat – as it were – in a piecemeal immersion in the Membership. The functionaries administering each dunking – though presumably idealistic volunteers like all the rest – received the pair's lowly business of recruitment with complacent disattention. No necessary material was ever right on hand, necessary people were always absent, no one ever knew where anyone else was, and everybody seemed to feel quite cheerful and self-approving about the whole thing. They had to wait half an hour for the necessary tenth member of the Witnessing Committee to be found. What ensued, with his indispensable aid, was an hour's casual chat among the ten, during which no one more than glanced at Hex – this though the ceremony's aim was to ensure, in case of spies, that at least ten crusaders knew any new recruit's face by heart. This done, he was allowed to proceed to the Notarizing Committee for his oath. The hired magus administering the oath, with a mild control-spell attached (who knew if it worked or not?), could not be found for almost an hour. Neither, when it came time to get Hex his membership token, could the woman who had last wandered off with the supply of them. The token, a medallion struck with a scythe symbolic of the crusade's 'harvest of justice', was essential for getting him in and out of quarters past the guards, and presumably the crusade needed recruits, but almost two hours were needed to procure him one.

But it was Kratsk and Benarius, presiding at the last tub he was dragged to, that galled Hex most severely. These, the Steersmen of the Crusade, had engineered the mechanics of merchandising the pirated peel and, being in their own right notable ideologues of the firebrand sort, exercised a kind of Duumvirate in the league. They presided – or rather, were petitioned and consulted – at the biggest vat in the picklery. Its circle of seats was thick with an impromptu court of lieutenants and acolytes.

The burly Kratsk showed a sombre, deaconish energy. He illuminated diverse issues for those who thronged nearest with their questions. Beside him, resting, the cross of leadership laid by a moment, sat the gaunter, paler Benarius. Slowly, eyelids shut, he massaged the back of his neck, wearied by his abundant load of cares. Sarf took Hex's business to Kratsk, pressed it not shyly – after a decent wait – on Kratsk's attention, was wordlessly bid hold a bit by Kratsk's left hand; waited, urged anew, was bid once more attend. Benarius' lofty weariness was not to be interrupted either. His self-massage was now devoted to his temples, with his head cocked back. The close air of piety, cloyingly pickle-scented, so goaded Hex he found a cask to sit on, pulled off one boot, and began giving his foot a massage – not without audible sighs, and demonstrations of eased distress.

The parody was felt, though the general pose of inattention to Hex and Sarf prevented its being openly resented. Kratsk turned to Sarf, forbearingly asked his business. Hex's name was entered in the membership rolls, and the pair waved away.

Self-importance being such a common folly, Hex had let the fundamental romance of the crusade carry his will. Its consonance – however marginal – with the bathcrone's hint was probably enough in itself to settle the matter. The congenial milieu of smart-mouthed academic idealists was a further seduction. Though such assemblages invariably included cynics out for monetary gain or glory, the cause at least was just and, given this, Hex found himself not too disturbed to note a certain gain-and-glory lust in his own feelings. This was natural, and at any rate he was doing no ill.

Now, however, the depth of his allegiance alarmed him. He *must* help this machine to kill, at risk of dying with it at Snolp's hands, should his ardour falter. Now the moral vagueness and petty vanities of the crusaders frightened him. Suppose they were stupid in bigger ways as well? Might not this venture pose a real threat to his own existence? Admittedly, the leadership had managed a sufficiently organized beginning. Rowing shifts were short enough to be bearable, provisions were abundant. No more than two-score mercenaries – rowers and archers – had been necessary to provide a backbone of efficiency. And the group as a whole had not done badly for starters this morning. While there was some hysterical over-kill in the recruits' bombardment, they had at least performed with a will, while the archers had feathered them with ghastly speed, till they seemed half avian – weird, bristle-plumed bipeds twitching against the skiff's thwarts.

But Hex recalled the half week they'd spent waiting to ship out – recalled some of his comrades' callowness, and was assailed anew by the worm of doubt. Discretion was difficult enough, of course, in that dense, reeking jostle of humanity. The quayside was a squatters' jungle of displaced slum dwellers. The parks and alamedas of the Heights were required by civil statute to accommodate riot refugees and provender their camps but, inevitably, the wharves absorbed the bulk of the dispossessed. By the cataclysm's third day the harbour had filled with ships awaiting discharge of their cargo. On the thronging docks balked merchants – bent in colloquy with irate captains – threaded their way through the bristling tent-towns of the citizens, loud and swarmish with children, and overhung by the garbage-piss-and-blood smell of mass misery. Environed thus, any secret might prove hard to hide. Alas, many of the crusaders seemed to find this group secrecy, this membership in a mystery, a heady thing indeed. Hex himself, whenever he had sat with a knot of them in any wineshop, had heard a score of indiscretions spoken, and none too softly, either. And who could ever tell who – in that hyper-populous surround – was listening?

True, the riot countenanced this rashness, to some degree. Beside the deep convulsion of that green world it was easy to feel invisible, and inaudible as well beneath that vast, rock-rooted thunder, the snap and groan and smash of the embroiled and raging titans, ancient First Citizens of this piece of earth. The inhabitants themselves seemed a gypsy camp of transients beside this primordial turbulence, and foreigners were the readier to feel like patrons of some huge, violent carnival – passing on the fringe of marvels, exterior to its terrors and outward-bound.

Well and good – if only there had not been more than three peelers in the shipping jam. This meant dozens of Snolp's employees must have been scattered through those crowds, drinking at those wineshops . . . it nagged his stomach now, that remembered looseness. Perhaps those peeler crews had been distracted, though. Two of them had been killed. Late in the afternoon of Hex's induction, from a wineshop he and Sarf had watched big rolls of peel being unloaded down the dock. The boat carried a large harvest, and some of the ten-foot rolls had been lashed on deck. These were now being offloaded down a gangway.

Refugees hemmed the operation quite densely and nearly – only the most minimal space was left for the cart receiving the rolls from the foot of the gangway. One of Snolp's stevedores misstepped, and trod on some by-squatters, and the crowd showed very nasty about it, not at all disposed to see it as an accident. Then, near the head of the ramp, two of the crewmen lost their grip on the wooden axle of a roll. With huge soft speed it thudded down and sprang into the refugees, killing a child and crippling two adults. The two crewmen were dragged down to the dock in five heartbeats' time – thrown down, one of them, who rolled into the water and swam free. The other was pinned to the dock with the stevedore, and instantly buried under a crowd waving knouts and hammers. Hex could still see the late, red-gold light drenching that scene, half-gilding the flickering clubs and toiling arms. Above the riot noise some trumpet melody was playing – a signal between those crews inside battling the riot. The green seethe of the furious trees was also beautiful in that golden light and, with the music, the whole murder had a gorgeous, ceremonial air, a ritual sacrifice of human life to the bloodthirsty deities, Pain and Fear.

This morning's snolpians had died similarly gilt with oblique sun, though nearness made that ceremony seamier – its blood more vivid against the skiff's bleached wood, the meaty noise of killing more distinct – *so* distinct, echoing between the two ships' hulls . . . So far, killing 'the minions of Snolp' was indistinguishable from the lynching of any defenceless victim.

Hex rebelted his pouch of notes, resheathed his sword, and went above. He found Sarf lounging portside watching the sinking of their prey, for the crusaders deputized to this were only now wiring the two men with weights and scuttling the skiff, likewise weighted.

'Are they still at it?'

'They've been retrieving the arrows – very squeamishly and with much delay.' Sarf laughed grimly at the memory, and they watched the silver-haired one sink.

'That one died hard,' Sarf added.

'A powerful man. "Snolp!" Remember? "We are Snolp's!" That seemed so poignant, somehow.'

'Yes.'

'Sarf. How do you think we will do?' They were looking at the almost circular little bay of the town of Polypolis which could be seen, two miles distant, through the rocks concealing their ships. Hex tried to wedge his imagination into that sharp little spit of silver – that headland of shiny slate rooftiles bright in the noon sun. How would he do there tonight? Sarf's answer was unexpectedly solemn:

'I think we'll do quite well, Hex. The more I think of it, the more impressive it seems to me – I mean all we might accomplish if we pull this off.'

'I'm impressed with us too, but also edgy.'

'Listen. If you stand quiet here a while, the breeze brings you snatches of the revels in the town. I swear it does. Our information's accurate – and what more likely in any case than that they'd drink deep and long before a harvest? I tell you I feel it quite distinctly. Hex – touch wood – we're going to find them ripe for taking, and we're going to take them.'

10
Two Musical Friends

The air was utterly clear – cool and dry, scoured by an offshore breeze. The full moon's light flooded Polypolis, bleaching the cobbles to knobs of bone, and burying half the world in shadows black as charcoal. The still, stony street echoed the pair's footfalls, though they tried to muffle them. The bulky smokepot they carried on a stick between them did not help.

'Wait,' Sarf hissed. 'Hear that?'

After a moment, Hex nodded. From two streets above there drifted the scuff and whisper of a large group moving parallel to their own course. The two looked a question at each other: Was the noise as loud in fact as it seemed in their anxious ears? No shutters opened. No heads were thrust from doorways. They moved on.

They had drawn, for their assignment, the Musicians Lodge. This stood – as did Peelers Hall – near the wall, but two streets downhill and shoreward of it. The Hall would probably hold every working man in town, and hence the bulk of the crusaders now approached it. But since their informants had indicated that some few of the harvest-eve's celebrants occasionally slept at the Lodge, the planners had thought it prudent that the Lodge be penetrated simultaneously, thus securing at a stroke every vigorous male in Polypolis, which their reconnaissance reckoned at some seventy souls.

The Lodge was a three-storey building whose dormered, slate-tiled roof overtopped the wall but whose lower floors were comfortably sunk in its shadow. Beneath one of its western windows, they set the smokepot gently on the ground. Hex tried the shutter. It swung open. The sash, pried with his shortsword's tip, slid up. This ease of access was almost daunting. Fumblingly, they fed one end of the pot's hose beneath the sash, and clamped the other to the smoke vent of the pot. Sarf inserted the bellows' tip into the intake vent and began to pump with a steady rhythm. Within the Lodge mute swells of thin, white smoke moved through the darkened rooms, as if seeking out corridors and stairways.

'Well,' Hex murmured, looking down the length of the narrow town that fell away seaward. 'At least it looks like the plan is well devised.'

The undulating rooftops of Polypolis formed a scaly, moon-silvered finger that ended in a claw – the landspit that hooked out into the tar-black sea. The wall ran straight down its southern side and even out along the landspit for a bit – for the killing-slope lay cheek by jowl with Polypolis, immediately beyond the wall. Side by side both slope and town ran upland, inland, to end at the skirts of the same tangled range of hills.

'Yes,' Sarf whispered, after a moment. 'A few archers can keep the whole wall clear.'

Hex nodded, mentally rehearsing the rest. Their two ships lay in the little harbour within the landspit's curve – he could just see their masts from where he stood. The town itself would screen them from offshore eyes should Snolp's ships come in view prematurely next morning. Meanwhile the town's few craft were in their control, so that anyone fleeing the place would have to go inland and through the hills. By that route it was a full day's journey to the next town whence the peelers might be alerted, and that posed no threat. Let them only get their fodder to the slope and chained down by sun-up, and the rest of the town could fly en masse with the alarm for all it would matter.

Sarf's touch on his arm made him start, and when he turned he flinched again at the leather-snouted monster he confronted. Sarf tapped the muzzle he was wearing. With a vexed nod, Hex donned his own. They had soaked them in seawater on disembarking, and the herb filling the vented pouches now gave off a bitter exhalation, a cold, scorched reek that made his whole face feel numb. Of course, if he went in unprotected by this effluvium, his whole *body* would shortly be narcotized by the slotherweed smoke that now filled the lodge. Sarf had the sash up high, and was climbing through. Hex hoisted the smokepot and helped get it inside. Then he grasped the sill and hauled himself over it.

He made more noise than Sarf had. This surprised him, for his spirit felt taut, gathered for action, athletic. Abashed, he crouched with Sarf, and they waited for any noise or light to answer his echoes from the smoky dark. Far, shuttered windows sketched by leaks of moonlight showed them a big room – the whole floor, it seemed. The tables of a refectory filled half of it, and a small performing dais much of the rest. Beside this rose a staircase to the upper floors, and up these stairs thronged the smokeshapes, bent on their soundless attack. The pair watched them rise and thin, and then carried the smokepot to the foot of the stairs. Now Hex worked the bellows while Sarf climbed up to the hose's limit, and directed the fumes towards the second floor.

As he did so he turned his face away from the streaming hose – and seemed to Hex a high-set gargoyle whose hideous, mouthless scowl presided over this bloody enterprise of theirs. To shake off this lurid fantasy he signalled Sarf to come down and help him take the smokepot higher. At the landing was a short stem of hall with a door on each side, which then branched left. They crept to the turning – the solid joinery silent as stone underfoot – and looked down a longer corridor, with two more doors on either side.

Sarf motioned vigorous pumping and Hex nodded. As

Hex applied the bellows with steady vigour, Sarf moved left and right, packing both halls with such smokes as would quickly paralyse anyone who emerged from one of the rooms. When this was done, Sarf laid down the hose and gingerly opened the first door.

An empty bedroom. He left it open, went to the next room, found it likewise empty, treated it the same. Hex for his part pushed farther open a door already ajar – one of the two in the short hall. Empty. He turned to the other. Even as he touched the latch he heard a snore within. He brought up the hose. Sarf, who had found the other rooms empty, plied the bellows. Hex pressed the nozzle to the underdoor gap and for five minutes they prepared the air within. Then Hex dared the latch.

The door gaped in on a misty chamber, its floor half covered by an avalanche of moonlight admitted through an unshuttered casement. A large bed with a carven headboard stood in the shadowed corner, its coverlet abulge with two snoring occupants. Their deep sleep heartened the invaders. Briskly they brought the pot nearer, saturated the bed with smoke. Hex and Sarf then withdrew to the hall.

'I'll check upstairs,' Sarf whispered. 'Get some chain on them.'

Hex nodded. Everything was taking on an ease that made him wonder if they were themselves drugged by leakage through their muzzles. Why should the third floor need less precaution than this one? But Sarf stole up the next flight without bothering with the smokepot and Hex himself, feeling light as a dancer, returned to the bedside. With a key he began unfastening and unwinding the manacles wrapped around his waist. He peeled back the coverlet. Two men slept on their sides, knees bent, snugly paralleled like two spoons. The one behind spoke a shapeless syllable in his sleep, his bearded chin stabbing the neck of his bedmate – a clean-shaven and somewhat plumper man who stirred, but did not wake. The bearded one's arm was draped over the other's shoulder, and their two right hands lay together. Convenient, Hex decided. With a short chain, he linked the two wrists. Once the other two were linked the pair would be locked in single-file. Their skin felt cool and faintly clammy, and their faces sweated. Perhaps they were getting more smoke than needful. He turned to open the window and a dark form lunged towards him.

He identified the returning Sarf long moments before his pulse rate had settled again. The top floor was empty. Sarf closed the smokepot's vents and Hex opened the window. They locked collars round both sleepers' necks and combined some shorter shackles to make three feet of lead-chain for each. They paused.

'Well,' Hex said, his voice unguarded for the first time, 'we'll have to get their left arms free.' His voice didn't wake them. Neither did the mild mauling involved in hauling their left arms out so they could be linked.

'They're really out,' Sarf said. 'If they weren't snoring so loud I'd think they were dead. Let's use the door to fan the room.'

Soon the smoke was all but gone, but the shackled pair still snored. 'Let's get some shoes and leggings on them as long as we're waiting,' Hex offered.

The notion, though sound, was faintly preposterous, and they laughed. Clothes lay on the floor by the bed. Dressing the two men was relievingly ludicrous and at the same time seemed to make their victims more properly theirs. Hex wrestled a pair of leathern pantaloons – rather outlandishly cut, in his opinion – up the slack, hairy legs of the bearded one. Chuckling, he told Sarf:

'"And there did nod, upon that vine, A pair of blossoms, tightly twined." Eh? You recall the Lay of Bobol? Oh, I forgot – you're a philistine.'

"Here, these must be *his* half-boots.'

'Yes. What a difference in foot-size, yet they look almost of a height.'

'Mmm. We're lucky they're both slight, in case we have to drag them.'

'Listen, those collars will compel full cooperation. Besides, why should they fight us and be hurt? They're only going to detention till they're ransomed.' This was the lie to be told all the abductees to procure their silent compliance in their transport, and Hex told it without looking up, because he had just felt a tension enter the leg he'd clothed. He looked up into the bearded man's open eyes. They were startlingly awake and conveyed to Hex a distinct impression of character, shadowed though the man's face was. There was ambition, effrontery, a sharp self-interest in that candid stare. There was also in the beard – spade-shaped, glossy with brushing, exquisitely trimmed – something self-coddling and finicky. Here was arrogance and timidity conjoined, and all this struck Hex instantly, so intimate had their doings made him with this stranger. He drew his sword and touched it to skin just below the hollow of the man's throat.

'Good evening,' he said. 'You are our prisoners.' His gesture was smooth. The sword point dented the throatskin with just the perfect tension – steel under firm command. His voice, masked by his muzzle, had an almost amiable remoteness – a calm anonymity that carried conviction. The man blinked. His bedmate began to stir – little paddling movements as though he were swimming up to consciousness. His eyes came open, though they were still glazed. In a child's voice rusty with sleep he asked:

'Bi-Bi?'

Unthinkingly Bi-Bi laid one hand on his bedmate's head, then looked startled by the click of chain this made.

'What do you want with us?'

Sarf answered, and Hex was pleased with how neutral and unalterable the muzzle made the words sound.

'You're to be detained at a camp we have arranged in the hills, and when Snolp pays your ransom, you will be freed. If you cooperate and come quietly you'll be treated well – sheltered and amply fed. If you resist we'll cut you. Get up now, and if you have anything like cloaks tell us where they are.'

'But we have none here, we slipped away from the Hall you see to be alone. We're completely *unprepared* to go out like this.' In his ardour to be believed he half sat up. Hex held the blade firm and cut the man over the collarbone. He fell back with a grunt, and looked at the two invaders, his eyes alert now.

'Tell me just one thing,' he said. Hex saw he had been right – this Bi-Bi was very nervy. Though lying obediently flat beneath the swordpoint he was talking fast and with brio. 'Are you or aren't you working for Rasp? It *is* him, isn't it? Because I'll double whatever he's paying you to do this to us. I'm paying him enough already and he tries to squeeze more out of us with terror tactics? Let me guess. You're getting five hundred each, eh?'

'I will answer you,' Hex said solemnly. 'We are not working for Rasp. We are working for ourselves. We are many. All your colleagues in the Hall are being taken too, at this very moment. Snolp will meet our demands because he must to get his harvest. So, good Bi-Bi. Take blankets if you have no cloaks, and cinch your boots. We must be moving.'

'My name is Oberg, if you don't mind. Umber,' – this to his bedmate – 'we have to get up now. Come on. Up.'

The smooth-faced Umber, once roused and clear-eyed, looked at the two invaders as through glass, or as though they were not quite in the same room. He hunched even nearer Oberg than their chains required, accepting his help with his blanket and the fastening of his boots. He was peevish and querulous about the awkwardness of these arrangements, but exclusively to Oberg, who absorbed his plaints with murmurs and deft, tending touches. Even while the latter's acid eyes kept flicking measuringly at the pair, his hands with unthinking expertise neatly knotted – from behind – Umber's improvised cape. Something in this almost maternal display seemed to irritate Sarf. Abruptly he took Umber's lead-chain and marched the pair out, Hex stepping in behind to take the chain trailing from Oberg's collar. As they moved down the stairs the symmetry of their procession was strange; it seemed the chains, combined with the bawdy link between them, had made a single entity of their captives: a two-headed creature leashed fore and aft, docilely shambling between its captors to its death. Yet at the same time Hex felt uneasy, as though it flowed to him through the connecting chain, the restless, weasely wit and brass of Oberg. In spite of himself he was impressed by the man's swift adjustment to this nightmare of narcosis and abduction. Downstairs before the door Sarf paused and turned. Deliberately he reached his swordpoint towards the cut in Oberg's neck, making the man lean back, jaw clenched.

'Now. Understand how serious your position is. While we're in town you must be absolutely silent. The least noise will force us to kill you to save the rest of our profit, and we'll slash your throats instantly.'

As they stepped into the street even the faint click of chains seemed proclamatory, and this moonlit act of piracy seemed stark, surreally blatant. Hex, seeing Sarf strip off his muzzle, did likewise, glad of the air, but feeling less well armed for coercion now that his face was visible. But they had their victims going now, still a little tranced by the sudden strangeness and moving obediently to the dream that had enveloped them.

They came abreast of the Hall – a yet more imposing

structure than the Lodge – and passed between it and the wall. They saw movement up in a dormer window, and the gleam of a dark-lantern in a ground-floor casement. The air smelled of slotherweed and the whole big edifice sounded discreetly astir with the creaks and thuds of some whispery business within. Two crusaders posted in the shadows of the main door raised their hands in oddly formal salutation. None of them, it appeared, knew quite how to carry off the role of plunderer naturally, and the fact that they were actually bringing the business off, through sheer method and boldness, now filled Hex with admiration. In the basement of the Hall, he knew, the purchased felons from the satrapies of Pil the Unkillable were prisoned. To have them docile for the morning's horror they slept drugged by the Slimshurians' narcotic of choice even while the latter – above their heads – were being numbed by slotherweed and chained to take their places. Those convicts would waken – not to the killing-slope, not to monstrous death worming from the sun-gilt sea – but to freedom. Ah, the moral symmetry of it!

Keeping always in the shadow of the wall they commenced, at its end, upon the road into the hills. This road, after a mile and a half of meanders, would pass by a certain gully. Down this gully a path had been improvised which short-cut back seaward to the killing-slope. Strung out in their chained pairs and trios, the crusaders' three score captives would let themselves be led quietly thus far into the hills, seduced by the fiction of detention and ransom. Once in the gully they would guess, but all along it were stationed crusaders with padded clubs, and as each few captives were snatched towards their true destination they could be stunned and hustled bodily along the last eighth mile if they set up an outcry. As Hex, trailing their prey into the first hill's shadow, reviewed these arrangements, he found he could not repress an empathic qualm for the chained pair. He needed to revitalize his sense of their murderousness. He opened his mouth, but just then, Oberg spoke:

'We're clear of town now – you'll let me make a new offer, eh? There's no harm in that, surely?' As he did not try to slow his pace, his captors said nothing. The road hugged a dark gorge. Ahead, it arched into visibility, wrapped across bleached hills pleated with blackness. Oberg's words, as he continued, seemed to scatter amidst these hills, grow aimless and feeble the instant they were uttered on this – for Oberg – final path. 'For you men to cash in, you don't *need* Umber. Let him go, he'll hide in the hills, and his lips are sealed till you've finished your business with Snolp – one Encourager less will make no difference when you're holding the entire work force for ransom. Meanwhile take me back into town by a safe route I'll show you and I'll take you to where I've cashed my savings. Almost two thousand dhroons in specie – I pledge my life on it!'

'First tell us more about Encouraging,' Sarf said. His lazy intonation surprised Hex, till he recognized in it his own desire to revivify their captives' crimes. 'What part does it play in the harvesting operations?'

'Bi-Bi's the youngest First Encourager we've ever had. He's only twenty-eight!' Umber offered. It seemed as strange that the man should address his captors at all as that the breathy disclosure should have such a cosy ring, as if all else were well.

Hex replied in the tone of exaggerated interest used for flattering children, 'So you're both Encouragers! And what do you do in the harvest?'

'Well we sing the oratorio, of course! We sing from the wall on our own special stage *above* the orchestra, though *I've* always felt we're just totally drowned out anyway because of *all* percussion and brass they give the orchestra. In any case Bi-Bi sings Shlubb the Primal in bass, and *I* sing under-tenor. I sing Slimb's part where he *addresses* Shlubb the Primal.'

And, incredibly, in a sweet cool voice without constraint, Umber sang:

> Advance, great Shlubb, both Dam and Sire
> Of all that thrives ashore!
> Ascend! Embrace what you desire
> Of fruit your own fruit bore!
>
> For all thy spawn are but at pawn
> Beneath the open air –
> Some few reclaim of those who've ta'en
> Their life from your deep lair!

The tune, while grave and hymnal, was decorously gay – such an air as might invite kings and dignitaries to some festival. The melody's eerie dispersal through the gorge, the singer's bizarre complacency – they were almost hypnotic.

'So,' Hex said, intending irony but his voice sounding mechanical, 'you warble the Shlubbups on their way up the slope?'

'It sounds,' Sarf put in, managing a better sneer, 'as if you're far too prominent to be missing from the ransom list.'

'Not at all!' This from Oberg. As he spoke he squeezed Umber's shoulder – a gentle turning off, as it were, of his lover's guileless flow of words. 'Umber's right about our inaudibility. The orchestra itself, you see, does the real work – it gives the beasts their rhythm. The oratorio sung by the five Encouragers is a traditional element only – the eponymous Slimshurian's first contact with the Shlubbups, that sort of thing. I'm not a native myself, but nowadays I can promise you it has as little consequence to most natives as it does to someone like me.'

Umber seemed about to make some denial of this theme of his inconsequence. Oberg squeezed his shoulders again, more peremptorily this time. 'So we're far from really functional to the harvest,' he finished. 'That should be the only point as far as you gentlemen are concerned.'

'But you're so *prominent*, aren't you?' Hex goaded. 'Your friend says you stand on the wall with the band and stand even higher than they! You survey the whole slope like lords as the big worms come toiling up, and you can be seen by the town as well.'

'But the beasts come to the fodder in any case! The music's not essential, it just *hastens* them, and *of* the music only the instruments are really heard. Snolp'll be paying for the harvest and he won't need Umber to get it.'

'The *fodder*, you say?' Sarf, never ceasing to march them ahead, let his mockery drift back. 'By that term, do you mean the prisoners from Pil's satrapies?'

'Well, certainly. The felons and – '

'It's true, isn't it' – now Hex thrust from behind – 'that in this fodder there are many individuals who were condemned for such atrocities as left-handed nosepicking and mispronouncing someone's honorific?'

A silence here. For the first time a hesitancy entered Oberg's compliant stride. Probing for sources of indignation, the crusaders had let show their moral opposition. And if they were more than simple kidnappers, then how much more were they?

'That is true.' His voice sounded almost absent, with his unspoken fears. 'But then, they're as good as dead, of course, aren't they? If they couldn't be sold, they'd infallibly be killed in the satrapies.'

'If someone besides you bought them,' Sarf retorted, 'they might at least survive as slaves.'

'Some people just run out of luck!' Oberg cried, a little frantic because he did not understand what they were probing for.

'That's true enough,' riposted Hex. This, with its grim undertone, hung in the air between them for a moment. And then Oberg balked.

'Wait. Please,' he said when Hex shoved him. 'I've lied about the money I have – nearly *three* thousand dhroons. And there's something else too I can give you, a vital secret, which is the location of the Place of the Touch. Just let Umber go here and I'll *tell* you where to look for the money, so you can deliver me and tell your friends I'm all you found.'

Sarf gave a rough pull to his chain which, in dragging Umber forward, made Oberg stumble after for a step. But only a step, for Hex, ignoring his friend, stood fast and brought Oberg up short.

'What do you mean, exactly, by the Place of the Touch?'

'It is where endless life is to be obtained. It is also called Yana.'

Sarf stared outrage at Hex for violating their unity of command, but held still lest he should emphasize the rift. For a moment Hex couldn't regain his poise – he felt himself still gaping, saw Oberg still reeling from the excitement he'd betrayed. Then he heard his own voice delivering a smooth and solemn lie:

'I know of Yana, and I take your offer very seriously. If your information is new to us, and sounds genuine, we'll be willing to believe you about the money.' He looked at Sarf, trying somehow to ask for complicity. His friend astonished him.

'Just ahead,' Sarf told Oberg, 'there is a gully off the road that angles back towards town. If my friend is satisfied with what you tell him, we'll take you both down it. We'll unchain Umber there and you can tell us how to find your money.'

The First Encourager's quick, pale eyes flicked between

their faces. 'Yana is near the mines of Kurl, on the West Shore.'

'The West Shore?' Hex asked doubtfully. Had the bathcrone's pointed ambiguity not been a hint? Or had perhaps his misdirected ocean crossing merely been the necessary payment that bought the luck of this next and genuine clue? 'Who told you this? I had indications it lay on the East Shore.'

'A man of the satrapies told me, one of the fodder.' (He emphasized the last word.) 'I was passing through the pens on a harvest eve and he reached through the bars and seized my robe, and offered, for his release, to guide me to where I could gain immortality. I was distracted with my own business, unimpressed, and to inflame my interest he told me it was the Place of the Touch, called Yana, near the Mines of Kurl. I turned away from him but next morning, after he was gone, I got the shipping roster for his batch, and it showed his crime to have been theft of a map from a wealthy collector of curios. Seeing his capture imminent, he'd been so furiously stubborn as to eat the map, boasting that no one else would have the treasure he saw he was going to die for. In the year since, I've asked here and there about the place, and I regret what I then refused.'

'But where are these Mines of Kurl, then? Are they north of here?'

'I've never heard of them. And since I've started asking of them, I've found no one who has. Now then. Will you keep faith?'

Hex nodded. Sarf said, 'Quick now. Before our colleagues catch us up. The gully is just past that bend.'

Now Oberg helped hustle Umber along with a will. They practically jogged round the bend. Umber lost his footing on the gully's seamed and crumbly slopes and tumbled them all into a dusty slide down to its floor. This brought at a run the first pair of crusaders stationed there.

'Quick!' Hex called, motioning them to strike. They wielded their padded clubs – not expertly, as these were their first subjects, but numbingly enough after two or three blows per Encourager. Hex watched, suspended. They'd made no outcry – it was the recriminations he'd wanted silenced in advance. The pair were unlinked. Hex and Sarf shared Umber, the others Oberg, and they hastened down the gully, other sentinels passing them to fill the point position. In five minutes the killing-slope opened before them.

Its stone was darker than the walls which marched beside it down to where the ebony ocean swelled and sighed. Yet the moonlight gave the slope a lustre that the wall lacked; its mottled silver had a scoured sheen, lovingly polished, like treasured plate. They carried their burdens out on to the head of the slope, which was somewhat more level than the rest, and where grew a little meadow of manacles anchored to eyelets and staples of iron sunk fast in the rock. Here they planted Umber and Oberg, relinking them and tethering them together to their fate. The latter was awake already, though his eyes were still dazed. Hex and Sarf withdrew, divorced from them now that they had been stationed for their new role in the harvest. Two club-men stood by them, guarding their silence. Hunched in their chains, they were silhouetted by the pale wall just beyond them. On its crest, not far downslope, Hex could see the platform, and smaller dais raised on that, where the captives had stood to sing for other harvests. He and Sarf stood talking with a pair of colleagues, waiting to enter the gully for carrying duty when the rest of the fodder should start coming, but his eye lingered on their late charges. Umber had waked now and, seeing their destiny, was crying. He was not very loud, and was struggling to control it, but their guards menaced, and so Oberg hugged his friend from behind, clamping his hand over his mouth, while Umber's tears made shiny snailtracks across his lover's fingers.

11
Men into Peel, and a Remarkable Change of Plan

At dawn, as the dark ebbed from the slope, and the ebony ocean turned steel-grey, an offshore breeze sprang up. This smeared and tore the smokepot fumes hanging above the thicket of chained men. Groggy struggles flared here and there, and muzzled guards moved through the meadow with clubs, while other crusaders formed windbreaks of their bodies. All Polypolis's harvesting gear had been handed over the wall in relay lines and now, near the thicket, the flensing knives and sectioning shares were being sharpened on treadle grindstones. These licked them sharp with spattering tongues of sparks. Fully thirty men were strung atop the wall with crank-load crossbows and baskets of darts. Others guarded the hills' approaches.

As the breeze freshened, more murmurs of woe washed through the field of shackled men. Beyond the wall the town could be heard wakening – the faint clap of a shutter thrown open, an isolated rattle of wheels on cobblestones. Soon the archers, who did not conceal themselves, would be noted, and the town roused. Glides rivered more thickly above the surf-line. Colour bled into things – the captives' clothes, the feathers of the archers' darts, the mosses on the offshore rocks. Crusaders clustered near the grindstones to receive their tools, or wandered on the slope with them, hefting them or pantomiming their use for each other.

Things grew livelier in town. Beyond the wall shouts of inquiry – blurred to the outsiders – were flung up at the archers. Faces showed at windows overlooking the wall, twisted with shock, and ducked from sight shrilling the news. Within its closure, Polypolis seethed with the realization that half itself now lay enchained on the wrong side of its bulwarks. Now the crusaders spoke more carelessly, traded shouts at need. The smokepots were carried off, for wakeful fodder best seduced the shlubbups, and pellucid saffron flooded half the sky, paling the moon now half sunk in the sea.

Truly sunrise was at hand. Though still in the hillshadow, the meadow had bloomed, and now the braveries of the victims' night dress – crimson, purple, orange – gave that congeries a festive air. Within the wall, a stew of noises boiled, shrill with juvenile and female voices, and the cracked ones of age. Random missiles arced feebly up at the archers, whose bows hummed, spicing the brew with piquant darts. The arrows slanted down from sight, each raising a separate splash of screams. The field crew's shares, crosscuts and flensers looked as fine-edged as the setting moon as they now began to drift en masse away from the wall and across the slope. Loosely though they deployed themselves, none took up a station less than two hundred yards from the wall, courteously allowing the marine monsters a wide berth whenever they should come. Already the hilltops seemed afire. The crusaders watched the sea, for the first sun to strike the bay.

Farther out – four miles – Snolp's fleet waited. Perhaps the crusaders felt curiously exposed on that vast rock stage – bizarrely open to the very ships they were in the act of robbing. At that distance, of course, one harvest looked much like another. There would be fewer people on the walls this time. On the other hand the fodder had totalled a surprising seventy-four men. An unusual number of shlubbups would be drawn ashore by the wrigglings of so much enticement, and the peelers would be too busy drooling over the size of the harvest to think of its spectators.

And of course by now the crusaders' third ship – bigger than the first two, but as shallow-draughted – would be in the harbour beyond the landspit. This ship bore Kratsk and Benarius and an auxiliary troop of mercenaries. Should the peelers send any boats ashore it would intercept them. Far likelier, though, that Snolp's captains would be alarmed too late to act. They would watch the peel made, hammered, stripped, and loaded on to the town's barges. The barges would unfurl their sails, head seaward – and then tack round the landspit and into the harbour. *Then* the captains would send boats in to make inquiries. These would scarcely have arrived before all three of the Cause's ships – with their peel and their forces aboard – swept out of the harbour, fat-sailed with the offshore breeze, and ran them down, with oar strokes hammering their bodies into the sea.

The crusaders' fleet would fly upcoast, hugging it miles nearer than Snolp's could dare to do. For transoceanic cargo ships they were quite shallow-draughted. In Slimshur this merely meant they rode high enough to get within barge distance of most of the cities of that highshelved shore. Scaled as they were for four- and five-city loads, they dared not get near the crusaders' fleet for a hundred leagues, long before which the latter would have gained the protected port whence the excellent Kratsk and Benarius had just now returned, having arranged harbourage, and the peel's sale. A shaft of sun smeared amber coruscations on the bay. An awed mutter, like a growl of readiness, rose from the slope.

'You know,' Hex told Sarf, 'somehow I'd be very reassured right now if I could see past that wall and be *sure* the third ship's here.'

Sarf laughed, picked up a pebble and worked at his flenser's edge. 'Those self-important bungholes! I think they're capable of any arrant cheat. But since this is the payoff, they'll be here, oh yes indeedy! Must one *be* half rat to fight the Reigning Rat? Those two have made me wonder.'

'Look!' Hex said. A frost swept down his nape, and he shuddered as it thawed again. Voices upslope were shouting 'Water broken!' A hundred yards offshore the gilt swell was torn upon a snag. Two snarls of foam clung to a rock that had not been there before. Then, from that black lump, two stalks extruded, and waggled wetly in the morning air. They twiddled shoreward, agile as the fingers of a lutanist – as if, instead of being eyes, they were a pair of palps that needed separately to touch each detail of the scene before them. A second fleshy crag marred the molten gold, and branched with eyes, and then behind this, simultaneously, a third and fourth.

Upslope the victims, motes of colour, swarmed with panic. Their chains stretched in parallel lines as they recoiled to the limit of their fetters. They seemed a bed of seaflowers or polyps whose stems the rush of an incoming wave pulls taut. As if the proliferating eyestalks had been striving – by their busy fingering – to achieve just this effect, the glossy armada began to move shoreward, even as other black turrets surfaced behind and to both sides.

These bifurcate but otherwise featureless heads drifted forward at the rate of a striding man. Behind the foremost there began to rise the dorsal hummocks of their colossal bodies. These lengthened into tarry, wrinkled islands as they advanced. By the time the first of them rode sloshing through the surf, they had slowed to the pace of a man crawling on all fours.

The shlubbup's form had the terrible simplicity of an immense slug's. It was a thirty-foot oblong, tapered more smoothly at the tail than at the head, upon whose clublike thickening the writhing eyestalks were the sole articulation. Their undersides were more complex, and the smoothness of their forward glide was in eerie contrast with the turbulent labour of their locomotion. They moved on scores of interleaving pads which, in their rippling toil, trod frenzies of white lather against the unsupporting rock. This sudsy slime was the colour of seafoam, and was produced with a clamour like that of the surf shouldering against a reef. As if each monster, in climbing, drew after it a tongue of the ocean.

Now guards stepped lively amid the fodder, clubs swooping to abort their attempts to give each other the undeserved mercy of a strangling. An even dozen of the giants came ashore. The fodder's wails raised a dismal cheer of agony within the wall. From windows that overlooked it came the voices of those wives and parents who, though the archers kept them crouching out of view, wailed out the names of those they were losing down below – and were answered hoarsely from the meadow. At the very last, one guard who stayed too late keeping the fodder alive was caught and pinioned by his arms and legs – dragged by the chained ones into the shlubbups' acid maws.

The sun was well above the hills when the ad hoc harvesters formed a line across the head of the slope, all hefting wooden mallets. Below them the last of the giants were just then gliding into the surf, and their scum-highway was already drying a yellow-brown behind them.

The chaining-meadow was completely dry. The pliant overlay showed – in bas relief – the snaky ridges of chains, a rib or a jawbone here and there – no more. A few rings and coins there would also be. This metal-studded stuff would be ripped up with shredding claws and sold for mattress stuffing. The hammering line, given its signal, moved downslope, beating the already leathery carpet, pounding into firm adhesion its two piles, the coming and the going layers.

Hex sank his mind gratefully into this labour. Finding his shortsword chafed him, he re-belted it under his doublet and leggings, snugging it to his thigh. Sarf laughed at this, as most of the other workers had laid their swords in heaps to one side of the peel swath.

'Well and good,' Hex told him, 'but I'm not about to risk this good weapon. Someone would switch it on me for sure.'

'Bramt Hex, swordsman-connoisseur,' Sarf chuckled.

The morning warmed. That downhill march, smiting the velvety substrate, was an almost voluptuous kind of work. The cutting and stripping proved tougher. The barges anchored close offshore. From windlass-operated drums they paid off cable, which crews of men hauled between them upslope. At the head of the slope they were hooked to the shares, round which the crews then clustered, steering them straight as the bargemen winched the cables back down. Hex, leaning beside Sarf on one of a share's handles and guiding its bite to one of the chalk lines a survey crew had just drawn down the peel, wondered if, after all, his friend might be willing to travel the course he had set for himself.

In Ungullion, when Hex had urged his news of Yana on his friend – indeed, solicited a joint search for it once the Cause's work was done – Sarf had demurred. At further urging he had grown sarcastic on the subject. It was some time since Hex, not to be mocked outright, had stopped discussing the matter with him. But surely Oberg's wholly unlooked-for confirmation of the place's existence had impressed Sarf; his quick assistance of Hex's play for information seemed proof of this.

The cuts were finished. The cables were run back upslope, and fastened this time to hooks set in each peel-strip's upper edge. The drums cranked and ten yards of peel were stripped from each cut. The sections were flensed through and dragged on to the barges. Then the cables were run back upslope and the hooks reset. In this phase, Hex and Sarf ran cable. In a rest, while a segment was stripped, Hex ventured:

'So *now* what about it, eh? About Yana? You were struck – I *know* you were!'

Sarf gave him a cool smile. 'You know, Bramt Hex, if Yana really exists, then I know more about it than you do. You've never heard of the Mines of Kurl, correct?'

'And you have? Come on, speak up!'

'Ah, the cable's free! Duty first – it'll keep.'

Newly excited, Hex let him have his humour. In a way, he didn't mind waiting for this next revelation – from Sarf now, no less! Yana! The way this rumour, having so suddenly possessed his imagination, grew and took on feature with such readiness began to alarm him a little. Was he, after all, the gull at the fair? Was he being shilled and cozened? Was some wizardly trap being laid for him? Perhaps the demon buyer of Poon's whorehouse had found a way to steer him, through others, to his doom.

On the other hand, was it not rather like some new word one has learned, unnoted before, then suddenly appearing everywhere you turned? In the end, he found himself inclined to the conviction he had begun with: Yana existed, and due to some inner merit of his own, he was being led to it.

When the stripping was nearly done. Hex's worry about the third ship was removed. A new troop of archers mounted the wall from its harbour end. They made the Cause's salute to the crusaders – all of whom were now bunched near the surf, and flensing through the peel's last sections. Cheery cries and slogans were traded, and the league's scythe banner was unfurled by the newcomers, who relieved the other mercenaries on the wall. These latter shouldered their weapons and shinned down a knotted rope to join the crusaders on the slope. The workers fell to wrapping things up with an eased air, feeling amply guarded from reprisal.

Sarf grimaced, looking up at the wall. 'With our own squad this makes more than sixty bowmen. Kratsk and Benarius must have feared some real trouble.'

'At least they could spread along the wall. Why do they bunch up near us?'

'Hex! Look!'

A ship like one of their own, but bigger, swept round the landspit – sails furled, oars flashing. The bowsprit carried the scythe banner, and a statuesque man in a bravely plumed hat stood in the bow, waving and cheering: 'Good News! Good News!'

The workers stood, rapt by the blatancy of this improbability – for this must prematurely reveal the crusaders' presence to Snolp's fleet, and show their hand before the booty was even loaded. The keel ground on to the peel-slick shore. Two dozen spearmen and a score more bowmen – wearing Snolp's blazon on their armbands – swarmed across the oars and on to the slope. The crusaders found the archers who had just quit the wall now so deployed as to hem them in against it – and their bows were drawn. Atop the wall the new men too stood at full draw, the huddled crusaders their target.

'Drop all your tools! Instantly!' the splendid man trumpeted from the bow. A snap, a hum, and a dart was planted tremoring in the chest of a man with a flenser – who may or may not have been about to drop it. As he hit his knees, all the other tools clattered on the rock along with his. The spearmen moved among the crusaders with chains and iron fetters.

The man in the bow was tall. He had great waxed moustachios and a nobly thrusting chin. He surveyed the shackled men of the Cause with a brightly amiable eye, a look of frank contentment.

'My friends, I am Forb,' he told them. 'We' – his hands

displayed the taut, encircling bows – 'are Snolp's. So are you, for you have just undergone a change of leadership. And indeed, it is touching this very fact that I've come to address you now. And I feel sincerely privileged, I feel honoured to bear you the message I do. It comes from a man we all respect. It comes from the venerable Kratsk.

'I stood in his cabin, as near him as I am you, when he dictated it, and I was deeply moved. Though fate has cast us in opposing roles, and I, as Snolp's man, must deplore your erstwhile leader's views, yet I still feel as I felt on meeting him: *here*, I thought, *is a man of my own kidney*.'

Forb's voice, mellow to begin with, had grown serenely sonorous. He drew a parchment from his fur-trimmed doublet. 'I pray you,' he said in Olympian tones, 'though my own poor voice must speak his words, picture him as you've known him, uttering them. Beleaguered man! What a load of responsibility he bears for love of his followers! He spoke so wearily, vainly smoothing his care-knotted brow with his fingertips. Hearken:

'"My fellow crusaders! It is a golden hour that I greet you in – golden, that is, for a heart enough at ease to savour it! As, from my cabin, I watch the sun-gilt waters, I sit in painful self-confidence, and I ask my heart: Can any end, however high, repay a man for the loss of the simple life? There was a time when I was free to muse upon such small, priceless things as the dancing of the sunlight upon the waters!

'"Ironic, is it not? It is to *Snolp himself* that we must sell our daringly won peel! Alas, Inspiration ever chooses its own time, and we had this one too late in the game to share it with the rest of you. Tragically, Snolp's factors have offered an unrefusable two hundred thousand lictors – yes! In gold! – for both the peel and yourselves. Their deluded reasoning is thus: with yourselves to give substance to a tale of vast piracies, they will conduct you on a pilgrimage to a much publicized place and hour of judgement, spreading a shortage scare as they go, and shortly they will double the price of peel on the open market.

'"Poor cynical fools! Do they think all justice sleeps? They do not grasp the incalculable impetus their own tainted gold will be giving our Cause! They but nourish the young lions that will devour them! Meanwhile, the pain that yourselves must suffer is yet another of the great burdens that we bear. It heartens us at least to know – had there been time to check this plan with you – what your ringing, brave, bold syllable of answer would have been. The knowledge buoys our spirits.

'"So now, with your heroic example, we set our jaws and face up to the tasks that lie ahead. For us, to steer the tricky tides of finance, and find safe harbours of investment for the Cause's funds. For you, to fling proud derision in Oppression's teeth! To mock its paltry torments with our watchword, reasonably sounded: *Swift Justice, and a Scornful Smile for Death!* Hail, and Farewell!"'

Forb let fall the arm which he had lifted in a last salute. He uttered an extended sigh. 'And so,' he said, with audible regret, 'there, my friends, you have it. And now? Now, my friends, you march.'

As the shackled line shuffled off between two ranks of bowmen, a cheer went up from the wall, where what remained of the Polypolitans now stood. They sent after the crusaders howls of execration, and some few heterogeneous missiles which, flung from that height, struck the line with good effect, and gave the men of the Cause a foretaste of the pilgrimage that lay before them through the cities of Slimshur.

12
Judgement, and an Execution

In the course of the next month, the crusaders came to feel very much like a troupe of travelling actors. Being always in the wains heightened this impression. At first Forb had marched them a good deal, leaving them on foot even when passing through a town, to wear them down and break them in a bit. But as they had a precise circuit to play, and time was limited, they were soon riding in the tumbrels even between the towns. When stationed in some public square where Forb read out his script, those creaking wains felt like stages islanded in a small sea of hostile audience. On all sides the compatriots of the crusaders' victims stood studying them. Their chains were compelling props – the very costume of Guilt. And they, in their muteness, felt like props themselves. Though they were enforced to this muteness, still they felt the eerieness of it, that they should stand there tongueless in an ocean of accusing eyes and docilely hear intoned Forb's preposterous declamations – each one tailored for the town that heard it – of their fictive crimes.

They were the survivors of a vaster force that had been killed in the quelling, Forb said. They had massacred the men of six northern towns, and outraged the chastity of their victims' wives, before even Snolp's unsleeping vigilance could prevent it. The particular victim towns might vary as the troupe moved south, so long as the nearest named was at least two weeks distant from the town they were playing. The fiction thus broadcast need not last. Its targets were the observers and purchasing agents of major peel markets who were resident in most of the major cities of Slimshur. Since these must, within a two-week period, bespeak their portion of the coming harvest, they could quickly be forced to ante up or be shut out of a share of the suddenly scarce fabric. Though none saw a shortage locally, they couldn't disprove this dramatized tale of general dearth, and they anted up lest their competitors should jostle them aside from the trough. That half-moon harvest was a landmark day in the history of peel profits. The troupe was then two weeks north of Hismin, at Slimshur's southern border, where they were bound for judgement in the Deputarium. Hence they were able – the rest of the way down – to till the economic ground for an equally profitable full-moon harvest.

Conscripted into such an inflammatory drama, the crusaders harboured the urge to protest their innocence. Alas, the knowledge that they would die for it was no more effective in silencing them than was the inevitable grotesqueness of any self-justification they might make: 'It's not true! We had no other forces! We only massacred seventy-four men and we never laid a hand on their wives!' Still, none could help feeling that each time they stood by silent at the reading-out of these lies, they sank by that much more into the characters which this play had billed them in. And how then, meeting judgement in those characters, could they hope to live?

Tirelessly, scant data on the Deputarium were pooled. Though communication was held to whispers and hours stolen from sleep, the mercenaries did not inflexibly repress it, and were even themselves occasionally the sources of some information, off-handedly given. Hex for one could not stop wondering what lies were being introduced by this channel.

'Why shouldn't they feed us pap to keep us confused? We did it to our prisoners,' he would hiss to Racklin, the man chained just in front of him.

Racklin, keeping an eye on the guards silhouetted by

the watchfire, whispered back, 'You've noted these chains that bind us? The guards equal our numbers. They don't *need* to fool us. They just get bored sometimes, and say what they know, or think they know.'

Sarf, chained behind Hex, reached over him to prod the speaker. 'That's the real point,' he breathed. 'Who knows *anything* sure about the Dapples? No one's from around here, our guards no more than us.'

Hex, in the bone-weary insomnia afflicting him these latter nights of their journey, struggled for hope, but remained inclined to Sarf's bleak agnosticism. Racklin's proximity tried Hex somewhat. Till their capture they had never associated although – and because – they were acquainted from Glorak Harbour. He was for Hex one of those academic Doppelgangers one never got friendly with but who was always popping up at the lectures and tutorials one took. A handsome fellow, undeniably, and very trim of body. Somehow Hex had just never taken to him. During the voyage to Polypolis he had contrived to be clean-shaven when everybody not already bearded had yielded to that condition.

But unarguably, Racklin's reading of Bindle the Black – whom Hex had long professed to admire – had been more thorough than his own, for Racklin was able to remind Hex that in the sixth of Bindle's 'Evensong Canticles' the Dapples were characterized as legitimate Great Survivors. The historiographer had acknowledged ignorance of the Dapples' ilk. As likely they were star-spawn from the Archipelago Constellation, as that they were benign demons from an arcane subworld. Still he judged it certain they had brought a more than human wisdom and mercy to their missionary work of offering justice to a thousand rude and criminal generations of restive humankind.

Racklin supposed, with an ironic smile, that Bindle could be trusted. Starting with that account, then, there was nothing in the current gossip that contradicted it. Bindle recorded no age of decline, but he had written two centuries ago. That the Deputarium for nearly half that time had been unvisited was one of the few certainties among the prisoners' information. It remained to determine what this desuetude reflected, and Racklin had no doubt as to which of the two current theories was correct. For in both Pil's satrapies and Slimshur's towns the apparatus of justice had long been the province of the respective polities' fiscal ministers. It had *been* a century since anyone hereabouts would think of wasting the guilty on the Deputarium's gallows, or risking their acquittal in its halls.

To Hex the competing theory looked more convincing – the reason, perhaps, he preferred his nescience. For it was insistently rumoured that, long before the modern technology of peel production was developed, the Deputarium itself had changed, grown draconian and bloody-hearted through long dealing with the race it had come to enlighten and elevate. By this account the Dapples, in their lineal succession – for each served singly, and performed one parthenogenesis near its life's term – had declined to such a pitch of black misanthropy as had made their gallows yard to flourish and expand like a stand of thriving timber. It was even said that one of this dour latter dynasty had gone abroad, and in a mood of bitter lunacy, had conquered and colonized where the satrapies now thrived. Here the Dapple renegade originated, it was averred, the legal system Pil had since so fruitfully developed.

When Hex argued that a man like Snolp would not trouble with any tribunal that might fail to take their lives, Racklin answered it was the publicity of being judged by the Deputarium that mattered to Snolp. The almost mythic aura that must surround a call-to-judgement of the long quiescent court – this was Snolp's goal, and was all but achieved already with its proclamation and their progress thither. And that the aura itself persisted could only reasonably be due to the fact that the Dapples, whatever the changes in their mood, had continued as incorruptible as Bindle had reported them. Snolp was gambling, then. No fix was in. And doubtless the very rumours Hex favoured led Snolp to count on death verdicts. But if there was any truth in Bindle – something scholars could better judge than pirates like Snolp, however cunning – then the Dapple retained his breed's superhuman discrimination, and would rightly weigh what the crusaders had done. If the dice fell thus, the Deputarium's protection would thenceforth envelop the acquitted, but Snolp could face this, knowing he could at least forbid them re-entry of Slimshur. Driven south, they couldn't harm his fable of dearth which, as pointed out, was all but accomplished anyway.

Such tough-minded and ingenious optimism always silenced Hex, because he craved its balm himself. When left to himself he managed not to debate the question at all, content with a sullen blankness of imagination that granted anything might happen, and thus sneaked in the hope that it would be lucky. Musing was in any case much inhibited two days from Hismin, for then Forb started marching them again. Hex feared he knew why – to wear them down and stupefy resistance as they neared their immolation. Hex's hidden sword, nested in the chronic sores and blisters it had long established on his flank and thigh, chafed and burned anew. Chained as he was to a master chain linking the waists of fifteen men, the sheer futility of this so painfully hoarded tool of liberty galled him almost as much as its steel did his skin. Still, in the terrible powerlessness of prisonerhood, though scarcely more than a symbol, it glowed like a secret comfort against his leg, and so he hugged it to him.

They skirted Hismin entirely, and on the third morning

of their march went straight up into the hills that backed it, where the Deputarium stood. Seemingly the trial was thought sufficient redramatization of their guilt in Hismin, without need of gulling the citizens in the streets. It looked rather a handsome city as it fell away below the centipedal procession of the chained lines. It stood where that vast, smooth littoral shelf defining Slimshur as a whole came to an end against a sizeable range of mountains, of which these were the foothills. Hismin's killing-slope was acres broad, its walls resplendent – a town ten times the size of Polypolis.

The sea looked glossy black beneath a high cloud-rack of iron-grey tufts and plumes, hurrying like one vast wing across the world on a cold, brisk wind. The air smelled like rain, but meanwhile visibility was vast and sharp. The shaggy, green-haired hills showed a first faint dapple of bloom – tight saffron flowers, not quite unscrolled from bud, as if distrustful of the gusty day. Their road wound round a first hill, crossed the saddle linking it to a second, and wound round that second, higher hill in its turn. Beyond it, in a further and far broader saddle, were the Dapples' gallows yard and, past that, the red sandstone walls and black slate rooftiles of the Deputarium itself.

But the building, at first, went totally unseen; the chained men's eyes were fastened to that little wilderness of racks and gibbets. For in that yard's mere aspect – the unelaborated image of it – was the refutation, the instantaneous extinction of every hope, each sunny supposition and airy argument which such as Racklin might have elaborated. Only crazed and homicidal castellans could have posted such grim sentinels – in such number! – before their citadel. The killing-engines, easily an acre of them, half filled the saddle, spreading right up to its sheerest side – for here talus slopes of a chalky pallor dropped sharply from its rim.

Forb, who rode point on a bravely fitted Slender, detained the column as it came abreast the gate of the yard. He rose in his stirrups, and swept a displaying arm.

'Behold these legioned machines, my friends! How much they have to show the instructed eye! See near the thicket's centre there, those frames of greater bulk and stature? The works of the Deputarium's earliest age. See the simplicity of line, the classic, unadorned strength of that Thrasher, or that Barbed Wheel just beyond it! In those days, my friends, the Dapples, in the first flush of their altruistic ardour, drew their conclusions in broader, firmer lines than they do today.

'For see! As one scans outward from that aboriginal grove, how much more involute and fanciful the garden grows! See the intricate, finicking symmetry of that Tenderizer's flared trip-hammers, the elaborate balance of that Sarcomord's toothed scrubbers!'

As he spoke a quick gust of rain swept over them. Black drops spattered suggestively on the bleached wood and rude old iron of those towering sentries. Their dangling chains and collars rattled laxly in the wind like a murderer's kite-cleansed bones.

'The conclusion's inescapable, is it not?' Forb was fluting. 'We see here Dapple jurisprudence mellowing through time! We see the very shape of Justice branch and twine, effloresce with ever more Baroque conceptions of reprisal. From this we must learn reverence for the noble Dapples' patient energy in studying the text of Mankind's eternally equivocal Brief!

'You know, since you've been my prisoners, I've grown rather fond of you all. I cannot help but hope your own cause benefits from the line of development we see before us here. But come, friends! Let us haste to judgement! Make way please!'

The latter was aimed at the townsfolk whom they'd found foregathered near the yard – perhaps two hundred people, none of them seeming very spirited. As the lines moved through them, they produced the by now ritual hail of clods and stones. It was ill-aimed though, felt rather listless, as were their outcries. It was not hard to think, as some of the prisoners did, that few even of the common folk of Slimshur believed Snolp's myth, or needed to. Enough that the lie was being told on the scale Snolp could afford, and it would become the truth. Still sodden with the shock of the gallows, the chained men marched. Hex marvelled at the leaden compliance of his own legs. The onlookers lingered by the yard, giving the sky vexed, pessimistic looks. Was this their certainty of the sentence? Hex reminded himself the Dapples were said to admit no public to their trials.

Forb plied the knocker of an iron door in the wall of the Deputarium's forecourt. When both valves swung open, his plume was fluidly doffed, but to no one. Far within, beyond the court and down a dark, porticoed gallery, a small shape waved them forward. Its voice loomed surprisingly large as it rolled out to them:

'Come in, then! Come ahead!'

As the lines crunched across the gravelled court, another rainspatter insisted on the coming shower. They clacked and clinked down the stony gallery. A she-dwarf stood before an inner door, again of iron. Her wild white hair made her half a foot taller, and her tunic looked thick and soiled as a mountain goat's coat.

'What *can* you want here?' Her big voice was tense and gloomy. 'Tell me you have lost your way! Say anything but that you've come for a judgement! Kroppflopp's in a rotten temper – it must be a century since he was anything else! He's dying of the mange!'

'Madam, we have come a long way. We have faith in the peerless Kroppflopp. Whatever his mood, he'll be just. We must insist on his service.'

'Are they charged with a capital offence?'

'Indeed yes! In fact, with the now fam – '

'Then begone! Kill them yourselves instead of getting *him* into a lather about it! Our gallows are full! Why pester *us*? We've done our share long since! What of your own courts? Is fodder no longer wanted down in town?'

'My dear dwarf,' Forb said, suave but visibly irked by her candour, 'your gallows are quite empty. We have only just – '

Profound affront had frozen the little woman's forehead into icy corrugations. 'My *name* is the Honourable Rem Ibnabib,' she slowly foghorned.

'Abjectest pardons, revered Rem Ibnabib! I recoil from the remotest thought of offending you. We – '

'You have my token then?' she asked, still ice.

'Oh yes!' Forb bowed, offering her a fat stack of coins that he dug from a poke in his belt. 'And we'd joyfully pay twice as much should you – '

'Do so, then.' She had raised one shaggy eyebrow, like the first crack in a thaw. Forb faltered, but bowed her the poke with recaptured poise. She scowled at her money a moment, then gave the kind of sigh that prefaces the undertaking of great toil.

'Wait here,' she told them.

The thunder of the door behind her made the chained men blink, as though they had slept while watching her. Hex found his guard's swordpoint to be now in actual contact with his neck. With unobtrusive firmness, as the truth came out, the steel of coercion had been drawn a little snugger against every man in the lines. From an echoing distance within the iron door they watched came a groan of other hinges. There was a pulse of voice, loud but confused, sustained through several seconds. The answer was a roar from lungs far huger than the human make. One of the prisoners' legs buckled and he had to be clubbed back to his feet by the guards.

That monstrous growl was also speech, but still indistinguishable for drowning in its own echoes, as though uttered from a well. Its ire billowed and surged a while until the dwarf's vituperative screech grew audible in counterpoint. The big voice rumbled down to simmer while Rem Ibnabib – unmistakably – railed and scolded. Again it thundered when she paused – peremptory now and curt. She counter shrilled and the far door drummed shut. The door they watched flew open – and so surprisingly soon, given the woman's rate going in, that Forb was knocked off his feet. Rem Ibnabib bowled out, wild and scratchy as a tumbleweed.

'So get up you pipe-legged idiot!' she raged at Forb. 'He's yours and welcome to him! Take them in!' She pointed across a wide and vaulted room, unfurnished save for murky tapestries laid slantingly across the floor by skylights of dark-stained glass. The door in the farther wall had bounced ajar and was framed by the rainy grey light of the day outside.

As the crusaders went rattling and rubberlegged towards that door, they smelled gusts of cold fresh air laced with whiffs of carrion. Forb strode ahead and pulled it fully open. Within, four slender-pillared porticoes rimmed a roofless pit. While they still approached, a hand a man could sit in rose from the pit and gripped its rim. It hauled into view the upper half of a face that looked as big as the rising moon. Its round eyes scowled on Forb. Its unseen mouth growled:

'Dung and Nosewarms! Bring the scum in, then!'

The lines were led cringing inside and arrayed round the pit – their guards at their backs and they amid the pillars, along its brink. The pit was near twenty feet deep and clearly the Dapple had not needed to leap to grasp its rim. Hex's legs crawled with the sense of their availability to those huge, gnarled bluish hands. The judge's scowl made them look all the readier to seize and tear things – as did, indeed, his pit's sole furniture, a big iron trough of raw meat, the broken limbs and ribs of hill plods.

Scanning them, the judge paced his cell's perimeter. His amber fur, whose black freckling named his race, grew thick on his chest, potbelly and thighs. At his elbows and knees it ended in ragged sleeves. The scabby blue skin it yielded to, and the judge's restless clawing at these receding frontiers of his coat, told that disease, not time, was denuding him. His dappled beard too hung in rags, his nose was a gnawed remnant round two gaping holes, and his ears were tattered, cheesy stumps. Though massive, his limbs moved with evident pain. His carrion breath came up to the chained men in gusts as he passed in his loathing scrutiny.

'Hail Lofty Kroppflopp, Arch-Juridical Dapple!' Forb said. He was not quite in voice – a bit dismayed to see his judge. 'These men, oh most August of Arbiters, are guilty of the now famous mur – '

'Silence!' roared the Dapple. The stone hummed with the voice's sheer eruptive force, and the prisoners' very chains seemed to chime with it. Silence, profound and perfect, ensued. Kroppflopp filled it – as mournful, now, as mad:

'You murderous, miserable human scum, do you come here *yet*? Your ghosts already pack and overflow the execution yard – the foul mix of their stench overwhelms me even here! Numberless filth, as many as the bubbies in the sea's foam, squeaking their hate and mockery of all the generations of my kind! Damn you, our gallows are glutted with you!'

Another rain-gust crossed the sky. The Dapple broke off and greedily raised his face to it till it passed. 'Why can you never be still?' he flared up again. 'You must be eternally busy undoing each other. It seems you can only build things out of one another's bones! Only water your gardens with one another's blood! No materials but these will do! Such a horde of little busy maggoty unmakers as you a world never swarmed with!'

Bramt Hex's spirit felt stretched taut between the charnel stench at his feet and the fresh, electric pre-storm sky overhead. A vast, sad resignation counterpointed the horror of his death. Strung dazedly between, his despair plucked his vocal cords, and he heard himself cry out:

'Great Kroppflopp, what of motive? We did not kill for gain, but for – '

'Moronic speck of slime! You killed to be right! The strongest greed infecting your vermin bowels!'

Lightning split the square of visible sky, and an instant later its thunder smote and skidded against the earth. The rain hit, and immediately doubled. First it clattered on the pit floor, and then embroidered it with the needle-fine spray of impact. The Dapple moved to its centre and raised his face. Rain hung in runlets from his beard's torn fringes, and darkened his fur to nearly solid black. He cupped his hands against the sky and gently laved his face and ears. Abruptly the rain dwindled, stopped. Kroppflopp's eyes returned to the accused while his hands still absently scrubbed each other. His hating rictus had relaxed to a bitter grin, and his eyes, from rage, were screwed to the sharper focus of remembrance:

'Alas, my poor forebears! Striving in their blameless, doomed succession to take the fairest measurement of your carnivorous souls! Poor Dapples, prisoners of their stubborn charity! It makes me itch with a rage far worse than this wretched mange! By the powers! Your guilt's almost no longer guilt! Scum stinks – why punish simple fact? And if only one, just one of you would affirm it! Would call himself in his heart the self-praising tyrant and murderer he is. By the Archipelago! I'd free that man and crown his head with gold! I'd shoe him in the

Sandals of Untiring Flight, and gird him with Faffnath's Unconquerable Blade!'

'Oh Kroppflopp, I am Guilty! Guilty! Guilty!' This was Racklin's impassioned cry. It was so vibrant and impeccably declaimed that Hex, after starting, grew impressed. His chain-mate's coolness made him ashamed of his own impetuous plea. 'I know in my heart,' Racklin shouted, 'the killer and the self-justifying despot that I am in my inmost self. I don't ask justice – that would condemn me – but only mercy; for that alone can the guilty ask!'

'But you don't believe it!' howled the Dapple. 'Not a word!' He surged at Racklin. The judge's fingers – each Hex's forearm's size – seized the pillar near his foot. A blue hand engulfed poor Racklin's middle, the chain was briefly worried at and snapped. Hex, fallen back against his guard, who had also fallen back, struggled to gain his feet without falling into the pit, where Kroppflopp now bit Racklin's head off, and stood a moment crunching it, as if in thought. As he took two further bites, Hex looked away, then saw him toss the red-stumped remnant into his trough, and gesture at Forb:

'One more there, ho!'

With the haste of weasels in a coop, Forb and some guards leapt to unchain the nearest man – but with such trembling that shortly the Dapple roared and helped himself, this time swarming up to grab a guard, already unencumbered by chains. The Dapple chewed a while, then threw another remnant in the trough, sighing.

'So. We've reviewed – sufficiently – both charges and defence, and now I think we may proceed to judgement. I must tell you beforehand what joy it gives me to render you this verdict. The ghosts of your ilk so haunt this hill, the addition of but one of you, let alone this crowd, must tip the scales and give it them, so that they quite unseat us, if not kill us outright. All this, gentlemen, all this!

And even *so* I dance, I warble, I all but cavort with joy to find you guilty, and send you to the Yard to die. And yea, though you were the guards, and your guards in chains, I would judge the same, and sentence you to die, and so, with godspeed, go you now, into the Yard to die.'

The aforementioned guards showed a laudable promptness and address in marshalling out the prisoners. The guards put armlocks on them and shoved them to a pace that kept them staggering. Hex stumbled with them, managing to hold intact a bizarre boon. It was the masterchain Kropflopp had broken to take Racklin. The sundered ends were both now hidden and held together by Hex's hand, for it was common enough for prisoners to grip the masterchain to keep better pace with the line. Yet another futile asset? Or was its futility merely his fear to use it? Stunned, he moved through the skylit chamber, the first door, the colonnade and then the courtyard, its wet gravel flashing underfoot. Ordained death was yards beyond the gate ahead, and the hills were his only slight chance of life. His free hand crept into his tunic, to the sweaty pommel of his shortsword. Just outside, he must draw as he dropped the chain, kill his guard and maybe Sarf's behind him . . . draw as he dropped the chain, kill his guard and – the gate, swinging open itself, showed the wains backed right up to its threshold, gangways in place for loading. Neatly, the lines were marched in and the tailgates locked on. In his wain, as it rolled towards the Yard, Hex still crouched with his two secret advantages clutched in either hand, like a mime frozen in a comic moment.

At the Yard's main gate Forb drew up. His gesture asked attention both of his own train and the townsfolk. The latter, many of whom crouched for shelter in the crooks and corners of the killing machines within, looked damp, disgruntled, and disinclined to oratory.

'My friends, I know that there are different currents of fashion among you. But may I now beg those of you with more rococo leanings to indulge an old campaigner's taste for the earlier, more classical instruments of justice? Note that I do not disparage the more elaborate aesth – '

'Do you think we care a pinch of flea-dirt?' shrilled a draggled woman. 'On with the show before it rains again!'

Indeed, the currents of fashion seemed to run so sluggishly among that crowd as to be undetectable. Forb looked to the wains, and there too beheld apathy.

'I thank you, then!' He bowed. The lynch party moved towards the oldest machines at the saddle's brink – the wains down a main path, and the townsfolk tricklingly on footways through the wood-and-iron copse. Forb deployed the tumbrels and their guards before a brinkside trio of venerable engines: a Gallows and a Lasher flanking an ancient Drubber's spiky clubs. From the elevation of the wains the chalky steeps just past that trio were obliquely visible – a rubble of rock and human bones, dropping more than half a mile to the hill-shadowed limit of vision. As the gangways were slammed in place and the tailgates unlocked there was a sudden, convulsive huddling of prisoner to prisoner. Into his friend's ear Hex said:

'Sarf. I'm holding a break in the chain. Let's try to run for that slope.'

The black glare of Sarf's eyes might have been trance. 'A break in the chain?'

The gate was hauled down and Forb was calling for four men from each cart. This left one man on the chain ahead of Hex. The guard on the gangway now held the lead end of it, and fitfully pulled it to keep it taut. Hex's sweating hand knotted and cramped in its grip he did not dare remove his other hand, from his sword. More rain was coming, visible now not many hills away – would he still be alive when it got here?

He scanned the crowd. Its callous ease appalled him. In the surrounding engines they arranged themselves with small, prosaic attentions to their comfort which pierced Hex with an exquisite bitterness. A woman spread her cape across two of a Hammer-tree's branches to roof herself and her tots; a young couple under a Toothed Coffin's overhang sat swinging their legs and sharing a cheese; an older couple made a fuss over the wife's white-haired parents, plumping up their cushions under a Tenderizer's arms. A man was being installed in the Lasher.

'My friends!' Forb cried from the Gallows' forestage. Behind him, a bound crusader stood noosed upon the trap, and over on the Drubber a man lay strapped to the bench below the clubs. 'This uncertain weather bids us haste, and leaves no time for a proper pause before each taking-off. So, in token for the rest of you, let this unfortunate on the Thrasher here receive it. Fellow, have you a last remark to make?'

The Thrasher was sometimes called the Snapping-Gibbet, that is to say, its four branches dangled chains for the wrists and ankles, and its occupant hung spread-eagle. Thus it was to the platform the unfortunate bellowed his last remark:

'Don't kill me!'

'Winch away, there!' Forb cried. The gears whirred. The branches snapped erect and plucked the victim skyward – snapped down and whipped him towards the earth, then brought him up again so short it broke him, neck and all, and he vomited a rush of blood upon the boards. The crowd raised only a feeble cheer, having braved this day for multiple, not single executions. Hex's bones seemed made of some grey spongy stuff, like so much raincloud, strengthless to save himself even clutching a piece of luck in either hand. Abruptly, painfully, his ears began to buzz – shock made his knees sag. What now? Was this some fit the face of imminent death woke in the irresolute? But hadn't Forb and his guards winced too, even as he waved on the other executioners? The drop clapped and the rope sang taut over the sudden-sinking felon. The Drubber flailed a meaty drumbeat, spiced with screams, and a rainy noise of blood. Now Hex's ears reamed his brain with outright torture. He could not think this agony born of real sound, though the coarse vibration drilled him with pain that seemed to *include* the range of sound. Forb was frankly writhing now, hands to his ears, and those guards and spectators nearest the three engines had fallen to their knees or bellies. Forb was sinking too, his dignity seeming merely slower to erode. Hex twisted, and howled aloud – as much because this wrenched his body free of fear, it seemed, as out of simple pain.

Of that there was enough. It focused to an almost intelligible whispering that flooded – fang sharp – into his brain. A ratswarm seethed through him, whispering with leprous lips a rodent litany of pain and rage. It seemed his skull took on such a cargo of these hissing stowaways that he would topple – weak stemmed – with the load. Woozily, his legs held. His right hand had dropped the broken chain, and joined his left, and both dragged free his sword. As if to mow a swath out through the encompassing agony, he swung wide, his arms in the process knocking flat the man before him, his blade biting, like an afterthought, half through the neck of the guard at his side.

He lurched forward, his waistband slid free of the master chain, and the same stagger dropped him to his knees. Down the gangway a guard that looked as stunned as he felt returned his stare while beyond, the four arms of the Thrasher lifted themselves off their axis, and floated whirling out across the air, their almost invisibly spinning chains, in passing, smiting Forb's head from his shoulders. He had, in that instant, been gaping at the Gallows' rope which – detaching itself and snaking laterally – had noosed an executioner's neck and yanked him, thrashing, off his feet. Before Forb's acephalic hulk had even settled to the ground, the Drubber's clubs too left their anchorage and dispersed, acruise for living meat. The whole Yard stirred. Its chains, clamps, collars, fangs, barbs, clubs, and whips – its winches, cudgels, wedges, flensers, saws – its wristlets, anklets, armlets, hooks, screws, knouts, levers, beams, and hammers were all awake, freeing themselves of the frames they were part of and flying abroad to work their art. The audience – snugged into the very arms of the insurrectionary giants – squirmed red and broken in their sudden turmoil. Their mouths made screams Hex couldn't hear through the pandemonium with which his brain was swarming like a hive, a honeycomb of larval horrors each gibbering its individual woe. On hands and knees Hex crawled towards the gangway, down which the guard was tumbling, his skull struck wide open by a toothed wheel that had just discused past. A flying beam like a swung club spun against the tumbrel and bashed its side panels to a spray of splinters. Staying on all fours Hex scuttled down the ramp.

The din of the charnel horrors poured into his ears, drowning out the surrounding tumult. Lightning flared terribly near, but he never heard the thunder. As the drench of rain crashed down he saw come speeding towards him – low to the ground – a chain with snapping manacles. He rolled on his back, thrust up his sword two-handed, and just managed, wrists popping, to shed its onslaught with a spray of sparks. Again he was acrawl down the flinty path. A fleeing guard overleapt him, headed likewise for the Yard's brink. A Tenderizer's floating hammer took him, the blow itself too quick to see. Hex, as the hammer lifted from that red ruin of a head, veered right, wormed low as he could through the next gap in machines. Five strides away a low wall marked the Yard's rim and the steep slope of the bone dump. As he watched, a guard ran to that wall. While he paused to look over it the liberated axe of a Mincer cartwheeled by and clipped through the small of his back, so that only his top half actually made the dive.

Now Hex felt his mind to be all but blotted by the blood-lusting din of the ghostly legions. Amid engulfing Pain and Fear he stood, feeling like a frail and skinless thing bent on its salvation with a suicidal fervour. Sprinting to the wall, he sprang straight over it and the huddled red half-corpse against it.

Through a long, giddy drop the vertiginous white earth failed to meet his footsoles – a plunging, stomach-stretching pause – and then he sank thigh-deep in the loose spill of gravel and bone. Broadly, sluggishly, the talus slid, conveyed him down towards the shadows he craved. He wrenched free his legs and plunged with the slide, his impacts speeding and spreading its descent.

Across the slope another man – a guard – fled just as he did down the rattling slump. Above and behind them both a Fanged Coffin overleapt the Yard's wall and – bounding end over end – pursued the guard. Some yards above him still, the box's lid gaped wide as it launched its greatest leap, spun down, engulfed him and bounded without pause away, the bellowing victim and his death-cry locked inside.

The agony dwindled in Hex's skull. He began to hear the rain that still hammered his face, and to feel the flints and bone shards biting his feet deep in his overfilled boots. The shadowed gullies were now not far below him. As far above him, when he looked back, was the Yard – its wall minute, its din all but erased by the rain. Someone else had escaped as well – or at least, was less than a hundred strides above him. In fact – could that be Sarf?

13
Transport by Means of an Amorous Ogre

'What was the name of that fifth town south of Polypolis? That one where the killing-slope was so dark because they seeded the Shlubbups' beds with purple dye pellets?'

'You mean where they made "Scanlion Purple, the Prince of Peels" as that sign had it?'

'Scanlion! Of course!' Hex spat into his inkwell – a dead leaf wedged in the grass he sat on – and sprinkled in more ink powder. He scratched anew on his parchments – spread on his notepouch, which he'd laid on his lap for a desk.

Sarf stood watching him a moment. His look, though not unmixed with affection, was one of sour, disbelieving humour. He went back to his work. Since the grassy gorge they had been following all day grew cold once the fading sun deserted it – as had the others on both previous days – he was gathering droppings for a fire. These – big, dry skats that littered the gorge just here – he stockpiled under a large outcropping of the gully's wall. As he picked up each patty, from where he stood he flung it, saucer-like, at the loose pile accumulating under the overhang.

'You know, Bramt Hex,' he said as he worked. 'You sit there snug as a hog in mud. With your notes for a map of someplace we've *been*. And what we *need* to figure out is where we *are* exactly, and where we can *go*.'

'We're going south. Till we get somewhere, what more *can* we know? Meantime I might as well get some work done.'

Somehow the reasonable answer made Sarf madder. True enough, since they didn't want to enter either

Slimshur or the Satrapies, and the two together bulked uncircumventably to the north – and since, moreover, both had heard that a week south of Hissmin was a populous stretch of coast not wholly hostile to strangers, they could only wind south through these hills as they had been doing. But Sarf was very hungry, and this for him sharpened the already keen bite of the cold.

'We should be planning, Hex! Grant we reach some town – how are we to find our feet in it? What are they going to make of me with this iron belt on me? And don't look so smug. You're *still* lardy enough that it's easy for you to be casual, but *I'm* starving, and these damned wild onions are worse than nothing at all!'

Hex looked up, stung. Last night, on the end of their second day in the hills, he'd been able to wiggle out of the eyeleted waistband by which he'd been linked to Forb's master chain. Sarf's, fit to a middle lacking excess, stayed in place. Hex, having begun to dream of an heroic transfiguration, now heard truth in his friend's sneer.

'You followed this lardy frame fast enough when it led you to your life, Sarf Immlé. And if you think I'm not famished – '

'I'm not trying to insult you! But just look at your state of mind! You're feverish maybe – who knows? But your mind just isn't in the grim here-and-now, it's off in cloud palaces. Like when I told you about Kara – I still can't believe you actually clicked your heels in the air!'

Early in their progress through these hills Sarf had told Hex what he'd boasted of knowing about Yana that Oberg hadn't known.

'This Kurl he talked of. In Sakka Thorss where I grew up there was a child's song – a game of handclaps and dance steps went with it. Part of it went:
"If you through Kurl's Museums would stray,
You'll stop in Kara on the way."'

'Kurl's *museums* – not *mines*?'

'Museums. But "Kurl" conforms. And if it's right, then at least you know which coast Yana's on.'

'But how? I've never heard of Kara!'

'And you the antiquary, and would-be map-maker! Kara's an old name for Kray! So it's Kray Major or Kray Minor that's meant. Now. Isn't that a wonderful revelation?'

Saying this, Sarf fairly smacked his lips over the ironic contrast: this clue to the Ultimate Prize set beside their actual nomadic misery, roofless and routeless. Hex's glee at the news had kindled in Sarf the anger he vented now. It made Hex shrug.

'I started with a name. Since then every turn of chance has added something, and now from *you*, who were never more than smilingly sceptical, I now know very nearly where to go. At least I know it's back on the West Shore, and a thousand leagues or so to the north. I mean, aren't *you* amazed too, knowing what I've told you? Right – it won't help us survive now, but if we do . . .?'

Even at his most sarcastic there had been in Sarf, Hex felt, a sneaking ardour for this idea of Yana, and Hex probed for it now. Surely Oberg's fear-racked, moonlit confidences had fanned the latent flame. It made Hex realize he craved an ally.

'I'll make the fire now. I'm numb to the bone. And what skin I have *on* the bone feels thinner than one of your parchments there. Give me your sword for the steel.'

Well in under the overhang, with a flint from the Deputarium Yard, he coaxed some heaped dead grass alight and propped some big skats over it. They were easily brought – with more grass and some blowing – to a low, smokeless flame. Hex joined him under the low rock roof with an armful of the wild onions he had gathered as they walked. They made a hot, gritty meal, but it blocked the jaws while it lasted and muted the growl of hunger.

Neither attempted talk and Sarf – lying knees-to-chin to fit under his half-cape – quickly fell asleep. They were warm at least. Hex curled himself around the fire, and thought perhaps he *was* in a kind of hunger-trance, for he marvelled how swiftly, weightlessly he was dropping – zigzag like a falling leaf – into sleep.

Icy cold woke him – the dawn's chill. Out beyond the overhang he saw the grass – from star-silvered black – had turned ashen. Groaning, he stacked droppings on the fire, whose inmost core still glowed. He nursed the new blaze with his breath, then dozed and woke beside it, dozed and woke, weaving in and out of sleep with the fire's company as with a bedmate's. When at length he rose and crept out to piss in the dew-charged grass, the river of sky visible between the gorge's walls was slate-blue, with a blush of light grey stealing into it.

He sat by the fire, letting Sarf – whose caved-in cheeks he pitied – sleep some more, poking the coals with his sword and mutely, gloatingly sifting through the hoard of his hopes. From marvelling at Yana's sudden findability, he moved to imagining its finding. Thence it was not far to a whole galaxy of dazzling enterprises – all purchasable from his endless fund of Time.

Such bounty, indeed, made its prologue – that is, the near future – seem trifling, a foregone conclusion. After all, had they seen any danger so far? And the alleged coastal towns could no longer be far off. Meanwhile, what more protected highway than these gully-systems through the meadowy hills? Even the weather blessed them, cloudless days as golden as new-struck lictors, though chill in the shadow, as now. Now, beyond the overhang, the grass was fully green, and a patch of sun slanted down the farther wall, freckling it with fine-etched shadows.

He grew impatient to be off – soon he would wake Sarf. His idly prodding sword hit something hard in one of the burning skats. He twisted the blade, splitting the faecal ember. He found – white in the smoking matrix – a row of teeth. With his swordpoint he chiselled the remnant clean: three-quarters of a human jaw.

He raised the jaw. He studied it, hooked there on his sword-tip like an inverted 'J'. Slowly, a great bitterness filled him. Surely he *had* been lightheaded to have forgotten – these last few days in the empty green hills – what the world was like. Apart from its fearsomeness, there was a humiliating sense of demotion in this harsh reminder of his life's fragility – its liability to just such brutal interruptions, and undignified disposals, as those suffered by the former owner of this jaw. His interrupted fantasies mocked him now. Sarf's lazy murmur came so consonantly with his thoughts that it scarcely startled him:

'So. Good morning, fellow Meatbag. How many leagues more do you reckon it to Yana?' Sarf hadn't raised his head from the arm that pillowed it. Sleep seemed to have deepened his gauntness.

'Are you well?' Hex asked with a qualm more of fear than solicitude. He felt one drive only: to get out of the gully. The walls were steep. Could he manage if he had to help Sarf? To his relief, his friend sat up with his characteristic angry energy – leaned over, grasped his shoulder, and said, grinning, near his ear:

'We must be charmed. Think of our luck! Chatting as we walked! The gullies channelling our voices ahead of us, like dinner bells!'

'We've got to climb – ' Hex's voice, scarcely a murmur, stopped dead. A thud – one grass-muffled drumbeat – sounded somewhere just outside the overhang. They were only eyes then, their bodies vanishing in the perfect freeze of fear. Their eyes, quick as flames, felt at the same time anchored by their dread of seeing what they searched for. Nothing stood on the gulch's grassy floor. The sun now gilt all the opposing wall, showing the crumbly steepness they would somewhere, as soon as possible, have to climb. They saw a brown blur plummet to the grass, and repeat the drumbeat they had heard.

A paralysed moment of comprehension passed, then their bodies were theirs again. Sarf dragged on his stiff and dew-cold boots, Hex belted on his pouch and sheathed his sword. Liazrd-low they crept downgulch, staying beneath the overhang to its limit. Thirty yards from where it ended the ravine turned, and beyond the jut of its wall, they should be screened from anything on, or clinging to, the wall above their camp. They studied the intervening ground.

'The wall's still got some jut to it,' Sarf breathed in Hex's ear. 'Stay belly-flat against it and there's really only a few yards just before the turn where we're exposed above.'

With that he stepped sideways and began edging out along the wall, taking handholds on it where he could for steadiness. Hex blessed his brave momentum, and let it pluck him after before fear re-froze his legs.

Now he was aware of his persisting thickness – felt sure his backside bulked out into view. The least clink of Sarf's waistband on the rock, his own foot's slightest tearing of the grass stopped his heart, though the gully was ninety feet deep. Near the turning he looked back and up; he couldn't help it. Sarf had done the same, then flickered rat-quick round the turning to be hidden from what he saw. Briefly and indelibly, Hex now saw their near-catastrophe.

A huge old Ironwood tree crowned the rim of the overhang. Three of its most massive branches overjutted the gorge. On two of these a pair of figures perched – ragged heads atop vast, sloping shoulders. One's shoulder lifted, and proved to be a huge, draggle-plumed wing, fully twenty feet long. A stunted, haggle-clawed arm scratched the monster's underwing. Also revealed were the dreadful talons that clutched the bough – wrapped it round, in fact, though it was thicker than a man. Hex ducked round the turn.

They fled – pussy-foot at first, then at an outright trot. From now on they forsook the smoother ground of the ravine's centre, and stayed near its walls. The silence of wings! As though for the first time they contemplated this terrible commonplace. Often they stumbled, and sometimes fell, with their sudden scannings of the sky. After perhaps two miles, they felt safe enough to slow down. However, at just about that point, the lie of the land began growing ominous. The ravine began to broaden and grow shallower. Within another mile its walls, not thirty feet high, fell back to gentler angles, and got grassy. Ahead, through their widened frame, the pair glimpsed the green swells of rolling terrain that opened out just beyond. While the subsiding wall still provided them with a crease of shadow, Hex stopped his friend.

'We should wait till night right here.'

Sarf gave his head a fierce shake. 'I'm going on while there's even the slightest cover. For all we know there's enough we can *keep* going. I'm too hungry to wait, Bramt. An extra day in these – '

'Listen! Hear that?'

Sarf hearkened, blinked. 'A shamadka?'

As Hex nodded, their eyes trading amazement, the distant chords were succeeded by a rich baritone raised in song, so resonant they could almost make out words. There was a verse, more wisps of the silver strings, a second verse, and some further shamadka as coda. Throughout, they watched the sky, and the song called nothing into it. Its emptiness ended by giving the distant voice an air of immunity.

'A camp maybe,' Sarf ventured. 'If they know about those winged things they must be defended against them.'

'We've got to find out, I guess. I just hate losing this cover.'

Again they moved at a half-run, crouching, as if cringing from contact with the widening sky. Swiftly the walls collapsed around them as they ran, became flower-freckled hummocks not twelve feet high. Just past their farthest turning, broad, rolling green billowed out to the edge of sight. They paused.

'Just past there,' Hex said, 'it really opens out. You can see where the – '

His jaw froze, and both fell flat to the ground. A large quadruped ambled into view round the turning. It paused, stretched down its neck, and cropped the grass. Its flaglike earflaps and mournful, topset eyes proclaimed its breed at once.

'A hill-plod. That was a herder singing!' Something unpleasant nagged Hex's memory even as he said this. Sarf led off again. He seemed to linger as they passed the plod – perhaps he imagined it roasted. Another turning, and the walls were barely man-high bulges and the smell of a herd-filled meadow reached them from just beyond, when Hex, galvanized, grabbed Sarf's shoulder.

'I just remembered. Did you ever hear that on the *East* shore plods are most often herded by *ogres*?'

The shamadka rang again, stunning now in its sweet clarity, though seemingly still some hundreds of yards distant. The voice that followed it was likewise stunning, both for its uncanny resonance, and for the fact that such eerie, echo-textured tones could issue from only one source: the throatbag of a bull ogre. It was a scolding, sprightly tune, coyly counterfeiting ire:

Oh cease to dissemble, thou lovest me not!
Though hotly thou swearest thou carest no jot,
Wherefore woe is my lot!
Aye woe, bitter woe, is my lot!

To deceive me thou need'st more than swearings and sighs!
To hoodwink *me* thou must undrape thy pale thighs,
Add thy breasts to the lie –
For such breasts can give *weight* to a lie!

And if *thus* thout dissemble I'll credit deceit!
So long as thou giv'st it both body and heat
And *those* lips make it sweet,
Then good sooth! 'Tis a dish I will eat!

'Maybe,' Hex breathed to Sarf, 'those things will fear something an ogre's size, and keep away from the neighbourhood of his voice.'

'Let's hope we can get past him ourselves; let's take a look.'

They bellied up the bank, and gingerly spread peek-slits in the grass. The meadow they must cross was a broad shallow dish. The plods were scattered through it, grazing. The ogre and his wagon were near the farther, downslope edge. He was a prime individual, perhaps ten feet tall and half as broad. His shamadka lay by him in the grass and he was drinking from a fifty-gallon winesack slung from the side of the wagon. This posture, and his unbuttoned doublet, displayed to advantage his rosy-skinned, tumescent throatbag – an impressive appendage, big enough to have made – with tailoring – a hammock for a mid-sized man. He wore the hairy breeches so widely affected by ogres they had given them the name, in many parts, of 'shags'. Near the wineskin, a big crossbow leaned against the wagon. Just behind the ogre, a plod with blue ribbons tied round its earflaps stood hobbled to a stake. The pair watched for a long moment, then wormed back behind the hillock.

'I'm beginning to think we're still lucky, Sarf Immlé.'

Almost smiling, his friend nodded. 'Best keep in mind, though – he's got to be good and busy before we break for it. That bow must shoot six-foot darts.'

'At least we can assume those winged ones know about

the darts too. As long as *they* don't come around I'll take my chances with the ogre.'

A new flux of supple chords sprang from the shamadka – a melody of voluptuous brio.

'Fine,' Sarf insisted. 'The fact remains – ogres are said to have good eyes.'

'Yes, but we can at least get out of his field of vision pretty quick. Let's study the ground some more.'

The ogre, who had started to sing again, was moving in a stately pavan-step circling the beribboned plod, which gazed moronically at the sky, waggling its ears. The ogre's voice, though delicately shaded, thrust forth with a serpentine, persuasive vigour:

> All day in fragrant toil we've filled
> Our arms with flowers of every style.
> Now forbear to judge me bold
> If – pressing still our harvest goal –
> I beg: 'Do not, do not withhold
> The choicest blossom of the field!'

The shag straightened, tossed his shaggy head (only his tusks deprived his bearded profile of a truly patrician beauty), executed a reverse, and recommenced his pavan in the opposite direction.

'This will be the refrain,' Hex breathed in Sarf's ear. 'It's in the quadrone metre.' Just then he glanced overhead. Back whence they had come, a flake of blackness detached itself from the skyline. Hex jabbed Sarf. Both watched, frozen, as the ogre sang:

> Oh let it be now as I so long,
> So ardently have willed!
> Dispread thyself the grass upon
> And yield, yield, yield
> To *me* that chiefest blossom of the field!

The black flake swam across the brilliant air, almost to the meadow's skirt, its height alone affording hope to the two spies that it noted only the ogre and his herd. Still minutely high it wheeled, returned the way it came, re-merged with the hills. In Sarf's eyes Hex saw his own dawning hope mirrored. Sarf pointed down the meadow's rim.

'Let's curve out along there.'

Hex nodded. They could not avoid following the meadow's skirts without crossing hundreds of yards of rising and very open ground, whereas by skirting the herd they would still have distance from the ogre and could creep on ground low enough to escape his eye. The herdsman had paused to drink again before the second verse. He commenced it, bending a smouldering gaze upon the plod. The animal tossed its head, returning a look of unease, dubiety.

> Successive Flower Queens have crowned
> Thy hair, thy breasts – each was cast down
> By some more splendid potentate.
> A Zarl made Quimsy abdicate,
> Then fled thy brow, her honoured seat,
> Before still-reigning Fairy's-gown.

Again he performed his volte face and began recircling the plod, his movements more tremulous now, full of a restrained force.

> Depose her now, for she's surpassed!
> Thine own bloom unconceal!
> Enthrone *thyself* upon the grass
> And yield, yield, yield
> To *me* that choicest blossom of the field!

With the gesture of one discarding artifice, the ogre flung his instrument aside – indeed, his violence sent it entirely out of the meadow. He grasped the plod's throat-muff, gazed into its eyes a moment. His throatbag swelled, empurpled. He uttered a great, inarticulate yodel, hurried round to the beast's hindquarters, and dropped his hairy breeches to his ankles. Sarf and Hex swarmed over the hillock and rushed – almost on all fours – along the meadow's edge.

The violated plod bellowed and boomed its outrage, the ogre obliviously writhed astern and the pair, using the rest of the herd for cover, dodged past the uncouth tableau – but only just past it. For they had barely put the wagon between themselves and the lovers when the grass snagged Hex's foot and he went down, tripping Sarf as well. They had not yet found their feet when a now familiar shape re-entered the sky. A second blackness followed it and both now swooped towards the herd.

'The wagon!' Hex gasped. Both scurried for it. Had they already been seen? So vastly did the sky's openness press on them, as though it were one huge, lidless eye, that Hex scarcely felt the smaller horror of the ogre's nearness. Each hugged a wheel, and peered beneath the axle-tree.

In the foreground were six legs, the rearmost shackled by shaggy pants, while beyond, the herd milled on the sward. For a moment the pair didn't dare get under the wagon, which rode high and would reveal them to the ogre if he looked around. Then they saw a nervous ripple move through the herd. An instant later, a vast shadow skimmed across it. They got under the wagon.

The ogre, unalerted, did not cease his labours, but the plod, with its topset eyes, began to bellow in a different key. Seeing its fellows begin to disperse, it broke its hobble with a kick and ran after them. The ogre held on, oblivious, yodelling with passion.

'When they swoop they'll be low enough to spot us,' Sarf said.

'Let's get in here till we see what happens.'

There was a baggage rack, mostly empty, between the axle bed and the bottom of the wagon's chassis. The pair crawled into it. It was open at both sides and if the melodious giant survived, they had just climbed into a coffin, but now it would hide them from the larger, faster-moving eyes they feared more.

The ogre, still hugging his trotting paramour, lifted his head in a climactic ululation. Just then talons clutched his head, wings thundered, wrenched him from his obscene seat, and flung him sideways to the ground, where his song ended with the report of cracking bone.

'Brilliant!' cried a great voice from above as the striker rose from view. 'A dazzling lateral tournello!' The speaker streaked down in his turn and snatched the just-disburdened plod from sight. Another crack, and it sprawled back down upon the grass. Two shadows crisscrossed lazily on the meadow.

'Two more then?'

'No four. Gleeb's belly grows no smaller with the years.'

'Nor Squalla's. But how to carry them?'

'I have a way.'

The plods were widely scattered now. The shadows fell away to the right and left. Like scimitars their black wingspans swung down above the stumbling beasts, a plod vanishing with each upsweep to be broken in the air and dropped, an instant later, on the heap near the wagon. As the last plod hit the pile a suspicion of what the raptor's 'way' was awoke in Hex's stomach.

'And now,' came the voice, 'behold our quarry bag!'

Gusts tossed the grass round the wagon, which quaked and shuddered while the hidden pair strained with feet and hands against the ends of the rack to keep from spilling out. There was a splintering, and then the cart stood still and its roof crashed to the ground.

'Now turn it turtle and pluck the wheels off.'

There was no time for fear. The earth lurched out from under their bellies, gravity torqued their every muscle, and they were hammered down against their backs. Wood groaned and snapped, four times, and then the cart was flipped again. Hammered against their bellies this time they lay, both bleeding from the nose, watching the stars slowly clear from their eyes while something dropped into the wagon. Five further impacts followed.

'So,' came the voice. 'I'll take the yoke-pole, you break two grips in the rear wall there.'

'Here?'

'More left, I think.'

'Try it now.'

The grass flattened out for fifty feet to either side of the wagon. It rose from the ground, hung, rocking slightly, steadied.

'Perfect! Away!'

With a skyward heave that crushed the stowaways' lungs anew, the great wings fell into phase. The meadow below took a giddy drop, then sank away more smoothly. A wider and wider vista of green hills spread below.

'By the powers, Sarf,' Hex murmured in his friend's ear, 'has even the greatest cartographer, in his wildest visions, seen such a map as this?'

Though the creakings of the wind-torn wagon and the muted boom of the unseen wings above made this murmur safe, Sarf glared and would not answer. Hex looked back out his side of the rack.

Below, tree-shaggy mountains marched beside the sea, thirty leagues of them – with their most hidden valleys – to be possessed at a single glance. They had re-passed Hissmin, which they'd been three days working their way south of, in a quarter of an hour, and now, though it was still broad noon, all Slimshur was behind them, as well as three large cities – nameless to him – in these mountains. One scant inch of planking intervened between their little bodies and two miles of empty, wind-torn sky. Suspended in such perfect powerlessness, Hex felt oddly easy in his mind. So huge a leap *northward* – what but their luck could have snatched them up and hastened them on their way like this?

'So it is. In love.' The great voice jarred him, reminding him this marvellous transport was not simply to be walked away from, once it set them down. Hex could hear the labour of the monsters' wings in their broken phrasing.

'How so? As with the ogre?'

'Just so. One moment. At love's peak.'

'The next. Struck down!'

'What good. To soar in spirit? Death. Mocks flight.'

'And yet. Such song! To sing thus. Is to conquer. Death.'

'But his song. Alerted *us*.'

'All acts have. Echoes past reckoning. Should one do. Nothing. For fear of. Consequences?'

This went unanswered. After a moment a rusty, lugubrious baritone sang reminiscingly:

'Yield. Yield. Yield. To *me* . . .' and trailed off.

Hex was falling, tumbling into the void, his tiny limbs clawing the emptiness that swallowed him. Splinters bit his cheek as he woke with a start. Had his convulsion been felt? They were banking, dropping inland, putting the sun – just beginning its seaward decline – behind them. They crossed a great bay whose hilly shore was fringed with beaches from which jutted literally dozens of piers. As their sloping descent argued a landing soon they eagerly studied that pier-bristled arc and, as they crossed them, the hills inland of it.

Still inland they sank, till cave riddled ridges appeared ahead of them. When it was clear that one large cavern was their bearers' particular goal, Sarf muttered:

'I'd call it a day's walk back to that bay. I saw a stream course I think we could follow.'

Hex nodded, anxious as his friend to clutch firmly the

notion of escape, now that their hour of peril was at hand. The cavemouth yawned with the scalp-tickling speed of their approach, but then the wagon rocked with the great wings' braking, the black hole paused, and swallowed them far more slowly than it had threatened to do. The cart was set down, firm and square, with hardly a jolt.

'Squalla! Gleeb!' their bearers cried. 'A feast! Come see!'

Somewhere deeper in that dark a clap of wings and a scrabble of talons woke. Suddenly, the wagon violently rocked, spilled on to its side, piling Sarf on top of Hex and dumping from the cart meaty masses on to the cave floor.

'Watch out!' a huge voice boomed. 'He's still – ' A foghorn scream and a wet noise of rent flesh-and-bone followed. A resounding bellow, throatbag-born, made one huge bell of the stony darkness, which then was filled with the smack-and-flap of panicked pinions.

Hex felt his wiry friend twist, shove, and vanish from atop him. In his turn he writhed up out of the tilted rack, and fell free on to the floor of the cave. He found his feet, and sprinted for the ragged mouth of blue sky out of which Sarf was just then running – seeming, with his wide-flung limbs, to be executing a dancer's leap.

14
A Riddle's Painful Answer

Banniple left the Boasting Hall of the Huffuff pier just as the sun's edge touched the sea. As a passenger on a Huffuff craft (*The Glide*, sailing two days thence) he had been privileged to dine at the hall's head table next to Huffuff Hardkeel, Shiplaw of the pier and head of the Huffuff clan. The Shiplaw had left him with some misgivings about the stroll he was embarking on now.

Hardkeel was a massive man, tun-bellied, a prodigious (and gurgling) swallower of beer. Also laconic. Friendly grunts had been the sole conversation Banniple could elicit from him, until he had mentioned his wish to take an evening stroll on the beach. Even then Hardkeel's remarks were vague enough.

'Hum. Much better stay here, you know . . . Have a merry time . . . Some spirits, game of chance, eh?'

It seemed he saw some risk in an evening walk on the beach. Unfortunately this wasn't clear. The Huffuff ethic – and it was the ethic of all the other maritime clans whose piers thronged Score-and-Seven Bay – shunned any verbal emphasis of risk as an unmanly utterance. Pressed for clarity, Hardkeel got even vaguer, and his protests might have been mere graciousness, pressing continuance at the hall's convivialities.

But the uproar of these latter had, for Banniple, passed bearability, whence he now stood at the pier's railing, contemplating the shore. Just beside him the great, barn-like hall literally shook – a low, buzzing vibration – with the pent activity of the Huffuffish mariners. They gambled round the pits between the beer casks, had food-fights and arm-wrestled at the tables, swore at and cheered the crab-fights staged in wooden pens along one wall, and had belching and farting contests wherever they found themselves so inclined. Since, with all this, the whole building shuddered contrapuntally at the velvety impact of the swell against the pilings underfoot, the sum effect was to make Banniple giddy. It reminded him – devoted landsman – of the creak and surge of a ship. Having already come four hundred leagues by sail from his native Erkish, and facing a voyage of some seven hundred leagues more, he decided that now he was going to stand on solid ground, if only for half an hour.

So. He'd walk down to the Kraff pier. There it stood, just half a mile downshore. It was a corpse-pier now. Built in Score-and-Seven's more thronging era, its clan, shrunk and subsidiary, had long since merged with the Huffuff clan. In its epic age the bay had grown, beyond its eponymous twenty-seven clans, to a full thirty-five. Its present shrinkage to eleven (one of these moribund, with only half a pier and a pair of ships) had given to the bay its predominantly skeletal look – decaying piers and flotsam-littered waters. The Kraff, for one – a stately spinal column of unequal pilings, slashed by crossbars and odd diagonal braces – stood rooted in the flexing, coppery sinew of the gilded sea, looking like a line of urgent but arcane script, engraved on lustrous sheetmetal; a cryptic warning. The slow surf grumbled with the sodden, multiple drumbeat of buoyant trash that choked it. The intervening beach – smooth-worn shingle of rounded stones – was heaped with storm-piled trash from the pier's erosion. From dunes of wave-stacked detritus jutted broken planks and timbers dangling frayed tendons of cable and flapping tatters of sail like bleached skin.

It put Banniple in an elegiac mood. He raised a declamatory arm, partly in mockery of his own unheroic form, which was slight and a bit potbellied. He intoned to the briny desolation:

Ah Marmion, who stood so tall, so nobly with thy towers took the sun!
Has Time's tooth devoured all, and left of thee but these poor paltry bones?

A belch resounded at his back. He turned. Two women, having just emerged from the Boasting Hall, stood regarding him. Both wore coarse tunics, shortswords, sandals. The more thickset, and somewhat elder, had a staff as well. She leaned on it – grinning, nodding. Her flushed face reported more than one tankard of beer.

'Quite right, my friend! Old Time gobbled it all up – all but a few paltry boneheads such as you'll find in there.' And she jerked a thumb at the Boasting Hall.

Uncomfortable, Banniple smiled. 'You'll excuse me from taking sides. You see I'm a – '

'A foreigner, oh yes!' cut in the younger woman. 'One can see that! You're a lovely one too – smooth and pale! Isn't he a lovely one?'

'By the blackest Powers, he is!' declared the elder. 'Damn me but he's toothsome! We have a mind to eat you right up, little foreigner – and not leave even a bone of you either!'

Both women laughed hugely, nudging and thwacking each other. Banniple, extremely uneasy now, managed a join-in-the-fun chuckle. The russet fleece of his hair, mirrored by the corolla of his beard, lent something flowerlike to his small, snub-featured face. Though he assumed himself to be unprepossessing, the estrangement of the sexes in Score-and-Seven made some erotic adventure just feasible and this, in arousing, unsettled him. But more unsettling was the likelier development: some boisterous satire, with himself as focus, which could only embarrass him with his hosts, should any hear it. For these women, in the bare fact of being on the pier, declared a self-assertive mood. Confronting the hostile clamour of the Boasting Hall to claim the right of the Women's Draughts was a political, not a recreational act. The beer itself had been made on the women's farms in the hills, and there – for them – was where it was most pleasurably consumed as well. But the men must be reminded, it seemed, how wholly they depended for most of the raw materials of life on the women's landlocked productivity.

'Do you know any other lines of eulogy?' The elder, as she grinned this, stepped forward and displayed the wrack-heaped beach with a sweep of her staff that made Banniple step back and bump the rail. This, with his crooked smile and headshake, set them off again. The younger took the other's arm and led her off down the pier, for the elder seemed not quite as ready as her friend to abandon the jest.

Banniple looked at the strand again, and found it still made him feel elegiac. He supposed he must grant a justice in the situation. The men's fraternity of the sea, closed so long to women, now depended on them even for the skilled carpenters needed to keep their surviving piers repaired. Shipwrights the men had in plenty, but so adamant had been their long insistence that only maritime affairs had manly dignity, that men who could build a boat from keel to mast could not frame a window. The clans still won a living from the tricky tides, though their roistering, never-daunted ethic blinked at their declining status on seas now swum by greater sharks than they had ever been. The fruits of some trade, some carriage, some old-style piracy, they still brought home, but now the main part of their gold and foreign goods went to the women for bread, beer and plod meat – for skins, shoes and blankets, spikes and dressed lumber – for everything that came from the abidicated shore. Still, if he had a bias in the matter, it was the feeling that the women were rather rubbing it in – having so much of their own, and then to come in and drink their own beer in the poor boors' clubhouse Sanctum, just to show they had the economic power to command the privilege – it seemed so vengeful. Then again (here the hall behind him buzzed with a surge of pent noise) these clansmen in their heedless, cheery energy might permanently infuriate any long-associated soul. His fortnight coming hither on the *Glide* had shown him that. He set out down the pier, judging the two women now far enough ahead.

He wished for the brazenness to overtake them and take them up on their lascivious threat. The sun-flooded lane ahead was empty. The path that branched from the pier's foot down to the beach hooked through a small cluster of houses, and on the porch of one of them a woman sat waxing a bow. He made a cheery salute, she stared. When he was some strides past she called:

'Stranger!'

'Good evening?' He saw she was tanned, trimly solid, had short dark-honey hair bound by a fillet, grey eyes, cool in the sun-darkened face.

'Why are you going to the shore at this hour? Are you going swimming?'

Banniple said: 'A splendid idea!', trying for a roguish blitheness. The woman didn't smile, sounded irritated:

'Well then don't knock your head against some stray piece of Score-and-Seven's glory!'

The traveller faltered, decided no further pleasantry was offered, and turned away with an awkward bow meant to be ironic.

'Wait!' she said. 'Haven't those fools told you? What about the Riddler?'

'Riddler?' He was glad of a chance to show some wit. 'Respected Madam, your question itself is a riddle. Are you then the Riddler?'

'Idiot,' the woman muttered, returning to the waxing

of her bow. Angered, Banniple marched on, down to the shingle.

The horizon now bisected the sun. The sea wore half its light – a great fan of puddled fire. The hills and the beach glowed with the other half, whose radiance ennobled the dunes of trash; made polished ebony of tarry beams, and beaten copper of rusted iron shards. And, on those stretches of the beach that were unlittered, the shingle itself was sumptuous – black and grey, each eggsmooth stone distinct, each lovingly, singly lathed by the sea, and painstakingly etched with shadows till their shoals seemed treasure, a hoard of polished coin where the surf plunged its white fingers with a greedy whisper. Banniple began to walk, the stones shifting musically underfoot. What he felt was like a foretaste of Kurl itself, this fear compounded with cupidity the scene inspired in him. And in its way, this trash was like the texts and works of art so deeply honeycombed in the museums. For didn't these jumbled artifacts document – to the instructed eye – a human history as darkly bright as any other? And – as must those far more fabulous relics of buried Kurl – this littoral boneyard wore the melancholy dignity of all things overtaken by their ruin.

His wonder to be walking through this gorgeous desolation precisely counterweighed his fear, as if he alternated between them with every other step. The pier's skeletal script seemed more than ever to insist on its own deciphering, a riddle much depended on. Yes, surely this ghostly scene was an omen, an admonition to remember the audacity of his larger quest, and the fragility of all human ambitions. The sun was down now. Its afterglow had unexpected richness, like a brazen gong that sent out reverberations of pollen-yellow, rose and violet. The beauty here was only on loan from the sun and already it was leaving. In deep Kurl, of course, half an infinity of marvels burned inextinguishably with their own buried splendour while the dangers there – why, how much greater than those of an evening stroll here on a deserted beach!

He had to stop a moment, to give a headshake, and smile. Slight, bookish Banniple! Sober sub-curate in the Erkish Archivium! *Here!* Actually, in the flesh, halfway already to legendary Kurl. A daub of colour snagged his eye in the dunes of wreckage. Here, on the corpse-pier' shalf of the beach now, these lay thicker. They were already bled of their sharper hues and the little dazzle he saw, though two heaps inshore, stood out, being concatenated of gold, crimson and fresh green. Using his hands, he monkeyed up the nearest hillock, whence the thing looked certain to prove some flower of rare luxuriance. He thought he saw a negotiable path to it, and proceeded.

On his return he would present it to that woman with the bow, and by then would have thought of some remark that would make her laugh. Yet another premonition of Kurl, where the foray would be over far more treacherous ground. He could not know what path he would find, nor, therefore, what precinct it would take him to, so he could not guess his prize's form. He had his private fantasies, of course – certain of the more famous texts said to lie in the lava tomb – but whatever it proved, wasn't his real mission with it much like this of the flower? To spark a new light, a new estimation and acceptance in his colleagues' eyes, and, indeed, perhaps in Ruanna's most of all? (She was a palaeograph with the Archivium's Historical Seminary.) Luck would determine if the prize itself were great or not so great. But the prize of having brought it back – this, irreducible, would make him shine, ennoble him for the rest of his life. A laughing matter, decidedly, to see this schoolboy pattern behind his great exploit. Somehow the foolishness did not diminish his joy in it.

Yes, it was a flower. Standing in a little vale environed by the charnel heaps of long-dead enterprise, its brilliance amid that anaemic grey seemed a flame set burning on the fuel of the bleached bones of ships. Those bones creaked under Banniple as he clambered down to it. Its bloom was fat and fleshy. The amphora of its calyx disgorged, it seemed a meld of fragrances, each unisolatable, all sweet. Its fat root came effortlessly free from the woody loam. Happily, Banniple felt the heft of it. It should startle the woman from her peevishness if only because he would – by the principle of contrast – look rather amusing carrying such a splendid vegetable. Wood groaned, and he jumped. Two men were looking down at him from a trash heap. They were tangle-haired and dirty, and their stares looked as startled as his own felt.

'Good evening,' he said, hearing it echo idiotically.

'Good evening,' said the taller, bulkier of the strangers. The pair came down to him. Both were gaunt of face, with the lax mouths of chronic exhaustion. 'We were afraid,' the taller told him, 'that this whole bay was deserted.'

There was a noise like that of a banner in a stiff wind. As Banniple turned towards it, the flower was torn from his hand while cracking red pain scored his cheek, knocked him sideways and bleared his sight. Kneeling as his vision cleared, he saw the blossom hanging horizontally in the air before him, clamped between white, protruding fangs, to either side of which one red eye balefully glowed. Behind this apparition streamed a long flag of black, horrid hair snapping like an ensign in a gale, though the darkening breeze that combed the wreckage was gentle, and differently directed. The thing wheeled to lash him again. The little scholar was just quick enough to dodge the snap, though it left his ear ringing. The creature dived upwards and eeled away with its prize as two others like itself plunged down upon the strangers.

So numbed and gaping were the faces of those two – so outraged they appeared by this addition to their evidently much-prolonged woes – that it seemed they would never move in time, though in fact the big one fell aside and yanked his sword free with creditable brio as he dropped. His upswing missed the airsnake. His weaponless friend, rolling agilely aside, came up clutching clubwise a broken spar. The other quickly sheathed his sword, and both he and Banniple hunted up similar bludgeons, for now the dimming air above the vale swam with the creatures. They hung just out of striking range, sharking back and forth, liquidly dodging collisions. Banniple, though tensely poised, club cocked above his right shoulder, found the bigger stranger's behaviour almost as distracting as these voiceless visitants'. For the man, menacing his cudgel skywards, was grinding his teeth, and shouting with a voice so freighted with rage that it was almost like a groan:

'Oh endless, rotten, stinking, scabby luck! Rest? Respite? Ha! No respite! No, oh NO! What else are meatbags for but hounding? Oh yes! Just hound and hound them! Spare no effort! Why, shite and noseworms! We'll have no slackers here! After those meatbags! On them, lads!'

Ranting and roaring, this hairy, bulky man began to run zig and zag, taking mighty club swipes at the air when their sinuous, flyquick tormentors effortlessly hung above their reach. Then a voice welled down against the trio, and as one they turned.

'You stole my blossom,' it had said. The speaker was a hugeness that squatted on the biggest of the trash dunes circling them. His body – a bristly bulb of dreadful shapeliness – hung low-slung between the jutting angles of his legs, four to a side in the manner of all spiders.

And such he was, save that, just where a spider's eye-knobs would be clustered thickest, he had a human face – short-necked and aimed rather skyward, and with what looked like a beard of coarse brown bristles just beneath the chin. This face smiled slightly. It was a thin, ascetic face, bald-pated and pale, and its smile seemed distracted, mere politeness, like the smile of a man with a toothache. He repeated:

'You stole my blossom. You shouldn't steal.' His voice was dry. It had a cricketlike, chitinous undertone.

'I beg your pardon, sir,' said Banniple with great feeling. 'I honestly did not know the flower belonged to anyone. I took it to be growing in the public domain, as so many flowers do. I *am* so sorry.'

The painted smile widened an apologetic fraction: 'But you see, you *did* take it. It wasn't yours, yet you snatched it. You snatched what wasn't yours.'

'But *we* stole nothing at all!' shouted the bigger stranger. '*We're* guiltless!' He still seemed even more outraged than frightened – flung his voice with stubborn petulance against the manspider, like a prisoner hammering at his cell door. 'We just met this man this very moment, and we never touched your stinking flower!'

'That's the truth,' said Banniple, his heart sinking at his own self-isolating words.

'But you *would* have snatched it!' sneered that monkish face. Very subtly his great body tensed and sagged, tensed and sagged – a machinelike pulsation that suggested a just-contained lust to spring in the hideous arachnid frame. 'You surely would have. All men want what isn't theirs. Aren't you seeking Yana? And aren't you bound for Kurl?'

Banniple traded mute startlement with the strangers and, paralysed, they heard the manspider say on:

'So. For taking what's not yours, you stand in jeopardy.

You must now answer my riddle. You must answer my riddle, or become my food. Here, then, is my riddle:

> I'm each salt ocean's other shore
> Where tasteless tides of drought don't roar.
>
> Defining all like daytime's light,
> I'm all-concealing as the night.
>
> Fuel that feeds all urgent fires,
> Extinguisher of hot desires.
>
> I raise all wingèd enterprise –
> I am the gulf where nothing flies.
>
> What am I?

Well then! What's the answer? Eh? Speak up, any of you!'

The Riddler's lips pressed shut. His eyes were bright with pleasure-in-suspense. More than before, the subtle flexing of his frame seemed a scarce-chained hunger to lunge and kill. The three searched each other's eyes, stunned less by the riddle – which had scarcely reached their minds as yet – than by their situation. Now the airsnakes began to seethe, to dip and lash the trio again, shattering the air just by their ears and striking them half deaf.

'Yes, at them! Stir their thoughts!' the Riddler cried. With a whispery quaver of glee he repeated:

'I'm each salt ocean's other shore.
Where tasteless tides of drought don't roar.
What am I? Answer!'

The smaller stranger feinted, then planted a mighty swing against the muzzle of one tormentor. As the smitten thing rocketed – locks flapping – from the vale, others dived, one of them biting a chunk of earlobe from Banniple, another dodging the bigger stranger, who fell with the violence of his swing. The Riddler bobbed atop the wooden boneheap in his rooted dance, his voice growing louder:

'Defining all like daytime's light,
I'm all-concealing as the night.
Answer! What am I?'

The smaller stranger was shouting: 'Back to back!' As Banniple formed up with him he was lashed on his already torn ear. The galvanized fury of his counterswing missed, came around, smote the shoulder of the bigger stranger who had just joined their pattern, and knocked him off his feet.

Now the Riddler's pulsation looked like ecstasy, and his voice came faster, not pausing to separate the last two verses.

'Fuel that feeds all urgent fires,
Extinguisher of hot desires.
I raise all wingèd enterprise –
I am the gulf where nothing flies.
'What am I? Answer now, or you are forfeit, and my food!'

The bigger stranger had regained his feet and was scourging the air with a lunatic frenzy that did indeed clear it momentarily of the airsnakes, but also had his friend and Banniple crouching and cringing from the murderous sweeps of his whistling knout. The man was transported, lifting himself from the ground with half his swings, regaining footing each time by luck alone and the blind, dancing, inarticulately bellowing élan of his wrath. Distracted by the spectacle, Banniple felt himself seized by the back of his jerkin, and lifted into the air – just as he heard the Riddler's jubilant cry:

'Forfeit! Forfeit! Bring him to me first, yes!'

The little scholar flailed his knout behind him, felt it snagged by his raptor's hairbanner. Hauling futilely to free it, kicking mightily, still he rose smooth as a bubble towards the purple sky, now thinly flecked with the first faint stars. Below, the impassioned stranger gave a swing that toppled him at last, one foot snagging, ankle wrenching as he – roaring – fell, but this the floating scholar scarcely noted, as the Riddler, towards whom he drifted, engrossed him wholly. For that monkish face, with a smile now full and joy-foreseeing, was tilting back, and the bristly mass that had seemed his beard was now unfolding, splitting, reaching upward: two jointed, hair-sheathed fangs that probed and twiddled towards their gliding prey. The empty air between the former and the latter seemed a downward-sucking vacuum, and set Banniple a-kicking with a warding rhythm that matched that of the fangs. Behind him now, the fallen stranger gave verbal expression to his first wordless pain:

'STINKING SHITE-SMEARED DUNGHEAP DEATH!!'

Below him Banniple saw the pale face crumple as with pain of its own. The fangs froze in their waggling up-reach. Just short of where the Riddler crouched, Banniple was dropped.

His body was scrambling to flee even before it had the crazy planking underfoot. He fell, and before he could get up, noticed the emptiness of the air. The airsnakes were gone. The Riddler was still atop his dune but looking smaller because he was frozen and folded up tight, the angles of his legs interlocking above his abdomen, his eyes and mouth squeezed shut as with distaste.

The smaller stranger began to laugh. 'Bramt Hex, you clever devil! How intelligent of you to find the answer!' Hex, seated and still clutching his ankle, managed a chuckle through clenched teeth. Banniple, taking what seemed his first full breath in an age, joined in. A fourth voice joined them and all three fell silent.

The woman with the bow stood above them, balanced easily on a jutting beam. Her bow was strung now, with an arrow nocked to it, but only one hand clutched these easily at their intersection, while with the other, still laughing, she made a brow-to-bosom obeisance, accompanied by a half-bow.

'Gentlemen!' (Some further chuckles, decorously suppressed.) 'I'm glad you saved yourselves. I followed you, sir,' (this to Banniple) 'because I decided I'd been snappish, and you were at a risk that no one had instructed you to appreciate. I got here too late to do more than spy, and maybe learn the riddle. He can't be killed until he's answered, you see,' (she gestured with the bow) 'and even killed, he returns sooner or later – this much is known of him at least. I must say I'm glad of your deliverance, for I would have felt bad watching your deaths.' Something in her own utterance seemed to displease her, and made her rather frostier as she said it. Whether they found this dubiety of hers quaint, or simply felt an overriding relief, her hearers all laughed anew, even louder than at first. At first she scowled. At length she grinned.

'No no!' she cried with mock concern. 'Don't thank me for my tender feelings! Nonetheless, my friends, it is said that even though the Riddler be answered, if his head is not quickly cut off, then the moonlight soon revives him.'

The woman's knife and hunting savvy made a neat end of what Bramt Hex, with his shortsword, messily began, and the party headed back towards Huffuff pier, Banniple carrying the dripping head by one of the fangs, which they had wrapped in a scrap of sailcloth.

Their feet crunching tunefully on the shingle, they walked in silence after the first spate of introductions. Shyly, in rather a rusty voice, Banniple poked a question at Raymil, the huntress:

'Will you tell them in the hall what the riddle was?'

The woman stopped and stared sardonically, letting the unintended frankness echo.

'Why Banniple! I assumed *you* would! Why should *I*!?'

She smiled, further savouring the foreigner's assumption of her inhumanity, visibly enjoying his discomfort. He – flushing – nodded twice, cleared his throat, and spoke to Hex.

'Tell me, Bramt Hex. I *am* bound for the Museums of Kurl. Was the monster right in saying you were bound for Yana?'

Hex, his hurt leg angled back of him, leaning on a broken plank, smiled as he grunted to keep up. The smile was half hilarious, a bemused glee just wakening from the pain and shock that – almost visibly – still drained from his loosening neck, his ever more flexible shoulders growing winglike in the easy gusto with which they crutched him onward.

'Oh yes! And that's why I was so . . . so insanely angry! I thought we were so *close*, you see! For you must understand we *flew* here, yes!' (Here he held up a warning palm, delaying explanation.) 'And suddenly thinking we were stopped *dead* here . . .'

Banniple was nodding, his smile broadening, growing almost tender in his sudden sense of revelation so enswathed with luck it beamed upon and from him like pure sunlight. 'You know, I was going to tell you I had heard that Yana was thought by many to be merely legend, and then it hit me that my own goal was the same, that even the Museums of Kurl are dismissed as wistful vapours by some scholars. To be so delivered, and so accidentally! Doesn't it make you feel . . . feel . . .'

'Weightless! Yes, though I limp! Let's simply throw our luck into the same pot, good Banniple! An instance of my newly buoyant, trusting spirit: are we not on the Isle of Kray? Note I scarcely ask this, I all but swear it. Sarf says that while I slept we crossed some open sea, and *I* now do not hesitate to say we've crossed to Kray itself, where both our goals are located! Do I err?'

Faced with such ebullience, Banniple felt his reply

already half-plucked of its sting – felt eager for the energy he already saw this new ally must bring him on his voyage.

'You do not err. You may, in one regard, misconceive things: "Isle" is something of a misnomer for Kray. Kurl is no less than five hundred leagues north of Score-and-Seven, which lies on Kray's southern tip. The fabled Yana lies yet farther north than Kurl – at least if my sources are to be believed.'

15
An Interlude of Fleshy Pleasures

The bathing-shed behind the Boasting Hall was furnished with overhead tanks of cold water that had showercocks worked by pull-chains. There were no lamps but the light of the gibbous moon – for the shed was wall-less, open to the breeze – showed bins of scrubbing sand and sponges for drying. Hex and Sarf scoured their shivering nakedness, snorted, blew, and gasped as they drenched themselves. The sand was compacted with disuse, and the sponges were crumbling, and Sarf murmured: 'These Huffuffians and their manly rigours! And yet to a man of them they're years unbathed, I'd swear it.'

'And that Hardkeel! Give me a man of few words, by all the demons! A man of few words, sir!'

They grinned as they shuddered back into their clothes. The cold, which in peril and destitution would have been misery, was a kind of intoxicant. Now transport and protection, weeks of shelter and sure meals, stretched before them, a shining corridor of days with Kurl at its end. The Museums of Kurl, Banniple had confirmed, were, by report, at least, 'not far' from Yana, also called the Place of the Touch. Hex palmed a square of thornfish skin and started brushing his hair.

'Sarf. Answer me something. Admit it once and I won't bring it up again. It's *there*, isn't it? You feel it now too, don't you?'

Sarf returned him a head-shaking smile. '*I'm* in because there's a chance, no more, and we've already come so much of the way. Your powers of belief astonish me, Bramt. Your wish feeds even on contradiction.'

Banniple, at Hex's urging, had allowed that of the half-dozen commentators on the matter known to him from the Archivium's vast shelves, there *was* one who did not dismiss Yana as merely fabulous. Ongerlahd conceded it a possible existence. Hex, though he had never read Ongerlahd, knew his name through an admiring allusion to him in Undle Ninefingers' *The Tarquast Reconsidered*, and was at once convinced that this Ongerlahd had the truth of the matter.

'I won't say you're wrong – ' He laughed. 'But my belief *is* great! I feel like . . . like we're still flying.'

'Well, I wish these high spirits of yours a long life.' Dryly he then reminded Hex of his recent raging despair.

'Bah! It was hunger, and thinking we'd come to a dead city, and – and didn't it save us anyway? Each knock we've taken so far has also struck us off the coin of new luck – and *that's* fact if you will, and not wish.'

They felt skinned by the cold and cleanliness; just moulted, their bodies reupholstered with fresh nerves both inside and out. Re-entry of the Boasting Hall was a second drenching of sensation. Blinking in the roaring glare they regained their seats by Banniple at the Shiplaw's table. The kitchen heat and vapours, with the bodyfever raised by all the swarming business, had their brows already wet again. The caves of craving tissue that were their noses, throats and stomachs quivered, tightened and growled at those savour-sweating gusts that overswept them all each time a tableboy erupted from the double doors with some new steaming vessel.

Hardkeel, on seeing his guests seated, made some faint smiles and inaudible remarks to them. Then he rose – a blocky man with little squirrelish eyes – smote the table with his flagon, and bent a prefatory scowl on the assemblage. Hex asked Banniple: 'I hope all this celebration isn't on our account. What we did after all was really quite – '

'Oh no, I think not. It was just like this last night too.'

Hardkeel now delivered himself of some brief remarks about the trio's heroic slaying of the Riddler. Since neither his flagon-pounding nor his scowling produced the slightest alteration of the environing holocaust, some of his remarks were lost to the eulogized trio. Hex heard almost half the speech as he was just two chairs away and Hardkeel – however wooden his intonations – had a naturally loud voice:

'. . . far as these three foreigners go . . . no introduction needed . . . contribution these outlanders have made . . . their customs or morals or strange destinations might be, their contribution is undeniable . . . service done us by these three aliens . . . likened to the rock that a good navigator steers from . . . have to be an idiot to waste my breath telling you . . . so let's face it, what more can I say?'

At this, surprisingly, the whole table paused in its grabbing and guzzling to roar confirmation. Hardkeel sat down and waved for the the waiting tableboys with their platters. Pitchers of strong dark beer docked cosily near each plate. Hard by, bowls hilly with hot breadrolls were planted, near dewy lumps of golden butter. The roast, hacked into fat-rimmed chops, oozed brown gravy at its many wounds. Hex forked his plate full – it rattled with the impacts. He filled his cup, and poured his gullet full of beer. His fork then hotly plugged him with the gravy-drenched gobbets of meat his knife deftly sectioned off. Bread sopped the bleeding business, gravy-bloated spongechunks of it. A second flask of beer rivered down him in two breaths. Wine then standing by, he dumped a sparkling pond of it into his cup. Throughout these labours he traded smiles and nods with the fat, bald man opposite, whose sauce-splashing, guzzling vigour matched Hex's own.

Now the first toast glided through the hubbub, dented

pewter cups rafting overhead on agilely toted trays. Scarce turning round, the gamesters at the pits reached up expert hands and plucked the trays bare of the brandy. Again Hardkeel rose, his smile a notch wider and his face a shade redder. Jovially – perhaps even eloquently, it would never be known – he spoke, while the din erased his voice and all eyes not bent upon the games were fixed on an impromptu leg-wrestling match being held three tables over. Nonetheless, when he lifted his flagon, two hundred matching flagons were hoisted in lusty unison, and with one voice the hall thundered the pledgeword, too deafeningly to be understood. The flagons went bottoms-up, there was a vast gurgling, and then the vessels were flung through the air in one great blizzard which crashed with surprising accuracy against the kitchen doors. As tableboys regathered the cups in baskets, others sailed out with more platters.

The brandy's heat ballooning in him, Hex looked complacently over at the Riddler's head, where it had been nailed through one ear to the side of a beer-tun, with a pan set beneath it to catch the blood which, amazingly, never ceased to drip from its neckstump. And there by the tuns, amid several women taking their Draught, was Raymil. Fluidly, for all his injury, he was on his feet. Eloquence, like a part of the buoyancy that lifted him, welled from his lips:

'Shiplaw! Clansmen! You've honoured us greatly! But we'd never have thought of cutting yon trophy – ' A perfect silence had fallen on the hall, and every eye was on him. Hex blinked, smiled, and welled to his conclusion: ' – had it not been for the aid of a fourth who stands before you even now – whose care for a stranger's safety led her to the scene of our ordeal, and whose counsel guided us once there. I mean Raymil there, the huntress!'

He did not hear his own last syllable, so abruptly did

the general uproar recommence – not in applause, but in resumption of a hundred different businesses, as though he'd never spoken. Raymil, grinning, made him a bow which he returned, and sat back down. Banniple said in his ear: 'You've touched a bit of a nerve there, Bramt Hex. The sexes are bitterly divided here – have been for over a generation.'

'I see, I see,' Hex murmured. He drained his wine, refilled the cup. 'Fascinating. Fascinating.'

And, with a moment's thought, it *was*, he decided. Everything, in fact, was a little fascinating, slightly radiant round the edges when seen in the overall glow of their reversed fortunes. The big crabs' garish mutual dismemberments in the pits, the breadroll missiles hilariously lobbed by the tun-bellied roisterers, the rumbly music of the gamesters' barbaric oaths, even the Riddler's face, which seemed wryly to squint with the pull of its nailed ear – all was exotic, each detail of it a specimen of the world's infinite variety. All of it glowed with meaning, if only the meaning that it would all some day be part of Hex's consummate *Map of the World*. Or better, perhaps, *Map and Ethnic Atlas of the World*. Or even, conceivably, his *New World Map and Ethnic Atlas with Brief Historical Indices*. It would all be part, in any case, of that compendious net of lines and words – whatever its eventual title – in which he meant to snag and snugly wrap the world and deliver it, triumphantly, to its own stupefied gaze. A captured giant, yes!

And how captured, though men more talented than he had tried and succeeded piecemeal only? Why, snared in the snaky toils of travels through limitless time – the long, world-lapping loops, crisscrossing coils of his endless itinerary that must, if only by mere multiplicity, end with the huge prize's utter envelopment. What a spur to even moderate genius – the knowledge that it need only remain true to its work, and that the mere scope offered it must win the world. Of course, Yana was not yet reached. He knocked wood, but his secret gloating smile displayed his real belief.

He snatched a flask of berry wine from a man passing with a tray of them. Merrily he cried, 'Set to, my hearty!' to the fat man opposite, and filled his flask. He speared the last slabs of roast on to his plate, dragged nigh a bowl of kelp salad, as well as a platter whereon smoked a foot-long fish. His fork and knife hovered, then, from their opposing angles, dived. With soldierly gusto his weapons conquered and his jaws possessed him of this pleasant realm.

The second toast appeared. As this, traditionally, was to the coming voyage (in this case the one to Kurl, two days thence), it was a toast both to the winds and the tides – hence a double toast, by ceremonial requirement. A set of much larger pewter goblets rafted on their spinning rounds. The pledgeword thundered (twice as loud and thrice as indistinct as erst), a larger gargling followed, then the booming volley of the goblets on the kitchen doors. These cyclopean concussions, like a summons, woke a further wave of tableboys with smoking tubs of food. Hex gazed raptly at the twin porticoes of fish-ribs his hunger had unearthed; they hinted strange cities, the buried marvels of some nation's past. Immortal, he would know, possess such pasts almost as fully as he would the world's future!

He surrounded himself with new culinary territories: before him, a lake of soup. Beyond this on the same meridian: an isle of peppered yammash and a gnawed-looking block of plod-cheese. The pools of his drink moved as if tidally, the beer surging up in foam and draining down to froth, the swirling wine lifting and falling in his flask. A roaring in his ears now matched the environing roar and it seemed – in a silence beneath their mutual cancellation – that he could hear his own voice.

He began to explain to the bald fatman opposite him how it had been more luck than any *particular* heroism of his own that had delivered the Riddler into their hands. He – Hex – was a scholar by vocation, you see, and certainly no one before now would have thought of describing him as a man of action. In fact he had just lately, and most astonishingly as well, been obliged to leave, or been ejected from, that vocation of scholarship.

From many of those fervent parentheses into which Hex side-tracked himself, he never emerged. Undaunted, he explained on. Waving his knife and spoon, self-propelled on swooning waves of wine, he expanded on his ambitions. He explained to the bald man what endless time would mean to the intrepid cartographer, provided he unflinchingly embraced his challenges. As he spoke he annexed a schooner of ale and he explained to the bald man the kind of heroism that would be required to *really* do the job he had set for himself. With impartial fervour he extolled the self-transcending soul of such a hero. The passionate particularity of his paean, the intimacy with the subject it bespoke, incidentally bespattered him with some of its glory. The intent look on that bald, fat face was like a mute cheer, a cryptic stare of complex confirmation.

Hex drained a swamp of savoury tuber stew, while twin rivers of wine and beer sank jewel-bright down him to the sunless seas of his craving. Indeed, to get to the heart of the matter, would the fatman like to know the crux of the question? It was the map, of course! Were not maps the very bones of empires, the lifeblood of wealth? And *this* map, potentially the greatest the world had yet seen . . . Of course, it was best to say little of such matters.

Proceeding to say that little at length, Hex toiled, like a fearless expeditionary, through formidable compound sentences. These simultaneous feasts of food and speech inevitably overlapped. From his lips, plosive crumb-bursts decorated his diction. The bald man – the table being wide – stared undismayed, and Hex soared on the tonic of his fiercely interested gaze, until it was discovered that the man had suffered a stroke from overeating and, to judge by his stiffness, had been dead since the second toast.

The bald man was carried off, and Hex deflected the torrent of his ideas to someone else – anyone else. With benign, inspired directness that overleapt any need for tact, he seized upon and untied forever many knotty questions. These included all he knew, and didn't know, about the estrangement of the sexes in Score-and-Seven Bay, for at about this time Raymil was his interlocutor. Complicated though the matter might be, he assured her, it was a simple matter, and would be all right, perfectly all right.

He resolved many other things that night, though he was not destined to remember either the solutions, or the questions. His last memory was that he sat talking while all around him men sprawled on the benches, snoring in the reeking desolation. The snoring, his own voice, and the slow surf under all were the only sounds, save that now and then, over where the Riddler hung watching him with his antic squint, was heard the tick of his dripping blood. Then Hex saw, heard, nothing.

Unwillingly, Hex's mind approached its awakening, wincing in advance at what it was going to have to remember. He raised his eyelids. He sat up.

He was on the bench where he had dined. Chill, ashen dawn sifted in at the windows. Around him in the malodorous hall snorted and rumbled the paralysed clansmen. He viewed, on the table by him, the scummy hill of his empty dishes. And he inhaled, without wishing to, their bouquet. Hex felt queasy loads of excess squirm within him. Urgently he rose, totteringly crutched outside and back to the rear of the hall.

In the latrine shed he vomited and shat, then, shortly thereafter, he shat again, and vomited once more. He took another shower, cringing penitently in the purgative shock of icy water. Before dressing, he limped from the shed to stand at the rail, prolonging his cold to numb his shame.

He watched the surf creaming in, cleansing the fog-slick shingle, feeling the sight might expunge the fatuous highlights of his last night's performance which, irresistibly, resurged from memory now. The images would not be erased. And what a flabby soul, what a shabby little egotism preened and ranted in those tableaux! How far from heroic the whole history of that gluttonous posturer – himself – now looked!

It caused him something close to terror to have this faint glow of heroic exemption – which he had unconsciously allowed to persist in his thoughts – so brutally extinguished, so that now he reeled to view the unadorned memory of his deeds at Polypolis. There was a stark and moon-bled scene – a dank, seamed deathscape as cold as the black, brothy sea! It seemed the very embodiment of his guilt. There he – once more the greedy, hasty, murderous dupe! – there his *own* self-seeking little meat rack might justly be chained for destruction.

Indeed, what of Zelt and her workmates – so many!? There he had needed not even the tawdry draperies of idealism to beautify the brutal act he had embraced. The poor Loop's leer, her breast-wagging jibes – Hex could imagine her hooting the truth at him now as vividly as if she had actually done it:

'Heroic? The only thing *you've* done on a heroic scale, oh Royal Enormousness, is be gulled! Bamboozled! Blindfolded and buggered!'

Hex shuddered. Before the nullity he felt himself to be,

those he had destroyed appeared in flashes of irreducible beauty: the arch-footed, panther-smooth sureness of Zelt's legs; Umber's guileless contralto, warbling in the valley of shadow; Oberg holding him, knuckles silvery with his tears.

Hex's remorse was great, but greater, perhaps, was his sense of personal loss. For clearly, the world-embracing career he had dreamed of could not belong to a fool. In being less than that luminous soul he had fulsomely hymned, he was disqualified from the rarity of supreme achievement. It was like receiving some thaumaturgic measurement of his spirit – concise, magically definitive – to see in searing recollection this crapulous poseur parading so blithely the equipage of greatness, his soft, excessive character buffoonishly bulging from the seams.

So Yana, then, to him must be an irrelevancy – a will-o'-the-wisp all the sadder if real, for it could not be his. Any knowledge he gained of the place must be as futile to himself as Oberg's was to him. Yana might be real, but Hex saw he was doomed to be part of that murderous common mill of humanity who blundered together, colliding, churning each other to pieces, only tormented by rumours of immortality – like snatches of melody, unbearably sweet – while fated finally to sink – torn meat themselves – and rot on the sunless floor of Time's abyss. He deeply sighed, a sound of real pain which nevertheless rang rather comically from this large, moist, somewhat doughy man – half-baked, as it were – standing nude by the railing, leaning on a broken board. He saw this himself, and feeling his own ludicrousness put the finishing touch to his misery.

Slowly he dressed. Slowly he crutched back around the Hall, and down the pier, meaning to find some perch in the wreckage on the beach where he might lie in peace and – once the day warmed up – sleep a bit. The plank had already worn a raw spot in his armpit. He was using it gingerly and when, just ahead, a figure stepped into his path his prop skidded on the fog-slick boardwalk, and he only saved his balance by hurling his shoulder against the wall of a shed. Here he leaned till he had replanted his support.

'Sorry. Did I startle you?' It was Raymil, whose faint smile did not echo her question's solicitude. 'You're probably still pretty fuddled from last night,' she added, clearly amused. Her hair was wet – lay in shiny black feathers on her nape. She held a string of some half dozen small fish.

'I'm sure I said many idiotic things,' Hex stiffly answered. He was feeling less remorseful by the second. 'Pig-drunk people *do*, you know. Celebration was my sole excuse. We've been through some trying times just recently.'

His dignified and reproachful tone failed to make her penitent. She laughed. 'Oh yes, you told me at length. No doubt you don't remember a tenth of what you said last night.'

'So spit and roast me for a fool!' he said. 'I got sodden, so what? At least I remember one thing – trying to give you public credit, which you sneered at as promptly as your menfolk ignored it! Ridiculous I grant I've been. But churlish like that to a well-meaning foreigner, who could know nothing of your customs – I like to think I wouldn't be *that* however drunk I got!'

'What eloquence!' She was still laughing, yet this was not purely sarcastic. The cadence of his words seemed actually to tickle her a little. 'You know, that's why I listened to you as long as I did. Because who *does* listen to drunks unless for some kind of entertainment? Correct?'

For this amiable directness Hex felt, after a moment, gratitude. It invited him to relax from the swaggerings of self-justification. He released a short laugh in his turn.

'Quite right. I will abandon further injured posturings, as I am sufficiently crippled as it is.' He quickly added – indicating her catch and her hair – 'Did you dive for them?'

She got a good laugh out of this, letting herself go a bit. 'Am I an otter?' As though seriously researching an answer, he found himself looking her over. Her face was squarish but trimly modelled; her torso broad but also trim, and big breasted. More sea-calf than otter, though the suggestion of supple quickness was appropriate. Her eyes were grey. 'But wait,' she said with mock urgency, 'perhaps you're confused because you don't know how we fish here. Those idiots didn't tell you! All we need to do, you see, is beat a drum on the shore. This startles the fish sleeping in the surf. They awaken in alarm. In their panic, they bolt seaward, not looking where they're going, and more than half of them knock themselves senseless against some piece of all that junk out there. We just wade out and pick the little beggars off the surface. It's an easy living. Didn't you hear my drum just now?'

They had started moving downpier together. 'I didn't,' Hex said, 'but *I* won't say you're lying. It's an unusual place you people have here.'

'It is unusual in its women,' she said promptly, easily. 'The delusions afflicting its men are ordinary ones.'

Hex glanced a little anxiously at her. 'To be honest, Raymil, I don't feel in the right position to join you in mocking your menfolk. I mean free board, passage, trail gear, provisions – indebted to us or not, they're behaving pretty handsomely as the world goes.'

'Oh, certainly our men are upright enough. So is a mindless post, a rotting piling. And the Riddler's head can be sold quite profitably to a sorcerer, by the way. Where are you headed now?'

'I thought I'd sit on the beach, wait for the sun.'

'You should give your ankle a soak in our bathing creek. It's on your way – I'll show you.'

They passed the small group of houses at the pier's foot where Hex – from Banniple – knew Raymil to live. She led him along the upper beach to where a creek that entered the bay from the hills widened in a gravelly shallows. She watched him find a perch, unbind and immerse his foot – making him conscious of the awkwardness of his movements but not seeming to attend to it herself.

'The fools should have commissioned you some crutches from one of us – you'll need them on shipboard. Am I right in feeling you judge us sour, and our men not such bad fellows as all that?'

'Well. I don't know what's passed between you, but I never assumed it was only your doing. Your countrymen, estimable in many ways, do have a certain, mmmm, heedless vigour.'

Raymil chuckled. 'Heedless vigour. Yes. With the same vigour they built all this, they destroyed it.'

From something in the bitterly disdaining fling of her hand at the tide-rack and the corpse-piers, Hex realized that for her this vista of dereliction was not as he saw it. For her, its former self was also real, or at least not so long dead it had not touched her life. 'What was it,' he asked carefully, 'clan wars?'

'Not as you mean, but in a way it was. They were always competitive, but had achieved an overall coordination – held together with infinite treaties, pacts, much ceremonial harrumph and balderdash, oh to be sure! But fundamentally in league. A thousand miles of this coastline – as many more of the East and West Shores, why, they'd strung a web of carrying-trades big as any in this ocean, the greatest cargo-taxis of the northern seas. And they achieved it by learning to back each other up with convoys, trade tonnage, and the like. Still. In the end, when they needed to gather under a sole and effective command, to counter a powerful enemy, they just didn't have the give, the limberness to manage it. Chafed by the crisis, each clan chief swelled and swaggered. Such a jostling and shoving over admiralties and flagships, and the uppermost position of mast pennants! Such epic rumblings in the boasting halls!' She gestured with her string of fish at the Huffuff hall, a spark in her eyes hinting a comparison. A kind of narrative gusto made her now seem to find the tale almost a merry one. 'A tight, flexible command would have done it, you see, one that did not fear strategic withdrawal as a brand of shame, and which got quick compliance from its forces. Snolp might have been beaten back just far enough to leave their sphere of trade largely intact. As it was, they ploughed head-on forard, every craft they had. What followed wasn't a war, but a single battle, a decimation.'

'Snolp, you said? Arple Snolp?'

'Well, it was Krasp, in fact. But he's long been Snolp's underling or his partner – no one's sure which.'

'Fascinating! When did it happen?'

'A little over thirty years ago.'

'He would have been just a young man then! Snolp, I mean. Would you believe, Raymil? I have actually met Arple Snolp, and not many months past? I've stood talking with him, closer than we are, on a street in Glorak Harbour!'

'You mentioned the city last night. I never heard of it before that. It is strange, isn't it, that the great corrupters and destroyers are also ordinary little men as well, who can actually be met, and talked with on a city street – whose warts can be counted, and foul breaths smelled?'

This not only forestalled the enlargement of his experience, which Hex had assumed would be eagerly desired – it even seemed to *dismiss* the entire topic, and something in the pronunciation of 'men' suggested that it was sexually specific, and no generic term. He bowed ironically.

'*Or* little woman, as the case might be, of course. My own ejection from my home-city, in fact, was – '

'Madam Pin or something, yes, you told me last night. If you haven't bathed yet, that's how we use this very stream. You really ought to get them to commission you some crutches before you set out.'

She had laid her fish by, and was using both hands to squeeze the short feather-mane on her nape. This extorted some final run off, which snaked down to spelunk beneath her tunic, and meanwhile the operation proclaimed the midsummer swell of her breasts, the burgeoning, harvest-time curve of them out from the sturdy, embowering frame of her shoulders. The picture gave poignancy to her abruptly leavetaking tone. He had already had time to be a bit surprised at his own irritation's quickness. Again the Foolish Traveller, to a T. Reacting – as he had last night – with a blind spontaneity to cultural problems he had not first troubled to learn. And with fresh guilt came a corresponding gratitude to this woman for being as decent to him as she had been.

He laboured to his foot-and-plank. Conscious of the absurdity of his useless extremity – a blanched and dripping tuber curiously appended to his leg, purple round its stem – he hastened to render both thanks and apology at once.

'Raymil – you've shown me great good nature, considering how sotted I've been. What can I say but thank you?' He debonairly smiled this last – drolly conceding his awkwardness – and bowed, a second droll gesture. Unhappily, he was not quite braced for such comic flourish, and his sodden reflexes did not correct him in time. He leaned too heavily, and the fogslick shingle squirted from under the planktip. His prop left earth, stabbed air in a rising arc that left him to plunge shoulder-first to the bank. The plank, upflung at impact, twirled once, smote a rock, and flew in half.

It was, on the whole, a striking manoeuvre; performed with an abruptness, an economy of movement, that irresistibly suggested intention, even aplomb. It left Raymil laughing so hard that, as if felled herself, she had to sit down. She clutched her head as she laughed, as if trying to dump the humour out of herself. She stopped. Caught her breath. Exploded anew.

Hex joined her with what vigour he had breath for, and this equable reaction seemed to chill the humour for Raymil.

'Listen,' she was able to say, 'I wish you'd seen yourself. You'd forgive my laughing so hard.'

'I know! I can never help laughing when I see someone fall extravagantly.'

This made her yet graver. 'Look,' she said, 'I'll make you the crutches. I really shouldn't have laughed so hard.'

'That's very kind of you! I'll get them to pay you if I can. Do you mind my watching? It's worse than dull hanging around the Hall.'

She paused, blinking, long enough for Hex to blush for his hasty exploitation of her courtesy, but he didn't retract. Crutches would be a great relief, and so would connected conversation, as opposed to the croaked monosyllables of his crapulent co-celebrants back at the reeking hall.

'Come on then. It's just back this way.' She handed him another plank that was lying by. When he was afoot she gave him the string of fish to carry. 'You can split and gut these for me while I work.'

Her house was in essence a big workroom with a bedchamber and a kitchen appended. It was made of a close-grained yellow wood, snugly and solidly carpentered – its floors and walls of drum-tight tongue-and-groove, its workbenches and stools of dowel-and--peg construction, strong and shapely. The three walls of benches, varied in height and function, supported on shelves or racks the tools of half a dozen crafts. She made him a heap of coarse sacking where he could lie on the floor out of her way and prop his foot up. Gratefully he received from her a fish knife and her catch heaped on a platter. He was glad of a way to pay her for this respite.

'What a theatre of industry!' he marvelled, to ingratiate himself. 'I can see that you cobble, carpenter, braid rope and bowstring, spin thread and weave it. What a sense of freedom this kind of . . . omnicompetence must give you.'

Raymil, mounting a stool in her carpentry corner, answered this sunny fervour with an arched brow as she gathered augers, a short saw and a stone jar of glue near a vice. Taking two lengths of stout dowel down from a rack, she came and squatted by Hex with the rods, whipping out a poignard. 'Stick out your arm, please – I need your heel-to-armpit length.' Placing the rods flush to his heel she marked them with two brisk knife-flicks that almost made him wince. 'Thank you.' Returning to the bench she set a pole in the vice and took up the saw. 'Try to get the lungs out too,' she advised as she cut. 'Those purplish globes. And when you're done take this' – she flipped her knife to stick neatly in the floor beside him, and he *did* wince then – 'and cut some of that sacking in palmsbreadth strips. A tight bandage will take the throb out of that swelling.'

'Lungs?'

'Yes. They climb out on to the rocks to mate.' It seemed to amuse her. Sanding the ends of her cuts, she looked at him amiably. 'I'm glad my competence impresses you. I have to say your praise sounds pretty naïve. I take it this Glorak Harbour of yours is large and thriving.'

'Oh yes.'

'Then surely, on reflection, you can see that in places where trade doesn't thrive, certain necessities are unobtainable except by manufacture.'

Hex, concentrating on his second evisceration, managed it better than the first. 'You know, you sound almost as if that circumstance makes you angry at me.'

She laughed. She had taken down some square stock, and marked off two short lengths of it. She viced it, and answered while she cut them. At each saw-stroke her tunic brimmed sideways with her breasts, a phenomenon which had Hex's covert attention. 'You know, I believe you're right. Isn't that odd? Maybe – and don't think I'm trying to insult you – it's because there's a certain . . . greediness about you that reminds me of my countrymen. Does that offend you?' Her inquiring look seemed half to hope it would.

Hex countered with swift self-effacement – his strongest card, he knew it in his bones. If her anger made her harsh to him, her guilt would augment her hospitality, as it had done so far. 'Ah Raymil; I'm the intruder here. Because of the various misfortunes I've already bored you with, I'm in no position to resent insult. *Did* I tell you about how – '

'Oh yes. You did, you canny, fork-tongued foreigner you.' She addressed this smilingly not to Hex, but to the two square cuts – the crutches' caps – which she had viced. Hex felt a scared pang of awareness that she knew him beyond what he could recall having revealed to her. He watched her auger holes half through the middle of both caps. A faint, belated shame for his meekness nettled him.

'You know, Raymil, I'm a little confused when you talk of your countrymen. I'm not trying to be impertinent, but it doesn't seem you could have had much to *do* with them in your lifetime.'

'My father visited my mother's house, and often dined with us, till I was seven. Then Snolp, through Krasp, worked our mercantile assassination. At that age I loved my father wholly, uncritically. I hated my mother for losing him when the great estrangement set so quickly in. I grew wiser soon enough to ask her pardon, and love her rightly for a while before she died.'

She had plucked the cap-pieces from the vice, and reinstalled a crutch-post in it. The neat dispassion of her moves was like her voice, which laid out its sad matter in calm measures that bespoke a lived-with pain. She augered a hole into the post's middle, her cranking forearm rhythmically etched with fine muscle.

'Sorry to sound nosy,' said Hex. 'It sounds so . . . sudden and final, this estrangement.'

'Yes, though there was always a ritual separation of our activities.' She viced the second post. 'I commiserate. I really do. There they were, the remnants of the battle. Running empty-ribbed from port to port, starved-out wolves chasing the scent of trade. Scattered bones of it were all they could find and they had to sail nearly year-round to glean them. You can be sure the special dignity of the Male and Maritime took on a critical importance in those demeaning times. Meanwhile a major recovery of our fortunes was just then possible. The first seasons of starvation were enough to goad the women to a new plateau in their development in the land-bound arts. We'd long had the big, plod-drawn ballistae that make the mountain roads passable. Indeed they are one reason the Gronds forage far afield, as did those that brought you. Now steady trade and mutual habitation are long established between us and both Grandim and Kark Valley, neither one more than a day's ride inland. But from the first our men refused this inglorious landward turning. We had weaving and leatherwork, hides and saltfish to be produced, if we were to trade enough to buy even modest comfort. We turned away from our men because we had to, and they would not turn with us. Connubiality was already ritualized, as I said. A little drum hung from each wife's lintel. Her husband, in from the sea, must strike it and wait to receive, in a simple phrase, the right to enter the house and the right to enter his wife.'

She looked him casually in the eye in saying this. He, almost cutting his thumb, bent his eyes on the lungs he was excising. 'You can see,' she resumed, brushing shavings from the hole she had bored in the second post, 'how soon a chilling stiffness and withdrawal could divide two sexes so . . . formally linked in the first place?'

She viced a lighter grade of dowel. She sawed six inches off it, then six more. She clutched one piece by its middle and sanded its tips smooth, then dug one tip into the gluepot and gouged up a wad of milky honey which she, holding the peg upright, watched as it crept meltingly down around the shaft, towards her hand.

'Such a waste,' she said almost musingly. 'I remember the season of change quite vividly. The rains, when normally my father would be most in port. At first he hit the drum, she let him in. Late at night I could sometimes hear their voices raised. Then, all the rest of those wet months, the drum was not struck but once, and then my mother wouldn't answer it. Oh how I missed him, Bramt Hex! He was a proper Hall bravo, and a good skilled sailor, but he had a sneaking, indecorous affection for both of us that made him set dignity aside for the drollest kind of hearthside games. And how sad it is, after all, that all of our brothers are now so lost to us.'

Having screwed the gluey pegtip into the hole in one post – producing thus a hand-grip – she polished the second peg's end, and twisted it into the glue. Hex found his hands growing deft. He stacked the split fish neatly, meaty-shingles, on one side of the platter, and waited for what she meant to say.

'How unbreakably, it seems' – she twisted home the peg – 'men have to forge the framework of their self-esteem! We prosper now. More and more we mate and settle inland. Not leaving the sea, but founding our wealth on mother earth. This our fathers couldn't and our brothers can't do. Retreat one step from briny bravado? Forsake the poopdeck? Never! And what a waste! What do they have now? Largely, they carry for Krasp at a footling salary. They do some pirating but it is, from the poverty of their fleet, small and mean stuff as a whole. You would like to couple with me.' A statement, easily made. He had to clear his throat: 'Yes.'

She replaced the countersunk caps in the vice. She gouged a post into the glue, wrenched it into one cap's socket. Repeating this, she left the crutches standing there on their heads.

'I think, with that ankle, this will go best if you take it lying down. How do you feel?'

'That would be excellent.'

'Here's more sacking – widen the mat.'

She pulled her tunic off over her head, and the warm musk of her unpent breasts drifted down to him with her voice.

Afterwards both lay on their backs. Hex looked down at his wide, pale trunk. 'I'm a fat man,' he mourned, sad and slightly bewildered to find it still so. Lazily, she scanned him.

'Not quite. I expect you were more so when you left your city, from what you've said of your sufferings.'

'Ha! I prove a sottish whiner and complainer to boot! I find myself none too brash today, Raymil. I can't suppress this feeling that you've very much given me the benefit of the doubt.'

She laughed, slapped his thigh with the back of her

hand. 'Oh I *do* like the way you're so clever-tongued and greedy, Bramt Hex. You dirty, oily-tongued man! You did all the right things to get into me, which you plainly wanted to do from the first moment you saw me.'

This was not strictly true, but Hex nodded warmly. 'Greedy,' he said. 'You keep calling me greedy.'

'Well, while I won't call you out-and-out-fat, you clearly have much leaner times ahead of you. When I think of it, it's a greediness like my brothers'. A grandly wasteful craving for absolutes. As if glory lay in the power to disregard all things but one – a vow of stupidity that wastes the fruitfulness that life, even in emergency, offers. At least by your last telling of it you helped rather blithely to waste a number of lives. But if I thought you grasped that evil at the time I would not be coupling with you.'

The words were a reminder to Hex. The urgent issue raised its head again – was socketed, and demolished to their mutual acclaim. Thereafter Hex lay, feeling himself slide towards sleep, watching her bind his crutches' caps with fat bandages of sacking. She was saying: 'I'm sorry that your destination – ' Seeing that he dozed, she murmured for herself: ' – is so unlikely.'

16
Hex and Sarf Exchange One Vehicle for Another

The hold of that trim Huffuffian two-wheeler, *The Glide*, was built to take more cargo than it usually carried. This excess stowage accommodated several crab-fighting pens, and now the clamour of the off-duty crew welled from the open hatches. The working crew – deckhands, the stokers for the wheel-furnaces – tended to congregate at the aft half of the ship where, rather rakishly backset, the pilot's cabin crowned the bridge – for here the constantly ongoing casual betting on matters of course and speed, and animal or topographic sightings was centred, the pilot serving quasi-officially as its arbiter.

Hence the quietest lounging places were in the bow and here, this morning, the handiest seat was a big carven box, a vacant bier. It had borne, laid in state, a dead Frispian patriarch whose burial-at-sea had been the *Glide*'s last commission, and his city her last port of call on the northern coast of the vast Isle of Kray. On this bier, then, Bramt Hex sat. His crutches lay by him, their support largely symbolic now, with his ankle a month on the mend. His unbelted notepouch also lay by him, but for some while before he opened it, he gazed rather broodingly over the sea, and at the ship's slender-winged namesakes doing lazy acrobatics above her wake – for the *Glide* was a well-provendered craft, and cast astern abundant garbage.

The scholar's face had grown peevish, and once more a little puffy. Each day he forswore his pattern of morning indolence and a double breakfast, and each forenoon he gorged down redundant crumble and wine – feeding, rather than a real hunger, a nervous gnawing in his heart.

The notepouch that at length he opened was painstakingly double-lined with whorl-skin, all seams thickly gummed. That this uneasy waterproofing was his sole accomplishment in recent weeks was an irony that did not escape him.

For now, just when Yana had gained some substance – some learned testimony, however fragmentary and concise – just now he found his will to cartographic work weakest, most uncertain. He had months of rare impressions to record. The tumultuous raw matter of his recent mishaps had still to be combed through for the threads of geographic and ethnographic continuity it contained. But he had loafed in a lazy anxiety, done three pages of notes in as many weeks. Compulsively, he re-read and dreamed on Banniple's notes – as he was about to do again. Alternately, he mused in quiet misery on all that might befall them, allowing death to supervene and snatch the nearing prize of everlasting life. Sighing, he read again the footnote wherein Ongerlahd, during his extensive (and hair-raising) account of the Museums of Kurl, set forth all references to Yana that were known to him. This copy, in a squarish calligraphy faultlessly clear, was Banniple's gift, for he was carrying a rescript of Ongerlahd's work on Kurl. By now, perusing it, Hex was reading not so much the words as the echoes, the haunting intimations of miracle they woke in his mind.

'Concerning Yana or Yanai. Its locale is too uncertain for even conjectural location in my *North Shore Pantographicon*. I hold with the proverb that scholarship is no substitute for taking ship, and none among the following commentators even claims to have reached the place. Here then is what I have read of the matter.

'Six sources offer substantive remarks about the place. Two of these – Barklap's and the Elder Tine's in his *True Wonders* – are clearly derivative from the account of the

August Pluril, and so we may speak, in strictness, of only four sources.

'These reports, while highly discrepant, exhibit a certain resonance of conception. I guess a common source, some myth prevailing in the neighbourhood of Kurl, whose catacombs are such cornucopia of marvels. The accounts run thus:

'Farrowgag says Yana is a valley eternally mild with "golden weather". Entrants encamping here are seduced to copulation with its trees – made briefly compatible with flesh, and unnaturally beautiful. After, they are fixed forever in the age and state of their hour of rutting. The marvel is not relished by them, for their subsequent longings for those apparitions is also immortal, and forever unfulfilled.

'Kadash the Spiteful (in *Gnome's Index*, one of his more reliable works) calls the place Yanai, and says it is "a vale of damp climate". He holds that travellers who pass the night there are visited by dreams of such intensity they linger forever – ceasing to age but never waking.

'The August Pluril calls the place "the chasm of Yana, inhabited by winged things". Here a mortal will not have the power of flight, but he will have immortality – for while he falls he will not age, and never will he cease to fall, the chasm being bottomless.

'The plethoric Sannak of Tibia, as is usual with him, says least with the longest throat-clearing. All we learn of him is that Yana is a place of undying, reached by a passage "through shoals of the dead".'

Hex re-pouched the parchment, belted it back on. He sat drumming his heels on the bier's hollow sides, his stomach acidic with wine, his mind queasily lurching with the two-wheeler's surge, willing it to greater speed before the intervention of some slight, senseless accident, such as always pops up somehow from the world's seemingly endless repertory of Harm. He decided he would have some more wine.

He went down to his cabin for it, which lay amidships one deck below. En route he passed the starboard wheel. It was a spinning cage of hot metal, and within its steaming blur the giant head of the Gollip that drove it was visible above the gunwale. The beast's perennial exhaustion with its race to cool its feet showed in the slackness of its fang-jammed jaw, and the glaze of its one visible eye. *Pain*, said the black globe, big as Hex's head. *Futile toil. Pain. Death*.

He brought his wine back to the bier and now he lay back, steadying himself against the swell. Behind his closed eyes, he recalled the Frisp's burial. They had glided through a zone whose depth of clarity had made his armskin prickle. Thirty fathoms of lambent green and down there, breaking up through the smoky floor of visibility, were the peaks of drowned hills, big ones by their shadowy spacing. It gave him the sense of flight he'd known in Kabrow's sloop, over the shoals, but over these much darker gulfs it was an ominous flight.

To this the dumped decadent dived – a skinny, pale face above a massy tunic of gold brocade that insured against any serio-comic buoyancy the patriarch might display, to the detriment of solemn sepulchry. The surface caved in under him in a silver boil of bubbles. Shedding this silver, he sank, and with him slowly rained a school of ceremonial brass medallions, inscribed, by Frispish custom, with the man's great possessions and accomplishments.

Settling like dead leaves, they shrank with the gaudy mannikin. Slow and remote, they struck a hilltop. A slow green seethe of impacted silt swallowed them from view.

To fall thus amid the trashy glitter of ambiguous deeds – Hex's sudden pity had included himself. He sat up now to take another swallow, and flinched to find Sarf and Banniple standing near, smiling.

'Black Death! You gave me a jolt! Don't you believe in knocking?' They laughed.

'Maybe wine blocks your ears,' Sarf said.

'Tidings to be jotted in your journal,' Banniple announced. 'On this noontide of your twenty-sixth day out of Score-and-Seven, the pilot makes us less than a week south of Sirril.'

Sirril was the *Glide*'s northernmost port of call on the West Shore, though still fifty leagues south of Kurl. The information felt like a taunt, though he knew Banniple meant none, being himself an industrious journal-keeper.

'I find I keep my notes poorly,' Hex said. 'Perhaps I should just crib from yours again once you've finished the work.'

'Accept my sympathies, Hex. We've all known such doldrums.' The Erkishite blinked. Though he often wore a stunned, visionary look, now Hex thought to see something new – a sad constraint. Hex grunted.

'Surely I'm an ass! I sit around brooding on the length of life, dreading accidents, and doing nothing.'

'You know' – Banniple's eagerness to take this up surprised both his friends – 'I've lately been considering about this idea of immortality, the painful ambiguity of it. To what extent would it entail invulnerability? Leave aside Ongerlahd's sources, who seem to conceive this endless life as linked to some endless bondage or self-loss. Suppose it *is* a free gift, but a mere guarantee against Time, against death by age? Think how painful life then becomes! How much more constant the fear of catastrophe grows when you have immeasurably more to lose from death.' Already his friends had cooled, imperceptibly drawn back. The sub-curate hurried, to have the sadness past. 'I gather you've seen my drift. I won't go on to Yana with you – we'll be parting ways at Kurl.'

For the overland miles from Sirril to Kurl his company would be welcome enough, but it was past Kurl they really craved his help. The vast, volcanic slopes where the museums lay buried offered the only ingress to the interior of a coastline which opposed to the traveller impenetrable swampy vales for a hundred miles both north and south. Inland of the entombed city a route to Yana lay – vaguely attested to by Ongerlahd's charts, though he declined to mark the place itself. It was down this featureless path, neither its strict direction nor its length known, that the pair had wanted his aid – not so much his added sword as his agile, lore-stocked imagination. Hex blew his lips out and shook his head, not really surprised. Still, though he wanted to sound easy, he managed only a stiff smile.

'You're throwing away gems for pebbles. Artworks, texts, die as men do, merely a little slower.'

'Blubber-backs! Blubber-backs! To starboard!' the pilot bawled, raucously seconded by the stokers of the starboard wheel-furnace. The three in the bow looked briefly. A half mile off, two glossy masses snaked through the swell. Already alarmed, the beasts were making, it seemed, for a cluster of rocks perhaps two miles away. The babble swelled up around the pilot house. 'Stokers!' the pilot was barking, 'Full stroke!' The ship trembled with its surge to full power. The three, familiar with this sequence, sought each other's eyes again. Sarf's look of anger surprised both the others.

'You amaze me, Banniple! To weigh the matter and then solemnly choose to be a fool! The more of us, the likelier we reach the place, if it exists. No need to speculate – go and assess the kind of deathlessness obtainable! Because if, with luck, it's a livable kind, why then you can come back to your beloved Kurl, and spelunk in those putrefying, buried aeons till the whole foul anthill falls to dust!'

'Blubber's running!' howled the pilot. 'Burn their feet off to the knees!' This last referred to the Gollips, whose wheels now blazed cherry red, and who yodelled and groaned as they toiled into overdrive. That the Blubbers 'ran' rather than sounded meant that the ship now had a bettable race on. Erstwhile crab-touters swarmed out of the hatches and thronged the gunwales. Running meant that the Blubbler-backs had broken for some rock or islet, for if they could cling to such as these, they could stay deeply submerged for hours, given just a few moments to 'breathe-up' before diving. The goal of this pair was plain, the ship's speed just great enough to put the issue hotly in question. Banniple had to make his answer loud:

'Assess what's offered – that's perfectly right! Doubt of the kind of immortality isn't my reason for splitting from you. Kurl is a prior promise to myself. She is the accomplishment my life has built towards. The life I've lived becomes nothing if I jump now to another aim, however splendid. I'll be sadly missing your help too of course, down where – '

'Amain! She runs amain! Last bets before we close with them – speak up!' The pilot's voice was trumpet-clear. Seen through the cabin window, he seemed a man transported – his eyes two craters made by meteoric impact and still smoking, his huge, scarred knuckles white upon the wheel. His announcement conjured from his clansmates a screeching, booming, hooting, gabbling reply. They mobbed the starboard gunwale, giving the *Glide* a marked list as it surged forth, the pilot cheerfully counter-pitching the wheel, closing remorselessly with the labouring, glossy backed giants.

Now the *Glide* had achieved override. By the time they reached the rocks the Blubber-backs would have the ship too close at heel to breathe up. They would plough on, soon tiring. The betting shifted key as new book was made on the type and degree of injury the overrunning would inflict on the titans at the first pass. Sarf nudged the sub-curate, whose nervous eye lingered on the fugitives.

'Listen. There *is* an absolute good: to crack the game of life. Given only the time to study it all this' – here his handsweep at the ship eloquently implied not only this, but every turbulent idiocy that abundant History had produced – 'becomes controllable. Then you have what is truly meant by Power, and can build the world better than you found it.'

'I'm sorry. The power I'm after is more like that in art, which dies – yes – like a man, but which is also, while it lasts, an ectoplasmic monument commemorating some life's knowledge that it lived. I want more to – I say, isn't that a rock ahead? I wonder if the pilot saw that!'

While the other two were puzzling over what seemed a senseless question – for obviously there was the cluster of rocks just ahead of them – Banniple had gone aft with startling briskness.

'You know, Sarf,' Hex began humorously to chide, 'I didn't realize the enthusiasm you'd developed about Yana. You always act dour enough when I try to bring it – '

'You know, I think there *is* a low reef there, just off the big cluster. Watch in the troughs of the swell.'

Yes. A fanged sparkle of rock, barely glinting between the wavecrests. Even now the Blubber-backs, slightly swerving, skirted it. Unswerving, their keel ploughed after. The pair looked aft. Banniple's head, small, fleecy planet, bobbed utterly a-sea amid the jostle of shaven scalps and brandished arms round the cabin. They looked forward again. Plainly, while their course would skirt the big rocks, it was now dead-aimed to broadside the reef. Unbelievingly, standing quite calm, they watched the unwavering prow surge right across it. Then it seemed that the upthrust hand of a giant shoved the entire ship against the sky. Hex and Sarf tumbled through a long arc, as from a catapult, out of the bow. They sprawled down through the long rush of the empty air. Hex smashed the water, cringing from the fracturing thrust of rock, but meeting none. Empty-lunged at impact he started sinking fast. He wrestled out of his cape, fighting in a hornetswarm of bubbles, the dead Frisp in his mind. The cape's weight fell. He clawed through the ceiling of light, and breathed.

Not far off he heard screams, but the first thing he sighted was a carven, oblong box bobbing towards him, with a pale hand visible clutching its top. The bier.

'Sarf?'

'Yes! It floats well! Grab the other side!' Clinging to this funereal furniture, they watched the *Glide*, not far off. The reef had hoisted her, bucked her up and sideways and dumped her drykeel on to the clustered rocks. Both her wheels were broken open, and the greedy vigour of the two liberated Gollips, from whose champing jaws a dozen broken limbs already jutted, explained why not a single other passenger had so far joined the pair in the water. They hung there in a daze of anguish, until Sarf asked Hex if Gollips could swim.

The box was narrow and rode high. One man might have straddled it. A load or two invariably turned over. To ease their clinging to its slick surface they stuck their shortswords upright in it, and bound the blades with wraps cut from their tunic hems. Thus they could hold one-handed, or one of them lie atop the bier between these makeshift stays, while one took a turn drifting astern.

They had thought themselves to be no more than a day's sail off the West Shore, but as the day grew late, though they paddled doggedly, not even the slightest silhouette relieved the perfect flatness of the horizon. The liquid desert's vastness swallowed all hope. And all that waste, it seemed, had no other life but theirs to show. Once a line of shimfins passed. In the arcing manner of their huge cousins the Blubber-backs, they came near enough for the oddly commiserative expression of their eyes – close-set to their little sharp-toothed snouts – to be readable. In the after-absence, the pair's sense of futility grew almost paralysing. Sunset had laid down a highway of fire before them and they – impotent specks that moved by inches through this endless molten gold – gazed stupefied at that Solar Glory never to be reached by any of the lives it raises to seek it. The dark felt near – they felt it in the waters first. Their legs, prickling with a thought of lurking carnivores, keenly sensed the abyss that hugged them and teemed with appetites.

Never, it seemed to Hex, could two lives have been so good as gone – while not yet strictly dead – as their lives were then. He cleared his throat. In the sky-drowned silence it was a quaintly formal sound.

'You know, Sarf, I've been wondering.'

Silence. Then, flat and unwilling, Sarf's voice came from the bier's other side.

'Wondering what?'

'About poor Banniple's question. What do *you* think? Will we find vulnerable or invulnerable immortality in Yana?'

Silence again. And then, a rusty, slowly rhythmic noise. Sarf was laughing. Hex joined him. They laughed wildly, irresponsibly, in barking, pickled voices. Their laughter populated the air like a scattering of startled glides. The sun was down, and the dark moved in behind them from the east.

17
Kagag Hounderpound and the Shorewitches

Each bound one of his sleeves to his sword and off and on they slept, hanging like dead counterweights from the drifting bier. The sun was two hours high when they fully woke, feeling it starting to bake their salty scalps, while the arms they hung by were ice, lifeless things not their own but curiously attached to them. Their voices were agony to their parched and swollen throats, but then they found little to say. The horizon's circle was flawlessly flat, no smudge of land defacing it.

They paddled. Time, their strength, and the water passed. At least they assumed the water passed. The only thing whose progress was incontestable was the sun in its climb.

'Hex,' Sarf croaked. 'See how shallow it is.'

It was true. Below, through exceptionally clear water, he saw scarcely thirty feet down the black-and-silver of a mussel-crusted plain. They eagerly re-scanned the horizon.

'Nothing,' Sarf said. 'This is a shallow sea in many places, that's all. Not *too* shallow, oh no! There'll be plenty to drown in wherever we collapse.'

Hex summoned strength to speak some encouragement. But his mouth stayed shut, for he noticed that the crusted plain below already lay much shallower. He could now make out upon it the greyish lace of corals, and the movements of large crabs.

He looked dazedly around. Were they drifting faster than they guessed, that the depth-change should be so rapid? But already he had *felt* the answer – felt the water's whole vast fabric faintly grow dense beneath him, thicken and press with the gentle upswelling of something huge.

He gasped, panicked, thrashed to climb the bier, to uproot and retract his footsoles from contact with that dread substrate's rise. He slipped and sank and – trying simultaneously to warn Sarf – breathed in a half a pint of water. As he coughed it up, helplessly clinging to his sword, a soft, enormous voice surrounded them, bathing them in mellow volumes of greeting.

'Poor friends, good morning! Castaways in these deadly waters? How glad I am to have found you in time to help.'

Still coughing, Hex swung round. There, perhaps two shiplengths away, and perhaps five storeys high from chin to brow, was a beautiful pallid face. It was reared from the water at an angle suggesting a man who floats on his back and studies his chest. And indeed, not two fathoms down now, the shell-studded plain exhibited, but half obscured, the symmetries of an heroic musculature. Worms of fear burrowed swiftly up Hex's legs and groped through his stomach.

'Your aid!' Sarf's voice, though a surprising full-throated shout, seemed a piping accident of breeze after the giant's welling resonance. 'We are as you see, great stranger. We must soon die if we are not brought to land.'

The titan smiled. His long, coalblack hair, high cheekbones, tapering jaw and elegantly wide mouth, would have had angelic impact even on a human scale. As it was, their serene force smote the pair like a tidal wave – Hex felt as if he hung in touching distance of the full moon rising from the sea. Mellifluously, the stupendous voice smilingly tolled:

'What ironies the world is woven of! Behold this situation of ours! Look how powerless you are, with your slight frames, to reach even the nearest land before you perish – while I could carry you there so simply, and soon! And then look again! For once there, I would be – for all my might – utterly impotent to climb one step up the littoral shelf! For I am debarred by malicious witches who've got the upper hand of me, you see. And meanwhile your slight selves would be able then to swim and wade – oh how easily – to land! Now if *I* could get ashore I'd work my deliverance from those witches, and doing it would be so easy! Oh double – or is that triple irony? that once ashore I could be as small and feeble as yourselves, and still handily work my own liberation!'

Gently the giant shook his head, causing his hair to boil silkily round his vast shoulders, and the bier to rock. The fullness of this proposition, its coyly rich detail, were stunning, given the scale of their utterance. Swiftly, distinctly, Hex's ear had judged the suasive titan a liar. Yet, a lie so huge, he found, had all the planted firmness, the towering stature, of Truth. He grasped – amazed – that they were being bargained with by this sun-blocking phenomenon. It made him feel that he was himself surreally enlarged.

The giant asked, 'Where are you bound?' resuming in a new key, for now an ineffable irony quivered on his lips as he queried. And almost, Hex found, he could laugh – howl at it himself. He fought to draw a long breath.

'We are bound,' he cried, 'to the bottom of the sea, Great Stranger! This day or the next! As you've just indicated!'

The giant's smile stretched and he faintly sighed, sending a gust of low tide, of dead kelp and reeking fishguts, to roll down across the bier. 'Too true, I'm afraid. But of course, I'm asking where you *wanted* to go.'

'To the Museums of Kurl, and past them.' This – he thought as he spoke – was how lunatics felt, madly discoursing with the rising moon which, they fancied, questioned them. Meanwhile the longer he looked at that lunar visage the more he saw – underpinning its urbane noblesse – a subtle mordancy, a sarcasm dissembled but fundamental to the Titan's nature. The latter displayed gladness at Hex's answer.

'My friends, I must now think us even better-met, considering how disparate our courses might have been. There is a little beach at the foot of the cliffs where my adversaries must be met – and do you know? It lies well on your way to Kurl. It's just south of Sirril, in fact, less than a day's swim upcoast – for me, that is.' He paused. His gigantic calm made that silence tremendous. Hex and Sarf – who now hoisted their heads above the bier to look at one another – were awed to feel their own frail voices awaited by such a silence. Somehow, across the funereal carvings, their eyes traded full acknowledgement of the hand they had been dealt, and Hex was able, in a nod, to tell Sarf they agreed, and bid him speak.

'Great stranger!' Sarf called, and gratefully Hex heard the vigorous timbre of his friend's voice. 'You hint that you might save our lives. Our lives are all we have. We would do much to purchase them. You further hint – astonishingly – that such as we could help you, once ashore. We'd gladly do this if you put us there!'

'Oh, most excellent castaways!' The giant's brio set the bier a-bobbing. 'We must introduce ourselves! I am Kagag Hounderpound.'

'I am Sarf Immlé.'

'I am Bramt Hex.'

'Gentlemen!' Two nods, gracefully apportioned, though the pair must have formed a unitary jot to those great eyes, made the sea shudder them twice more. 'Well-met indeed, sirs. Felicitously met! If you'll forgive the liberty, I'll scoop you up and begin immediately to convey you towards our mutual excarceration. You've no objection?'

'None! Not at all!' they jointly cried, yet felt – both –

only terror at the prospect. Giddily they viewed the pale, colossal hand, an island-sized hydra, slide beneath them. It raised them off the sea in a captured lake the size of a town square. The fingers flexed to let the imprisoned brine drain out. The pair and their bier settled on the broad, whorled hillocks of Kagag's padded palms. The low-tide stench, more haunting than overwhelming, exhaled from the waxen micro-furrows dizzyingly patterning that dermal hollow. Some dozen yards above the swell Hounderpound palmed them, the remote thunder of his legs' slow kick following them as they skimmed at a wave-smashing pace across what now seemed minor wrinkles in the open highway of the sea.

Head inclined, Kagag told them sadly from his briny cushion: 'To starve is like being devoured, but slowly. Look, friends, upon my shameful emaciation – shameful to my tormentors, not to me!' Rolling to his back he lifted high his other arm. Thicker than a big house is high, the dire, massy block-and-tackle of its sinews shone brilliant with corals in the broad noon. 'I am, you see, a peaceful grazer – I browse the multitudinous tiny life that throngs the sun-warmed littoral. My food are the green dust-mote hosts that make pastures of the shallows. But every morning these two witches – a warlock and his stinking dam, blood-sworn against me for my chaste abstention from their mephitic arts – these two chant, every morning, an incantation which bars all that coast to me where I might most profitably feed. They damn me to a creeping inanition, to wearying migrations to glean at large too scant a sustenance.'

Looking to Sarf, Hex caught an almost angry glance from him, one that touchily protested: *and why shouldn't this be true?* But indeed, he'd felt the same. Fearsome and strange though this skin meadow was that they were camped on, it hovered firm and dry, one vital remove above sodden death, and the muddy nibbling of fish in cold darkness. In this, oddly, they felt their pride restored, which had been so sorely bruised by disasters. How restorative – just when Chance had again reduced them to flotsam, bobbing wreckage – to be offered a job! The hostile cosmos had discerned a use in them. They had some weight to pull, some power that could buy their lives. Goals, aims, ethics apart, how tonic that was just in itself!

'Great Hounderpound!' Hex shouted. 'It seems to me these nighthags who torment you, are the most vile and poisonous sort of vermin!'

The fierce, angelic smile this won from Kagag thrilled the mendacious scholar. Truth after all *was* anything that loomed this large, and saved one's life. Even a bloody job seemed right now no more than a just vengeance taken upon their long-term helplessness. These witches – any witches – would surely kill *them* to survive. Inspired, Hex pulled their swords from the bier, sheathed his, and started tumbling – with Sarf's quick-comprehending help – the bier towards the great hand's brink. They shoved, it struck the sea and sped back to their mighty wake.

'Our pledge!' Hex cried. 'You are our vessel, we will be your sword.'

Kagag laughed, a drumroll of mirth. 'Ah friends! How can mere physical scale divide, where there's a kinship of the heart? But now, I swim best when I attend below. We'll talk before you go ashore, near dawn. The day and night are yours for rest. Move as you please, I scarcely feel you.'

Kagag Hounderpound submerged his head, and was thenceforth a mute blur underneath the swell. His forearm alone broke the crests. His cupped hand, like a finger-ribbed aerial boat, sailed them frictionlessly forth with the smoothness of unstoppable mass. Fearing finger-twitches, the pair walked astern across that eerie leathery plaza, and up on to the fat, sternward hump of the thumb's base. Here their view commanded the whole horizon, and the warm winds scouring them proclaimed their membership, dubbed them fellow-traffickers of the glides, who had looked so poignantly exalted from down in the water all those hopeless hours.

Hex looked at his friend. Sarf's eyes shocked him a bit. Renewed life thrilled them, but they also had a cutting edge of truculence, sharp for a glimpse of some reproach.

'Sarf. Listen. When I did what I did for Madam Poon, I forswore canting ethics for a life of heroic opportunism. I was like a child, not knowing what I did. But now I do. And now I know that rakish opportunism doesn't win your fortune. It just barely buys your life, as this world goes.'

Uncannily, Hex found that this was as plainly as he wished to speak, as though the fleshly planet they were camped on might hear through its skin. So he shrugged, and made a rejoicing gesture at the sky, the glides, the breeze. Sarf nodded. Having found accord, he was now willing to show his own misgivings. Pointing to their vessel, he shook his head, eyes grim. Hex nodded in his turn.

They lay back, two creatures restored to the solid world. They reposed their weight and lo, it did not sink. The breeze laved them and very soon, in the hand of the giant who needed them, Hex and Sarf slept.

They first knew of the land's nearness by a raggedness in the rim of the starry bowl ahead of them. Behind them, the horizon's line got faintly silver with the hint of dawn. Then, after a time, when the glacier-slow pallor had begun erasing the eastern stars, the coast took on some hints of mass and feature, and they realized they had drawn quite close to it. Frighteningly, Houderpound's voice welled up from below.

'Prepare to disembark, gentlemen. This rock ahead

should accommodate you while you learn the balance of our pact. I can approach the shore no nearer.'

The rock they jumped down to was broad and white with guano. The giant, turning belly-down, crossed his forearms on a larger reef nearby. The dawn, gathering strength behind his head, made his face hard to see.

'You are upright men, Sarf Immlé, and Bramt Hex. You can't know the chagrin of being forced to skulk, and hire henchmen. Murk, indirection and intrigue are not my way, sirs, for upright I too have always sought to be.'

Oddly, the pair found the mellow boom of the voice somehow diminished here. The surf's wide mumble, though middlingly distant, seemed to nibble its resonance away. His words, here and there, crumbled at the edges into the sound of wind and sea.

Hex cried consolingly, 'The forces of destruction surround all lives, great Kagag! That we can help – '

'How true that is, good human! How well you put it! And if you had cruised the Abyss as I have done, how much more strongly you'd feel it! What an impudence, an insouciance Life is! The universal Rule is Void. Gaping, freezing blackness without feature, without force, without end. Yet here, there, everywhere this buffoon Life staggers, struts, swells and plumps out its plumage, rearing its grotesque elaboration screechingly, shamelessly from the vast environing Nullity! All this, while at every step the slightest tremor shatters it, the merest squeeze annihilates it – '

Hounderpound's head was reared back. He had raised one hand against the silver backlight of the dawn, then sighed. 'Ah, Life! Brave bagatelle!' and chuckled. Replacing chin to hand, he now plunged the other underwater, and seemed to rummage. He brought up, on his forefinger's tip, two black stones that were sandgrains on it, but big as goose eggs to the pair to whom he delicately presented them.

'These must be your weapons. Please tuck them in your belts. You'll find if you throw them hard enough, it won't matter what part of the witches' bodies you strike. More of that anon, but first, gentlemen, as all of us hate to be misjudged, I apologize to you in advance for a little demonstration I must make at this point. Please note your arms.'

The directive was superfluous, for the pair had already dragged back their sleeves with cries of loathing, and begun, helplessly, to scratch themselves. Foul, weeping pustules clustered wherever their nails raked, but they could not desist.

'You sample my one poor compulsion over you,' Hounderpound said. 'I can afflict you with it wherever you may be ashore, on any part of your persons. Do forgive me – ' Already the pair found their skin whole and clean again. ' – but these witches, though loathsome, are on your scale. Ashore, you might feel quite alienated from the needs of one such as I, and might find it easier to neglect the killing of those whose crimes you've never borne the weight of.'

Hex, whose pulses had scarcely ceased racing, shrilled: 'We're in no position to resent this doubt of our honour, Kagag Hounderpound! You are mighty, we are slight! I can only say you'll have no cause to regret engaging us. May I voice one misgiving?'

'By all means!'

'We are not Thaumaturges. Won't our lives be seriously at risk, attacking witches with stones?'

'None, I'm happy to say! No risk! You must heed my prescription closely of course. Here it is then, in sum quite a simple matter. If you swim to this nearest cove you will find a spring to refresh you. Then make your way north – the little spits are easy to overclimb – and several coves upcoast you will find the witches' tenement. A rock stands near it, where you can hide. At sunrise they will come out, and will perform an incantation over the surf. It has three verses. Before these verses are finished, rise and hurl the stones at them. Aim as best you can but remember force is most important. This last thing above all: When they fall, drag them inland on to thoroughly dry sand. Don't let their bodies fall into the sea.'

Shivering in advance, Hex and Sarf lashed their boots to their belts. It was with great loathing they re-entered the sea. The swell, at least, seemed bated, as though just here the titan behind them could cause the sea to hold its breath.

Greedily at last their footsoles greeted the little crescent beach. They squeezed the coarse sand in their fists as lustily as they drank from its stream, and then bathed in it. They wrung out their gear and dressed. A kind of bitter cress grew on the banks, and they found their stomachs held it down with a good grace. Now there was enough light to reach each other's eyes closely. Hex saw that Sarf was ready for the killing, and, knowing this, he realized he was too. Sarf led off, and they climbed the first landspit.

The dawn's fan was saffron now, and subtly gilt the foam-lacquered sand of the next beach. The holes their feet punched out as they crossed it were like script in linearity. Above all else, Hex found, this killing felt like a passport for re-entry of the world – a vengeful demonstration of identity and mission here at the gates of a land that was sure to prove as dangerous and apt to cast them down as other lands had been.

'In order to get back in the game, one antes up a bit of blood,' he said aloud. Sarf shrugged, attacking the next landspit without glancing back. Hex understood his friend's impassive stride – he felt a touch of trance himself, for amazement at the stupendous being who had taken them in hand still buoyed them, as the hand itself had done. Evil both men felt he was, but, by sheer presence he diminished the stature of any opposing beings the pair could imagine. After a second empty beach they topped a further landspit, and ducked back, their goal before them.

At the beach's centre, where the sand met the grassy bluffs that walled it, stood a hut, an ill-joined box of driftwood fragments. Beyond this were drying-racks hung with rags of netting, and, keel-up on the sand, a punt of the same miscellaneous wood as the hut, and as ill carpentered. About halfway between the hut and the avengers' covert stood the rock that Hounderpound described. The pilgrims leapt off the landspit and made for the rock. The rag that draped the hut's door shuddered. They hit the sand, but it had been the breeze. They scuttled ahead to cover.

Peeping from here they saw fish skeletons littering the sand before the hut. A stench, too, hung round the hovel. It was ranker than Hounderpound's had been and its persistence, in the presence of the onshore wind, was uncanny. The east was now a multiple arch of light, each concentric curve a gradient of gold. A flicker of movement overhead made Hex's heart thump.

It was a river of glides, a hundred feet above, flowing along the rim of the bluffs on the updraught they made. The birds hung cruciform, perfectly synchronized, the stream of them endless. Their beauty, the clarity and directness of their movement through time, gave Hex a pang, made him feel deep-sunk in the flounderings and muttering pauses of men. There was a crisp sound that Hex knew was a foot treading dried fishbones. Low to the sand, the pair looked out from either side of the rock.

It seemed to be the witch who came out first, for the ape-jawed, bowlegged hulk had dugs. That it was the warlock became clear when his whitehaired spouse, with far bulkier paps, followed. Loin-wraps they had, no other clothes. With an idle, shambling disunion they moved towards the surf and as they did this the torch of the sun's rim kindled on the horizon. Hex pulled Hounderpound's stone from his belt. At their nearest pass he noted that the witches' lower canines were so pronounced, they made little dents in their upper lips.

For a moment they were simply an old couple pottering among the seawrack. The witch wet her feet, and stood scratching her ribs and staring at the particle of new sun. The warlock bent with a grunt and picked up a mussel shell. Holding this out towards the sun, he tilted it. A dash of water fell from it, into the inrushing surf. The old woman spat into the same wave, and then cried out in a voice that was rough but precise, like a coarse saw sinking into soft wood, stroke by decisive stroke:

> 'Curse you, Kagag Hounderpound!
> We damn and ban you from this ground!
>
> On ruin, Hounderpound, you gloat,
> And under swarming shipwrecks float
> to see the dead rain dreaming down;
> The storm-broke hull
> Soon crowns your skull;
> In your museums of the drowned
> Long galleries of trophies bloat.'

And Hex felt them like sawstrokes, cutting the sinews of resolve, for the indictment resonated with his own unarticulated judgement of the giant. But how could he dare do other than serve the monster? Did Sarf feel this? The woman spat again, as the warlock tilted a second libation from the shell, though he had not bent to fill it. Again she confronted the growing sun, now a thick bar of fire, a melting ingot.

> 'Curse you, Kagag Hounderpound!
> We damn and ban you from this ground!

For in the wrestling sea and storm
All crafts or lives escaping harm –
All such survivors wake your hate!
All ardent wills
Whose ships and skills,
Whose dwarfish toils outswim their fate,
These gall you, these unbroken forms!'

Hex clutched Hounderpound's stone as though it were his sole handhold on this shore. What were they themselves, he and Sarf, if not flung stones – found and saved by the giant to be hurled against his enemies? And, powerless things that they were, they should fly obediently to their targets, for granting at length they found their immortality, what would it be but infinite dolour, poxed by the titan's revenge? He dared not look round at Sarf, and yet he waited because he was hoping – he realized – to hear his friend leap up, and see his stone fly, and then he would be freed to do the same. Already the hag intoned the third verse of her malediction.

'Curse you, Kagag Hounderpound!
We damn and ban you from this ground!

Withhold your huge, unmaking hand!
This patiently wave-hammered sand –
This smithied gold – won't feel your touch.
No, nothing that breathes
Outside the seas
Will strangle in your envy's clutch,
Nor shall your claws unshape this land!'

While the indictment rang, Hex could not cease to listen and receive it, and at the same time his fear set his rage a-boil at the witch, her paralysing of his body with the sound of truth. Finding he had let her speak, had let pass the time the giant had bid them strike, his terror galled him, goaded him to his feet. His arm cocked back to throw, and just then the last quatrain's meaning caught up with them. In a kind of perfect perplexity between attack and fraternity, Hex's hand subverted its own cast – balked and flung awry – almost straight up.

But, as if alive and craving its target, the stone swooped impossibly, its swerve so severe it actually struck the shoulder of the hag, even as Sarf's stone, thrown with more purpose, whirled out and jarred off the warlock's head. The witches fell as though abruptly legless. They thrashed where they lay with a horrible, helpless energy. The old man spanked the sand with chest and loins, his eyes sand-blind, his mouth a gasping hole, his arms appearing welded to his sides. His wife had fallen closer to the water. She writhed in the same fluid, armless way, her hip and flank wet with foam. Her face strained towards the sea as if she would drink it. She seemed stronger, her eyes more brightly desperate than her mate's. And then, overwhelmingly, Hex felt with her, wanting only one thing – that she reach the sea.

He launched too suddenly, lurched to a fall near her feet, which he shoved as he went down. Rising, he found Sarf beside him now, and they staggeringly hustled her out into the surf up to their hips. She had grown heavier, her thrashing more powerful and rhythmic. The wave receded, and the foam as it drained off her was dissolving her hair, and eroding her shoulders. Galvanized, they dropped her – a silver streamlined shimfin now bucking forward into the resurgent surf, and out to swimming depth on its recoil.

Uprooting their feet from the sea's tangle, they dashed to the warlock. The piscine force of his floundering had enfeebled shockingly. The sand clotted on him, caking him like grave-loam as they hoisted him. Offshore the metamorphosed hag's silver muzzle, flanked by the two huge, knowing opals of her eyes, broke surface and cried out to them, the grainy fluteburst like melancholy itself above the breakers' noise. They charged the surf with the he-witch to ram him home with one grand thrust.

He went under like a stone, the sand smoking off him. As the suds sped past their middles they watched him through the clearing water. There was no dissolution of his form. His head rose weakly to look down through the water. Shakily, his hands began to drag them there, strengthless crablike hands laboriously climbing towards the abyss. The surf dragged out again and Hex and Sarf, panicked, fought beachward.

For the shimfin had erupted much nearer, and hung watching them. She seemed, so tapered and compact, a single, silver muscle, an ancient, perfect thing taut and strike-ready with their punishment. But impassively she looked them ashore, and then dived towards her mate. Neither reappeared.

Retreating to mid-beach, the pilgrims stood. The cove's new and terrible emptiness held them like a detaining guard. An appalling beauty flooded this empty stage. The sun was up, and the sand glowed like an infant's skin. The bluffs, furred with varied grasses, burned sweet-green, ochre and a smoky silver. Still rivering past their crests, the glides shed their benediction of silence on the ocean's patient lamentation. Hex drew back his sleeves and viewed his arms. With cautious hope, he quoted:

'"Nothing that breathes/Outside the seas . . ." Could she be wrong here, and still have the power to hold the giant offshore? I think he would have stricken us by now if he truly could.'

'Why did you throw?' Sarf's tone was almost grieved.

'I didn't grasp the sense in time. You?'

'I let your cast trigger mine. I was too unwilling to begin.'

'Do you think he will live?'

Sarf shook his head, but not in answer. A faint, sickening tension had entered the air. The surf, they realized, had ceased to come in. They saw that the waters lay in jumbled, retreating ridges that ponderously recoiled en masse from the shore. The travellers sprinted towards the bluffs.

The most creviced and gently pitched of these rose behind the hut. Here they flung themselves on to the bluffs' knees, and began to climb. Hex was hindmost. As he gained six, twelve, twenty feet of elevation, he saw the ocean, like the gathered-up skirts of an immense mantle, pull twenty, forty, sixty yards back from the beach, leaving rags of foam on the weedy, gutslick floor. Twenty-five, thirty feet up. Something was wrong with the horizon, too. After a heartbeat, Hex knew what it was: the sun was again half-sunk below it. Thirty-five, forty feet up, nails splitting, mashed knees seizing purchase when soles or fingers slipped. Too far to climb – oh, much too far!

For now, front concave, the skyblotting wave moved forward with titanic pomp, and now with his eyes too he clawed at the slope. He seized the earth in mad, wholesale embraces, fighting to heap space beneath himself. Fifty, fifty-five feet, sixty. . . . The huge tactile aura crushing against his back became a sound, a hiss. He saw the tops of the bluffs still far above, the rim of their grave. The hiss became a vast, velvety rumble, and then he was exploded at the sky.

He was a wheeling, blind nothing ascending, a jot of foam in a geyser. A touch to the rockface would erase a limb, but lacking the touch, he was immaterial, disengaged, and had long instants to visualize his back-fall, a hundred feet back down, to be milled between the ocean and the earth. Praying, as the upsurge slowed, he twisted in the cliff's remembered direction. The climb slowed, reached its peak, that instant's stasis. Hex clutched for earth, and hugged a sudden massy knob that miraculously greeted this grope. His fingers sank deep into the matted roots of grass. Flat as a starfish his middle pressed harsh granite, and he fought to shed the wave's retreat, ton by ton. The pressure wrung soul and sense from him. But then, gasping, he lay in the light again. He was at the bluffs' crest.

Sarf, dropped farther inland, was already afoot, and shouting:

'It's Hounderpound! Run!'

Half a mile offshore the giant stood visible to the waist. His barnacled shoulders flashed fanglike in the sun as he bellowed wordlessly, shaking his fist at the shore. Then he struck the water and a wave as high as his own chest sprang up to the limits of vision in either direction and grimly rolled towards the land. But Hex too was up now, broad meadows stretched before them, and they knew that this wave they could outrun.

18
Stilth

Kneeling in moonshadow, Bramt Hex worked up a gob of spit, and with his forefinger rubbed it into the latch and rusty hinges of the shed door. Clustered at the farm compound's farthest corner, the hounds already bayed where Sarf, skulking in an outer ravine, taunted them with hisses and flung stones. Soon the farmhouse door would open; right now, Hex got the door of the chuck-chuck shed open without a sound.

Through the acrid dark within he moved along close to the wall, where floorboards were most mute and firm. At the rack of perches where the sleeping fowl drooped, he paused to gloat an instant over this deftness he and Sarf had gained in recent weeks, like the great Tricksters of legend. He smiled to think this, and at the same time fancied the thought.

With a single pulse of speed – it must surprise even himself to be perfectly smooth – he snatched a chuckchuck from its perch. The birds slept with their stemlike necks looped backward, heads tucked under wingtops, and as he plucked up this one he wrenched the neck into a tighter circle, breaking it. He stifled its feathery, hammering throes against his chest, and hooked its neck through his belt. Then he snatched and killed its neighbour. Securing this, he crept back to the door. Still the spell of legendary figures seemed to lie on this thieving, so timed-to-the-whisker was it. For commotion now spilled out of the farmhouse, and sleep-blurred shouts moved towards the dogs. Hex grasped the door's handle – and froze.

Repeated midnight thieveries had given him faith in the slightest crawlings of his skin. And now some infrasensory goad told him, with a pang, that someone stood just outside the door. Its panels showed him a dark outline that featurelessly faced him. He brought his sword out, not otherwise moving. Was he going mad, waiting here past the critical point when nothing stopped his exit? Sarf would have already retreated up his ravine. Outside the door, a man cleared his throat.

That was all. Perhaps a breath was drawn for speech. If so, the would-be speaker changed his mind. There was one faint footstep, clearly part of a retreating series, and no more. Now doubly afraid he had hallucinated, and dreading that the hands would be thinking to check the shed by now, he opened the door. Outside, only the fences' silhouettes, shadowed on the bone-pale dust. He ran to the fence and heaved himself over near the cornerpost. A cone-shaped object capped the post – he had not seen it going in.

Indeed, it was a cap. Of leather, conic save that its apex was a limp knob, not a point. Not pausing to wonder at the act, he snagged it and pulled it on as he ran for the shadows beyond the farm. The perfect fit of it gave him a thrill of pleasure even as he dodged and hunkered. Under it his very thoughts almost seemed clearer, distincter – in its envelope – to his inner ear.

Two days later, at sunrise, they gnawed and sucked bare the last of those pilfered chuckchucks' bones. When they had washed their hands and faces in the dew-charged grass, Hex unbelted his pouch, whose contents had survived the shipwreck no more than damp at the edges. Sarf laughed.

'Really Hex! It's right there after all, plain enough, isn't it?' He meant Kurl. The grassy coastal hills they had followed so long, and now camped in, ended perhaps twenty miles north. Hex looked across them, their green bulge intermitted by hollows, their snaky shoreline lace-trimmed from the sea's froth. Then they ended – the shore became a straight edge and the terrain a vast flatness blackly sloping to the water: the ancient lavaflow of Kurl. Hex nodded, but pulled out Banniple's rescript of Ongerlahd anyway. The gentle sub-curate had traced on its reverse the cartographer's scarcely more than conjectural sketch of Kurl. It was the terrain inland of Kurl, where names alone hung, unattached to any graphics, that Hex wanted to brood over again.

'I said it yesterday, and today I feel even surer, Sarf,' he announced. 'Banniple once had an instructor comment on this map, and his impression – I think – was that Yana actually lay well *south* of Kurl, and it was only because of the Borborg you had to go through Kurl at all.'

'What help is that? I don't want to go through Kurl either, but I'll do it sooner than go path-hunting in that swamp.'

'"Unlovely truth, hence hag!" as the poet said. We should go, I guess? It looks like we'll be there by dark.'

They broke up and buried their exiguous fire in the event incensed rustics pursued them. In moments they were on the road, a foot-track, really, though well worn for so sparsely populated a region. The breeze now blew offshore, and brought them, as if it had for weeks, the stench of the great Borborg Marsh, which lay just inland of this range of hills, and stretched unbroken a hundred leagues both north and south. Kurl was one of the region's few portals of easy penetration inland. The same volcanic holocaust that had buried Kurl had bridged the Borborg. The mountains had shed their molten stone to both sides, and while eastward it had sealed the great city a mile deep and sizzled into the ocean, to the west it had cauterized and paved miles of the bog. As if remembering that incendiary day, the rising sun now minutely pricked out a glassy dazzle from those dark igneous slopes.

'Think of the stench and steam!' Hex said. 'I mean when – '

'Wait! Stop! You two, there!'

They turned, grasping their swordhilts. They saw a gaunt, grey man gee-ing his mount – a crop-eared azle – towards them. Flight seemed pointless. They saw no weapons on him, nor could they outrun the azle if he lashed it on. He ambled on, though, and they watched him come. His profuse silver muttonchops revealed only the hedged-in essentials of a face: bright black-eyes – not quite in phase – which crooked brows gave a sharp-peaked look. These lurked close to a high-ridged, drooping nose that overhung a narrow mouth.

'You, my friend,' he told Hex as he came up, 'have my cap on your head. It's been mine these hundred years and more, and is mine now. You'll have to give it back to me.'

It was disorienting to return the stranger's strabismal gaze. When Hex focused on one eye, the face looked mordantly amused; but shifting focus, he found it more dazed and bilious, a vindictive codger's. His voice fit neither of these faces, being cool and easy, and firm as a younger man's. As soon as the man had got near, Hex had sensed power in him, knowledge in abeyance. He bowed.

'Sir, I won't deny this *could* be yours, for, frankly, I found it. But can I be *sure* it's yours?' With a flourish he doffed and examined it. In shade and wear it matched with the worn leather of the man's jerkin and breeches. 'Be so good as to describe where you left it last.' Hex felt his conclusion ring a little lame. The man smiled affably.

'I'm sorry. I was professionally engaged, and my oaths forbid discussion of my work. You see, you must simply believe me. The cap is no mere adornment. It is my witguard. I must pass through Kurl soon. It is essential that I be at my very sharpest if I am to survive. Kindly return me my property.'

Looking to his friend, Hex could see that Sarf – to whom he'd detailed the cap's odd provenance – had registered a sequence of doubts much like his own. The man had practically described himself as a possible guide through Kurl, and he must, by the ploy of the cap, have been following them for at least three days. This close fit of his to their aims smelled of a trap. Hex struggled to remember if they had told Kagag Hounderpound that they were going to or through Kurl. He and Sarf had long discussed the only real danger from Hounderpound: human agents, enlisted for shorework as they had been. Hex bowed once more.

'Your honesty is plainly printed in your face, sir, and I'll ask no further text to prove you true. Are you perhaps a farmer, sir?' Never thinking that he was, Hex waited. Receiving the hat, the stranger shook his head.

'No, friend. My name is Stilth. I'm a traveller. Do you know a curious thing? I have an idea about the two of you. Not far back, I met a giant whose nodding acquaintance I am, one Kagag Hounderpound. Spoke to him a bit – he offshore, I on, of course. A bad fellow, but I'll trade amenities with anyone on civil terms.' He donned the cap. It completed him, sat like a crowning insolence atop his now sarcastic hatchet face. 'Kagag was gnashing his teeth, in a fury. A gale was blowing and it seemed to suit his mood. The breaking waves leapt round him, like a hunting-pack entreating the master to loose them.' His voice trailed off. His face, senile again, wore a look of pleasant, fuddled reminiscence.

The pilgrims traded a second look, granting there was some reassurance in Stilth himself bringing up the titan.

'You didn't finish, good Stilth,' Sarf prompted. 'I, by the way, am Sarf Immlé. This is Bramt Hex. What did the giant say?'

'Why just so, then! You're the two he spoke of! He said you'd broken a contract, and owed him your lives. Now there's a nasty matter. Neither of you should go sailing for a while. In fact, I would think twice about taking a swim.'

'Well, neither of us craves a swim, nor will we, I think, for quite some time.'

They had all eased into a northward stroll now. The pilgrims wanted Stilth to say more, but said nothing of it. The old man gee-d in the azle to their pace, and rode wordless and calm, occasionally snuffing the early air with appreciation, seemingly unperturbed by the whiffs of swamp.

At last Sarf prompted: 'You said you are passing through Kurl. Where are you headed beyond it?'

'Nowhere at all. I am going to the head of the Old Highway, and from there, I am returning south. I'm not going to Kurl for *its* sake, you see. I go to the Old Highway and home again – it's a penance I perform every third lustrum. I offended a certain lady of considerable powers, you see. I go through Kurl only because the Old Highway begins in the mountains above it.'

'What an interesting life you must lead,' Hex cried convivially. 'What is it you do on your travels?'

'Come, gentlemen,' Stilth said promptly. 'You shouldn't pry. Am I asking you endless questions about yourselves?'

After this, they asked him only about Kurl, wherein too they could somewhat test him, having Banniple's stories to compare his to. On this topic he was genially prolix. His tale rang more than true – it dauntingly fleshed out the gentle Erkishite's sketch of the dangers there. Meanwhile something in the way Stilth spoke, his occasional laugh as he laid out his facts, fed the pair's trust of the man. At length he paused to give them his azle's bridle while he went into the high grass to relieve himself. The friends found that a conference needed little time.

'An agent of Hounderpound wouldn't say that anything was none of our business,' Sarf pointed out. 'More likely he'd have something plausible cooked up.'

When Stilth resumed his mount, he resumed his story. The Dynasties of Kurl, throughout the millennium of their naval empire, had exercised a broadly tolerant rule over their client states and cities, while showing a remarkably consistent preoccupation with the rarest fruits of culture. The inevitable harvest of artworks and libraries that accompanies the military establishment of empire was but a nucleus which all the dynasts, through the centuries when their keels and coinage were the lifeblood of a fourth the known world, augumented in their turn. And, inevitably, a tolerant capital which is the repository of such materials becomes the cynosure of the greatest talents throughout its territories. And most who came there to study stayed to enrich the mountain-flanked mecca's stores.

Kurl had no decline; she died a sudden death. One summer a scholarly coalition from one of her academies sank a new pit high in the hills of what was sometimes called the City of Galleries. This was the foundation for the ill-starred Last Incubarium. It was not meant to be the last, certainly – merely the latest of a number of ectoplasmic libraries where thaumaturges might – at their own risk, of course – study incarcerated specimens of almost any species in the vast ghost-taxonomy still known in those days. Kurl's architects had for centuries extended new building underground as well as overground. The mountains at Kurl's back, which cradled her against the sea, wore as many of the capital's splendid structures within their bowels as upon their flanks. The pit for the Last Incubarium sank only one level farther towards the mountain's roots, but struck a living nerve, a vein of lava.

The Kurl Range fractured through a mile of its length. The empire-ending avalanche of magma took only a day to reach the sea, searing away all life and structure on the highest levels of the megalopolis, but cooling so quickly it sealed in deep, undamaged layers of the city. When that vast gout of cthonic vomitus reached the sea – when the surf, along a seventeen-mile front, froze the skirts of the boiling rock – the Museums of Kurl, the City of Galleries, began their new era as the Mines of Kurl.

The survivors organized to repossess their capital, but the factionalisms between governmental agencies flared into life amidst these desperate remnants. Emigration, civic violence, and foreign raids decimated these survivors. The vestigial population quickly developed a rudimentary, parasitic society which lived by selling the licence to plunder the mother-city's immense corpse – which men of all nations flocked to do – as well as by preying on those who refused to pay their extortionate fees, and sought to plunder Kurl by stealth.

These bandit heirs of Kurl's greatness, organized into the Tax Squads, were one of the major dangers of the place. They made the right to spelunk, or 'mine', so expensive as practically to compel even the affluent to become 'sneaks'. Yet those who did pay, should they bring up anything of unusual value, were as sure to be killed and robbed by the Tax Squads as was any sneak who got caught.

That the Squads should do little direct spelunking themselves, and prefer to fish in this way for the buried goods with the lives of foreigners, ought to give pause to the delvers' greed, but the place so thronged with venturers, licensed and sneak, that no one, Stilth observed, seemed to give it much thought. Indeed, the Squads knew some fragments of the buried maze, which was to say more than most save thaumaturges, and they knew just enough to grasp that the thronging predators in those catacombs – their restless movement and explosive, bloody interactions – rendered impossible any trustworthy map of dangers down below.

Deep in the galleries, vaults, shafts, and chambers of that stupendous inhumation a host of entities had taken up residence. These included men, as many of the temples and libraries still offered ideological centres around which troglodyte cultists and enthusiasts clustered, guarding their deep shrines from neighbours, human and otherwise. Mindless hungry things abounded: Torks, Albino crushers, shaggy Spidurbbs. And also hungry things with excellent minds, among them Ghuls and Broad-jawed vampires (far more intelligent than their chinless hill-cousins). As if this did not suffice, there were yet other denizens, the ones, perhaps, most in harmony with the mosaic tiles and sculpted symmetries of the sunken hive. These were loosely called 'animate artifacts', entities that were immortally, or at least indefinitely, about the business for which their long-dead creators had fashioned them.

'I can hope,' Stilth said by way of conclusion, 'that you, my friends, aren't would-be miners. You have no gear for spelunking, nor conveyance for anything you might bring up. Put my mind at ease, and tell me you are not.'

'We're not,' Sarf said. 'We're passing through to the Old Highway, for I take it that's the inland road from the pass above Kurl?'

Stilth, incongruously with his stated concern, had plucked a little clay flute from his belt and was extorting a nimble, pleasing little squawk from it. He nodded, finishing the air before he answered: 'I rejoice. Merely crossing the slopes is extremely dangerous, but nothing to what you face below. And of course, on the surface you'll have my guidance, and therefore an excellent chance of survival.'

'You are very generous,' Hex said. Stilth shrugged, fluting again. Then he stopped, as with inspiration.

'Let's have some wine and crumble. Find us a cushiony spot on that bluff. I'll unpack the goods.'

The pair lounged in the springy, milky grass, sweet-smelling past the swampstink's erasure. The hilly coast lay by the sea like bathers' limbs sprawled in careless sensuality. Thighs, torsos, jutting knees of this milky golden green, and the whole calm orgy of them tufted with the glossier greens of thickets, groves, and dales. Beyond this, looking much bigger now, was the bright tilted plain of the lavafield, above which fragmented images from Stilth's account seemed almost still to hang like slow-dispersing mists.

'He's flatly challenging us to trust him, Sarf.'

'He's certainly let us know he won't explain himself.'

'So . . .'

'So let's ask bluntly why he's helping us, see how his answer sounds, or evasion.'

'And if it's another evasion? What I don't like is that it would be easy for a malefactor to know that no explanation's more convincing than many.'

Stilth, having hobbled his azle, set the wine and loaf on the grass, and sat with them. Speechless guzzling followed. The wine jumped in a glittery arc from the squeezed bag into their throats. Sighing mightily, Hex said: 'Bless you, Stilth, for this refreshment! Why are you helping us? Why are you going to guide us? The questions aren't courtesies – we have to know, you see. For you *could* – ' Hex tried a suave, discounting smile ' – be an agent of Hounderpound, and mean to lead us to harm, heh-heh.'

Stilth, throughout the last of this, was wringing dry the

wineskin into his bobbing throat. Smacking his lips, he dropped the deflated bottle on the grass.

'How amiably insulting you are, Bramt Hex! It's quite disarming, really, your flagrancy. *You* gentlemen *did* have a business agreement with that loathsome enormity. *You*, I believe, even killed for him! Yet *you* ask *me* – I, who've never lost a chance to do that monster secret harm – if *I'm* Hounderpound's agent. Drink! I must toast your effrontery.' Hex caught the wineskin – now, somehow, fat and wobbly full – and dazedly drank.

'Listen,' Stilth said as Sarf took his draught, 'are you two disbelievers in coincidence? Far-travelled as you look to be, can you not have met with it? I will tell you one thing more on this matter, and then you may do as you like. Had you not half-undone your commission for Kagag, you would have been involved in a far more melancholy coincidence, for, assuming I had learned of your act, I would have seen you dead three days ago.'

The old man's asynchronous eyes gave two different inflections of mirth to this avowal – one foolish, the other carnivorously bright. Hex bowed ironic acknowledgement. Nothing had been proven, but in some way this threat of death stilled his distrust, and made its questionings academic.

'I can only say, Stilth, that I'm glad of your aid – Sarf? – and that we are lucky to have a guide if all you say of Kurl is true.'

19
The Ghellim Visits the Ghul

At sunset they sat on a deep-grassed hill at the lavaflow's border, and gazed across Kurl. For almost twenty miles, broad slopes joined the sea with the mile-high mountain crests that rose perhaps four leagues inshore. Here was no Slimshur. Here was ragged-toothed rock whose shape recalled its once-liquid state. From between the fingers of the fractured peaks, it poured in gnarled currents, great ropy tendons of magma that fanned towards flatness near the shore, but whose upper reaches were seamed by deep rifts and glens and sulci. Now before the westering sun, the shadows of the peaks marched oceanward, miming the ancient disaster. Thus dimmed, the higher slopes began to show beacons and torchlight here and there, sketching a rather sparser bristle of structural detail than that the trio saw more nearly, down on the sun-flooded shore. Here, some of what they saw – parapets, minareted towers, broken polygonal steeples, all half-melted by millennia of rain – were clearly protrusions of Kurl's buried architecture. Other forms – blocky huts and houses of weathered wood – were as plainly the stations of the Tax Squads. Stilth fluted a mournful little meander as they watched.

'Look,' said Sarf. 'I can see someone going down.' Something crawled into a broken cupola, looking like an ant toiling its way into a fractured eggshell. Three more ants followed, linked at the waists by a just-visible, vanishingly-fine filament.

'Poor fools,' Stilth paused to say.

'For any particular reason, beyond spelunking at all?' Hex asked.

'Well, first of course, they've paid the Squads, since they're working in broad daylight. As I've indicated, to do this is simply to alert, formally, an added set of predators to your presence here. But secondly, more cogently, they're fools for going down through any portal near the shore.'

'Yet the protrusions, the structural adits, look much thicker there.'

'Of course! The lava's shallower there. The Kurlites built large, monumentally. A lot of those things stood intact against the lighter flux here. Whole neighbourhoods – street level and deeper – have been tunnelled clear here. These shallow mazes are – ah! – so thickly nuggeted with repositories, archivia still unexhumed, though hidden by mere inches of stone, and easy to crack for someone with tools and time enough. But just there – it's the *time*, you see. Indwelling predators ambush these zones so thickly that you may rest assured: those miners you saw will be on street level in ten minutes, and in something's jaws – or worse – in twenty. Upslope in the deeper tunnellings, many accesses go unwatched, if you know to find them. In short, spelunkers who mean to *find* something, and are determined to stay alive more than an hour, must use wise indirection, and prepare to spend days getting down and in.'

Again Stilth fluted. The stubby-pipe – pleasingly coarse, flatulent in a friendly, low-comic way – rendered a jolly little jump-up very much in the southern mode. For an instant, Hex closed his eyes, and thought he might be in a Glorak tavern, down by the Academy quarter. He might just be waking up from a light beer-doze, coming out of a dream and back home to his vinous, lazy, loudly merry schoolmates, surrounding him in full carouse. The truth he reopened his eyes on, the wide, sighing vista of wave-lathered stone and darkening lavaseams, took on an edge of sadness. What a satanically intricate universe it was, a world away from youth's ardent, disordered rallyings under the sheltering banners of ideals.

The all-but-sunk sun tossed over the mountains' fanged crests a terminal flood of gold that fell far out to sea. Gently it sizzled there on the whitecaps the rising onshore winds had kindled. All in mountain shadow now, the slopes of Kurl were quietly winking alive. Far upshore, halfway to vision's limit, the lanterns of the harbour works sparked serially on, pricking out the lines of piers and docking floats. To these, dark ships nosed thick as gnats. The clustered craft seemed the more poignantly doomed in that, Kurl's natural harbour having been buried, this one was a thing of wood and buoys, and clung by cables, an appendage to the fire-sealed shore.

'Stilth,' he asked. 'What places lie along the Old Highway? Just what *is* inland of Kurl? Do you know?'

'Well, let's see. First, as I recall, are the Woods of Amberdowndown. Wodeling is the major city there. A civil place, but glum. Nice enough I suppose if you don't like sunshine. After that, the Sparg Flats. Detestable vegetable! And the highway, remember, is long unrepaired. Even when I last passed there – is it thirty years already? – there was plenty of sparg to be hacked through right in the roadway. You've heard of sparg? "Mouthed bramble"? I hated the sucking of it worse than the stabbing of it, I'll tell you! After that it gets hilly. The ground starts rising towards the Demonlace Mountains. How far inland are you going, anyway?'

Nonchalantly Hex picked up the wineskin – still full, though they had drained it all day. 'To a place called Yana.' He drank, awaiting reaction. Hearing nothing, he looked up to see Stilth staring at him. His look was calm – a shade amazed at one focus, sardonic at the other, but unperturbed. Still his silence, Hex decided, showed he was impressed. Gradually, the old man smiled.

'Perhaps, oh excellent Bramt Hex, your information is

confused. You seem to think that Yana lies along the Old Highway.'

'It doesn't? You've heard of it? It exists?'

Sarf almost laughed wth Stilth, but he craved the same answers. Stilth bowed slightly: 'I've heard of it. I presume it exists. It does not lie on the Great Highway.'

'We heard it lay beyond Kurl, inland . . .'

'It does lie *beyond* Kurl, oh yes. But its portal is *in* Kurl. Deep in Kurl.'

There was a long silence. Sarf touched the old man's shoulder. A strange gesture, Hex thought, in that tight-tempered, inward man.

'What do you know, Stilth? Is it real? Is endless life obtained there? Not some wizardly bondage, but endless life with freedom?'

A kind of crazed tenderness almost aligned the centrifugal planets of Stilth's eyes. 'I've never gone through the portal, Sarf Immlé. I can say nothing for or against your wish to do so. That gamble must be yours. Some few things about *getting* there I do know.'

'Will you help us get there?' Hex hadn't weighed the question, though he was suspicious of the man. Slowly the old man nodded his head, turning his flute round and round in his fingers.

'I don't know. Primarily, I don't know that we'll get that far alive. This wouldn't be worth anything as a pilgrimage for me if there weren't always a real risk, you see. And the portal lies quite deep in the peak-wards reaches of the slopes. The added risk of such a long descent is something I'll have to think about. I suppose' – here he sighed – 'that I will direct you the way, whether or not I guide you myself.'

Full dark was very speedily on them – or perhaps it was just that the two friends were stunned. Kurl had been a nest of dangers they were to skirt – en route to other dangers, surely, but vague ones. Now, all they had heard of Kurl – had gladly glimpsed at one remove, as not *their* problem – loomed dead ahead, their own next step. The now-black slopes were thickly constellated by the smutty orange firebaskets of Tax stations, and slim chains of torches that marked established pathways over the glittery steeps. Stilth rose, nudged to its feet the azle, which lay snoring in the grass. Cinching the saddle, he said over his shoulder: 'Look for small lights moving – just glimmers, some of them – hooded lanterns, globes of foxfire, the like.'

'Yes,' Sarf said. 'Everywhere. Full-size torches too, groups of half a dozen here and there.'

'Those are the Squads, and a few licensed fools. Though the Squads sneak offtrail too without lights. Once the moon's up only the most reckless, or powerful, will use any lights at all. There are far too many things, right out on the surface, which delight to be informed of human presence. So. Are you ready, gentlemen? A single caution. Do only what I tell you. There may be occasions when flight will strongly recommend itself to you, and yet not in fact be called for. Indulge an old man then' – a smiling bow here – 'and heed him strictly.'

They skidded softly down the loamy bluffs that terminated the hills. Shortly, they were marching across the skirt of that starry volcanic mantle. Their steps grew audible, made a faint, frosty crunch on the ancient slag, the lava, a bizarre, contorted enemy. Its largest quietest paths were milky threads of flatness that the eye could follow a mile off in starlight alone. The web-fine skulkers' paths, ducking through glens and shadowed seams, threatened differently: their less-trod stone snagged and gnawed at bootsoles, making Hex and Sarf stumble repeatedly. However, the azle – for Stilth sat so nonchalantly it seemed the beast steered – went amblingly, easily slantwise upslope, and used both kinds of track with apparent indifference. It snaked them through echoing dells (from one of which a shattered belltower jutted, a rusty chain ladder like a dead tongue hanging from its rain-smooth sill) – only to lead them next most blatantly across a star-washed knoll, with torches flanking their almost polished path. The pair found too that easily though the azle ambled, it set a pace that taxed even their trail-hard legs. On one of these broader tracks, four fleet shadows crossed their path, the last of these nine feet tall, and dragging the lax body of a man briskly by his ankles. The slack head jarred across the pavement, the group plunged down into the off-road dark. The pair, irrepressibly, had stopped and drawn, while the azle sauntered unfalteringly ahead.

'Come, gentlemen,' Stilth turned to admonish, not reining up. 'If need be, hold Hamandra's tail, but in any case keep pace. We will need to work shifts, deceptions . . . Surely you appreciate that these call for unity, for orchestrated behaviour?'

Stung, the pair kept up.

Now, entryways to the depths more thickly featured the slopes: circular towers umbrellaed with ancient lead shingles; the broken crown of a gargoyled campanile, its dial runed with a forgotten measure of time; the jutting corner of a buried mansion's roof, a rain-scoured jawbone toothed with the broken stumps of balustrades. And, along with this thickening city-jut, there were more frequent shaft-mouths too: square-cut into the epoch-ending stone, timbered or lintelled with masonry. Some of these portalled gentle inclines down into the city, and some framed pits, with hitching posts for ladders and lines anchored near their lips.

'Listen,' Stilth murmured. 'Both of you: keep one hand on Hamandra's flank. *Don't pause*. Grin as broadly as possible. Do not cease to grin at their eyes, and say nothing.'

A torchlight approached their path, coming out of a

confluent defile ahead. The pair touched the azle at either haunch, and grinned. The torchbearer turned and bore down on them, followed by four other men. All had torches, steel gauntlets, knouts, and swords. But oddly, these bravos – hungrily alert to them at the first sighting – began to slow, with a clumsy piling-up effect, while their leader addressed the trio in a vindictive boom that dwindled almost to a whine as the azle bore the trespassers steadily forth:

'Travelling without a squad, are you . . . eh?'

'Yesss! Yesss!' Hex, not turning, knew it was Stilth who spoke, but the voice now spidered along his spine. It was a facsimile, a lizard-dry voice as creaky and clean as a decade-buried bone. 'Greeetingz, Sssweeet fellow humanzss. Come, give us your handszz, Sirzzz!' During this statement Hex thought he saw Stilth glowing with a faint yellow light and more – thought he saw the same glow on his own insanely rictused cheeks. The lead squadman, hearing this greeting through, screamed, flung his torch away, turned and fled. He would have overrun those behind him had they not fled even swifter than he.

The trio proceeded, the old man lax as before, and definitely not aglow. 'What did you do?' Sarf asked.

'There is a denizen of these parts,' Stilth said, geeing Hamandra to a slightly brisker saunter, 'called the Quash. It tends to travel in threes. Its human disguise is remarkably good, though marked by certain well known deficiencies.'

'The Quash? What is the Quash?'

'Give the name a rest,' snapped the old man, glancing nervously round, 'lest it bring the thing itself.'

They crossed another knoll. Now they saw a good two miles of jewelled lava plunged to the sea behind them. Far upland ahead of them the dark peaks – shadows sharply bitten from the clustered stars – appeared no nearer. Softly Hex said aloud – not to tell but to hear the truth himself – 'We cross the field of a million-million men's dreams of greatness. Does anyone ever retrieve anything, and escape with it alive?'

'Oh yes! A tidy few!' Stilth grinned. 'And I might say that not very many of them come here looking for Yana. I suppose it is not widely known.'

'Is it *real*?'

'I've already told you what I'm going to. I can give you one other bit of news. The portal you must seek, though deep, is at least not much ambuscaded – for so few willingly go there. Of course, that's a mixed consolation.'

'I suppose it's right that the portal should be here,' Hex offered. 'Where better than here might eternal scholarship commence? Where else does so much lie – '

Into the gully they now followed a bigger gully debouched just ahead, and from this came – suddenly audible as it rounded some turning – a horrible sound, a noise both complex and at the same time hideously, clearly readable: a multi-voiced chorus of human agony, groans and gasps of effort. Behind this there approached a massive, grinding noise, the single tread of some following colossus. It was something big, driving a sweating chorus of human captives.

And there they came – first, the struggling crew in bonds. Towering after them, a huge beaked head, fifteen feet in the air, its eyes red globes of flame. Hex's feet were triggered, as if they alone were conscious, and capable of saving the rest of his stupefied body. He sprinted for a shaftmouth just below the path and to his right – its deep-set frame could shadow him from the monster's gaze. Just as he leapt for it, he glimpsed behind him the clustered victims squirming under the beast's outstretched claw, heard Stilth's startled, preventive shout, and tripped – all three at once. His leap was now a dive. Airborne, helpless, he flew towards the pit within the portal. Only a stone anchoring post stood at the pit's lip, and desperately he hugged that in midair. His shoulder, with his full mass's thrust behind it, felt the stone solidity even as – struck quirkishly awry – the post snapped clean off its base. Insanely, he still hugged the post as they pitched down into the perfect dark. Teeth clenched, clutching his anchor, he writhed and fought to pull his body up and back off of gravity's sticky pull, to hang back from the blotting smash below.

But the impact – though it smacked his lungs flat-empty like a bellows – was soft. He had one pain – in his ribs, from the blunt end of the post, which was now sunk full length into the pillowy mass he sprawled on. But even as he realized he was safe, the springy substrate heaved, the slippery shoots that furred it squirmed violently under his cheek and palms, and a stinking syrup welled out from around the newly rooted stone. With an explosive twist of loathing, he scrambled and rolled till the grateful shock of clean stone bruised his tumbling body. On all fours he scuttled from a thrashing bigness till a rough wall stopped him. There he crouched, straining his eyes.

At first the thing's struggle was noise only – a flabby smacking, a chitinous rattle. But above it, a conic section of starlight screwed down through the entry-shaft's throat, and after a moment this shed some faint form on the tormented being. A huge bulb, hirsute, tapered, at whose tip a clutch of polished, jointed legs rattled in a spastic bouquet. Sword out, Hex backed along the wall. The thing heaved towards him. Hex scuttled faster. The hand that felt his way thrust into emptiness – a tall vent of a natural fissure in the lava. A few strides down its ribbed length a yellow light glowed that limned its twists. The thing, though nearer, lay now in another spastic pause. Hex hesitated. It heaved nearer, and he slipped into the fissure.

The light came from a hallway. He stepped wonderingly down on to its floor. This, though pocked and scorched, was all arabesques of mosaically laid bricks. He moved towards the light source, noting that, the walls being hewn lava, and the paving's pattern irregular, this was probably a tunnel across what had been an open space, some plaza, or great hall's floor.

Rounding the next curve, he saw this confirmed. The light source was a wide, open space ringed with torches. It sprawled one short flight of marble steps below Hex, who cowered to see two ranks of giants flanking these steps, facing the plaza beyond. No. They were statues, theriomorphic sentinels of stone. He crept up behind the nearest, from its shadow peeked down and out across the rotunda, whose rough-hewn walls were apertured by rude tunnels all around their circuit. Probably, he was on the higher of what had been a series of broad squares, only the lower of which was widely excavated. He scuttled down to the next statue's shade, then the next's. Now he could see that the ragged-rimmed pavement's containing wall presented, among the tunnel mouths, one proper door, or gate, rather: two majestic valves of bronze, their hinges huge, as big as wine-tuns. To three times a man's stature they rose, blushing bright gold when the torches stirred in the black, subterranean breeze. The brazen torchsockets that ringed the plaza were of this portal's make, for two larger versions supported huge flambeaux that flanked the door. Clearly, it was the door's keeper who maintained this nexus of light, where so many ways converged.

A multiple tread sounded from one of the tunnel mouths. Hex, sneaking between statues, plunged and rocked the next one with his hasty crouch behind it. The big archaeolith heartstoppingly teetered on its base, then stilled. A man in billowy robes emerged from a shaft across the rotunda from the door. Out he marched, followed by three pairs of men, each of which carried a covered litter between them. The man in the lead, in his awkward stride to the great doors, stumbled twice. He seemed to have trouble with his robe as he led the others across the burnt flagstones. At the door, his worried briskness contrasted with a lagging manner in the litter bearers behind him. When they were stationed by the door he turned to them with shooing gestures: 'Let's be at it then! Come on!' The voice was frail and cross, fragmenting against the torchdecked, blackmouthed walls. With ostentatious delay, yawnings and stretchings, the bearers set down the three litters, and undid the bolts which fastened the cabs of these conveyances to their bases. They lifted the cabs off, reducing the vehicles to three stretchers, each enthroning a single occupant, slouched in a chair. Two of these were nubile girls, the third, a pubescent boy. All were frozen, nude, a green neckscarf the only garment of each.

While the bearers were uncovering their charges, shambling about, the robed man stood aside, his nose pressed close to a parchment page, his lips visibly rehearsing the shapes of words.

'Shall we call for *your* understudy, Understudy?' The question, from one of the bearers, raised a snicker from the rest. The understudy glared back and shook his fist at them, crumpling his page with the gesture. He turned and marched to the bronze door, anxiously smoothing the parchment against his hip. He plied the knocker three times and at the first crash Hex gave a jump, distant though he was.

The understudy stepped back and one of the great valves swung mutely foward a short way. From behind it a lithe, white ankle followed a tasselled blue slipper into view. Next to emerge, at somewhat less than a man's height, was a white head, a hairless bulb. It was inset with eyes like great sentimental opals, and underslung by a shrunken little chin and jaw the size and texture of a large prune. Then the little figure stepped fully out.

Slender, whitely nude, he wore besides the slippers only a scarlet breechclout. His crooked jaw drooped with astonishment, and his seamy lips framed a musical exclamation: 'Oh! Oh! Oh! Who, then, are these? What visitors these, at the Ghuls' gates? Whoever might they be, these callers at the gates of the Ghuls, which are also the doors of the Archives of Tam where, humbly entrenched, the mild and goodly Ghuls have continued these three hundred and seventy-one years?' The egg-skulled Ghul's voice was tender, liturgical. He spoke as if to a middle distance, and not to his callers at all. The understudy, drawing a deep breath, held his page close to his nose and began to read loudly: 'Oh oh it is we we who implore and abjure. Your sufferance for our plea oh please hear our simple. Request. Namely that you receive these whom we have brought these fair ones here. As it happens by a stroke of luck precisely – Oh, I'm sorry! That's the *next* one. . . .'

But the slippered Ghul seemed still not to see the man, and exclaimed smoothly: 'Are fair ones mentioned? Fair ones? Could it be that you have brought, that you have with you, dear visitors, such ones as we delight in, such ones as we adore?'

'As it happens by a stroke of luck precisely such as you say – sit here yes fair ones sit here on whom sits all loveliness behold!' The understudy swept his arm at the last word. One of the men by each litter, with a tug, slipped the knot of its occupant's green neckscarf. Only one of the three, a girl, was faced in a way that presented the throat to Hex's view. A red but oddly clean gash crossed its width: a second mouth, slackly open, as if shocked, while the face above it, fine-featured, merely slept.

'Oh what is this?' the Ghul trilled. 'What offering is this, worth priceless pages to the adoring Ghuls?' He swept towards the nearest bier, the boy's, and lifted one hand towards the corpse. The hand, like a hummingbird pausing by a flower, hovered at the youth's throat, then, with a forefinger, touched it. The Ghul drew back his hand and applied, with virginal amazement, his red fingertip to his tongue.

At the taste, the Ghul turned his huge eyes on the understudy and the litter bearers, seeing them all for the first time.

'We are well met my friends, my goodly friends of the fair ones! Could it be there are some texts, some pages in our endless stores thereof, that you desire to own? Some spells or legendaries, some lines of close-linked syllables constraining powers untapped, commanding wealth or –'

All heads (save three) turned in sharp unison towards one of the shaftmouths. Hex followed their look, catching an instant later than they had the grinding footfalls that approached. He remembered the stony tread of the thing that had caused his fall to this place, and waited in horror. But the thing that emerged from the tunnel was little more than nine feet tall.

It had the form of a naked man save for two features. Its shoulders were surmounted by a sarcophagus mask, a broad, embossed abstraction of a face, the mouth a slot. And it was sexed with what looked like a spindle, a conic spike with a grooved handgrip near its base.

It paused in the shaft mouth and greeted the party before the door with a deep bow. Stunned, they half-responded, and the giant advanced. It moved with a dry friction that suggested a sculptor's pumice stone polishing a statue. The thing was made of flexible rock. Its voice was boomingly distinct: 'Good evening. I rejoice to find you here. I need seven whole lives, a set of wits from one man, and the eyes and hearing of another. I thought you were eleven. I note now, alas, that three of you are dead. We must make do. Have you concluded your ceremonies?'

The litter bearers shifted on their feet, the understudy stood with a limply working jaw, and the Ghul had already begun a gradual retreat, with subtle writhes that it disguised as bows and obeisances to the giant.

'Alas, we are not in fact finished, benign giant,' fluted the Ghul, bowing yet again towards the open valve of the door behind him. 'For what do you require these lives and . . . other things?'

'My master's soulscape, Ghul, for whose continuance he fashioned me, and whose epic scope I have unflaggingly expanded, these eight hundred years since his demise.' The giant had paused some score of feet from the party, and as he spoke, he was unscrewing his spindle from its socket in his crotch.

'Indeed!' cried the Ghul. 'Surely then you are the renowned Ghellim, created by Mahood the Inspired?'

'I am,' replied Ghellim. Even as the Ghul uttered his question he had sprung for the door, and Ghellim, as he answered, flicked the point of his spindle like an angler casting. There was a small, clear sound of meaty impact, and the Ghul's body froze in mid-air, a foot above the spot he had leapt from. Hanging thus, his chest swelled into a spine-reversing bulge towards the giant.

The seven men were fleeing in as many directions. As the knot of them fragmented, the giant snapped his spindle again and again; with each flicker of his wrist a man was snagged from his flight and hung straining in the air. He had all seven hooked and dangling before they had well dispersed.

Now Ghellim began rolling the spindle back and forth between the flats of his palms. It was a busy, patient motion which did not draw the eight suspended forms any nearer, but tautened their limbs, and bowed their spines more and more radically, till they were impossibly curved, like fighting fish. Then Ghellim gave a tug to the spindle; there was a snap, and all eight collapsed to the pavement.

Six lay as they had fallen: heaps, jointless, jumbles of flesh and rags. One of the litter bearers, and the understudy, struggled onto their knees. The understudy made it on up to his feet, palping frantically at the dry, vacant orbits of his eyes, and at his ears. The litter bearer remained on all fours, where he began to drool, rave, and hammer the floor mechanically with one fist. The giant patiently wound his tool.

'I can't see! I can't hear!' screamed the understudy. 'What? Where?' He tottered forward and stumbled against his gibbering confrere. 'What's happened?' he asked, gratefully embracing the living motion of a comrade. The witless one, galvanized by the understudy's touch, seized him deftly by the throat, and throttled the astonished man. The giant began screwing his spindle back into his crotch. The madman dropped the understudy's corpse and seized himself by the throat. The giant paused in his screwing-in, and then began unscrewing again.

'How fortunate!' the Ghellim cried. 'I did not notice you there!' (The madman, purple, uttered a terminal gurgle and dropped himself to the floor, leaving the three nudes, enthroned, in serene domination of the littered plaza.) The giant had turned towards the stairs Hex crouched on; his granite hand flicked and Hex felt a light *splat* against his breast. A red taproot of pain sank to the centre of his lungs.

Even as he felt this, a hand grasped the invisible line right above the hooked spot in his ribs. Stilth was standing beside him. The old man's grip on the line was remarkably strong. It was braced against the giant's tug, intercepting the agony of the hook's pull. His voice too was strong, plangent in that mausoleal air:

'Seven questions, Ghellim! Seven questions!'

The Ghellim's form and face were impassivity itself, yet still it subtly bridled, its bigness restless, resentfully constrained somehow by Stilth's words.

'Seven questions, then, Trickster.'

'First then. Are you well, good Ghellim?'

'Yes, thank you, Trickster, I am well.'

'Secondly. Must you use my friend's life in your soulscape?'

A gritty shrug. 'I will, because there is no reason not to – and yours as well, Trickster.'

Hex was clinging to Stilth's shoulder, sweating freely, barely keeping his legs under him. The old man's hand, without seeming to move, was covertly wiggling the hook to free it. The barbed pain, ratlike, worked in his raw heart muscle reiterated wounds. He fought not to betray the covert operation, though the sweat runnelled off his face.

'But what of your work's form?' Stilth asked in amazement. 'How can it not matter what goes into it? And what of great Mahood's unequalled elegance, his commitment to concise expression?' The cunning squirm of the hook sent out waves of sickness that half-unhinged Hex's knees.

'That's third, fourth, and fifth,' the Ghellim said, holding taut his line. 'As a man who loved the ephemera of his restricted span, Mahood considered events and objects to be grave, important. His selectivity served his passionate attachments. But naturally, selection has no meaning in an infinite flux of endlessly unique experience.'

'What!?' Stilth trumpeted. 'Are you not, then, making a trash-heap, a sprawling psychic junkyard, of Mahood's great, deathless epic?'

'No doubt. To match the trashed plains of eternity.' Hex's knees now did collapse, as the hook came free. But his grip on Stilth's shoulder held and he did not sink. Not once had Stilth's hand moved perceptibly, nor did it now. 'That is the sixth, Trickster. What is your last question?'

'It is this. How can you betray your maker, Mahood the Inspired, as you do?'

Even as he asked this Stilth jumped sideways and pulled a statue down. It fell crosswise in front of them as the pair fell back, and pinned Ghellim's invisible line to the step. The giant reeled in powerfully, but so quick had Stilth been to snag its hook on one of the statue's fangs that the giant's pull only noosed the statue tighter, and hauled it down a step. Yet he was still compelled, and though his voice raged, his words obediently answered, their echoes chasing the pair as they fled – Stilth half dragging Hex – the way they had come: 'I can't betray him – I am he, and do no other than he would have done in my place, for he furnished me with his own memories and desires, ending himself in making me begin.'

A noise of shattered stone followed, and a grinding thud, a massive sprinting sound, came after the pair. Fear had returned Hex his legs. They rushed through the vent – a bruising passage for Hex. Beyond, the star-sketched ruin of whatever he had landed on, now inert, was like a ramp that Stilth unhesitatingly ran up, to grasp a glowing purple filament hanging in the shaft. Loathingly, Hex followed suit. Stilth climbed two-handed but no sooner had Hex clutched the cord than it retracted, and drew him smoothly up. Like a hail of drums the giant's echo-muddled voice sounded in the deeps behind him as he rose towards a seam of stars. There the azle stood silhouetted, the cord re-coiling itself round its saddlehorn, ceasing to glow as it did so. Once above ground, Hex made to bolt further, but Stilth stayed him.

'Peace, Bramt Hex. The Ghellim cannot surface. Catch your breath a bit, and meet the one whose acquaintance, for some reason, you so precipitately shunned.'

Gladly Hex snuffed the upper air, and good-humouredly

met Stilth's mordant eye. There, in mid-glen, stood a statue a storey and a half high, set on crude wooden wheels. Its gem eyes flashed with oily life. It was carved crouching, with an outstretched paw, from whose talons dangled the abandoned harnesses of the men who had been pulling it.

Sarf presented the statue to Hex with a courtly arm-sweep. 'His companions,' he suavely explained, 'startled by a most unearthly glow that afflicted their flesh, did not stay.'

Hex made the monolith a deep and solemn bow.

20
Slove's Enthralment of the Squotobe Host

'Well, Bramt Hex,' Stilth said when they had resumed their slantwise upslope march. 'I grieve at the lack of faith in me this flight of yours betrayed.'

'Listen Stilth, it was only the smallest part of a betrayal. My feet alone were faithless. They took flight. The rest of me stayed calm and true as steel.'

'I'm relieved to hear it. In any case, good came of it after all. Your fall killed a durb – the biggest one I've ever seen. Its stonework was flawless. No one could have told that den from a genuine portal.'

'I refuse to accept credit for the deed. I felt it was the least I could do to atone for my feet's defection.'

'Well, don't tax yourself. I enjoyed the exchange with Ghellim. S'Death! I handled that one neatly, don't you think?'

'With all my heart!' said Hex. 'We're fast learning to value your judgement, Stilth. Forgive one question, which I can't repress. You know of Yana. Why haven't you gone there?'

'What an idiotic question! I'm scarcely a century and a half old! I've got at least a century more if I keep my wits about me. Why should I need even to think about immortality yet?'

'Well, wouldn't you want to perpetuate a . . . younger self?'

'This is ridiculous!' Both Stilth's aspects seemed truly peeved, and looked more querulously senile, withal. 'I don't even *look* old yet!'

'Well, elderly,' Hex said stoutly. Stilth spat, and said nothing. His protracted silence distinctly bristled. Now above the relatively coalescent apron of flatter lava near the sea, they moved up and across a great frozen tendon of rock. Stilth's hand came up for their attention, though the azle did not pause.

'We are now in the worst kind of danger. We'll be branching off ahead there on to open ground – I think there's a Tax Station above and we're going to go past it, though I'm sure that won't help us shake the beings who are about to join us. Stay close to the azle, move calmly and unconcernedly, and say nothing. We're already being observed.'

As they moved farther up the great hogback of ashen stone, they saw there was indeed a Tax Depot ahead: one large, and several smaller buildings of weathered planking. Fire baskets raised on posts lit the compound. They burned a cheap fuel whose yellow light looked unclean in the star-vaulted night.

'In a moment,' said Stilth, 'there will be much talk between myself and certain squotobes. Throughout, remember to stay mute, walk smoothly, hope.'

Hex immediately violated Stilth's second command, and jumped nearly a foot when a slight, pale figure landed on the path in front of them, loose-jointed and light, having jumped, it seemed, down from the air. Two others followed, one appearing at Hex's side, and one at Sarf's.

'Why, good evening, fair squotobes!' Stilth cried with pleased surprise. He nodded at each, a courtesy Sarf and Hex aped with ghastly smiles as they viewed – with a dismay they could not hide – the features of these new companions. Their greasy white hair grew in lank tufts and tongues widely separate across their bodies, and their skin was rubbery and pale between the patches. They were shovel-jawed, and their white lips' bespittled slackness showed their jutting mandibles to be crowded with crooked, carious fangs. Their eyes were lemur-large, and hot with a light that seemed almost lambent. Though a shade less than man-tall, their walk – a disgruntled slouch, really – expressed a fluid, reptilian strength that made the two pilgrims they flanked profoundly uneasy. But it was particularly Stilth that all three squotobes had their eyes on as they walked.

'Why so sombre?' he rallied them. 'Is it not a splendid night? The air like wine?' The creatures grunted a sullen, perfunctory assent, and kept staring at Stilth. Now they were passing before the Tax Station's main building – an act that would have dismayed Hex moments before, but now seemed insignificant. The building's front door stood wide open.

Inside, four men surrounded a table that stood endwise to the doorway, and whereon someone lay who presented a pair of wildly kicking bootsoles. Three of the squadmen held this person down – the fourth worked, furiously with unseen hands, where his face would be. 'Scum!' this fourth was shouting, straightening, stripping off thorn gloves whose barbs were clotted with new gore. 'Get me some coals!'

A brazier of live coals fumed on the porch. A squadman, striding out to fetch it, saw the trio and their squotobe escort. Horror shook him – he stumbled as he stepped, and pitched face-first into the coals. His friends now, too, had seen and, howling, slammed and barred the door, leaving their tormented mate to writhe outside. His cries dwindled astern as the azle Hamandra ambled on upslope.

'Well then,' grumbled the squotobe who walked in the lead of the beast. 'Tell us a story, traveller. A good story.'

'Yes,' said the one by Sarf. 'Tell us an interesting story, traveller.'

'That's right!' chimed Hex's pallid neighbour. 'An *interesting* story!'

'What's this? You say you'd like to hear a story?' Stilth spoke in tones of awakening pleasure. 'Now this is really lucky! This is delightfully opportune! You see as it happens, my dear squotobes, I am no mean narrator. In fact, in all candour, it's amazing how I can weave myself in and out of a fiction – what twists I can give to the threads of a plot! My friends here, unaccountably, say they think me tiresome and, to make a long story short, I have sat bottled up for this last hundred leagues. I'm sure that connoisseurs such as yourselves can appreciate how an accomplished tale-teller pines to speak, how he swells with his undischarged narratives when he is denied an audience. He moons and mourns for all the unborn felicities of expression, the delicate internal resonances of theme and image which, lacking issue from his fecund mind, must inflate him till he – '

'Enough!' shouted the lead squotobe. 'Get on with it! I do hope you *can* tell a story well!'

'Yes!' cried the one by Hex. 'I do hope you *can*. You sound like a terrible windbag!'

'Yes!' chimed Sarf's pale Doppelganger. 'A *dreadful* windbag! Why don't you get on with it?'

Stilth was enraged. He actually reined up Hamandra. 'I'm dead and roasted if I'll suffer such abuse! Go fish other waters for your story! And you're great losers by all your ill manners, I'm glad to tell you, for I had in mind to tell you the story of Slove's Enthralment of the Squotobe Host.'

'"Enthralment of the Squotobe Host"?' Bah! There's no such tale!' The lead squotobe was outraged in his turn. But then he turned to a distraction. Their path had now dropped down the tendon's farther side, and plunged them in the shadow-cleft dividing it from the next great magmatic sinew. Thus, they stood with high ground to their left, and now, from this, a Tork sprang down on them – a stump-legged whip-tailed maggot as big as a wolf, jawed with ragged black carapace like a termite soldier's. These, once locked on prey, fixed it as the axis for the larva's python twining, and oviposition, after paralysis.

Sarf's squotobe caught its gaping jaws in either hand, broke their joints, and used them for handles to pin the glittering head to the rock. But the squotobe's jaw dropped to a second, lower hinge – clamped, and, with one pressure bit clean through a maggoty neck as thick as Hex's thigh. Tossing the head aside, the creature fiercely echoed:

'Exactly! There is no such tale at all. There was only Itzpah's Enthralment of the Squotobe Host!'

'That's right!' cried Hex's squotobe passionately. 'Only Itzpah ever enthralled the ears of the squotobe host!'

Stilth crowed derisively. 'Ah, you're such perfect examples! Glib error always goes with haughty manners! I might have expected you to drag out that tedious Itzpah chestnut! Let me just ask you this: does the story of Itzpah's enthralment of the squotobe host contain the *tale itself* whereby he worked this alleged triumph? Oh no! As all the world knows, it does not! It merely alludes to it!'

'What of it?'

'Yes, suppose it doesn't, what of that?'

'Yes, what difference does it make if it does or not?'

'It signifies, oh arrogant squotobes, that the tale's apocryphal. The *Slove* cycle, meanwhile, recently recovered from among the Quimble Bay Parchments, is the true original of that tale. And it is its own proof of this fact, for it contains the tale wherewith Slove enthralls the minds of the squotobes, and any of that race who hears it stands himself enthralled, the living proof of the story's genuineness.'

Though the squotobes' answering chorus was derisive and sceptical, it horrified Hex to detect in them a hideous, unearthly interest – an unholy lust to hear – which the old man had kindled in them, and which showed itself in ever hotter flashes of orange-and-amber light coruscating across their eyes.

'Bah! Impossible! Out with this tale!'

'Unheard of! Let us hear it at once!'

'Immediately! Out with this supposedly genuine tale.'

Stilth seemed to waver, grew decisive: 'Absolutely not! You called me a windbag. I'm not about to give you the choicest story unearthed this century in return for *that*.'

Now the squotobes' eyes blazed outright. 'Insulted you? Bah! I spit on the idea – PTAH! You're clamming up because there's no such story!'

'Slove's Enthralment – rubbish! You won't tell it because you *can't*!'

'What?' Stilth roared, towering in his stirrups. 'Because I *can't*? Can I not indeed, you presumptuous neuters! By Plague and Flame and the Dry Rot, you'll have it then! Prepare to hear, and be humbled, you who have begged your own ensorcelment.'

The wiry, pale bodies, falling in step again with the azle, gave an unmistakable shiver of delight, understanding that Stilth was now composing himself to proceed with the story. The dreadful saurian power of that suppressed convulsion awed Hex, renewing his sense of how powerfully the love of narrative gripped these squotobes' explosive hearts. He would not wish himself to have to tickle, with his spoken words, such volcanic sensibilities. Stilth cleared his throat with quiet ceremony, and Hex cast a look around. The harbour shone like stitchery on the ocean's absolute black. Would he ever take ship from there, bound back to Glorak with the harvest of his venture? The moon now gave some feature to the peaks they climbed to – they were much nearer too, of course.

'When Slove the Canny was twenty-four,' Stilth – not unmelodiously – announced, 'he had achieved wealth. In that year of his age, all four of the Season Kings had received him in their halls,' – his voice, indeed, had a brimming mellowness. 'And all four of them sent him out again laden with gifts.

'In the lying bouts of Spring's court, he won five hundred years from Life. From Summer, for the obscenities he intoned before that full-fleshed assembly, he received nine chests of breeding-gold, which had moreover the faculty of shrivelling the hand of any but its rightful possessor.

'In Fall's court, Slove pitted his curses against those of Druil Faff, who was a great master of the form.' Here Hex saw the squotobe nearest him nod and murmur with the absent corroboration a rapt reader gives his page. 'Here Slove won his fleet of triremes, and his seven hundred swords. With Winter he had especial luck. His dirges pleased Wolf, Winter's chamberlain. Wolf plied an interceding tongue anent his Majesty's icy ear, and Slove was given the power to change his shape.

'Now when Slove the Canny had these things, he sought out a removed place, and bethought himself. And he considered that, as he stood now before his twenty-fifty year, it was time to begin his work in the world.

'Therefore, Slove hung in doorways as a spider, and outside eaves as an owl, and heard what people said of the world at large, and in particular, what wits were held formidable, such that honour and glory lay in confounding and defeating them. Slove heard, and weighed, at length. At first, he thought to challenge Avatar the Confounder, and tourney with him in the Lists of Ancient Dreams.' (Hex saw his squotobe shake his head with absent protest.) 'But at length, he determined that he would go seek out the renowned squotobes in the dead city of Kurl, and enthrall them with a tale. For, though this was a thing attempted by the best, the attempt had unfailingly ended their lives, and remained to that day unaccomplished.

'First, to prepare his spirit for this contest, Slove the

Canny went into the hills, and lived there for a full springtime in the form of a snake. At the summer solstice he was ready, and had made a tale of marvellous simplicity, with marvellous power to enthrall withal. Ye gods! I have made a terrible mistake!'

The squotobes' bodies were wrenched in unison, as if they had been seized in their vitals. 'Fool! What did you say wrong?' wailed the lead one.

'Everything! I've put it all in the wrong style! So remote, and uninvolved! It hit me as I was telling about the months he spent as a snake.' Stilth slouched in his saddle to do a mocking version of himself: '". . . and had made a tale of marvellous simplicity . . ." Bah! It's wrong, I tell you! What was the *quality* of those spring days? What were Slove's *feelings*? Where is the man in all this? We don't want just an empty cipher! I must start over and tell it right!'

This made the squotobes epileptic with rage and pain. They fairly danced. Their eyes blazed fever-orange. Almost, Hex felt pity to see their loathsome bodies so racked.

'No no no!' they howled as one.

'We *hate* starting over! It's horrible form!'

'We can't *stand* starting over! It's deadly boring!'

'Don't start over! Go on, go on, go *on*!'

'Be reasonable. I must at least tell over his months as a snake. Think of the charm of that time, the peace Slove enjoyed, the obscure unity with the sunny grass . . .'

'No! Never!/Absolutely not!/It's not done!' they simultaneously shouted.

'Very well,' the old man said stiffly. 'But from this point on I will insist on an appropriate style.' The squotobes assented. Still tremulous with their late upset, they resettled to a hearkening stoop as they paced alongside Hamandra. Stilth cleared his throat.

'Having at last his tale, his magical germ of art which

he meant to sow in the squotobes' ears and reap glory from – having his tale, I say, Slove the Canny took ship and set his sails for Kurl.

'Surely these ships, Slove considered, were the very image and emblem of his inmost longings: they swiftly rode the waves, as did his hopes, and they were as trim and crafted to their purpose as was his own young frame. Through the long voyage Slove stood in the bow of his trireme, the wind bathing him, taunting him, even as his ambition softly taunted his deepest desires.'

The squotobe nearest Hex groaned softly and gnashed its teeth. Stilth paused at the sound, then continued calmly:

'Slove reflected on this wind that bathed him. Somehow, through all the world's changes the wind, an endlessly changing thing – indeed, the very symbol of change! – remained the same! And that, in a sense, this was the very same wind that had bathed him through the long days he had lived as a snake. And as he stood there in the bow, those recent days returned to him in a rush. As in a dream, he relived the long, sliding tickle of the grass-shafts against his scales, the tactful touch of the earth against his segmented underside, the peaceful, obscure unity with the sunny meadow that he had enjoyed. And now, he told himself, this same wind was bearing him to his destiny, wafting him to – '

A snarl of anguish burst from the jaws of the lead squotobe.

'Stop! Cease! This cannot go on!'

'Yes! Stop at once! That's a *dreadful* style!'

'Damn you then,' Stilth roared, 'that's my limit of abuse! You'll hear no more from me!'

The creatures commenced a shuddering dance that appalled the pair flanking the azle. The light of the squotobes' eyes was so intense Hex saw it actually sweep his body, like light from a crazily agitated torch.

'S'Death! Calm yourselves!' Stilth cried in consternation. 'I did not guess you were so high-strung. Come come! I won't be petty, since it affects you so! I'll tell you the rest. To accommodate your rustic ears, I'll abandon the lyric style. But my first style was unacceptable. I won't return to it. In a spirit of compromise, I'll give you the rest of the story in the original scansion, as it appears in the Quimble Bay parchments. Do you accept this?'

The squotobes groaned with relief.

'Willingly!'

'Absolutely!'

'Get on with it!'

'Very well then. It runs as follows. Though of course I must first point out that it is Beedle's recension I am following here. I'm aware that in the late controversy the Quimble Cabal – as they are rightly named! – have done their scurrilous utmost to discredit Beedle's scholarship. But I for one, sirs, will never prefer such mincing, tintinnabulous doggerel as *they* provide for an alternative, the work of their much-trumpeted Haggle, a scholar of dubious genius. I know that you will join me in deeming Beedle's manly, strophic measure to be a seemlier mode for so – '

'Beedle is fine! Fine! Proceed!'

'Get *on* with it!'

'Beedle will do *splendidly*!'

Stilth nodded, then bethought himself anew: 'There *is* of course Thurrible's recension, which is not utterly devoid of – '

But the squotobes' paroxysms now compelled compliance. The creatures seemed endlessly irascible, knowing no relaxation of spirit, each succeeding fit keener, more excruciating for them than the last. For the pilgrims the delirious play of their eyelight was a frightening, almost palpable caress, a premonition of explosion. Stilth cleared his throat. As befitted epic verse, a certain pomp entered his posture as he intoned:

> '. . . Thus his keels cut the brinehills
> his course to Kurl bore him,
> til he crossed the foam border
> where the combers fall broken,
> and the sea weaves white lace
> on the skirts of wide lavas.
> Then down on his foredoomed spot
> where those firedrowned spires and domes
> lie sepulchred in ash, there Slove
> lightly sprang, and stood on Kurl,
> on the pride of its towers, stone sunk,
> entombed by the peaks' streaming sap.
> Yes, down leapt that slyboots
> like a dancer so lightfoot
> and, his mind on his quest,
> he turned quick to his mission.
> He crowed o'er that red waste –
> his cries they went winging:
> "Dire Squotobes, I challenge ye!
> You will hearken till helpless
> my harmonies hold ye
> and like stone you stand,
> stunned with my story!"
> The first these boasts conjured was Quaspar –
> dire Quaspar, the fiercest, the kingly!
> Arch-wit of all Squotobe learned,
> arbiter most quoted and loved – '

(Here Hex detected another absorbed nod of confirmation from the creature nearest him.)

> ' – yea, now skullish Quaspar darted
> from a gully's darkness, and gasped:
> "Slight skulker, you lie!
> Sleight-of-talk you lack for it!
> You are tongueless to charm us!
> Your tale will chain us!
> All assemble! To the heights!
> Of Seven Hairs Hill!"

> Thus he squalled up his cousins,
> and pale squotobes came scuttling,
> pallid as fungi
> they popped from each fissure
> fleetfoot as rat hordes
> they flowed from ravines – '

(Here Hex noted in his creature some vexation with the imagery, but saw this was completely outweighed by the squotobe's raptness with the tale.)

> weasely and white
> they wormed out to witness,
> and flocked up to Seven-Hairs
> where, with flourish, and sprightly,
> already young Slove . . .'

Stilth paused. He cleared his throat, and repeated:

> 'and flocked up to Seven-Hairs
> where, with flourish, and sprightly,
> already young Slove . . .'

The squotobes' eyes, deliriously ablaze already, fixed the old man, malignant satellites to the bushy orb of Stilth's puzzled face. He was pulling vexedly at his beard.

'Well I'll be roasted,' he muttered amazedly. 'This is not possible. I! I, who have won renown for tale-telling from Quimble Bay to Boguspolis!'

'What are you saying?' bleated the lead squotobe. An eerie plangency, as of exquisite pain scarcely contained, haunted its voice. 'Get on with the story!'

'Impossible! I've forgotten the rest!'

'Forgotten?' Three inhuman voices chimed this, yet it was the merest wisp of sound, for something had broken in them.

Stilth exploded: 'Yes, fools, *forgotten*! Do you know the word? *I* have forgotten a tale! Don't stand there drooling! Help me remember!'

A spasm of hideous power shook the chest of the lead squotobe, and shuddered through the length of its body. Even as its legs gave way, the light of its eyes went dark. It lay in a heap, and its hands twitched once. The other two were already down.

'Are they dead?' Sarf asked quietly.

'Yes,' said Stilth, geeing Hamandra up. They put the three corpses behind them.

'How did they die?' Hex asked.

'Frustration. It's said to be the only way you can kill a squotobe. You can try to enthrall them, of course, but they are such finicking critics that it's doubted whether any tale can succeed in this. Many argue that the Itzpah tale itself is merely a myth they circulate to encourage people to try, because the squotobes love to hear a story before dining.'

21
The Voyage of the Necronauts

Just under the mountains' highest crags, in a shadowed groining where two confluent tendons of lava met, the trio sat watching the dawn. Behind them, sprawled doglike on the ground, Hamandra snored. Farther back within the vale raggedly yawned the wide mouth of the shaft that plunged, half a mile straight down, to the Incubarium of Dazu-Zul.

As the dove-grey light fanned up from the horizon, the harbour's torches paled, its maze of floats and piers grew more distinct against the silver of the water, and some unusual flux of business could be seen there: more than a dozen big ships docked as a group, disgorging cargo and men, and in their midst, a smattering of bigger shapes they appeared to manage and shepherd on to shore. The three men watched this, though they were more engrossed in their talk.

'How do you know,' Hex was asking, 'that in this . . . grappling, they have no power to win?'

'But they *have*, of course!' Stilth snapped. 'If your nerve fails, if they cow and terrify your will, if you can't firmly tell them *no*, then they will *take* possession, and enter you, and warm their deathly chills in the glow of your life. And then too,' – his voice softened here, and he smiled – 'there will perhaps be one you *choose* to admit, a ghost that perhaps you regret. I couldn't say, not knowing whom you've killed.'

'I'm still not clear in this,' Sarf put in. 'If we *did* take on, accept, one of our own, then we would be protected from the rest?'

'With certain qualifications, my friend. If you go in all

bold and flagrant, you will be mobbed by all who see you. If you swim humbly through the waters, offering yourself to your own. Oddly, the man who's never killed is most at risk. The murder latent in the souls of all but the rarest is a handle any ghost can take him by. But if you have dead, and take one on, it's said to be protection, provided it is a spirit of weight and force enough to hold you against others.'

'And if we say them *all* nay?' Hex asked. 'How soon then does the general host descend on us? For you've said there's no set distance or direction we must swim – that we reach the Portal soon or late, so that we swim at large, and randomly?'

Stilth shrugged. 'For all I know, you'll swim till your own dead are denied, and the rest swarm you to death. I never heard Yana was promised to all – only that all who could swim long enough reached it. Were you never given to understand that this enterprise was in the nature of a gamble?'

A silence followed. Inch by inch, from the docks, the microscopic mob they idly watched began ascending the slope in a column.

'My dead aren't many,' Hex muttered. 'The ones I'm sure of were so . . . scattered. Could they all be here?'

Stilth smiled. 'You haven't grasped the situation. *All* the incubaria are gates to Yana. All, far from being closed boxes the wizards trapped their ectoplasms in, were the nature of antechambers to the ghostly realm, which is all one and unitary, a single zone such unanchored souls all share at large. This place's space and time lie at an angle to the space and time we move through. When the governing magi who built these . . . adits to the dread motherlode died or abandoned their outposts, then whatever artificial, partial separateness these latter had enjoyed relapsed, and they entirely rejoined the ghostly main. I've chosen this place in particular because

Dazu-Zul's outer gate remains intact; the spirits can't spill out and range abroad, so entry's simplest here. But wherever you went in by, you'd have all your dead to deal with.'

Hex was trying to catch Sarf's eye, and failing. Were his friend's dead more numerous than his own? Strange not to know, yet trust the man as he did. And how many, exactly, *were* his own? Did *all* Polypolis lie to his charge? For he had aimed at and strenuously aided the entire killing, as a chosen mission. Would he be mobbed below? The far procession had now drained from the docks, and as it trickled up the slope its minute march proclaimed a striking energy, snaking smartly over the terrain.

'It's a little army, nothing less,' Stilth mused, not unimpressed. Hex, feeling gloomier by the moment, wished they had an army of their own as escort on this last leg of their trek. What host of uncouth shapes, down in that pit behind him there, was he about to meet? What of dead he might not guess at? Had any in Poon's whorehouse died when he had brought about its hideous transposition? What more likely?

His situation, which he saw now as some stranger's, stupefied him. To have come so far, for so mad an aim! Unending life. The gluttonous mania of some twisted soul. Yet what else was left him to do, but go down that shaft, and through Dazu-Zul's door?

This particular annexe to the ghostly realm had been, Stilth told them, designed as a vast lake, whereon chained demon giants floated. To this undying fodder the gibbering, faint-bodied hordes had flocked. Differences in the demons' species had sorted the ghosts according to their tastes in feeding, and wizards seeking specific grades of spirit could take ship to the appropriate, bevampired colossus.

Dazu-Zul, alas, was just outside the incubarium when the mountains ruptured – mounting its front steps, in fact, scant yards from the safety of the ghost-dimension. The lava – monstrous and sudden – caught him in *this* time and space, and even senior thaumaturges, when their bodies are converted to ash, cease to live. And now, within his perduring gate, the vengeful dead raged and swarmed in a vast, anarchic zoo. Jammed with the bones of men dragged down alive, that bright-skied sea was now an endless swamp, an ectoplasmic hell and feeding-ground. And the only guarantee for those who swam here was the prior claim of their particular dead. Hex's own, in a vague-shaped, faceless line, wound tauntingly towards his inner eye – even as the newly landed army wound towards them still.

'This is remarkable,' Stilth said. 'Titanoplods.'

Clearly now, all varnished silver by the sun's approach, the army's polished weaponry detailed their quick-time march. The bigger shapes within their line were titanoplods, and big saddle-packs could be seen to bulge from the beasts' sides. Some smoke went with the line, and at length the three could see that censer-bearers flanked it and dispensed a saffron fog that uncannily hugged the slopes despite the morning breeze. Skirmishers, both mounted and foot, could also be seen scouting in advance. The watchers viewed a miniaturized drama: six like-clad human jots – a tax squad – flushed, cornered, and exterminated with arrows and – finally – axes, in a shallow gully. It was, in its conciseness, the absence of discernible waste-motion, a chillingly workmanlike performance. The line, free of the time-consuming ploys of self-effacement, set a blistering but effortless-looking pace. Soon – since it still came in their direction – they began to hear it. A frail, bright clatter of steel and lacquered shields reached them. A tiny worm of flute music also began to twist towards them, and a minute clash of cymbals. A decorous and pompous march began to piece itself together through the brightening air – just such state music as precedes a royal progress. Another tax squad was flushed and dispatched. Stilth's expression had grown a touch dreamy.

'My friends, if you find no particular need for hurry, let's wait a bit.'

Hex laughed despite himself. 'I must confess, I itch to be down and doing! It seems I can hardly wait to start my swim through the lovely, writhing muck you've described to us! But wait for what, then?'

'Am I going blind? Don't they appear to be headed this way?'

'They're hours off! Who could say?'

'I think we'll wait. We may get lucky, for this shaft is not unfamed. And where the great precede, they widen the gate.'

Both Hex and Sarf lounged back more comfortably, glad to accept the odd calm that the old man's voice worked on them. Not that he seemed in error, for that force (they now could distinguish the slingers, the peltasts, the ranks of heavy-armed with their leaf-shaped spearheads and round shields) was with a dreamlike tenacity persisting – through the roll and pitch of the terrain – in their direction. What was strange was that he calmed them with the belief that these at least five thousand skilful killers were headed for the very spot they sat on. Hex smiled at this thought.

'You don't fear they'll turn out to be folk we should rather escape than wait for?'

'What need harm us – so grand and well-mounted an expedition as that? That smoke's a spell-ward that costs thousands of lictors an ounce. Look at the gear they're bringing. Wherever they go down, they're going to open things up and set their neighbourhood astir. We can risk waiting to find out how.'

The sun appeared, and for a while made a gold-scaled dragon of the supple, armoured line. The line had a distinct head: a quincunx of titanotheres. By the time the sun was an hour high the beasts were near enough for the centremost's superior age and size to be seen, as well as the richness of the brocades in the canopied pagoda it bore. Two men were throned beneath the canopy. All five beasts were helmeted and greaved and belly-armoured for battle, and the four that surrounded the chief one bore cranes and ballistae on their swaying backs. Hypnotically, they did not cease – through all the ground's deflections – to approach the watchers. And when the moment came that the latter found themselves rising to salute this giant vanguard as it mounted to the vale, Hex and Sarf exchanged a marvelling look. But it was Hex who was to be the more amazed – for he now discerned that the smaller, plumper of the two men beneath the regal canopy was Arple Snolp.

Incredibly the magnate met his gaze, his eyes kindled, and he shouted convivially down: 'It's the scholar! Good morning, young man! This is most surprising! You must never have found your way to Madam Poon's – otherwise I don't see how you could still be alive! You, ah, *are* still alive?' Snolp's eyes had flickered thoughtfully towards the mouth of the pit beyond them.

'Oh yes, respected Snolp!' He felt absurdly flattered and grateful at this cordiality and recognition of a man who sat so obviously at ease in the world's dire scramble. 'I reached her house, you see, even did business with her, but by blind luck escaped alive. And lest you fear that the incubarium back there leaks ghosts, we are assured by our knowledgeable guide, Stilth here, that Dazu-Zul's outer gates are still intact.'

This suavely offered comfort seemed to infuriate Snolp's seatmate – a far older man with a bony red nose.

'Of course they are! Is he an incompetent, to let them decay? Do you take him for a fool?'

'No more,' declared Stilth, with a graceful bow, 'than we could take the great Raddle of Ploys for a fool. We are honoured in this meeting, Mage. My friends, though well meaning, are imperfectly educated, and do not know great wizards when they meet them.'

Thoroughly mollified, the wizard waved off praise with a gruff chuckle, and Snolp seemed no less pleased. 'That's well said, sirrah Stilth. I have spared no expense in this expedition, least of all in the matter of wizardly expertise, you may be sure. Quartermaster! Our breakfast pavilion! Over there! Hogwand! Deploy our perimeter, and then have the chief pioneers and engineers attend me at table.'

Attendants swarmed. A capacious, pennanted canopy sprang from the stone and overspread a table groaning with gold service and surrounded by plush couches. Wonderingly, the pilgrims forked meat from smoking heaps of it, and guzzled wine as golden as the cups, and saw the dangerous waste that had so recently surrounded them transformed into a bustling, ordered camp, a place of safety.

Indeed, the transformation went further than this, for the whole prospect of a descent to Dazu-Zul's incubarium was changed into an easier, sunnier thing than that which Stilth had so sombrely depicted to them. For one thing, Snolp's terse directives, delivered between greedy mouthfuls, kept his engineers hopping to and from the pitmouth, which soon seemed a much tamer portal, for three great cranes sprouted round its rim, and dangled basketfuls of workers into it who walled its shaft with ladderways and scaffolds, and conducted downwards great bundles of material for assembly half a mile below, before the gates of the ghost-keep. Meanwhile, Raddle was remodelling the travellers' conception of the incubarium itself. To be sure, Stilth had not urged his differing view. With a smile of charming diffidence, seeming to foresee the storm he raised, he had only said: 'You know, great Raddle, on our way here we heard the oddest rumour – that peerless Dazu-Zul actually *perished* in Kurl's holocaust, and that his – '

'What?! A learned man like you, believing such tavern talk as that!?' The wizard's kingly arch of nose and ancient cheeks were all patched and veined with the purple of burst veins. His eyes displayed a sublime disdain, so bright it half-seemed lunacy, at least to Hex. Fiercely he drained his cup, as if thus disposing of Stilth's outrageous notion. 'Have I not hunted here with him myself, on the high ghostly seas we both so loved? Ah, the song of the harpoon's cable paying out, the grunts and gasps of the crew, the surge and splash of the barb-snagged prey! Did he live for anything else? Ha! And would indeed have *I* lived otherwise, had I had choice? You no doubt know I have been . . . out of time. A black-luck sojourn in a lower world. But of course, down there – ' the wizard indicated the pit, where lamps now blazed on catwalks coiling down past sight, ' – Daz himself has stood apart from time, and lives there still. Ah, how sweet return will be! Youngsters like you can't know the clarity one's finest years retain down through the longest lives! I can tell you, in perfect truth, that with all the centuries of rare balms I have snuffed, the hot stench of the rendering vats remains for me a cosmic landmark, a plane of consciousness apart from humdrum reality!'

Already calm – yea, mellow and exuberant – the wizard settled with that Bore's address, that quick pleasure in his theme which, three phrases into it, forgets all other souls, and is past hearing answers to its flow. With easy, laughing strokes, he drew a world of wild intoxication. Stilth had made the pilgrims aware that the bigger necroplasms were widely hunted by wizards for the raw necromantic power they contained. Ghost-mass depended on moral and mental force; great murderers figured large among the murdered. Since geniuses of conquest, wizards of the sword, were mankind's most abundant crop of talent, Dazu-Zul's lake of the slain had always teemed with slow, remorseless leviathans of slaughter – so fat with other lives they could fuel a million spells for the magi who speared them and cooked them down to ichor. These ichors were the very stuff of man-compelling spells, for if ghosts were anything, they were the interface of sentience with world. The plucked nerve, jangled ear, and oft-sleighted eye of a soul – this was the true ghost substance. The echoing record of a still-vivid, unconsummated life. With such matter, armies of the living could be driven to the wielder's slightest wish.

And, undeniably, Raddle could saga such sea-hunts as Dazu-Zul's vaults had abounded in before the mountains spewed up an empire's end. He could make the travellers see the brain-pierced giants that were – one instant – writhing gargoyles hideously distinct and – other instants – huge, convulsive dents in the sea, with no shape or colour, only voice.

But his talk's fervour soon unsettled Hex. Too clearly, a subtle madness underlay it. The least gainsaying of the wizard's vision brought this out in the angry fervour of his reiterations. Couldn't Arple Snolp see this? Hex and Sarf looked to Stilth, but the old man, eating steadily, gazed rapturously at his plate, leaving in doubt if it was Raddle's story or the meal that enthralled him. As for Snolp, if the wizard's monologue caused him anything, it seemed to be boredom at needlessly repeated facts, no doubt.

'Ho now!' the magnate cried. 'Raddle's ready for the dessert wine. Can't you see that, boy?' The diversion worked. The wizard, who throughout had made bold with the wine, looked around with sudden interest for the treat.

'You know,' Snolp cried, thwacking Hex's shoulder, 'I *am* so glad that you've survived, and that I've run into you again! From the first, you've struck me as such a *plucky* jot of scum! And here you've survived Poon, proving it! She's vanished, you know.'

'I am no jot of scum!' His voice, in his own ears, had an ineffably ludicrous sound – comically baffled. It sounded like the denial of a jot of *something* which was only undecided whether it was composed of scum, precisely, or of some other, equally inconsequential waste-material. Suddenly vivid came the memory of the big wave thrusting him straight up the face of the cliff, and the slight atom of awe he had been in that blind unanimity of brute material power. A moment passed, and then he saw the entire question was tertiary at the most. He laughed.

'Where did she vanish, exalted Snolp?'

'The most amusing mystery! You were *Bramt Hex*, yes? Amazing, what I can remember! Mystery, yes dear Hex! She went to a certain shameful property in Shoreditch – rightly rumoured to be her own – and vanished, with the building itself, quite suddenly one rainy afternoon last autumn! But of course you don't want to discuss *your* insignificant affairs – you want to know what *we're* doing here, and how you might benefit by it!'

'Exactly, oh most unspeakably inexpressible Hugeness! For you see, we're going down into the incubarium, and I'm sure you'd make it easier if you took us along with you!'

Amazingly, to judge by his benign nod, Snolp heard no sneer in this. Suddenly Hex grasped why the magnate heard no madness in Raddle; he was deaf to the betraying dissonances of the mad because they chimed with his own serene self-exaltations. Thus easily, then, Hex had his wish – escorted entry to the incubarium. He had to ask himself just how happy this made him. The evident power of their hosts soothed the doubts these hints of lunacy raised. Could Snolp, so consummate in atrocity, mount any kind of fool's errand?

The magnate, leaning back, was now expounding his mission: 'The question, you see, which even the greatest – *especially* the greatest – must ask themselves is: "Where have I failed? Where have I fallen short?"' He paused so meaningly here that all three of his guests hastened to make protesting sounds which he contentedly gainsaid: 'No, even *I*, I assure you, even *I* was forced to propound this question to myself. We all omit some form of accomplishment, and in my case – shall we proceed as we talk, friends? *Hogwand!* The basket! – and in my case, the answer was suddenly evident. I had omitted nothing in the way of exploiting the living, but I had *done* next to nothing by way of exploiting the dead.'

One of the cranes swung a basket to one side of the pit, and the five climbed in. They swung back over the bottomless, torch-freckled bore of the shaft, and smoothly sank into it. Raddle, as a man nearing home, sighed happily and, having brought the bottle of dessert wine, took a lusty draught.

'So consider my joy,' Snolp was saying, 'when I learned that by doing the latter, I could wring even *further* profit from the living! And I mean *cities-ful* of the living. For you can swindle a city, or sack it with mercenaries, or delude it into forming an army for your uses – but to compel and enslave it, each man, woman, and child of it, into utter, unanimous obedience to your purpose? This is a whole new magnitude of power, potentiating rapine on a scale undreamed of!'

Ramp-and-ladder networks starred with fire slid all around them upward to a shrinking patch of sky. Snolp looked ruddier in this light, quite jovial and avuncular. Hex, who sat next to Raddle, could hear that the wizard was humming some sailor's shanty under his breath, and could see – with some unease – the reflected torches, tiny squirmings in those deep-shadowed, drink-oiled eyes.

'It's the particular energy, you see,' Snolp said, 'which all these vengeful dead have – that baffled rage at interrupted life, that aching, ragged edge of mind, torn off by death, where every brutally discontinued lust, ambition, spite and tender urge throbs inextinguishably!'

'Are all the dead thus?' Stilth asked. There was a fatuous fascination in his manner which Hex felt sure was false.

'Oh no.' Snolp waved dismissively. 'Many die fulfilled and they vanish somewhere that is not ascertainable, or so I'm told. But you seem to miss my point – it's these bitter ones, you see, whose ichor works such thraldom on the living. For they are human longing in its essence, and nimble nightmare at its most metamorphic. They can instil a host with any obsession you choose for them, and make them inexorable as zombies in the execution of it.'

'They're a heady treat, by the One Black Crack!' Raddle shouted this, then drained his bottle and tossed it from the gondola. 'Daz and I used to drink it boiling hot from the rendering kettles – a boyish prank, bravado you know . . . foolish of course but, damn me, those were the halcyon times!' From far below, there came a tiny smashing noise, and a minute curse. They passed a tunnel mouth in the shaft's wall, and saw men with sarissas stabbing at some frenzied, spiderlike thing inside it. 'Ah, those hallucinations, those alien urges! What sport!' Raddle's voice dwindled to a less expansive note – perhaps he had bethought himself of his age. 'I hope, Snolp, that your engineers have fully met my specifications. I'm going to go over her thoroughly. I don't want Daz, after all this time, to see me steering anything second-rate, or makeshift!'

'How could you think it!' Snolp's plushy tone of courteous blandness was a little threadbare – his dislike of being interrupted peeped through. For an instant the two partners shared a look of politely mutual detestation.

'At any rate,' Snolp told his guests, 'I'm sure you'll see the power of these essences if you just consider your own diverse attachments to the world, the poignancy and hopeless disorder of them, and then imagine death's blade lopping them off all unresolved. The resultant psychic amputation will cling to any living mind it touches. I don't know why you have come here – it is a matter without the slightest significance, of course – but *I* have come to take at least a million gallons of Power's purest nectar from Dazu-Zul's deep hive. Ah! Now you can see her, gentlemen – the *Necronaut*!'

They sank into a great vault hewn raggedly from the lava. It was big enough to have contained the Glorak Academy's main hall thrice over. What it did contain was a tall-masted, portly ship, now all but assembled by swarms of engineers on the scaffolding encaging it. Its keel sat on rollers, and its proud, curved prow was aimed at a vast door of polished bronze. As they approached the floor the pilgrims saw that some of what they had taken for masts were wooden arms supporting scoop-nets or, alternately, swatters of woven wire. Big ballistae of a curious make were mounted on the foredeck, and the sails were black and saggy like sheets of soft tar.

'Esteemed Snolp – ' Stilth bowed. 'I'll bid my friends good-bye – I'm not contracted to go with them.' Distractedly Snolp waved them off as he climbed out after Raddle, who already was striding towards the scaffolding. Stilth led his friends aside, where they found seats on the ground out of the way, and watched the work. Stilth said nothing, but sat serenely full of unspoken truths. At first the pilgrims resisted questioning him, as he so plainly knew they longed to do. Then Sarf tried chummy nonchalance.

'Well, we'll miss your company, Stilth, beyond that

door. Because I think this pair could be more than a little crazed.'

Stilth grinned unpleasantly. 'Miss my company, hmm? A *little* crazed?' He turned to look them over with an unsettling thoroughness, as if finally noting them for his mental record. Then he seemed to have, in quick succession, a nasty idea, and a humane second thought. 'Listen, my estimable, dense friends. I flatter these ninnies to procure your passport, because they *will* make your entry easier. But once you're in, I have just two words of advice: abandon ship. Hit the dip and start swimming. Because if the swarm that hits them gets thick enough fast enough, you'll be sunk and torn to bits by its sheer weight before your own dead's prior claim has time to work. Raddle is centuries past his prime, and doomed by an infatuation with his youth. No!' Here Hex had tried to add a question. 'I won't say more than this! Those waters are such as you will loathe to enter, but you must dive, or die there. So. Where will you meet? For I believe, if you attain Yana, you are returned, immortal, to your place of choice.'

'Glorak?' Hex asked his friend.

Sarf nodded. 'There's lots to work with, there.'

Hex briefly wondered what his friend meant by this. And then they watched the swarm of engineers, for plainly, Stilth meant to say nothing else. Already the crews were mainly busy with the scaffolding's disassembly. Workmen, with their pulleyed baskets of pegs and spikes, melted down from the ship's tall rigging. A huge, wheeled Thruster had just shed its own assemblers, and even now the titanoplods to push it were craned down – one after the other – being uncabled, and led to their engine. Once harnessed to its stern they shoved it so that it rumbled till its padded tip just touched the stern of the *Necronaut*. Now the staging fell away from the craft's hull in tall, stilty sections, and they could see a seaman beckoning them to a ladder that dangled from the gunwale. As they rose, the pair spoke awkward good-byes that were not answered, only smiled at. They climbed aboard on to drum-tight decks, that rang with a perfect rigidity of construction. The crew – some in the rigging, most in the mizzen-deck ranged along the rail awaiting duty – rocked only slightly, so good were their sealegs, when the plods pushed the Thruster cautiously, snugly against the stern. Raddle marched pompously down a special gang-ladder from the bow, and up to the mighty, one-valved door of bronze. Though he gave his gait a priestly emphasis, eager haste showed through. He flourished a small hammer at the mighty valve, and shouted – impressively for lungs so old and drink-pickled:

'The dust of a grave required here to open thee, I now supply.
As all Kurl's now a grave this, her glassy mantle, is its dust!'

Then he smote the lava underfoot with the hammer and, dislodging thus some igneous flakes, pinched up and flung these against the bright door's lowest hinge. He retreated, and remounted the ladder. The immense gate swung outward with a tearing, sucking sound, like the unpeeling of an old, infection-crusted bandage. A wall of murky water, stable, though it shuddered and wrinkled softly, filled the brazen, rune-graved frame.

'It's a window, you see, set into the floor of the incubarial lake,' Raddle enthused, rubbing his hands. 'Well, come on there!' he roared at the Thruster's drivers. 'Do you want us to sit out here all day?' The old man bustled in joyful circles on the foredeck, somehow unstaggered by the ship's forward surge on its rollers. From his girdle he plucked a little bone flask chased with silver, drank, and gazed longingly at that uncanny water-wall. Hex guessed the old wizard was alone in not sharing the drivers' hesitation. The prospect seemed to touch everyone else on the ship, with awe and gloom. A faintly rotten-smelling cold breathed from it. It had a vague translucence, as if some vast, dim light shone beyond it, at an unguessable distance.

Their prow had almost touched it when Raddle shouted, 'Hold! Just there!' He took another long pull from his flask, draining it, and then, with a whoop – as startling as a thunderclap in this moment of general awe – flung it at the water-wall. It struck, and was sucked straight into it. Raddle shouted a harsh, uncouth polysyllable, and made an out-flinging gesture with both arms. A spinning disc of glassy plasm formed in the air before him and smacked flatwise against the centre of the water-wall. It still spun, bulging against that upright flood, pushing a glassy, growing dome into it. 'Forward slow, now!' Raddle cried, repeating that shooing gesture which, each time he made it, swelled the dome. The plods eased them forth. Their bowsprit entered the dome, then their foredeck, their mainmast.

Still wildly conjuring with his arms Raddle – crackling with delight and now facing sternward – wove the bubble round them.

'Now then – one mighty shove!' he shrieked. The ship lunged entirely through the doorframe, and with a great sweep of his arms the wizard sealed the bubble shut astern. In that instant the eerily suspended ship pitched violently through a quarter-turn to present its keel to the antechamber still barely visible behind them – or rather, beneath them. For what had been forward was now overhead and, as Hex and Sarf picked themselves up, the bubble snatched them all with smooth power in that direction.

Through the shuddery flash of the bubblewall, increasing light filtered as they rose. 'Look! Ah, look!' the wizard cried triumphantly to Snolp who, rather slumping at his side, seemed not to share his joy. 'That lovely mellow violet of the sky that Daz made! It shows through already!'

But the magnate plainly saw what all the others did – a carious brown-yellow light, a sickish glow.

'Is he now mad outright?' Sarf asked.

'I think so – see the waters?' As through a twisted pane they could now see the ghastly, sodden trash which the airbulge shouldered aside. Skulls and fragmentary bones danced, in a kind of reversed hail, against their wobbly envelope. The light increased.

'Hold tight!' Raddle bleated. They erupted into air, crashed down, rocked crazily. The breaking bubble fell to pieces all around and hatched a view of all-embracing murk. A sky of torn and dangling clouds bled muddy-yellow light upon an endless, muddy-yellow swamp. In one direction there were silt-bars overgrown with shapes the eye at first shrank from analysing. Open water stretched away to port. Dead ahead, halfway to vision's limit, a colossal cadaver, or part of one, thrust stark ribs against the drizzly sky. Raddle's delusion had shattered with the bubble. He stood gaping, irrevocably enlightened. Horror had weakened everyone's knees except Snolp's, whose plump face darkened with congestive wrath.

'Dazu-Zul *alive*! *Alive* you said!' he bellowed, sweeping an arm round at the scene. 'You call this *alive*?!'

22
In Yana, the Touch of Undying

Oddly though, it *was* alive – most horribly. Their keel, scarcely moved by the slack, tarry sails, cut through a soup of soft concussions and twisting shoves. From the rail all eyed the main, wherein a host of presences stirred. No one of these had shape in more than blinks, and they teased the mind with a fleet, melting multitude of fanged and snouted things. The siltbars too were alive with mournful, anchored movement, char-limbed things that had been men writhed there, rooted at waist or knees, and strange shapes squirrelled amid their blackened arms. The stark-ribbed giant too – legless, and with just one wolfish lower jaw thrust up, a fanged tower where its head had been – was doubly alive. Numberless ghosts maggoted its hide, or wheeled restlessly in winged flocks from perch to perch on it. Moreover, with rising gorge Hex saw that – though dismembered, though half-mummied, hardly fleshed at all – the anchored demon actually breathed, the laboured bulge of its thorax – gaunt coffer of its ensorcelled life – disturbing the bloodfly swarm not at all.

Snolp, whipped to a fury Hex had never guessed was in him, lunged to seize Raddle's throat. Scarcely thinking of it, Raddle made a warding gesture that flung the magnate through the air and tangled him high up in the rigging, while still the wizard's rheumy eyes looked round in dismay.

The pilgrims watched this dumbshow only half attending, for the sheer spiritual mechanics of their situation crushed them with dread. A score and a half of mercenary soldiers, the red-handed Snolp – all entering here alive together. Stilth had made plain the rush that must ensue – not only the convergence of their *own* dead, whose aggregate must be legion, but any others drawn by the smell of life, for they were out of water, and free game. And yet, though the friends searched each other's eyes, they could not find the desperate courage to jump.

The crew were mobbed together in such fierce, recriminating babble as men fall to when disaster strikes them. Some few looked up at Snolp's howls to be helped down – and then these cried out, and made their fellows look, and all were staggered. Snolp's entanglement was not what he himself still took it for; the rigging *moved* to weave him in. Ropes broke, raised frayed heads, and snaked to web his writhing plumpness, while the tarry sails bulged into animate tatters that spidered down to seize him. This raised his roaring to a different pitch.

But now the crew howled equally, for some of the rigging broke free and fell on them in phosphorescent skeins, and like swift fungus rooted in their flesh and sprouted shaggy myceloid shrouds. The netting melted from the scoops and swatters and rolled – now glowing too – in amoebic blobs that sought the wizard where he stood still brokenly regarding the vast ruins of his hope. The anchor chain poured into the air, a slick tube of gut now, throbbing with hellish ichors, and slung its hook through a man's chest. The remnants of the sails – those parts not devouring the squalling Snolp – also pulsed translucent, thick with veins, and peeled down to enfold the struggling seamen. The iron rending-vats made mouths and bellowed and, bounding free, swallowed fugitives and snatched them overboard. Meanwhile a hideous polymorphous riot now converged on the ship from the air.

'We *have* to jump!' Sarf's urgency was suddenly facilitated, for glittering, clawed flippers now clutched the gunwales, and the ship began to list as the aquatic dead mobbed up its side.

'They'll break like glass on impact!' Hex screamed this to make himself believe it, meaning the shape-jammed waters they now vaulted into.

They thrashed in the teeming stew, their violence as much a tearing aside of it as a means of making headway. They milled their arms and legs to pull them free of the gelatinous, fleet nudge and rub that swathed them. The liquid was less dense than water – volatile, spiritous, its exhalations faintly stung their nostrils, and its buoyancy was such that even their sodden gear did not exert much drag on them. Rather, its saturation made them feel bubble-light, and moreover seemed to inscribe upon their skin – even upon its most intimate inches – swift sensations, horribly particular and distinct.

At first, though the eloquence of these ticklings was felt, it was not readable, for their first agony of loathing kept them ripping and bucking at the waters, fighting for distance from the doomed *Necronaut*. But shortly, they could feel the flux they swam grow less turbid, the queasy impacts far fewer. Facing back, they gaped to find themselves almost a quarter mile away. The craft's net and swatter arms waggled in the air, masts – uprooted – danced with an obscenely expressive jubilation, all of them furred and studded with thick-clustered ghosts. Even as the swimmers watched, the *Necronaut*'s ballistae fired off harpoons that looped up towards the clouds and wrote liquid, cryptic scripts of writhing cable against the grey, sweating air. Winged, crested, fiercely snouted, squat and busily multibrachiate – all seething like ants on a honeydrop at noon, the lust-crazed dead so densely thronged the listing craft it looked like a ripe, wind-blurred thistledown globe whose fragments ambiently smoked and swarmed – save here was convergence, not dispersion. Hither hastened numberless airborne shoals to heap the decks in drifts that deepened by the second.

The pair swam easier now. Tall kelps and oil-black, multifoliate seaweeds were the main inhabitants of the waters, as though the ship had drawn off the moving traffic of half-visible things. And now the water's ticklings, its creeping evocation of memories in the skin, grew frighteningly distinct.

'Do you feel them, Sarf? My hands, palms are . . . *remembering* the feel of the cask I threw when I crushed the head of that man in the rowboat.'

'Yes. Mine feel – feel *exactly* the chains I clamped on to those musicians.'

'And my right arm. At the same time. The blows I gave them down in the gully to stun them for the killing-slopes.'

'And also, Hex,' – Sarf's voice shook slightly here – 'also the feel of the rock I took from Hounderpound.'

'And so do I,' Hex realized, awed. He hung treading water. 'Could it mean that *he's* one of my dead too? It was you that hit him!' They gazed back at the *Necronaut*. All but shapeless now, it seemed a floating hive that fumed and dripped with toiling wasps. Dozens of new nightmare anchor lines now bound it to the main, squirming fetters of braided ghosts. Bramt Hex screeched aloud.

This did not startle Sarf, who did the same, for the same reason. Their legs were seized, greasily tourniqueted by snake-tough bights of seaweed. Loops of it captured Hex's shoulders, cobraed from the water before his face, whence his hands wildly slapped them aside. Socketed in each oily, pennate frond of the ghost, a jewel-bright eye flashed bale – the eye, a hundred-fold, of Oberg, the Polypolitan conductor. Each muscled leaf of him that clutched Hex thrust an icy nerve-root into him. These ghost-pangs sketched in his mind a tenuous map of agonies he had never guessed at – the being's death-pains, Hex understood. He wrestled furiously, counter-strangled with fevered hands. *Fight back, and as long as you do, it can't take you. At your first passivity, it has you for its lodging till you die.* Stilth's voice, unreal footnote, hung round the margin of his horror, his bodily explosion of resistance. Central in his mind, uncannily interior to it, was Oberg's murmured voice, whose text the coruscation of his multiple stare counterpointed with flashing hate:

'Take me on. The shrunkenest, meanest little corner of your life! I'll curl up, be content to thaw in your blood's heat. Take me on, you scum! You chained us there! I had to strangle Umber to spare him pain. I sank alive in the acid maw of the Shlubbup! Smothering foulness! Snot-thick caustics rubbed all my flesh from the bones! Take me on!'

Pity as devastating as his horror half paralysed Hex. Clearly he saw the small bright-clothed shapes chained to the killing-slope in the early morning. To shout 'No!' – as, groaningly, he did, was a thing as hard to do as nocking, drawing, aiming, and loosing an arrow deep underwater. Cumbered by his own woozy terror and compassion, he let fly the negative. Fractionally the liquescent necroplasm melted to a slighter grip on him, and he bellowed again.

'No! And No! I do refuse you! Release me and retire!' He saw now that the whole weedy floor of this tarn shivered and danced like flames, and flashed with constellations of hating, craving eyes, but then he was released, and Oberg shrank down to the impotent level of what, surely, were his townsfellows. A bar of bare, bone-studded silt defined the limit of this shallows, and Hex swam for it. On the gravel of vertebrae and cranial shards he sprawled, gasping, and only Sarf's arrival at his side reminded him of his friend's existence. They lay catching breath a while. At length Hex told his friend: 'I danced with the conductor.'

'I fought his catamite.' A shudder. 'So slippery and cold a thing!'

'They are bigger, the stronger their souls. Have you thought of that? And I keep feeling the giant's rock on my palm.'

Sarf nodded, not answering. Plainly, the warlock had been a man of Power. After a moment he said: 'If we don't continue, we'll grow afraid to, and die here.'

Grunting, they rose and heaved themselves into the deeps beyond the bar. The *Necronaut*, crumbled, a puddle of swarming fragments, now left their sight. The far sky was feverish with sluggish lightnings which backlit, near the horizon, more demon fodder: a colossal, rat-gnawed spine – whence some few hook-footed limbs branched, remnants of a centipede's array – that was skulled at either end by sharp-beaked raptors' mummied heads. Feebly, their legstumps stirred, and rippled the inky flood they rode; feebly their beaks gnawed the air, and now and then crushed tardy members of the aerial hosts that rookeried them even to the point of filling their eyesockets, and painting their cruel cheeks with streaks of phosphorescent guano. Still the swimmers felt blubbery bignesses flirting with their kicking feet; still, through the turbid flux, quick, melting faces feinted near their own – tusked muzzles, barbed probosces, slitted yellow eyes flirted against their cheeks. But now, having felt the nearness of those with claim on them, they swam less fearful of the general shoals. The mudreefs and sandbars they here and there passed still made their eyes cringe – from the charred, truncated eloquence of fingerless gesturing arms; from cairns and the broken walls of cloacal shrines, all graffitied in scripts of varied muck and drying blood, calligraphies as stark and menacingly sharp as silhouetted lines of demon-troops. But their bodies, meanwhile, recoiled less and less as they swam. They understood that however they wandered, they would be found, and re-embraced.

The water was alive with vaster tactile memories than their own. A kind of neural mutter moved through it; murder in a thousand vivid forms crackled around them, to be erased by a random counterwave, the pangs of a thousand species of disease.

'Hex. The water's colder – feel it?'

Hex groaned for answer. Fear was big in him again. The water was not only colder, but had a new emptiness that felt premonitory – even bony trash thinned out. There was something big coming, he felt, and it was for him. He howled half with relief when he was seized, so sure he'd grown he would be taken.

A glowing pincer had his middle, a serrate claw that lifted him out of the swell. Two stalked eyes – slanted ovoids tapering to points – thrust up to view him from the huge crab's carapace they crowned. Hex knew Zelt's eyes, and dreaded them. Her mouth, underslung to the carapace, was a wide seam, puffed into a crimson bivalve whence a thin stream issued through the water, smelling of sulphur and burnt bones. Again, the tongue she spoke with was no organ of her own, but a suddenly animated valve within his mind.

'Let me in, oh Enormity! There's more than room enough in your warm blood. How agilely I plied your pump – remember those drunken nights? We'll twist that spigot and I'll pour into you the way you poured out into me. So easy! A little itch, a faint burn, that's all I'll be! So spacious is your fat-arsed vitality! You pig! You facile swine! You signed my life to hell as easy as a coin passed for a dram! I had to leap into a fire to die! I – '

Black fur sprouted from the water, a reeking lawn of squirming hair. Something huge and otter-lithe had looped round both Hex's legs and Zelt's claw, on which it gnawed with great fanged jaws. It had no eyes, but both its mouth and snout, even through the gorgon coilings of its beard, were unmistakable enlargements of the Lady Poon's. Though her bite cracked the harlot's pincer, it did not let go. Poon's length sufficed both to grapple the free claw and to clamp with python force the scholar's lower half. The big necroplasms tore and tumbled madly through the water and – now sunk, now hoisted high – Hex was mill-wheeled endlessly across it. And throughout, the contestants' voices fought within his mind:

'Loose him, slut! He's mine! Evicted me from mansion, from fortune, from my life! He'll house me now. Yes, *you'll* be my mansion now, officious fool! I had to slit my throat because of you! We'll couple now, and you'll warm me through all the years you have left.'

'Ha! You'll split him like a growing wasp its spider prey. Your gluttony for possession will worm his brain hollow – he'll have nor dreams nor nightmares but your own.'

During this battle, another raged in Hex. His every inmost sexual channel recalled, each pulse of lust he'd ever known. Even as he tumbled, mad with these volcanic she-powers, he saw for what it was the delusion of possession that sexual crisis had always brought him. The puny egoism of desire now mocked him as these two libidinal juggernauts ploughed the seas with his little share of skin and mind. And even so his lust prevailed, was what had locked his jaw thus far. When he saw this, he found his voice at last.

'No! I deny you both! I tell you no!' He kicked feebly, yet their grip attenuated. 'And no again!' His kick felt strong now – Poon's viscid clasp grew more liquid, and his hands could start to pry Zelt's claw apart. He roared again, thrust wide his arms, and was floating free, alone.

Gasping to breathe, utterly shaken, he felt for the first time a yielding to this swamp, an acquiescence. Sarf was he knew not where, but they would find each other, and Yana's door, or they would not. In this new vista, the only demon fragment was a clawed, stump-wristed hand; piebald with a fur of parasites, it clutched in spasms while – too quick for it – the scythe-beaked flocks on their leathern wings boiled up, slipped between its fingers, resettled. Mists were thicker here. In crooked pillars they wandered over the waters whence, here and there, shapes boiled up into them, filling the foggy frames with incandescent viscera. Scarcely trying to steer past these, Hex swam. An architectural corner of the Incubarium was at last evident: half an arch of stone, crown lost in clouds, its raggedness all starred and tented with spiderwebs. Under this the waters seemed to echo with some faint tidal noise and a current, just detectable, moved towards it. Uncaring, Hex moved with it. Another of his dead laid hold of him.

This was homunculus, a third his size, hanging just under the surface. From its shattered skull a sticky weave of brains and ropy tissue had snared Hex's feet. His counterkick and shout of refusal sufficed to free him. The dwarfish phantom would have been the man in the rowboat. Immediately he felt a gnawing on one ankle, and found a tiny frog-shape had him there. He sent this fleeing with a second kick, telling him that this ectoplasmic minnow must be the guard of Forb's that he had slain in the Dapple's killing-yard. Almost, the meagreness of these dead of his made him groan aloud. So many, great and small, torn raging, uncontented from their lives! A universe of them. And in this cosmic slaughter-fest, what signified his own brief, greedy damages? His own scant bill of dead? Could any man move, act at all, without killing? An immense loneliness bore down on him, a sad powerlessness that he felt no length of life could cure.

A raging voice reached him, gasped denials, a bubbly noise of struggle. He paused in the gentle drift. Clearly, it would take him under the arch which towered near now, dark spiky shapes discernible in the webbing that partly curtained it. He heard more torn water, and a shouted 'No!' He drifted a little longer. Sarf, as lax and worn as he felt, drew near. He seemed himself a ghost – and what was a man, Hex thought, but the sum of phantoms that haunted him, as much those he denied as those he admitted?

'Hail, fellow ghost!' Hex said, to see if he still had a voice, and what a joke would sound like. It sounded like a croaking in a tomb. Sarf's mouth was slack with exhaustion, but a stubborn fever in his eyes filled Hex with admiration. His friend had felt no slightest acquiescence to these horrors, no kinship. Only an uncrushable will to reach their goal.

'The worst is coming, Hex. No others are left – at least for me.'

Hex blinked, then remembered. The black tide now moved them at a walker's pace. The great arch loomed above and dropped behind them. To their right, far mists and clouds were vision's limit. On their left, a towering cavern wall, along whose bayed base the current snaked them sluggishly. And, in the big embayment it now bore them to, it briefly seemed that something moved beneath the water.

'The man-witch.' Hex's voice came almost stillborn. He'd thought himself emptied, all power to fear wrung out of him yet now his legs began to move in wild retrogression.

But it was as if he kicked against thin air, and that black lagoon were a place he fell towards. They saw what seemed a bouquet of pallid kelp filling the great pool; seemed thus until it stirred and thrust with silken muscularity against the flow, probing greedily towards their coming. The tarn's floor deepened under them, sank to a depth they could not have guessed through the murk, save that the pallor of an immense torpedo body – a body where those shuddery tentacles were rooted – moved within the chasm, and showed its scope. A tentacle took Hex's middle, another Sarf's. They were lifted from the water and brought to hang above the surface where, like a weedy shipwreck resurrected, the ghost's tapered body rose. One of its eyes turned to them. Though big as a warshield, it was the warlock's eye.

'No!' Hex cried. 'I never struck you! You're not – '

'I am yours too.' The voice filled not just the captives' skulls, but resonated through their bodies, shook them as a gentle surf might do. 'You buoyed each other's purpose. You launched the giant's hate for him, you set it on the wing, however confusedly. And now my mate must live out her life alone, and ward the monster by herself. Yet, if you take me in, you could go back to her, and clasp her hand, and thus I could pass into her, and at least that much restore our union.'

Sarf's strangled negative came as through a dream to Hex. The enormity of taking in so vast a being made his throat cleave shut, and it stunned him so precisely because – yet greater enormity! – he found he *wished* to do so. It devastated him, this aberration, this alien impulse in the mind he had thought to be his own.

It was the eye that caused it – that barbarous orb whose pupil's tiniest contractions seemed to gnaw his image from the air, and devour with that image the form and feature of his soul. Yet at the same time a monstrous beauty in that eye made Hex feel he looked – not into it, but *out* from it. Here was no longing hate, but a sardonic love, a superhuman appetite for the All, for Earth Sea and Sky, and Hex seemed to look out on these things, on every vista he had ever seen, and feel that love himself – a giant's love, far greater than his littleness was framed for. He hung in stupefaction, already aware that the critical moment of passivity was past, and he was the warlock's. The eye, he thought, now held a smile.

The tentacles tremored. The body grew smoky, vague. A sharp pain now girt Hex's ribs, matching the ghost's grip. Sarf fell to the pool, released. The molluscoid melted and contracted, and the tentacle it held Hex by throbbed like a pipe up which pulsed the phantom's dwindling mass. The eye was last to melt; then, pain gone, unsupported, Hex too splashed down to empty water. Sarf swam to him, touched his shoulder. Again the current took them, Sarf half pulling his friend along. The cavern wall receded. Just detectably, their flow-rate quickened.

'Sarf,' Hex breathed. 'It is . . . astonishing. Yana's very near. It is . . . a green place that we fall to without harm. The warlock makes me see it. But . . .'

'But what?'

Slack-jawed, Hex shook his head. Yana's gate was the simplest vision given him. And it was, he now understood, a gate at which, with the gain of endless life, he was about to lose all the life he had had. For the rest of his revelation was no less than that: an upwelling of a million things and faces he had seen, thoughts he had read, fleet, inexpressible tastes and touches of the world and all the imaginings it had kindled, and the countless musics of wind and word and sheer sweet noise it had made to him. It was as if the aggregate of his finite time formed a great chandelier of flashing crystals, sharp-edged instants each of which, approaching extinction, flared alive in him with a new radiance born precisely of its singularity and its fragility. Had the understanding of this radiance been the warlock's strength that made him so firm against Hounderpound's tireless hate? He saw the witches' cove as – in some part of him beyond his fear – he had seen it on that morning of the killing: the sun-gilt glides in their flawless aerial river, the sand like beaten gold. That splendour, that sufficiency! Thus had the warlock possessed the treasure of his time. They were drifting much faster now, and a soft roaring could be heard ahead. A great terror was awakening in Hex.

It was not terror of what he could envision even before they saw it – though they saw it almost at once: the black flux, nacreous with sudden turmoil, plunged down a slope, and ahead appeared a wide wheeling of waters round a monstrous pit in the ghostworld's floor. But his terror was not of the fall ahead. It was of the deathlessness he now knew, past doubting at last, that they would fall to.

'No,' he mouthed without voice. It was as if the warlock, by showing in its true light the world Hex's life for thirty years had failed to embrace, had back-lit for him the true size of his soul: a jot of gluttonous plasm. And this soul now speeding into the swirling rim of waters, was spinning around the very brink of an unholy enlargement, a prolongation that would make its maggot's smallness huge – an empty gorging on a world it could not taste.

The waters flung them down into the pit, whose floor was a sunlit sky of royal blue, where the black flood's spin whirled to mist that fed clouds white as hoarfrost. Through these stately, scudding clouds they fell, towards a green land miles below, a gentle-hilled paradise of silk-fine meadows brocaded with flower-studded trees and minutely stitched with silver streams. The body-panic of so great a fall was almost at once mollified by the sheer upwelling glory of that place. Yana's beauty lifted to their eyes a balm that promised impact not just harmless, but bosomy and tender. Hex dropped towards immortality's awesome magnification. All power to possess his life would die there with his power to die; there, a monster with an unassuageable hunger would be born. Huger than the ghost had felt entering him now swelled his fear as he fell. It filled his lungs and cracked his jaws wide open and burst out in one outcry that seemed to ring as wide as all that world.

'NO!'

He was in utter darkness, tumbling in an icy hurricane. He was a dead leaf swooping, smashing and crumbling frail as eggshell in the wind's pummelling. He was no longer body, but a thought of motion. He was lying on cold stone, shivering in his sodden clothes. He opened his eyes.

He lay on the floor of the Incubarium's antechamber. Crews were breaking down the last of the scaffolding round the empty rollers. Stilth sat not far off, smiling strabismically at him.

'Change your mind?'

Slowly, slowly, Hex sat up. He drank long and repeatedly from a winejack Stilth handed him. At length he sighed and shivered.

'No,' he said. Then more decisively: 'No. I've just decided to come back later. I have some things to do first.'

He realized he had never heard Stilth really laugh before as he sat listening to the old man's mad cachinnations. Hex waited calmly, then asked: '*Can* one return?'

Grinning, Stilth shrugged. 'Survive the trip here? That's as may be, of course. Re-enter the portal itself? I've never heard it was impossible. Just what is it you have to do first?'

'Hard to explain. Learn how to taste the life I have before I take a second helping.' He could not read in Stilth's continued smile if the old man mocked or liked this notion, or even if it came as news to him.

'And Sarf?'

'Well, I *am* going back to Glorak, retracing my route somewhat. There's one cove in particular where I have to stop, south of Sirril. But of course, Sarf will be there so much sooner, and he'll have rare projects to pursue . . . Why did you laugh so hard?'

'He'll be there already, no doubt about it.' Stilth got up, suddenly bright and brisk. 'Well, it's time I headed south myself, so I can give you some company. Let's get you some new gear. Hogwand!'

The tusked, bullnecked hybrid marched up and delivered a smart salute.

'Did you see to my azle's foddering, Hogwand?'

'Yes, Trickster.'

'Good. Now my friend here will need new trail gear – stout leather and sailcloth, for rough wear. Give him your boots, Hex, so he can match the size. When you've brought that, we mean to sup topside, so bespeak the meal while you're up there, and arrange to have a basket ready for us.'

'Very good, Trickster.'

'And have the captain over there bring us that brazier. My friend needs drying out.'

'Yes, Trickster.'

When he was gone, Hex smiled. 'You cut a wide swath here it seems, Stilth.'

'Ah well. Raddle carelessly left a leak in the wall, you see – caused a bit of a bother here. I closed the door for them. Here's some fire. I'll leave you to make yourself more comfortable.'

He strolled off towards the crews, and watched their work like any idle old man. Sighing comfortably as his mind ranged over all the dangers that lay before him, filled with a serenity he could in no way justify, Hex stripped off his doublet. He found his notes only slightly damp, and ranged them round the coals to dry them. He smiled as he did so because, as he had unbelted his pouch, he had made a discovery: he was a thin man now.

Isaac Asimov, grand master of science fiction now available in paperback from Grafton Books

'Foundation' Series

Foundation	£1.95	☐
Foundation and Empire	£1.95	☐
Second Foundation	£2.50	☐
Foundation's Edge	£2.95	☐

Other Titles

Opus: The Best of Isaac Asimov	£2.50	☐
The Bicentennial Man	£1.95	☐
Buy Jupiter!	£1.95	☐
The Gods Themselves	£1.95	☐
The Early Asimov (Volume 1)	£1.50	☐
The Early Asimov (Volume 2)	£1.50	☐
The Early Asimov (Volume 3)	£1.50	☐
Earth is Room Enough	£1.95	☐
The Stars Like Dust	£1.95	☐
The Martian Way	£1.50	☐
The Currents of Space	£1.50	☐
Nightfall One	£1.50	☐
Nightfall Two	£1.95	☐
The End of Eternity	£1.95	☐
I, Robot	£1.95	☐
The Rest of the Robots	£1.95	☐
The Complete Robot	£3.50	☐
Asimov's Mysteries	£2.50	☐
The Caves of Steel	£1.95	☐
The Naked Sun	£1.95	☐
The Robots of Dawn	£2.50	☐
Nebula Award Stories 8 (Editor)	95p	☐
The Stars in their Courses (non-fiction)	£1.50	☐
Asimov's Guide to Halley's Comet (non-fiction)	£2.50	☐
Counting the Eons (non-fiction)	£2.50	☐
Asimov on Science Fiction (non-fiction)	£2.50	☐
X Stands for Unknown (non-fiction)	£2.95	☐

To order direct from the publisher just tick the titles you want and fill in the order form.

SF181

The world's greatest science fiction authors now available in paperback from Grafton Books

Philip José Farmer
The Riverworld Saga

To Your Scattered Bodies Go	£2.50	☐
The Fabulous Riverboat	£1.95	☐
The Dark Design	£2.95	☐
The Magic Labyrinth	£2.95	☐
Riverworld	£2.50	☐
Gods of Riverworld	£2.50	☐

Other Titles

Dayworld	£2.50	☐
Dark is the Sun	£1.95	☐
Jesus on Mars	£1.50	☐
Riverworld and other stories	£2.50	☐
The Stone God Awakens	£1.50	☐
Time's Last Gift	£1.50	☐
Strange Relations	£1.95	☐
The Unreasoning Mask	£1.95	☐
The Book of Philip José Farmer	£1.95	☐
The Image of the Beast	£1.95	☐
Blown	£1.95	☐

To order direct from the publisher just tick the titles you want and fill in the order form.

All these books are available at your local bookshop or newsagent, or can be ordered direct from the publisher.

To order direct from the publishers just tick the titles you want and fill in the form below.

Name _____

Address _____

Send to:
Grafton Cash Sales
PO Box 11, Falmouth, Cornwall TR10 9EN.

Please enclose remittance to the value of the cover price plus:

UK 60p for the first book, 25p for the second book plus 15p per copy for each additional book ordered to a maximum charge of £1.90.

BFPO 60p for the first book, 25p for the second book plus 15p per copy for the next 7 books, thereafter 9p per book.

Overseas including Eire £1.25 for the first book, 75p for second book and 28p for each additional book.

Grafton Books reserve the right to show new retail prices on covers, which may differ from those previously advertised in the text or elsewhere.